P9-CEC-212

Tap City

TAP CITY

Ron Abell

LITTLE, BROWN AND COMPANY • BOSTON • TORONTO

COPYRIGHT © 1985 BY RON ABELL
ALL RIGHTS RESERVED. NO PART OF THIS BOOK MAY BE REPRODUCED
IN ANY FORM OR BY ANY ELECTRONIC OR MECHANICAL MEANS INCLUD-
ING INFORMATION STORAGE AND RETRIEVAL SYSTEMS WITHOUT PERMIS-
SION IN WRITING FROM THE PUBLISHER, EXCEPT BY A REVIEWER WHO
MAY QUOTE BRIEF PASSAGES IN A REVIEW.

FIRST EDITION

Library of Congress Cataloging in Publication Data

Abell, Ron, 1932–
   Tap city.

   I. Title.
PS3551.B339T3 1985   813'.54   85-7062
ISBN 0-316-00200-3

DESIGNED BY DEDE CUMMINGS

Published simultaneously in Canada
by Little, Brown & Company (Canada) Limited

PRINTED IN THE UNITED STATES OF AMERICA

FOR CHARLES R. SWIFT

Now you can really read me like a book

This is a work of fiction. The characters and events portrayed are imaginary and are not intended to represent any real people, living or dead. There is no Taj Mahal casino-hotel in Reno.

PROLOGUE

Part Two

RENO
August 20

H E was called Stretch Jackson and his markers were honored from London to Las Vegas. He weighed a hundred and fifty-five pounds and would have stood six and a half feet tall if he ever straightened up, but he had a lazy-man's posture. He never stood if he could sit and he never sat if he could slouch. He had a hollow chest and almost no waist and when he walked he went slowly, like a man moving through water. He wore faded Levis and white-on-white western shirts he bought at J. C. Penney's, but his feet were encased in eight-hundred-dollar leather boots and on the small finger of his left hand glinted a diamond ring he could have swapped across the board for a Rolls Royce. On the back of his head Stretch Jackson wore a cowboy hat with a rolled brim, always. From a distance he looked like a rodeo performer but from up close it was obvious he was pushing sixty. He had good teeth and an easy smile and his gray-blue eyes were every bit as compassionate as a wolf's. Five years earlier they'd made a movie about him and ever since he'd been the most famous poker player in America. He claimed the reputation didn't help him any. "A movie and five bucks'll buy you a bowl of chili," he'd drawl. "I've made more money in one hand of poker than I ever did in the show business."

"And lost more," a crony would remind him from across the table.

To that, Stretch would just smile and say, "Pardner, a man who never loses ain't gamblin' — he's cheatin'."

It was an early evening in mid-August and Stretch Jackson was slumped on his tailbone in soft leather in a conference room of the Taj Mahal Hotel in Reno, Nevada, his long legs extended and the heels of his boots buried in carpet. Outside in the high desert the temperature had begun to drop rapidly from the day's high of ninety-three as the sun moved behind the mountains to the west, but inside the fifteenth-story executive offices of the Taj Mahal, and in fact throughout the entire hotel-casino, air-conditioning kept the temperature perfectly within the comfort zone. That was taken for granted. Such mundane matters as temperature, humidity or time of day were never allowed to interfere with the concentration required by guests of the hotel in their primary pursuit. Which is to say gambling.

In the conference room with Stretch Jackson were two men in business suits. One was a lawyer and the other was the casino manager of the Taj Mahal. Their negotiations completed, they raised their glasses in a toast. The lawyer was working on a Scotch and water but the casino manager took straight tomato juice. Stretch was drinking his usual, which was coffee with cream and sugar. The lawyer said, "I'll get a contract drawn up."

Stretch didn't answer. The casino manager said, "That's probably not necessary. Stretch?"

"We don't need anything in writing," the tall man drawled. "If I can't trust this billion-dollar saloon, I got more trouble than I want to know about."

The lawyer said, "It's customary procedure. What if we all dropped dead tomorrow?"

"Then I guess we'd be playin' cards in a lot hotter climate,"

Stretch said. He stood up, and the effect was like the slow unfolding of a carpenter's rule. "Your word's good, pardner. No offense, but I learned a long time ago it wasn't a plague of locusts the Lord sent down. It was a plague of lawyers."

Something about Stretch's easy-going manner made the lawyer feel good inside. There weren't many of the old road gamblers left anymore but the few who came around were a wonder. They were like the mythical gunslingers of the Old West, ready to put everything on the line at any time. When they gave their word on a deal, that was it. Despite his disapproval of the casual arrangements, the lawyer felt privileged to shake the slim man's hand. Being called partner by Stretch Jackson was like being blessed.

"He's quite the gentleman, isn't he?" the lawyer asked after Stretch left the conference room.

The casino manager, whose line of work over the years had endowed him with all the emotions of a rock, said, "Beats me. I'm not personally familiar with the word."

The arrangements they'd just arrived at were simple enough. In January the Taj Mahal would host the First Annual Stretch Jackson Seven-Card Stud Poker Classic. January was a slow month in Reno and a poker tournament would create some action. The hotel wouldn't make any money from the tournament itself, but it would benefit from the ripple effect. With high rollers in town for the side games, everybody from the cocktail waitresses on up would share the wealth. The bulk of it would end up in the casino safe, of course, but nobody seriously objected to that because everyone understood it was inevitable. That was Nevada's first commandment: in the long run, the only winner there could ever be was the house.

When it came to poker, Reno couldn't compete with Las Vegas. The larger southern city was the poker capital of the country and the operators of the Taj Mahal didn't have pretensions of challenging Vegas's World Series of Poker. They played all the games at the World Series, but thanks to publicity the event had become famous essentially as a hold-em contest, so a tournament in Reno that was strictly seven-card stud made some sense, especially with a celebrity like Stretch Jackson as the host. It would be a three-day tournament with a ten-thousand-dollar buy-in and if they attracted fifty players, the final pot would be for half a million bucks. The Taj Mahal would get its crowd.

"But what's in it for Stretch?" the lawyer asked.

"Twenty grand," the casino manager told him. "What you called the honorarium."

"Does he need it? A man like him?"

"I'll let you in on a little secret," the manager said. "The card player hasn't been born who can't use twenty grand."

Meanwhile, Stretch Jackson had ambled down the hallway to the elevator bank and descended to the street floor of the Taj Mahal. As he exited from the elevator, the casino's din assaulted his ears but he scarcely noticed the noise; the sounds were always there, the background music of his life. Moving amid the summer vacationers, he made his way through the crowded casino to the poker area in a far corner. Until his plane left for Vegas, poker was as good a way as he knew to pass the time. He took a seat at a hold-em table and peeled five hundred-dollar bills from a money clip he extracted from the pocket of his Levis. He gave two bills to the dealer for chips and placed the other three on the table in front of him. Using his thumb to push the cowboy hat an inch farther back on his head, he slouched in his chair and looked neutrally once around the table.

"Stretch," the dealer said, acknowledging his presence.

The other players knew who he was, even the tourists, and that was fine with Stretch because it gave him an edge. When the cards were dealt, he raised on the first round of betting and everyone dropped except for two players. When he raised again after the flop, the remaining players folded and the dealer pushed the pot over to Stretch. He gathered the chips and tossed his hole cards in without exposing them. They were garbage — a two and an eight of different suits. Stretch settled more comfortably in his seat. His bluff had been a cheap trick but it often worked on the first hand in a game like that because the others were intimidated by his reputation. Until they settled down, he'd use their worry to his own advantage. Stretch Jackson had learned long ago that you didn't necessarily need good cards to win at poker. Poker had almost nothing to do with cards. It had to do with people.

Part One

Gamblers

LOS ANGELES
September 20

J ERRY CORBETT fanned her cards on the table and flicked an index finger in their direction. "Trip kings," she announced.

The bald man across from her threw his hand in disgustedly. "Beats," he said. "Damn! I had a hunch."

Jerry Corbett scooped the pot in and muttered, "Hunches are for dogs fucking."

The comment raised some eyebrows among the regulars at the Gardena cardroom. Jerry Corbett wasn't a prude but no one knew her to be coarse, either. Still, she'd seemed edgy lately. The regulars had been waiting for her sour mood to begin affecting her game, but so far they'd waited in vain. She was a winner again that night — two or three hundred, it looked like from the pile of chips she was stacking in front of her.

Jerry caught the floorman's eye and called, "Seat open." She left the table, a thirtyish, dark-haired woman slightly above average height with regular features and a solid chin. She was handsome but somehow not sexy, and if any of the men in the cardroom looked at her with lust as she threaded her way to the exit, their longing was strictly for Jerry Corbett's streak of luck.

In the parking lot outside the cardroom, Jerry unlocked her shiny red MGB and lowered herself behind the steering wheel. An ocean breeze had finally broken the September heat spell and now at two o'clock in the morning the temperature in the Los Angeles basin was down to a tolerable level and the air was almost fresh. Drained as usual after six hours of poker, Jerry drove west a couple of miles, then north a few blocks on a side street. She pulled into a driveway beside a wooden bungalow with white paint flaking from the siding. The front lawn was sparse and dry and a single palm tree, looming crookedly from the parking strip, rattled in the wind. Jerry pulled open the screen door and entered the living room. "Chris? I'm home."

From the kitchen came a woman's voice. "How'd you do, hon?"

"I'm a goddamn machine. I caught shitty cards all night and won a couple of hundred anyway."

"Super."

"You mean predictable."

A trim blonde in her mid-twenties, suntanned and startlingly attractive, entered the living room. She was barefoot and wearing blue jeans and a well-filled tee shirt that said Hussong's Cantina. "Don't be sour," she coaxed. She kissed Jerry lightly on the lips and broke into a smile.

Jerry disengaged from her and said, "Give me a hand with the toop."

"I wish you weren't in a mood." Chris carefully removed the dark wig from Jerry's head, revealing the curly, close-cropped hair of a man underneath. Jerry turned, offering his back so Chris could unzip his blouse and unhook the brassiere, which he shrugged out of, falsies tumbling from the cups.

"In a mood?" Jerry asked, standing exposed in his masculinity from the waist up. "Why can't I get through to you? A *mood*? God, how weary, stale, flat and unprofitable seems to me all the uses of this world," he declaimed. "It's an unweeded garden — a *Gardena* — possessed by things rank and gross in nature!" He stepped out of his sandals and said irritably as he walked towards the hallway unzipping his slacks, "I'm going to the can before my bladder ruptures."

They'd met in acting class. Chris had unblemished good looks of the sort that would stop traffic in any city in America except Hollywood, where she was just one of a thousand other equally talented and flawless industry hopefuls. After a disappointing year of no parts and no income, she'd gone to work as a makeup stylist. Her employment was sporadic, just picture to picture, and Chris recognized that short of a movie contract the best thing that could have happened to her in L.A. was linking up with Jerry Corbett. He was smart and ambitious and she loved him. But he'd been so out of sorts lately. She worried about losing him.

Jerry came out of the bathroom wearing a pair of khaki trousers and a short-sleeved shirt. Cold cream and soap had relieved his face of its heavy burden of cosmetics and the countenance he showed to the world in his natural state was more impish than handsome. There was something mischievous in his expression and something intimidating, too, in the flashing alertness of his large brown eyes.

"*Mon petit chou,* I'm starving," he said, entering the kitchen. "I can't eat when I play, I can't drink. Getting nephritis is bad enough but what happens if I have to take a dump some night? They'll bust me. The cardrooms have cans for men and cans for women but they sure as hell don't have any for transvestites. Jesus, I hate what I'm doing. Whenever somebody bets a queen, I think they're talking about me. Ha." He opened the refrigerator and looked inside.

"I can fix you a beef sandwich," Chris offered. "And I'll bet there's some cheesecake left."

He shot her a look over his shoulder. "You'll bet there's cheesecake? I'll call and raise."

She stuck her tongue out. "Smarty pants. Sit down and I'll deal you some food, okay?"

"You're on." He pulled her to him for an embrace. "I love you, hon, but I swear you're killing me. I've turned into a wage earner."

"Such wages, though."

Jerry sighed. "The one point I can't argue with." He sat at the kitchen table while Chris fixed a sandwich. "I broke up a pat full house tonight," he said suddenly. "Goddamndest thing. I kept trips and took a card so I'd get a call after the draw."

"That's nice. Did it work?"

"You're not listening again, sweetheart. It wasn't nice, but I made sixty bucks more than I would have by playing the pat. I was sitting right but the thing is, it was too sophisticated. I'm getting so good it scares me sometimes. I wish you knew the game so you could appreciate what I'm talking about."

"I play poker," she said.

"Everybody plays poker," Jerry said. "I'm talking about *knowing* the game. More and more I wonder how good I really am." Almost in a whisper he added, "It might be I'm great."

Jerry Corbett's bizarre gambling career had originated half in earnest and half as sheer audacity. Earlier in the year he'd played the lead in *Charley's Aunt*. Chris had done his makeup and Jerry had been terrific in the part. He'd played it against the grain and what people couldn't get over was the way he'd pulled off the aunt's role. "You have to believe in it," he'd explained. "I don't play it like a guy in drag — I play it like a woman. Physically it's tricky but if you can do a faggot, you can do a female. The voice is the key. Olivier said when he played Richard the Third he just tucked his foot sideways at the opening curtain, left it that way all night and the limp took care of itself. I do something like that with my voice. I soften it to the point I want and then forget about it. Ha. Maybe I can do Camille next. Or Blanche DuBois."

Jerry Corbett had a reckless streak. On closing night when the cast dared him to join them on the town wearing the aunt's costume, he did it without hesitation and stayed in character all night long, too. Later he remembered that occasion when he decided to try his luck in the Gardena cardrooms. Playing poker was a desperate way to try to make money, but he and Chris were broke and had debts all over town. As soon as Jerry decided to try Gardena, though, he became a victim of his own logic. As he explained to Chris, gamblers live in a world of machismo. "If a woman knows how to play poker worth a damn, she's got a hell of an advantage because men simply won't believe a female can play cards in their league. So what if a guy disguised himself as a woman?"

As soon as he proposed the theory Jerry recognized how ridiculous it sounded, yet he was trapped by his own argument; if it was valid it made sense for him to act on it, ridiculous or not. After all, playing poker was strictly an economic venture for him; the object was to make some money. So with Chris's help Jerry made himself up, not as Charley's Aunt but as a female version of himself, and on his first night at Gardena he carried off the impersonation perfectly. But he learned absolutely nothing because he fell into a phenomenal run of cards. Buying into a small-stakes game, he drew cinch hands one after the other and cashed out a big winner after only an hour. He knew skill had nothing to do with it because with lucky cards like he'd drawn, even a terrible player would have won. Yet that first flukey night determined his course of action. Jerry shrugged and told Chris, as gamblers have conceded since time immemorial, "You can't get off a winner."

Thus began Jerry Corbett's gambling career as a female impersonator. After a while he could have written a book about the war of the sexes, except that wasn't what interested him. What interested him was the game of poker. And what he soon learned was that serious poker wasn't a game. If anything it was a craft, almost a science. Ultimately, he decided, it was an art. A creative art. The deeper into the game he plunged, the more he understood the kinship between acting and poker-playing. Quite simply, in draw poker Jerry Corbett had discovered his métier. Beginning in late spring he played at Gardena five nights a week and the game absorbed him totally. He had his share of losing nights, like any gambler, but there were fewer and fewer of them as the months passed and his style took shape. In his mind Jerry could picture his learning curve at poker and it was as stupendously vertical as the trajectory of a rocket launch.

Over the summer Jerry had paid off their debts and credit cards with his winnings, which was tax-free income, as Chris liked to point out. They'd shifted to a cash basis and even stashed two thousand dollars in a safe-deposit box, and that was only a start because Jerry was working his way up to the bigger games. If his luck held, by Christmas they could have a real bundle salted away, and they needed it. But they had a problem: Jerry wanted to quit the cardrooms. He hated Gardena. He couldn't stand the place. By September he knew deep in his bones that he didn't belong there. He couldn't get Chris to understand why, but there was so much about the game that he couldn't share with anyone that he felt frustrated trying to explain.

"It's not a card game, Chris," he argued, munching his beef sandwich at the kitchen table that night in September. "I've told you before. Cards have almost nothing to do with poker. You only use the cards to move the money around. It's a game of psychology. But every good player knows that, so what makes me so successful?"

"Probably because you're smarter," Chris said. "And maybe luckier?"

"I worry about luck. I could be on a five-month rush and be too damned arrogant to recognize it. But I doubt it. Luck doesn't hold up that long. I'm convinced I play at a higher level than the others. They might as well hang signs around their necks advertising their cards. It's like there's a window in their foreheads and I can see right through. I'll tell you what it is," Jerry said. "You know how dogs can smell things and hear things humans can't? That's how I am at a poker table. I pick up clues other people don't see. Or hear. Or sense, whatever the hell it is. It's body language, nonverbal communication, I don't know. All I know is that being an actor has a lot to do with it. I control what I send out and read what other people send out. Am I saying anything that makes sense?"

Chris loved it when Jerry went into one of his monologues, his ideas popping like a string of firecrackers, one thought feeding another. He was so alive when he was talking a blue streak, more interesting to her than anyone she'd ever known. She could listen to him forever. In bed later that night, she came out of her sleep and snuggled to him when she realized he'd been lying awake. "Thinking?" she asked, and felt him nod his head in response.

"After New Year's," Chris whispered, "when we have our nest egg? You can use it all to get back into acting. If we're careful, we can make it last a long time. It doesn't matter about me anymore. I want it for you."

"That's not our deal."

"I know," she said, "but I don't care about me. I love you, hon." She kissed his forehead. "There. I give you my share. I want to see you in a part."

Jerry was silent for a while and then said, "That's what I've been thinking about. I'm in a part every night. I'm in a long-running play except there's no audience, which is a substantial annoyance. My act's wasted on those Gardena lowlifes. You don't understand how obnoxious that scene is, hon. Gardena's the skid row of poker. It's not a place where gamblers go — it's where they end up. I can't take it anymore."

"Just 'til the holidays," Chris urged. "Finally we're saving some money."

"I want to go to Vegas," Jerry said.

She held her breath. "Alone?"

He shook his head. "With you. I need to go up against better players and Vegas is where they are."

"Then let's go," Chris said. "We have fun on the road. We had a good time in Ensenada, remember?"

"That was vacation. This would be work. I heard about a poker tournament in Reno in January. That's what I want to aim for."

"Sounds good to me," Chris said. "I've never been to Reno." She kissed Jerry good-night and moved contentedly to her side of the bed.

But Jerry lay awake. Reno sounded good to him, too, except there were a couple of things he'd neglected to point out to Chris. One, he'd been playing draw poker all summer but the tournament was going to be stud poker, which was a different game. Jerry wondered if the risk was worth it, because the second thing he hadn't told Chris was that Stretch Jackson's tournament would be a ten-thousand-dollar buy-in and even if his luck held up for the rest of the year, that would be the most they'd be able to sock away by January. He could blow their whole nest egg in the first hour of the tournament. It would be a betrayal of Chris's trust in him but as near as Jerry could tell, he was willing to take the chance. The money didn't matter to him anymore. Money wasn't the point. The only thing that mattered to him was finding out who he was and how good he'd be when he went up against the best in the business. It was the challenge that counted, the testing of his nerve and his brains and especially his talent. What counted was the game he'd chosen to play. Or maybe it chose me, he thought. Maybe I don't even have anything to say about it. Maybe this is the role I've been auditioning for all my life.

☜☞ O R O V I L L E
October 20

W HEN he plodded out of the motel office with his room key in his hand, he smelled the rich Sacramento Valley aroma, the thick redolence of irrigated crops, the vast fecund land throwing the heat of the day back into the air at twilight, and it reminded him jarringly of an earlier time. The only thing that still seemed to work for Lee Sherman Tobias was his honker. His teeth and eyes were shot, his hair was gone, his bones ached and the old pump was running down for sure, but at least he could still smell things. Not that it gave him any pleasure to be reminded so unexpectedly. How old had he been the first time he was smacked by the smell of the big agricultural valley? Twenty-nine, maybe thirty? It was before the war, he knew that, because he'd been driving a '38 Packard convertible, one of those long green sporty jobs with spare tires upside the fender wells. He'd climbed north out of Los Angeles over the old Ridge Route at about midnight, the convertible top lowered in the blast furnace of summer, and dropping down the Grapevine he'd rolled into the heat of the central valley to be walloped by the uprushing sweet composty smell of California's immense breadbasket. He remembered the odor, which was the same then as now, even four hundred miles north, but a difference was that Lee Sherman Tobias was almost half a century older now and felt every day of it. He didn't kid himself about that, not since his last time in the hospital.

They could keep the West Coast, he thought. He'd never liked the place. He'd driven the Packard out on a lark that first time, to pick an orange off a tree and take a swim in the Pacific Ocean like he'd promised himself, but once he crossed the desert into Los Angeles all he wanted to do was get the hell out. It wasn't his kind of a town. Years later at a golf club in Hollywood, when he had a name, Lee Sherman Tobias had won a bundle off some movie big shot at gin rummy and mailed Edith a six-figure check, but he couldn't say it was fun even then. The producer had brought a crowd of people in to watch and was more interested in showing off than playing cards. "I flew a monster to town," he kept complaining. "At gin yet! It's not enough he's the best poker player in the country, but he schneiders me at my own game! How do you do it?"

One hand at a time, Tobias could have told him. The producer was probably the better gin player of the two but that didn't matter because he was an amateur and that doomed him from the first shuffle because like all amateurs, he couldn't keep his mind off the stakes. He cracked for good when it finally dawned on him that Lee Sherman Tobias couldn't be rattled. The gambler was an elemental force. It was like playing cards against the Rock of Gibraltar.

"What did they name you Sherman after?" the producer asked. "A tank?"

Lee Sherman Tobias was still solid then. He was barrel-chested and thick-armed and had a large square leathery face unmemorable in its Missouri ordinariness except for his steady eyes, which were brown and deepset, and the two lines, straight as furrows, which ran from the outside of his nostrils to the edge of his wide upper lip. "Go you double or nothin' on eighteen holes if you want," he offered.

"Horse puckey," the producer answered, which was just as well. Tobias was a lousy golfer.

And now he was back in California, none the happier for it. He was too damned tired and sick even for an old man. Edith had phoned him in Vegas a few days earlier and told him C. R. Cooley was in a hospital in Portland and asking to see him. "He's got a cancer," she said. "There's no one to look after him but a niece. Lee Sherman, I don't want you goin' there unless you feel up to it."

Tobias could hardly believe his ears. Any time his wife started to pussywhip him she was asking for more trouble than she knew how to handle. He hung up on her. Later he landed at Portland in a blustery October rain and took a cab to the hospital. The girl wasn't C.R.'s niece, it turned out, but his step-granddaughter. She was his only kin and grateful that Tobias, or anyone, had showed up to help her keep vigil.

"It's a wonder he's lasted this long," she said. "The doctor says he's got a fighting heart. He's between medications now, so this is a good time if you want to talk to him."

Well, shit, Tobias thought. He hadn't bargained on the last rites. C.R. looked as bad as a man could look without having lilies on his chest, but he was propped up in a hospital bed and jabbing at the television remote control, as yellow and shriveled as a dried-up gourd.

"Well, looky here," the dying man said when Tobias entered the room. "Lee Sherman, you look like death suckin' a pickle. I heard you had a heart attack."

"More like lung trouble."

"What I figured. I never knew you to have a heart. Nina," he said to the girl, "shake this man's hand. It ain't every day you get to meet the champeen poker player of the whole country. Three times runnin'."

"Three out of five," Tobias said, but it meant nothing to the girl. She turned off the television and pushed a chair over for Tobias. He eased himself into it as the girl started to leave the room, but Tobias motioned for her to stay. It had been a mistake coming here.

"You look like hell, Lee Sherman, if you want the truth," Cooley said.

Tobias answered, "You want a mirror?"

Cooley's face crunched in a spasm. When it passed he said, without elaboration, "Tap city."

The words lay awkwardly between them. Tobias had nothing to offer. He wasn't that tight with Cooley. He'd known him for years but only as a face across the poker table, that was all. A face and a voice and a pair of hands and a set of habits, the chief one being that he bluffed too much.

"It ain't so bad," Cooley said. "I been hurt worse in crap games."

Tobias sat patiently. When you're all in and holding an empty hand, he thought, there isn't a whole hell of a lot you can do except tap out. Father Time runs the game and he's no gambler; he just keeps takin' the odds until one day he's got 'em all.

"Tell the girl how I got my nickname," Cooley said. "I always liked to hear you tell that story."

Tobias shook his head. He wasn't a storyteller. An ego case like Stretch Jackson could take a yarn and string it out forever, but Stretch was a natural-born bullshitter. He could start up a conversation in an empty room. Tobias had more of a retailer's personality; with cards and words both, he followed what he understood to be Wall Street's advice: buy cheap and sell dear.

"Tell her," Cooley said, and turned to the girl. "Nina, it ain't everyone gets nicknamed by the world champeen. You listen to this." Another spasm creased his face but he shook it off. The girl stole a look at her wristwatch and then focused her gaze politely on Tobias, waiting.

She doesn't care about it any more than I do, Tobias thought. But silence filled the room and he decided the hell with it, I'll humor him and then get out. "I'm a bettin' man, Missy, and that's a fact," Tobias said. "But your granddaddy there, he'd bet on anything. I used to tell him he was so crazy for action he'd bet on a cockroach race."

The girl smiled but Tobias knew she wouldn't understand. He felt too tired to go on. He wasn't sure he didn't belong in a bed down the hall somewhere himself. "I meant it as a compliment, understand," he said. "I used to tease him he'd bet on a cockroach race. One night in Vegas, I guess about ten years ago, he pretended to get mad —"

"Bull," Cooley interrupted. "It was Hot Springs and it was thirty years ago if it was a day. And you didn't know I was pretendin'. Tell it right, Lee Sherman."

"Could have been Hot Springs," Tobias conceded. "That goes back, C.R."

"Way back," Cooley said from the pillow.

Hot Springs, Saratoga, French Lick, New Orleans. It could have been anywhere, Tobias thought. Back before Vegas there used to be lots of stops for road gamblers. "Anyways, your granddaddy slammed his cards down and said, 'Goddammit, I've heard that from you for the last time!' Pardon my French."

"I had you goin'," Cooley said.

"You tell it," Tobias said. He felt fatigued.

Cooley said, "You."

The girl smiled again but Tobias knew she was just being polite. Cooley'd been a crazy bastard in his time and of course he'd figured the next time Tobias saw him, he'd make his usual crack about betting on cockroaches. So Cooley was ready. He'd left the table but came back with a little wooden matchbox with two cockroaches inside and he'd just raised all kinds of hell. He slapped a thousand bucks down and challenged Tobias to a bet. He made such a big production out of it that everybody in the place was watching. Tobias was in a bind — he had his reputation to protect, but Cooley had rigged things so he could look like either a coward or a damn fool.

Tobias was getting caught up in it now. "Say a cockroach's got eight legs," he told the girl. "All you have to do is break two of 'em and you got yourself a four-to-three proposition. Or you could maybe use glue on one side — the way I figure it, that insect's just gonna run around in a circle. I had to do somethin', though, because your granddaddy was screamin' so loud for action. So while I'm figurin', I take the matchbox and close the cover nice and careful and I say, 'Mr. Dealer, I believe we're playin' straight poker here. Ain't supposed to be no bugs in the game.' I get a little laugh out of the crowd for that, but C.R. acts like he can't believe it. He says, 'Are you tellin' me that a man of your notorious character and reputation ain't gonna give me any action?'

"I said, 'You got the picture. And you want to know why?' See, I got the crowd with me now. I said, 'It ain't that I don't trust you. And it ain't that I don't trust them cockroaches.' I give it a pause for the build-up then. 'What I don't trust,' I said, 'is them tiny little jockeys of yours.' "

"Little jockeys," Cooley giggled. "You can't get ahead of Lee Sherman."

The girl was still waiting for a punch line. Tobias said lamely, "That's when they started callin' him C.R. For cockroach."

Cooley grimaced again and the girl asked, "You gonna ring for the nurse?"

"Not yet," Cooley said. He asked Tobias, "Know what my real name is? LeRoy. It's frog for king."

Tobias pushed himself to his feet and said, "I guess they didn't know the word for ace, huh?"

Outside in the hallway, the girl thanked him for coming. Tobias reached into his pocket and pulled out a money clip, peeling off some hundred-dollar bills. "Towards a stone," he said, folding the money into her hands when she protested. And, his gait slow as he plodded down the hospital corridor, he left.

And rented a car, which was another mistake. He wasn't in shape to drive. South of Portland he pulled over in the drizzle to pick up a hitchhiker, a bearded young man in work boots. "How far you goin'?" the stranger asked Tobias, throwing his bedroll in back and sliding into the driver's seat.

"South." Tobias tried to get comfortable but his chest was heavy. "You?"

"Cancún," the hitchhiker said. "Mexico. Why the hell not? This winter I'm gonna tan instead of rust."

The interstate led them south through a persistent mist. Tobias could see wet green fields on both sides of the highway but if there was any scenery beyond that, it was obscured by the low clouds. "You got a line of work?" he asked after a while.

The younger man grinned. "I deal a little."

Instinctively Tobias looked at the hitchhiker's hands even as the delayed message reached his brain that the kid didn't mean he dealt cards. He chuckled to himself at that one. Times don't change so much, he thought. There's still hustlers on the road, guys living on the edge. Tobias had the sense of being there before. It was where the kid said he was going that put him in a reverie. Cancún. Tobias had played coon-can as a kid. That's what they gambled at, so he'd learned it. Coon-can, dominoes, pitch-to-the-line, dice. He'd hustled pool for five years but meanwhile he'd discovered poker and by the time he was twenty he was playing in the East Texas oil fields, big games, for a kid like him big beyond belief in those raggedy-ass boomtowns. He had a regular circuit — Tyler, Henderson, Kilgore, Longview — and by God, the money he made and spent. And got robbed of a few times, too, until he learned not just how to make it but how to keep it.

And then, during the war, there was Norfolk. Talk about boom-towns — the Norfolk docks made the Texas action look like peanuts. Between the longshoremen and the steelworkers and even the sailors sometimes, Norfolk was gambler heaven. The games were huge and twenty-four hours and it seemed like every high roller in America came through Norfolk. Tobias would never see anything like it again. No telling how much money he sent home to Edith.

It was afterwards that he was a road gambler. Edith stayed in Joplin and Tobias got there whenever he could, at least always at Christmas and almost every year in a new car. He had a reputation by then and he came to understand that there were people, rich people he'd never heard of, who played him cards expecting to lose. They had mental problems as far as he was concerned, because Tobias never got in a game he expected to lose at. Which isn't to say he never lost. But over the years he never ran into a player who could beat him regularly, and gradually he accepted what everybody was saying about him: that he was as good as there was. Tobias never looked at it that particular way himself, though. The only way he saw it was that he was a poker player. It was what he knew, so it was what he did. That world championship business didn't signify half what people made it out to be. In Vegas they said Lee Sherman Tobias could see around corners, but Tobias knew he'd just been sitting in the right seat at the right time in the tournaments. Half the game was patience and the other half was luck, and anyone who was patient enough would still be sitting there when the luck came. Poker was that simple. The rest was instinct.

It was all Vegas now, he thought, but Tobias didn't miss the old days; a game was still a game to him, wherever they played it. Edith stayed in Joplin and Tobias still mailed her expense money, and when he went home he was as comfortable in the nondescript cottage as he was in the Vegas hotel where they kept a suite for him. He figured Edith could afford better but if she wanted to stay in the cottage, that was her business. His job was earning the money, hers was keeping the house, and after so many years of habit it didn't even strike him as strange that his wife had never set foot outside the state of Missouri.

When Tobias had been sick the last time, they'd asked if he

wanted to send for his wife and he'd said, "I ain't dead yet," and that took care of it. He had what they called congestive heart failure, but he couldn't make much sense of it when they said the heart problem caused his lung trouble. They put him on oxygen and gave him pills and finally turned him out of the hospital, but he'd felt like hell ever since. When the heavy feeling came, he couldn't catch his breath. He was winding down and he knew Father Time had the long odds on him now too, just like on Cooley.

It was Tobias's health that made it a mistake to rent a car, but he felt better when they crossed into California. The weather was dryer and warmer, downright hot, and when the hitchhiker said he wanted to detour into San Francisco, Tobias let him out of the car and took the wheel himself. He made it as far as Oroville before the heaviness came over him. In the twilight, he checked into a motel and that was when the Sacramento Valley aroma struck him, the thick, rich smell of farmland remembered from a time so long ago. He wanted to get dinner but once he propped himself up in bed in the motel room, panting, he didn't have the energy to get up. He decided he'd drive into Reno the next day. It was just a short push over the Sierra, and when he got to Reno he could decide what to do next. He figured, depending on how he felt, that he'd either check into a hospital or buy into a poker game.

&⊙& L A S V E G A S
November 20

SHAYNA LEVINSON'S first memory was of kicking her older brother in the nuts when she was four years old. He was a wimp and so were her parents, her father an engineer at Boeing who fished weekends in Puget Sound and her mother a long-suffering housewife, period. Shayna Levinson cared for her family only in the way she might have been fond of home appliances, in that they made her life convenient. But they bored her to death. Shayna learned early that there were only two kinds of people in the world: there were people willing to be pushed around and there were people born to do the pushing. She was one of the latter. Shayna was aggressive. Although she had ordinary looks, with pale blue eyes and washed-out blonde hair, people had always noticed her from the time she was a child because of a peculiar alertness she had, a predatory glint common to the kind of small animals best kept in cages.

For as long as she could remember, Shayna's one driving ambition had been to escape from Seattle. The place was a prison. Seattle was a hick town in the farthest corner of the country, light-years from the mainstream. Its weather was punishing — wet, cold winters that began in September and lasted until May, unending months of rain when the sky was dark and heavy and so low you felt you could reach up and touch it — and even its geography was oppressive, with mountains and water crushing in from all sides. Shayna wanted freedom, freedom from Seattle and license to do whatever she wanted.

She was a whiz at math and she had a mind that was immediately brilliant at chess, music, puzzles and any card game she was exposed to. Her father hoped she'd aim for a college like MIT or Cal Tech, but Shayna knew herself better than that; she was street-smart, not book-smart. She enrolled at UC Santa Barbara, where she said she planned to major in finance and surfers.

The surfers were easy; Shayna never had trouble manipulating men. But Santa Barbara turned out to be as dull as Seattle. With the Pacific Ocean lapping at its edges, it even reminded her of Seattle, except for better weather. More alluring to Shayna was the incredible megalopolis farther south, Los Angeles. But L.A. made her nervous; with its reach, its population, its unknowableness and its wealth, L.A. only drove home to her what a hick she really was. Inland, though, there was another city just as impressive in its sweep and even more alluring in its glitter and garishness. It was in the desert, where the air was clear, where the climate was dry, where the only standing water was chlorinated and usually kidney-shaped, and where such things as rain forests or log trucks were as unthinkably alien as a kind word or a decent act. One trip to Las Vegas was all Shayna Levinson needed to recognize that she'd found her home. Las Vegas was a city without heart or soul, a city with no reason for its existence but lust and avarice, a city where dreamers were losers and losers were swept out with the garbage. Shayna Levinson quit college in her sophomore year and moved to Vegas. It was predestined. She was a piranha; she could swim with the rest.

Tips were good for cocktail waitresses but Shayna soon figured out there was no future in depending on tips for a living. To succeed in Vegas, she needed to learn gambling. So she went to dealers' school, and in a long year of dealing twenty-one and craps and roulette, she learned that the games were strictly for suckers. The lesson came as no surprise, but the message she took to heart, the cold knowledge she absorbed for all the time, was how merciless the house percentage really was. She learned that losers in Vegas weren't beaten as much as they were pulverized. The mills of the casinos grind slow, but they grind relentlessly.

Inevitably, Shayna became a poker dealer because she'd discovered there were only two ways a gambler could make money in a casino. The first was by counting cards at twenty-one but that was a dead-end career because of Catch-22: if you were good enough to beat the game, the casinos banned you. The second way was by playing poker. Poker was the chink in Nevada's armor. It was different from all the other games in a casino because in poker you didn't play against the house. In poker, you played against the other players and the house didn't give a damn how much money you won since the house took its edge right off the top, by raking a percentage of every pot. In poker, the casino provided you with a table and a dealer and a game, in effect renting you a seat from which you could help to pulverize the suckers.

Shayna thought she knew the game. Trips beat two pair and a

28 //

full house beat damn near anything. Basic. But when she started dealing, she watched and listened and realized she hardly knew poker at all. She was missing something. She felt a rhythm but didn't know where it came from. She saw the same players win day in and day out and she knew they were defying the laws of probability. It didn't make sense. Then one day Shayna got ahead of the rhythm. She'd been dealing poker for three months when it struck her that she was a beat ahead of the game. Her hands seemed to be moving on their own, anticipating the action, and at that moment everything came clear to her. Subconsciously, during her long shifts of dealing, Shayna had penetrated the mystery.

She'd found the missing piece of the puzzle, which was that the rhythm of a poker game didn't come from the cards. It came from the winning players. They didn't defy the laws of probability — they denied other players access to the odds. They dominated the game through their style. Oh, they were clever. It would take a genius to spot some of them. Some were quiet, some noisy, some jovial, some shrewd, but Shayna could pick them out, and her heart lifted when she saw through to the core of the game: despite the odds and probabilities, a winning style could triumph over losing cards. Her insight was paradoxical enough, smacked enough of Zen, so that Shayna knew there wasn't a player in a hundred who could appreciate it. But she understood she'd seen the truth. Now she was ready to start playing. If she'd been a piranha when she came to Las Vegas, she'd evolved into a barracuda.

Shayna kept her job. She dealt days and she played nights at other casinos. The odds were second-nature to her, the game automatic — what she developed was a style. She could beat the tourists but that was easy; if the locals couldn't beat the tourists, they wouldn't stay locals very long. What Shayna did was to beat the locals. She did it by beating their spirit, breaking their will. She didn't have to fake a poker style; it sprang naturally and full-blown from her personality. Dominating a poker game was no different to her than kicking her brother in the nuts; she won by aggression. She challenged the virility of male players, rattled women players with feminist cant. She was noisy and obnoxious. She sprinkled her chatter with racial and ethnic innuendoes. Winning a particular pot didn't matter to Shayna; she played to cash out winners over the long run, and that meant she had to destroy the other players, crush their egos. She hurried the slow players, stalled against impatient ones. She unbalanced a table's equilibrium. She wouldn't let other gamblers play their own cards — she intimidated them into playing against her. She wore a tee shirt when she played, boldly printed *Ms. Deal*, but the nickname didn't catch on. What they started calling her around town was Doctor Death.

At first Shayna kept her dealing job for the income, but later she kept it for cover. If the other gamblers thought she needed the salary, they wouldn't suspect how much she was winning on her own. She even kept her winnings secret from Frank Bartelli, letting him believe she won maybe a couple of hundred a week tops. In his scheme of things, that was chicken feed. Frank Bartelli was a pit boss Shayna lived with in a rented house west of the strip. If her parents ever laid eyes on Bartelli, Shayna thought, they'd die. He was a real greaseball, as Italian as linguini and Catholic to the core. What Shayna liked about him, aside from his looks, was that he was shrewd and calculating and just as cold-hearted as she was. They belonged together. They were a couple of armor-plated survivors.

Bartelli worked nights and Shayna worked days, so they only got together in bed or on weekends or over breakfast sometimes in their kitchen. It was a good period of time for Shayna, comfortable and steady and lucrative. And then overnight her world fell apart.

"You've been fucking your ex," she told Bartelli at breakfast one morning.

He said, "That's a lie."

"She told me."

"You believe that bitch?"

"She's got the IQ of a cactus," Shayna said. "She doesn't have enough brains to make things up."

Bartelli shrugged. "A couple of quickies," he admitted. "For old times' sake. It's no big deal."

"Six months is no big deal? You've been cheating on me since day one."

"I don't like that word," he said.

"What're you gonna do — break my legs? You son of a bitch. I'm lucky I don't have some kind of disease from you."

"Don't swear at me," he said.

"Asshole."

"I warned you."

"You're making me a laughing stock. You've been jumping anything with a body temperature."

"Hey, I don't have to apologize," Bartelli said. "It's a long time since I was a choirboy. Tell you the truth, it's hard to be grateful you do me a big favor twice a week."

"Pit bosses," Shayna said. "I trust one guy in town and he turns out to be a snake."

"Yeah? You're never home. You're out playin' poker all the time like a goddamn tourist. The gash around this town, what am I supposed to do? I never said I was a priest."

"That's for sure. Your brains are all below your belt."

"You never complained."

"Don't flatter yourself," Shayna said. "Man, how you make me look. Can I pick 'em."

"We get along, kid. Don't mess things up."

Bastard, Shayna thought. Don't mess things up, he says. As if she could salvage anything out of the disaster. Bartelli had ruined her gambling career in Vegas, that was all. With the insults Shayna handed out at the poker table, she got her share back and most of them referred to the lack or depravity of her sex life. She always ignored the comments as futile attempts to rattle her, but now she wondered how many in fact had been sly references to Bartelli's screwing around. Probably the whole town knew about it but her. She couldn't win money at poker from people who were laughing at her. You can't intimidate people when you're a clown. The insults would continue, Shayna knew, and now every one of them would hit home with exactly its intended effect. Her game would be shot. So long, poker winnings.

What a joke. Trust a man to fuck things up, she thought. Shayna couldn't get even with Bartelli; she had no leverage to use against him. But she did the best she could. The next day she called a second-hand furniture man over to the house. She left Bartelli his wardrobe and jewelry but otherwise sold the house out to the bare walls for cash. Furniture, TV, appliances, kitchen stuff, the works. She packed her car, drove to the bank, took thirty thousand dollars in bills out of her safe-deposit box and got on the highway. A stake like that would set her up fine in Reno, thank you. They didn't know her from Adam up there, and after Vegas she was ready to eat that town alive and spit out the bones. Shayna Levinson wasn't a barracuda anymore; she had become a shark. She put the gas pedal to the floorboard when she cleared the Vegas city limits, speeding north into the desert and destiny. She was all of twenty-four years old.

✒◦✑ HONOLULU
December 20

*B*RIAN BATES had nineteen-inch arms and a forty-seven-inch chest, no small achievement for a man who stood only five-feet-six. He bench-pressed two hundred and eighty pounds in the gym, pumping ferociously, and after his final set he finished his workout with a brisk two hundred sit-ups on the slant board. He stripped for a shower in the locker room, pausing to strike a pose in one of the full-length mirrors. His body, suntanned and shiny with sweat, was approaching competitive shape. It was bulky and symmetric and slabbed with muscle, ribbed and bulging and striated with muscle; if he'd begun bodybuilding at an earlier age, Bates thought, he might have made it a career instead of a hobby. Not that he was too old at thirty-five, but competitive training would require a major commitment of time and Brian Bates had other, more important matters demanding his attention. His divorce, for one thing.

A half-hour later, dressed in blue-denim trousers and a silk aloha shirt, Brian Bates sat in his lawyer's office in a high rise in downtown Honolulu, venetian blinds drawn against the slanting Pacific sun. "Temporary three thousand a month is generous," Bates said. "It's more than she'd get in a settlement."

"I still say you're going at it the wrong way," the lawyer said.

Bates ignored the remark. "You know what to do about the lawsuits."

"You told me. Fight everything. How long will you be gone?"

"I don't know."

Like most people, the lawyer found Bates's abrupt answers unsettling. Bates would sit still, without even blinking, as if he were in meditation, and then when he spoke, he went right to the point in complete sentences. His voice had the soft huskiness of an adolescent's but it discouraged argument. Bates didn't ask questions; he gave orders.

The lawyer said, "We can settle the suits at twenty cents on the dollar. It'll get the litigation out of your hair and clear everything up. Except the orthodontist — he's furious."

"Forget it," Bates answered. "They don't have a leg to stand on. The dentist, either."

"What if the D.A. gets interested?"

"He won't indict."

Brian Bates had regular features and with his sandy hair, clear blue eyes and unlined face, he could have passed for ten years younger than his age. He had a handshake you could trust, the lawyer thought, and a confident manner that gathered you in. On top of that, he somehow managed to convey a wounded, little-boy look, and that was the clincher. Beneath his self-assurance he let you glimpse a vulnerability, and that's when you got in trouble, the lawyer thought. When you felt sorry for Bates or thought you could take advantage of him, that's when he reeled you in.

The lawyer said, "You'd just better hope that orthodontist isn't descended from samurai."

"He's loaded," Bates answered. "You didn't meet that Jap. He held me up for eighteen percent on his loan."

"My luck, I'll meet him in court." The lawyer gathered the papers on his desk and asked, "When's your plane leave?"

"Couple of hours."

"And you don't have a forwarding address."

"I'll phone you."

"Can I know where you're going?"

"Reno. Nevada."

The lawyer stared at him. "You're crazy. In December? Your blood's not ready for that. You'll freeze. What are you going to Reno for?"

Bates stood up and walked to the door. "I did time there once." At the look on the lawyer's face, he added, "Don't worry — it wasn't for fraud. I punched out a cop. Be sure you serve those papers on Marlene tomorrow." He left.

Contrary to the lawyer's belief, Brian Bates's vulnerability wasn't feigned. Life was a constant struggle for Bates; his nickname in the Marines had been Dumb Okie. Bates knew he was a simple man in a complicated world and needed all of his concentration just to stay on top of things. For his own self-protection, he had to think through everybody's lies and figure out what was really going on. It had taken him most of his life to learn even that much. It used to be that Bates believed the lies, and that was when he always got hurt. They'd told him the orphanage would only be for a while but after they'd put him in, he never saw his mother again. They'd told him a little guy could be good at sports, that it wasn't size but skill that counted, and then they'd made a monkey out of him when he tried to play basketball. They'd told him the Corps would turn him into a man and then thrown him in boot camp with a bunch of gorillas. When they'd sent him to Nam, they told him it was to win the hearts and minds of the people for the American way. That was when Bates started to wise up. By believing what smarter people had told him all of his life, he'd managed to end up in a foreign jungle with nothing to defend himself with but an M-16 rifle and an eighth-grade education while most of the gooks in Asia were ganged up trying to kill him.

After the Corps, Bates went into sales. He did fine. He was earnest and patient and could tolerate having doors closed in his face. It was a simple formula — make so many calls, you'll make so many sales — and everybody understood the rules: you sold at a markup over cost and the difference covered your commission and the company's profit. Nobody argued with that. But it was different in real estate, which Marlene urged him into after the first kid. In real estate, rules weren't rules if people thought they could chisel around them. And real estate had another important aspect to it, too, which was greed. Brian Bates gave a lot of thought to how greed fit into the formula. He decided it helped him because he figured out that greed was a weakness, and weaknesses were one thing he didn't have.

It was Bates's habit to concentrate on one thing at a time. First had been bodybuilding. Then his courtship and marriage. Then real estate. After the other kid was born, they moved to the Islands. When the recession hit, Bates came into his own because he wasn't rattled by adversity. All he'd ever known was adversity; he thought it was the normal state of things. He turned his concentration to what people called creative financing, not knowing it was a complicated subject. To a dumb Okie, everything was complicated. Bates thought his way through it and within a few years he was on his way to becoming a millionaire.

He did it with mortgages. Bates would buy a condo by agreeing to the asking price and making a big down payment. He'd give the seller a second mortgage for the balance. Then, with the deed in his hands, he'd borrow money from a private investor and give him a first mortgage. Bates would cover his down payment with part of the first mortgage and pocket the rest of the cash. Then he wouldn't make any payments. When the investor foreclosed, the original seller, stuck with a worthless second mortgage, would lose his shirt while Bates walked off with a bundle. He wouldn't own the condo, but he didn't care about that because he'd clear fifty thousand bucks or more on the deal. And he wouldn't even owe taxes, since all he showed on paper were debts. The transactions were legal, but Marlene, and his lawyer and everyone else, kept telling him they were unethical.

"They're greedy people," Bates would answer. "It's like poker. When they think you're hurting, they pour it to you."

Bates had formed his philosophy in the Corps but he'd only heard it put into words when he watched John Wayne's last movie. "I won't be wronged, I won't be insulted and I won't be laid a hand on," the Duke had announced menacingly from the silver screen. "I don't do those things to other people and I require the same from them." That said it all to Bates, and to his way of thinking, he'd been wronged by his wife. She'd married a man, not a pussy, and now she was trying to change him. She wanted to make him weak.

"We were kids, Briny," Marlene argued. "We were lovely, innocent kids. We put each other on pedestals. You were Sir Galahad and I was Snow White and it was wonderful, it really was wonderful. But we grew up, don't you see? At least I did. I'm not perfect. I'm just me. I've got cellulite and I have bad breath in the morning and I have to shave under my arms and . . . I'm just a human being, is all. I'm nobody special."

"You're my wife," Bates said. "You're the girl I married."

"I'm the woman she became. I've got fears and doubts just like everyone else and it's not my natural cheerful disposition to stay home all day and be a mommy and a housewife anymore. I'm entitled to a life."

"I give you a good life."

"You give me money and a place to live. You don't give me a husband. Not a partner. You think you married a princess and I'm supposed to pretend I married John Wayne. Those aren't real people. They're not us."

"You know who I am," Bates said.

"I know you could be gentle and understanding if you'd let yourself. I don't need a tough guy. I need a partner, someone who can allow himself to be soft, who can share his problems. Share with me, Briny. Talk to me."

She wants me to cry, Bates thought. She won't be satisfied unless I break down and make a fool of myself and blow my nose and tell her I'm afraid of the boogie man. What bullshit. Well, she'd brought it on herself. She couldn't say he hadn't warned her. He'd warned her they had a deal and she was backing out of it. She even wanted him to give the money back to the people he bought the condos from. She accused him of robbing them.

I won't be insulted, Bates thought. That's how I am. I don't do those things to other people and I require the same from them. Especially from my wife. Airborne later, the Islands below him and an hour back, Bates sat stolidly in a first-class window seat as the big United 747 flew east high over the ocean towards darkness and the west coast of the continent. She won't be expecting divorce papers served on her tomorrow, he thought, but she did it to herself. And with three thousand a month until we go to court, she can't blame me for anything. I'm treating her all right.

Yet Bates felt an unfamiliar twinge of regret. He knew he wasn't a man who could be hurt — after what he'd been through in his life, nothing could hurt him again — but Marlene had reached deep inside him. He didn't have the words to describe it, but she'd touched something otherwise untouchable within him and he felt a strange sadness because she'd ruined everything by changing.

Flying to Reno was an impulse. Bates had a grudge of long standing against the town and wanted to settle it finally. They'd busted him in Reno once for vagrancy, although it had taken three cops to do it, and now he was going back a rich man. Sitting in the window seat, Bates flexed his upper arm and watched as the muscles bunched and grew. That's who I am, he thought; I won't be wronged and I won't be laid a hand on. His arm filled the sleeve of his aloha shirt and threatened to burst the fabric. His Hawaiian clothes wouldn't do in Reno, but he had a layover in San Francisco and could buy a sweater there. Tomorrow he'd go shopping in Reno. And then his plans were to throw money around the casinos like the wealthy man he was and see if it felt as good as he expected it to.

Part Two

The Tournament

➤◦➥ *Monday*

*A*RT EPSTEIN's office was oversize and on the spartan side except for its heavy leather furniture and the bright acrylic abstracts that splashed color on the walls. A large, broad-shouldered man with blue eyes, Epstein sat behind a big walnut desk in front of the picture windows, talking on the telephone. His office door opened and his secretary poked inside, pointing at her wristwatch. Art Epstein held up his free hand, spreading his thumb and fingers. Five minutes. The secretary retreated and Epstein continued his conversation.

"Listen, amigo," he said, "I'm late, I've got a car waiting and I haven't been able to find my wife all morning. I can't believe we're quibbling over a lousy million bucks. What do you say we split the difference?"

He grinned at the answer he received. "Right, Uncle Sam gets it all anyway. In a pig's eye, pal. No," he said, "*you* write the deal memo — I'll be out of town the rest of the week."

Art Epstein replaced the receiver and punched out his home phone number, swiveling his chair to look outside while he waited for the ring to be answered down on the peninsula. From the thirtieth floor, his view was northwest towards the Golden Gate Bridge. The sky was blue and clear but he knew aloft it would be windy.

"Lupe?" he said when the phone was answered. "If you hear from Miss Gaines, ask her to call Connie at the office. I'll be home Friday unless you hear otherwise. Thanks."

He hung up again and buzzed for his secretary. Connie re-entered the office and Epstein asked, "Anything that absolutely can't wait?"

She handed him some messages. "The governor's office called. That arts commission thing."

"The governor or his office?"

"Just the office."

"Call back and tell 'em it's under control," he said. "It isn't, but what the hell. All they want's a donation — the rest is window dressing. If it comes down to it, I'll write a check."

"In six figures," she said dryly.

He shrugged and sifted through the messages. "These can hold," he said, and stood up. "I'm off. No calls now. You don't know where I am to anyone except Jackie. Tell her I'm at the Taj and she's warmly invited."

"Will do," Connie said. "Good luck. Bring back a trophy this time."

Epstein paused in his stride across the room and gave her a guilty grin, like a schoolboy playing hooky. Then he left the office and rode the express elevator down to the parking garage.

Arthur David Epstein, Beverly Hills High '66, Yale '69, Harvard Law School '72 and Stanford MBA '75, was six feet four inches tall with two hundred and twenty pounds packed solidly on his frame. He had blond hair, pale eyebrows, a strong jaw and an athlete's grace of movement. When the elevator doors opened in the basement, he was greeted by a black man in chauffeur's livery. "Sorry to keep you waiting, Earle," he said.

The chauffeur touched his cap. "Morning, Mr. Epstein," he said. "No problem. Your bags are in the trunk."

"Great." Epstein climbed through the open back door of the Rolls and said, "Oakland airport. *Vámanos.*"

The automobile maneuvered quietly through the garage and as it entered the outside street with a cushioned bounce, braking for the downhill grade, Epstein reached for the daily *Variety* waiting beside him on the backseat. He cracked the window to let the tangy air blow through. As the Rolls proceeded through the late morning traffic towards the Bay Bridge, Epstein suddenly put the newspaper down and reached for the telephone. When he got through to his office, he told Connie, "It just struck me. Jackie might have gone down to Carmel. Try her at the Lodge, will you? And see if you can reach Capello for me."

The peculiar status of Epstein's marriage was no secret to anyone who knew him. His wife, Jackie Gaines, *née* Judith Gintz, was a movie actress who divided her time, when she wasn't away on location shooting, between the Bay Area and the purlieus of Hollywood and Malibu. It was Epstein's fate to worship his wife and what Jackie did with her private life during her absences was something he didn't want to know, although he assumed the worst. As near as Epstein could tell, Jackie didn't have a jealous bone in her body and was still as head-over-heals in love with him as she'd been on their wedding day, but she just liked to live too much of her life away from him. Epstein couldn't fathom how he'd drifted into such a crazy situation. His marriage was either perfect or perfectly awful and some day, he thought, he might discover which it was.

But meanwhile he ached for children, and time was growing short for that. Jackie was as sleek as ever, but she worked harder at it now and had begun to talk about soft-focus closeups with a particular sneer in her voice. She was currently annoyed with Epstein because she wanted him to put together a movie deal and he wouldn't touch it, arguing that even her agent balked at casting her as an ingenue at the age of thirty-two. Epstein knew Jackie wouldn't stay angry, but for the moment he didn't even know where the hell she was.

The phone in the Rolls beeped and Epstein grabbed it. "Capello?" he said. "I've got a brainstorm. Let's take an option on that building we don't want. Offer twenty thousand for a month and I'll bet they grab it. They've got a cash problem." He laughed when the other man objected. "Of course it's nutty," he said, "but look at the leverage. Where's your imagination? I can't resist controlling ten million bucks with twenty thousand. Besides, I'm on my way out of town and I need an omen. None of your business where I'm going. I'll talk to you Monday."

Epstein replaced the telephone receiver, knowing he'd just thrown away twenty grand. But the gesture helped to put Stretch Jackson's poker tournament in perspective. Epstein had to be oblivious to the stakes when he began playing tomorrow.

At the airport, Foley, the co-pilot, was waiting outside on the ramp next to the Lear. "Well, look who's here," Foley said with his big grin. "Stretch Epstein. Hi, boss. We're fueled and ready."

"Sorry I'm late."

"No sweat," Foley said. "Beautiful day to go up."

"Windy," Epstein said.

"We'll be over the weather." Foley, who was wearing harness boots, blue jeans and a nylon parka with zipper pulls all over it, was a six-footer with round cheeks, curly dark hair, green eyes and the gift of a wide, dazzling smile that was created for no other purpose than to disarm people. He reached for one of Epstein's suitcases and the two men climbed into the jet. Inside, Foley went forward and left Epstein to discover a girl sitting in the cabin, legs crossed elegantly and a large handbag on the seat beside her. "What the hell?" Epstein pointed towards the cockpit and asked, "Are you with him?"

"He says I'm with you."

Epstein couldn't help grinning. "No offense, honey, but are you a hooker?"

She gave him a blank look. "Are you a cop?"

"Wait a sec." Epstein went to the cockpit, where Foley was settling into the co-pilot's seat. The pilot, Virgil, a small man in a suit and tie, was in the other seat, concentrating on setting frequencies. Epstein asked Foley, "Did you pay her?"

The co-pilot, his green eyes merry, said, "Me? I'm just a working stiff."

"I know about the stiff part," Epstein said. He went back to the cabin and gave the girl a couple of bills. "My friend has a sense of humor," he said. "This'll get you back to town." He helped her outside. "Maybe some other time."

The wind blew her hair. She pushed it back from her face and looked up at him. "It's like fishing," she said.

"How's that?"

She shrugged. "The good ones always get away."

"It works both ways," Epstein told her. She fluttered her fingers at him and walked off towards the terminal. Epstein climbed back into the plane. "Foley," he said when the co-pilot came back to close the air-stair, "you're hopeless."

Foley was enjoying himself. He got away with his attitude simply because he was Foley and nobody who knew him expected anything different from him. "Me?" he said. "You won't see me turning down carnal activity with the likes of that one. Did you catch her figure? Try to do a guy a favor and he doesn't even say thanks. There I was, flat on my back at twenty thousand feet —"

Epstein had followed him forward. "Which is when you leave poor Virgil here alone at the controls, right?"

"No way," Foley grinned. "Virgil's a horny little bastard. What do you have against parties all of a sudden? It seems to me I remember a time or two when you got your knob polished on these jaunts. Here we got us a little gambling trip, a little nooky, a little whiskey if you want —"

"Foley," Epstein said, "my father warned me about two things in life. He said never drink with an Irishman or dance with a Greek, because you'll sure as hell hate yourself in the morning. You owe me two hundred bucks."

"You hear that, Virgil?" Foley said. "Here I was going to get us all blown out of the sky and Scrooge puts the kibosh on it."

Virgil waved him silent. He was talking to the ground controller, preparing to taxi. Epstein went back to the cabin and buckled up. When the plane lifted off in its steep climb, banking to the east, Epstein looked down and saw the bay and the cities spreading below. Then he leaned back, relaxing to collect his thoughts. The crucial point, he reminded himself, is to stay alive Tuesday and Wednesday. Give the weak players time to knock themselves out. What you'll have to do is get a reading on the strong players. And keep them guessing, which means you'll have to run some bluffs. So pace yourself. You won't need the biggest bankroll going into Thursday's round but you'll need one big enough to mix things up. Which means Wednesday night will be the critical time.

Art Epstein had done everything he could to put himself in the right frame of mind for Stretch Jackson's tournament. He was rested, his mind was clear and for business purposes he was incommunicado. Now the result would depend on his skill, which was the way he wanted it. Except you could never tell about luck. Even the best players needed some of that.

Foley came back and sat down. "In your mood, you probably won't even go to the whorehouse with me," he said.

"Poker and sex don't mix real well."

"So shoot craps. It doesn't take brains. I figure a cathouse beats a full house any time."

"Did you ever play bridge?" Epstein asked.

"I hope not."

"I did, in college. In high school I played basketball. I was too big to be a guard, too small to be a forward and too quick to be left on the bench. The coach didn't know what the hell to do with me."

"He could have sent you to the football team."

"That would have been worse. I hadn't learned it yet, but I don't mesh with teams. I'm a buccaneer. I figured that out playing bridge. Bridge is just logic and arithmetic. Playing bridge is like four people solving algebra problems together. For that, who needs the other three? Nope," he said, "I get off on poker."

46 //

The plane lurched. "Hell, I can't play with my friends," Epstein said. "I don't want to take their money. It's the pros I want — against them, it's uphill. Playing on their turf, that's a challenge. They creamed me the last two years in those Vegas tournaments but with half a break in this one —"

"Foley!" Virgil called on the intercom.

"Weather up ahead," Foley said. He went forward and in a moment Epstein felt the plane go into a climb. The plane bounced, dropped and kept climbing. The clouds outside suddenly turned dark. Epstein saw snow. Then a lightning bolt exploded brilliantly off the right wing. The plane dropped until it seemed to hit something solid, then lurched violently upwards again. Through the windows, Epstein saw bolts of lightning flash through the blackness. The plane plummeted abruptly and then shuddered and lifted as if weightless. For a long minute it bounced through the dark in roller-coaster hops. Then, as suddenly as it had entered the storm, it broke into daylight, and through wispy clouds below him, Epstein saw the eastern slopes of the Sierra Nevada and the high brown desert unrolling ahead in the bleakness of winter.

He went forward. "Still got your lunch?" Foley asked. "I've heard of dropping in on Lake Tahoe, but that was ridiculous."

Virgil said, "Sorry for the scare, sir. It wasn't on the program. It'll be rough going in. You'd better get buckled up."

Epstein went back to the cabin. Looking down, he picked out the clump of foliage and architecture that was Reno. As the plane descended, the downtown high rises tilted, taking on perspective. Then Epstein could see the neon lights and he swiveled his gaze away from the swerve of the aircraft, staring intently at the town as the plane entered its approach for landing. In his mind he was already walking into the casino of the Taj Mahal, feeling the warmth, inhaling the scent. He could hear the unique sound of the casino, any casino, all casinos, the magic white-noise mix that pulsed almost tangibly, like ocean waves, the sounds of slot machines and keno calls and roulette wheels and stickmen chants, the shrieks and groans and ululations, the rattle of chips.

And the clean rasp of cards being shuffled for the deal of a poker hand. Art Epstein took a deep breath as the plane touched down. For the first time since he'd awakened that morning, he felt a stirring of excitement in his blood.

Shayna Levinson was killing time in a ten-dollar stud game at Harrah's, too bored even to get up and leave the table. She'd wandered into the casino a while earlier and bought into the game when she'd noticed two unfamiliar faces playing. Tourists. But they'd been plucked clean a half an hour ago and now only Shayna and four other locals were sitting at the table, pushing chips around without interest. Shayna wasn't even trying to rattle the other players, since there wouldn't have been any point to it; they had the personality of tombstones. What she felt like doing was going back to her apartment and taking a nap. The town was dead except for the Taj Mahal, and Shayna was forcing herself to stay away from the Taj because when she went there she was going to have to pungle up ten thousand dollars.

Ever since she'd arrived in Reno, it had annoyed Shayna that Stretch Jackson's stud tournament was going to be taking place there without her participation. She was aching to challenge the hotshot pros, to humble them in the full spotlight of public attention, but not at the risk of ten grand of her own money. Three nights earlier, though, she and seven others had bought into a private stud game of their own for twelve hundred and fifty bucks each, winner take all. The final pot had been for ten grand — the entry fee for Stretch's tournament — and Shayna had won it by catching a fourth queen on the last card against a made flush. It was a sweet win, the more so because for the first time in her life, Shayna had people on her side. The other seven let it be known that they considered themselves entered in the tournament vicariously through her. It was a new sensation for her, having a rooting section for once, but that was Reno for you. It was a tank town compared to Vegas, but it had a heart sometimes.

Still, Shayna couldn't bring herself to part with the ten grand yet — tomorrow morning would be soon enough to pay the entry fee — so she stayed at Harrah's, killing time at a boring poker table. She glanced at the outside windows and saw snow flurries. Or maybe it was just rain. Whatever it was, it was cold and gray outside and would only get worse by nightfall. She ought to get up and go home, Shayna thought.

An awkward kid with a lock of shiny brown hair falling over his forehead dropped into a seat at the table, plunking a bottle of Coors down next to him. He was a type to Shayna; for kids like him, it was always their first time in a casino and they usually traveled in packs. With this one's arrival the other poker players came to life, although their quickened attention would have been no more apparent to a casual observer than the slightest flick of a feline's tail.

"Ever play here before?" the dealer asked.

The kid said no.

"It's seven stud, one to ten. High card must open for at least a dollar." He shuffled and cut the cards but paused before dealing. "Need some chips?"

"Oh," the kid said. He leaned back, reached into his trousers pocket and pulled out some red five-dollar chips that he dropped on the table. Four of them. He looked towards the rail with a naive grin and Shayna saw that he had three friends watching, another young guy and two girls.

"Five minutes, Doug!" one of the girls called. "You promised. Then we have to go eat."

"Ace bets," the dealer said, indicating the kid's up card.

The kid, Doug, looked at his hole cards. "Is it on me?" he asked. "How much?"

"You can bet one to ten."

"I bet a dollar." Doug pushed a red chip across the table with his forefinger. The dealer scooped it into his rack, made change, dropped a dollar chip in the center of the table and slid four chips back to Doug, all in one fluid motion.

Shayna folded. The old man on her left, irritated, threw a dollar in. He was always irritated; if he held bad cards he was irritated that he couldn't bet and if he held good cards he was irritated that he had to. The only difference in his play was that the longer he scowled at his cards, the better they were; he was about as hard to read as a billboard. The player on his left folded and Rafe, an overweight man at the end of the table, got in for a dollar.

The dealer burned a card and dealt a round of cards faceup. "Ace still talks," he said.

The kid, Doug, bet another dollar. The scowling old man called and Rafe, throwing two red chips at the pot, said, "Play for ten."

Startled, Doug looked at the raiser. What he saw was an obese man of about thirty in a canary-yellow shirt, wide red suspenders, a gaucho hat, a Fu Manchu mustache and aviator sunglasses. The getup was Rafe's idea of how to look inscrutable. Doug looked at his hole cards again, shrugged, awkwardly pushed two red chips at the pot and gulped from his bottle of beer.

The scowling old man threw his cards in as if they smelled bad. On the next card, Rafe, showing two hearts, caught the queen. The kid caught a ten to go with his unmatched ace-deuce.

"Still the ace," the dealer said.

Doug bet a dollar again. Rafe, his attention apparently wandering to a distant part of the casino, threw chips in and said indifferently, "Ten better."

Doug gave his friends behind the rail a look of resignation. He leaned back to reach into his trousers pocket but the dealer extended his hand to stop him. "Table stakes," he said. "All you can bet is what's in front of you."

The kid pointed to his chips. "There's seven dollars. Can I call with that?"

The dealer nodded and Doug pushed the chips at the pot.

"He's all in, Rafe," the dealer said, sliding three dollars back to the fat man. He quickly dealt another up card and a final down card and said, "Okay, let's see 'em."

Rafe turned his hole cards over. "All purple," he grunted.

"Heart flush," the dealer said to the kid.

Doug frowned, as if things were going too fast for him. He turned his first two hole cards over one at a time and said, "I had three aces."

Shayna had a feeling. Full house, she thought, and sure enough, the dealer turned over the kid's last down card and it was a deuce. He separated the three aces and two deuces so Rafe could see them, then pushed the pot over to Doug.

Now Doug had forty-some dollars in front of him. He said with a huge grin, "It's been like that all day!" To his friends, he held up an index finger and called, "I did it again!"

"Five minutes, Doug!" the girl called.

Time to go, Shayna thought; in his ignorance, the kid was un-balancing the equilibrium of the table. Shayna was scarcely aware that she was analyzing the dynamics of the game, but she knew without thinking about it that Rafe was pissed off now, that the other players were anxious to nail the kid in a hurry before he cashed out, and that the kid himself was oblivious to all of it. Trip aces wired and he bets a dollar, she thought. "Does your mother know you're in Reno, Dougie?" Shayna asked, but he just grinned at her and drained the last of his beer.

Shayna was dealt a small pair in the hole on the next hand. Rafe, showing an ace this time, opened for a dollar. He got a call from the player on his left, an octogenarian with shaky fingers and a stubby cigar plugged in the center of his mouth like a cork. The kid, Doug, called with a three of spades showing. Shayna called and the irritable man on her left, studying his hole cards as if they were inscribed in runic, finally threw in a red chip and said, "Raise it four." He had a king showing and Shayna folded, figuring him for a pair. The others called.

The raiser caught a second king showing on the next card and bet five dollars again. "With trip kings?" Shayna sneered. "They'll never arrest you for gambling." Rafe called but the old man with the cigar silently turned his cards over. Doug, who caught a four of hearts to go with his three of spades, called.

Nobody helped on the next two rounds and the kings bet ten

dollars each time. On the last card he bet the limit again. Rafe called reluctantly. Doug, showing no apparent strength, said, "I guess," and threw in ten dollars. He won the pot with a hidden spade flush.

"Honest, it's been like that all day!" he laughed. "I can't lose!"

"It's not because you're not trying," Shayna said, but Doug didn't hear her. His girlfriend was calling to him and he stood up, stuffing chips into his trousers pocket.

"Gotta go," he said.

Shayna, who'd lost exactly a dollar in the two hands, figured it was cheap entertainment. The kid didn't know anything except that he was hot, but that was all he needed to know; he'd just taken a hundred bucks off the table. Now the others would tighten up even more, and that finally got Shayna to stir. Standing up, she gathered her chips and told the dealer, "Seat open."

Young Doug McGowan, meanwhile, joined his three friends and the quartet made their way through the casino, Doug's enthusiasm pulling the group forward. "It's like I told you," he said. "They *give* money away here!" He stopped impulsively at a roulette wheel and asked, "When's your birthday, Gail?"

"April third," the girl said.

"Perfect! April's the fourth month, right? Four and three — that's a lucky number." He pulled a red chip from his pocket and threw it on the seven. But his bet was too late; the croupier flicked it off the layout as if swiping at a fly.

The ball landed in twenty-five. "See, what did I tell you?" Doug said. "Two and five!" The croupier swept the layout clear and Doug put his chip back on seven for the new spin. This time the ball skittered around the wheel and plopped into the seven. Doug's girlfriend squealed and grabbed his arm. The croupier passed four black chips and fifteen red ones over to Doug — a hundred and seventy-five dollars, if he'd bothered to count.

"Look at that," he laughed. "Can't miss. Can*not* miss! Let's go eat."

But first he stopped at a twenty-one table and slapped down a chip. Only when he lifted his hand did he see that it was a black one, twenty-five dollars. His friends, caught up in the magic, pressed close to him.

He was dealt two face cards. The dealer, showing a five, turned over a six, hit a ten and swept the table. Doug lost. "A fluke," he said. "Double after trouble." He put two black chips down and this time he was dealt a fourteen. He stood on it and the dealer busted. Jubilantly Doug scooped up his winnings.

At the cashier's cage, Doug McGowan emptied his pockets, dredging up more chips than he remembered stuffing into them. He felt drunk and not-drunk at the same time, intoxicated on adrenaline and his own metabolism, and beyond that he felt safe and euphoric, as if he were in two parts, half of him detached from his body and floating protectively nearby. Nothing could hurt him. The cashier piled his chips, knocking them down into stacks of five for counting, and paid him off. Doug's winnings came to more than four hundred dollars. "And that's just the start," he told his friends. His optimism wasn't unreasonable, considering that he'd started gambling only an hour earlier with a two-dollar roll of nickels at the slot machines.

Doug McGowan was slim, with healthy coloring and eyes soft enough to belong to a girl. People who'd been to old-time film festivals told him he looked like James Dean, the movie actor. At midnight Doug McGowan was going to turn twenty-one years old, and he was in Reno because of that special occasion. As he'd told his friend Terry, who worked at the pizza joint with him, for as long as he lived he'd never again have the chance to drink and gamble in a casino when he was underage; it was now or never if he was going to have stories to tell for the rest of his life about carrying on in Reno when he was legally too young. He'd talked Terry into joining him on the adventure and then, when the girls had agreed to come along, it made the whole thing incredibly perfect.

Doug and Terry had flirted with the girls at work but inviting them on the drive to Reno had been sheer bravado. Gail and Lisa were roommates at San Jose State and only nineteen but, being female, as usual could anticipate no problem with I.D. And, being female, as usual had also quietly worked out between themselves whatever proprieties were going to be observed on the trip. The group had rented two rooms at the motel, ostensibly one for the girls and one for the boys, but during the few hours since then Doug had come to understand that things would work out better than that. Lisa had fastened on Terry, and Gail on Doug, and that was just fine with him.

Something about the way Gail was hinged at the midriff appealed to Doug's sense of aesthetics. She had long thighs, a flat stomach and a natural swivel when she walked. She turned him on. She had a pretty face or he wouldn't have asked her on the trip in the first place, and now, with the brisk mountain air heightening her complexion, Gail's carefree animation matched Doug's own. He put his arm around her shoulders, she hers around his waist, and they crossed the intersection in stride, leaning into a slanting drizzle that carried a definite scent of snow down from the mountains. What a day, Doug thought — the booze, the slot-machine jackpots, the poker win, the roulette win, a sexy girl's hand tickling his hip bone — and it was just beginning, too. In seven hours, at the stroke of midnight, he'd be in bed making love to her. That was Doug's plan and he didn't question that it would happen. The terrific way things were going, the special magic he was touched with, anything he wanted to happen was going to happen.

But first there'd be dinner and more booze and more gambling and more winning. "Magic time!" he announced, pushing open the glass door to the casino across the street. The four of them rode an escalator up to the second floor and were escorted to a booth in the restaurant. "Dinner's on me," Doug said as they picked up their menus. "Anything you want."

A keno runner walked past and Doug stopped her. "Can you bring us drinks?" he asked.

"Sorry," she said. "Did you want to play keno?"

"Sure. How do you play it?"

"It says in the booklet." She pointed to the keno tickets and paraphernalia that occupied a compact place on the table, like a centerpiece. "I'll be back."

Doug plucked a leaflet from the pile and unfolded it in the air like a small road map. "Okay, group," he said, "the game is keno. Let's see now. You can bet a dollar and win three dollars. Or you can mark more spots and win more money. Or you can — wait a minute." A dreamy look came over his face and he said with awe, "Jesus Christ, you can win fifty thousand dollars in this game!"

Brian Bates had found a congenial companion for dinner, a middle-aged psychologist named Carroll Shepherd. Shepherd was pink and bald, except for a fluff of cottonlike hair around his ears, and he had a pleasant amiability and something of a look, too, with his wide-set eyes, that reminded Bates of a big friendly fish. Bates figured the agreeable expression was Shepherd's professional mask but what the hell, the old guy seemed genuinely curious about him and Bates welcomed some company for a change.

They'd met that afternoon in the health club on the fifth floor of the Taj Mahal. Bates had finished his workout with the weights and was taking a sauna when this other guy sweating in there asked, "Didn't I play poker with you last night?"

"Could be," Bates said. "Over at the MGM?"

"That's the place," Shepherd said. "You play a hell of a game, son. I hope you don't mind my asking, but are you a professional?"

Bates laughed at that. He said, "Sure. In real estate."

"You could have fooled me." Shepherd had an easy manner that encouraged conversation. "You seem to remember cards awfully well."

Bates had to think that one through, since he wouldn't have described his playing in those words himself. Finally he said, "It's work, like everything else."

"Discipline, huh?" Shepherd made a gesture that obviously was meant to include Bates's overdeveloped physique as well as his card-playing. "You here by yourself?"

None of it was any of the stranger's business, but Bates was glad for a chance to talk. A sauna was no place to carry on a discussion, though, so the two men agreed to meet for dinner. Bates recognized that getting picked up in a steam room by an older guy wearing nothing but a towel definitely could have its faggot overtones, but in fact nothing like that was happening. Shepherd had volunteered that he'd come to Reno by himself for a few days of what he called recreational gambling and, like Bates, he was tired of taking his meals alone. Besides, he said he wanted to learn more about how Bates played poker.

Later, over dinner and drinks in the subdued atmosphere of the Taj Mahal's steak house, two floors removed from the casino's din and the churning of slot machines, a relaxed Brian Bates found himself expounding volubly. It was uncharacteristic of him but he appreciated being taken for a gentleman for once in his life, instead of for a hustler. He told Shepherd about his experience in Reno years earlier, when he'd been broke and brawling and finally had done thirty days and gotten floated out of town. "In the back of my mind," he said, "I had an idea of looking up that judge and, I don't know, bragging to him about my net worth or something. But that's crazy. All these years I thought he wronged me and then when I came back here I realized I'd been asking for it. Hell, it's a good thing they picked me up. I could have killed somebody before I was through."

"Literally?" Shepherd asked.

Bates shrugged and reached for his wineglass. "I was pretty flaky after Nam. I wouldn't say I still don't have violent thoughts sometimes."

Brian Bates admitted to Shepherd that he was getting bored in Reno. He was down a few thousand in craps and blackjack, nothing he couldn't afford, but the inevitability of losing to the house had finally been driven home to him and he didn't see any future in trying to get even. But the thing was, he didn't know where to go if he left Reno. Or what to do. Bates saw a problem building on the horizon because the weather was sure as hell going to drive him away soon; he never got outdoors except to walk to a different casino or take a cab over to the MGM. Poker was what occupied him in Reno and he stayed with it because he was winning, but how much poker could a guy play? When you have twenty-four-hour action and can find a game anytime you want, poker begins to lose its appeal after a while.

From talking about poker, Bates suddenly found himself telling Shepherd about the orphanage. "Clubs were black guys," he said. "You know, because of the way their hair looks. They should have been spades maybe, but I never heard that word until later. Spades were shovels, so those were guys I worked in the fields with. Diamonds were girls." Bates had never learned a real card game as a kid but he'd invented his own fantasy game using the cards as people. At the orphanage he'd lost himself in the game for endless hours, even sleeping with the shopworn deck of cards under his pillow until he reached the point sometimes where he couldn't tell what he'd dreamed and what he'd made up.

Shepherd asked, "So the cards all have distinct personalities to you?"

"It probably sounds funny," Bates answered. "But like I said, I was pretty much of a loner."

"What if I said the ten of clubs?"

"Roosevelt Garnett. Big sucker with a purple birthmark. He hit me on the arm once and it hurt for a week."

"Deuce of spades?"

"Bobby Dee. The twos are little kids. Bobby Dee wasn't around long. He lost some toes in a shop accident."

"Eight of diamonds."

Bates said, "You'll laugh. Doris Day. It was a jerk-off card."

Shepherd stared at him. "Outstanding. Did you ever hear of cognitive psychology?"

Bates shook his head.

"Loosely, the study of thinking processes. The cognitive boys get into recall a lot. Memory, mnemonic systems and so on."

"What's that mean?" Bates asked. "I'm a nut case?"

"Hardly. If you can use recall to your own advantage, wouldn't you agree that's intelligent behavior?"

"It's work, I know that."

"But I don't get how you keep track," Shepherd said. "I assume you play stud because you can follow the up cards —"

"It's hard to explain." Even without the martinis and the wine, Bates couldn't have adequately described the dormitory because it was a dream dormitory but based on a real one; he could see the dark interior of the sprawling old building in his mind but he couldn't convey the picture to Shepherd. Everybody had his own bed and the beds were in four sections, one for each suit. "What it's like," Bates said, "is when I see the up cards, then I know who's home. It sticks in my mind. If I want to make a hand, I have to go outside the barracks for who's still not home. So do you. Like say you're showing deuces, but I happen to know that on the first round somebody tucked Bobby Dee in bed. Well, he's home, so you can't get him. That means your chances of filling aren't real good and if you try bluffing me, you could end up in trouble."

"You invented that memory system?"

"It's not a system," Bates said. "I played *with* cards before I ever *played* cards. It's just how I remember 'em."

"If I spread ten cards on the table, real fast, and then turned them over?"

"I could tell you who they were. As long as I got a look."

"Twenty?"

"I think so. But you won't see that many in a hand of stud."

"I'll be damned," Shepherd said. "Last night sometimes you took a long time to bet. That wasn't strategy. You were recalling cards?"

Bates thought about it. "I guess. Oh, another thing about poker — I practice. In my mind, I mean. I do 'what if?' situations."

"Tell me what you mean."

"Well, what if I'm losing and another player's got my number?

You know, beating me every time. Do I back off? Start to bluff? Lay in the weeds? Or what if I get a full house and I'm maybe looking at four of a kind? Do I fold? Or what if I get a hell of a hand? How do I bet to keep people in the pot? I practice stuff like that in my mind. It's what you do in sales."

"You lost me," Shepherd said. "Do what?"

"Rehearse ahead of time. You damn sure do it on patrol. What if we get ambushed here? What if there's a sniper there? In body-building, I do a set in my mind before I do it with a weight."

"Visualization."

"Huh?"

"It's like Zen tennis," Shepherd said. "They've done experiments with athletes — shooting free throws, driving golf balls, et cetera. Mental practice can enhance future performance."

Bates took a moment to digest the information and then said, "It figures. I have to learn everything by myself. Nobody ever tells me a goddamn thing. That pisses me off, you know? You want to see something?" He fished a metal gaming token out of his pocket, held it out between his thumbs and index fingers and bent it in half.

"How to double your money," Shepherd said. "What was that about?"

Bates laughed. "I don't know. I'm drunk."

"You want some coffee?"

"Hell, no. I want some gin."

A few hours later Bates was in his room at the Taj Mahal, flat on his back in bed with one foot on the carpet to stabilize the whirlies, and wondering what had prompted him to open up so much to a shrink. I'm not that bad off, he thought. Bored is all, maybe a little lonely. Because he and Shepherd had agreed to go partners, eighty-twenty, in a poker tournament starting the next morning. Under the influence of alcohol, Shepherd had insisted on putting up two thousand dollars and backing part of Bates's action if Bates would enter the tournament. That's not too shabby for a dumb Okie, Bates thought, having a doctor in my corner. Marlene?

Momma. Bates didn't want to go home for a nightmare again but the shadowed dormitory came unbidden to him in his sleep. Bates ran terrified through the dark corridors, taunted by exit signs that led him only deeper into the labyrinth. The niggers and girls and cotton-choppers slept, oblivious to the deuce of hearts as he cried for his family. Momma? If he could find the door to Heartland, if he could reach the handle, he could enter and experience once again the love and joy of the family that waited for him only at night. His nightmare would end and Brian Bates could crawl into the peaceful warmth of the bed of the queen of hearts. "Momma!" he cried, embracing his pillow.

Outside, the wind had calmed and it was snowing steadily in downtown Reno, big wet flakes descending through the neon illumination. The muffled quiet seemed to have penetrated the casino of the Taj Mahal, where the crowd was thinning as gamblers called it a night. There would be a brief surge of activity later when the midnight show let out, but for now the noise level was dropping and even the commotion of the slot machines had begun a gradual diminuendo. Throughout the casino, life-sized silhouette posters of Stretch Jackson were on display, showing the gambler in a white jacket with rhinestones and fringed sleeves. Stretch was smiling, the corners of his eyes crinkly, his right hand extended in welcome, and from time to time one of the posters would startle a distracted patron who veered away from what appeared to be a realistic but curiously flat gambler accosting him from against a pillar.

Up the main aisle of the casino, his curly hair sprinkled with the shiny dew of what moments ago had been snowflakes, walked the unemployed young actor Jerry Corbett. When the poker tournament got underway the next morning, Jerry would resume his masquerade as a female, but at the moment he was dressed normally, as he had been since his arrival in Reno two days earlier with his girlfriend Chris. Feeling apprehensive, Jerry paused on his way towards the rear elevators. Near the center of the casino, several rows of slot machines had been removed and temporarily replaced with extra poker tables, where side games were now in progress. Above the tables a banner extending twenty feet in length proclaimed THE TAJ MAHAL PRESENTS THE FIRST ANNUAL STRETCH JACKSON SEVEN-CARD STUD POKER CLASSIC. A purple velvet rope, waist-high, encircled the playing area so that only the tables on the perimeter were conveniently accessible to spectators. Those were the smaller games; the high rollers bought themselves a measure of privacy at the inner tables. At that time of night, the poker area was the only busy part of the casino and even there the noise was muted. Craps tables would have created a din, but poker was a quiet game and the tableau that Jerry Corbett paused to observe was almost as still as a scene from a silent movie.

A western, he thought. At least half of the players wore costumes ranging from rodeo-macho to Dallas boardroom, with pointed boots, wide-brimmed hats and huge metal belt buckles in plentiful evidence. The rest of the gamblers were wearing everything from dinner jackets to what looked like Goodwill castoffs, including three-piece suits, golf outfits, jogging ensembles, polyester clothing of unnatural hues, and shirts and blouses either buttoned to the choking point or casually open to the sternum. Some wore outfits that only a wardrobe master or United Nations delegate could appreciate, and as a group the players bore up under the weight of enough rings, wristwatches, cuff links, bracelets, pendants and neckchains to founder a galleon.

Jerry Corbett drank it all in like a star-struck fan, grateful to be present at the spectacle but at the same time sick with the fear that he was in over his head. How many of the players would be in tomorrow's tournament he couldn't say, but just pausing there at the rope he could pick out a handful of professionals for whom a ten-thousand-dollar entry fee would be the merest pocket change. Jerry Corbett had learned a few things during his autumn in Las Vegas, and one of them was that real poker players, the guys who played no-limit, were unfathomable. Comparing himself to people willing to push fifty or a hundred thousand bucks into the pot for the turn of a card, Jerry thought, was like comparing a hang glider to an astronaut. Himself to Brando. He couldn't compete with gamblers who lived in such a rarified atmosphere. They'd murder him tomorrow.

Since the previous September, when he'd abandoned the draw poker games in Gardena and moved to Vegas, Jerry Corbett had come a long way. Continuing to impersonate a woman in Vegas, he'd soon decided that his instincts had been right, that the Gardena clubs were the chain gangs, the salt mines of poker. In the small-stakes games he could pry out a living an inch at a time by figuring the percentages, by waiting for the nuts, by playing with the patience of a spider. But for that kind of gambling, he might as well have carried a lunch box to the casino, punched a time clock. Stepping up in class, though, he escalated the risk. Vegas was like an ocean feeding ground where the big fish ate the little ones. The tourists fed the ten-dollar bettors, the ten-dollar bettors fed the hundred-dollar bettors, the hundred-dollar bettors fed the thousand-dollar bettors and at the top of the chain the biggest predators, the no-limit guys, the great white sharks like the Stretch Jacksons and Vic Houstons, preyed without fear on anybody who dared to enter their territory. And meanwhile the house chummed the water and took its relentless rake, fattening on them all.

Jerry Corbett had arrived in Reno with Chris two days earlier but hadn't done any gambling yet except for some keno and slots, which didn't count; keno and slots were so ubiquitous that playing them was as incidental as lighting a cigarette or waiting for a traffic light. So far Jerry had merely gotten acclimated to Reno, taking in a couple of shows, catching a movie, walking around town with Chris, enjoying himself — or trying to, with Chris in a mood. The side games had been going on when he'd flown into town and each night there'd been more of them, with higher stakes, as tournament gamblers assembled at the Taj Mahal from wherever they called home. Jerry recognized a few players from Gardena in the smaller games, but Vegas people were more in evidence. He knew some of them from experience and some only by reputation. That bitchy dealer, Shayna, was in a game right now, wearing her *Ms. Deal* tee shirt and hassling somebody as usual. It occurred to Jerry that he hadn't seen Shayna for a while. In Vegas he'd played against her a few times and on balance she had the edge on him, although Shayna was annoyed by other women players and Jerry had managed to get under her skin once or twice. He wondered sometimes if she weren't putting on a better act than he was; with her mouth, she belonged in improvisational theater. Now Shayna folded her hand and as she leaned back to glance around the casino, her gaze fell on Jerry Corbett. She didn't recognize him as a male and her own expression was neutral for the brief moment that their eyes met, but Jerry felt a twinge of anxiety. She had his number, all right.

But the hell with her. The moment passed and Jerry's attention was drawn once again to the center table, where six men were seated at a stud game. Jerry didn't know the denomination of the chips they were using but the chips were stacked in ramparts, mounded like sand castles, and he knew there had to be at least a couple of hundred thousand bucks on the table. Yet from the players' expressions, it was just another game of poker. Three of the players were unfamiliar to Jerry and for all he knew they could have been dope dealers or Arab oil billionaires, but more likely they were professional gamblers like the other three at the table, whom Jerry did recognize. From Vegas. The round-faced gambler with the spectacles was called Hoo-Hoo, because he looked like an owl, and the unflappable black man was known as Sandwiches, from his girth. The third player, and he was the reason Jerry Corbett lingered at the velvet rope to watch, was the legendary Vic Houston.

To Jerry's overactive imagination, Vic Houston could have been carved in granite, a Mount Rushmore sculpture brought to life. Houston was a big man with a solidness to his bulk, as if a swung two-by-four would break against him before it knocked him down. He was wearing brown, a Western-style suit with stitching on the lapels, a lighter brown shirt, a string tie and a brown cowboy hat with a deep center dent, and he even had a robust brown tone to his skin, in contrast to the indoor pallor of most of the other gamblers. His eyes were strikingly blue and suggested a hint of generosity that seemed incongruous in a man who was arguably the best poker player in the world. But the word on Vic Houston was that he was different from the other professionals — when he smiled at you, they said, sometimes he actually meant it. As a Vegas cab driver had once told Jerry, "Back home it's a different story, but out here there's Wayne Newton, then there's Vic Houston, then there's Jesus. That's how it is in Vegas."

Jerry let go of the velvet rope and turned to walk up the aisle towards the elevators, weighted with doubts. During his autumn of poker-playing in Las Vegas, his relationship with Chris had deteriorated. Watching Jerry play stud poker in drag eight hours a night wasn't Chris's idea of a good time, and the alternative, waiting around for him in an empty apartment in a strange city and then sleeping half the day away, was even worse. Their solution had been for Chris to move back to Los Angeles, where she had friends, while Jerry stayed in Vegas trying to build a stake. In that he succeeded, except that his bankroll suffered from the cost of maintaining residences in L.A. and Vegas both and shelling out for airfare between them once a week.

In Vegas, Jerry had discovered that his natural talent extended to stud as well as to draw poker. But he couldn't risk the big games; one bad night at even a hundred-dollar table could have wiped him out. So he'd plugged along in the twenty- and forty-dollar games, which would have been high-stakes gambling anywhere else in the world, and he'd watched time and again as Las Vegas proved its reputation as the graveyard of hometown champions. Jerry saw them when they arrived, the confident car-dealers with their sunglasses and pinky rings, the poolroom sharps with tattoos and pomaded hair, the gum-chewers, the finger-snappers, the paunchy Elks club shrewdies ready to show Lost Wages just how dangerous Main Street USA could be when it came to a game of poker. And Jerry saw the same guys when they left, older by ages than the two or three days or a week it took them to tap out, putting their hotel bills on charge cards and taking the longest, bleakest drive there is in the world, the one out to McCarran Airport sitting on an empty wallet.

The losers came and went, the winners stayed and flourished, and Jerry Corbett survived. He was a hell of a poker player, he learned that, but he happened to have put himself in a city where everybody and his dog was a hell of a poker player. By the end of the year, Jerry had accumulated his ten grand and a small cushion on top of it, not enough for comfort, and in the course of the grinding marathon he'd begun to wonder if Vegas had changed him. Inside, he felt as ebullient as ever but he wondered if modifying his behavior, subduing himself during months of poker, had turned him into one of the others. He felt weary, just as they looked pale and weary. All they knew was poker. All they did was poker. All they understood or cared about was poker and gambling. Between deals one night a player had said, "I tried fuckin' a few times but it didn't do much for me — there's no money in it," and such had Jerry's frame of mind become that he couldn't even tell if the guy was serious.

Upstairs in the Taj Mahal, Jerry opened the door to his room. Chris was waiting up for him, the TV on, and she asked, "Well? Did the walk clear your head?"

"It's snowing," he said. "Vic Houston's playing downstairs. And about twenty other killers." Jerry punched the TV into silence and sat down on the edge of one of the queen-sized beds. "Honey, I already put up the entry fee. I'd feel like a damn fool asking for a refund."

"Losing it won't make you feel any smarter," Chris said. "You told me yourself you don't have a chance."

Jerry took his shoes off. "That's terrific. I need Lady Macbeth in my corner and you give me Cassandra."

"Sweetheart," Chris said, "it's not like you'd be quitting. You're a success at poker. You set a goal and made it — and not against turkeys, either. But tonight's a turning point. Right now we've got enough money to live on for six months. What happens after you lose? Do you go back to Vegas and start over? Where does it leave us?"

"I'm sorry about the audition," Jerry said.

"You ought to hear yourself," Chris answered. "The whole idea was to win enough money to buy some time until you got a part. Then you had a chance at a part and turned it down. But it's not just the audition. I get the feeling you don't care. That's what frightens me. I don't understand you anymore. Are you an actor or a gambler?"

"Both, maybe." Jerry stood up and approached the mirror over the bureau. "They all are." He examined himself in the glass, making faces and assuming poses. Over his shoulder he could see Chris sitting cross-legged on the bed. She seemed far away. "You ought to see them downstairs," he said. "Cowboys, hippies, jet-setters — there's every costume down there but a goddamn circus clown. They're all actors. They're all doing *schtick*."

He made a face in the mirror, softening his features and pursing his lips in a pout. "And what am I — chopped liver? I'll give 'em acting." Jerry turned around and said, "Sure I'm nervous. So what? Did you ever give a good performance without stage fright?"

Chris said, "This isn't acting, Jerry. It's gambling. I don't know what Las Vegas did to you. You're a professional actor. People are supposed to pay *you*, not the other way around."

Jerry Corbett lay back on the bed and closed his eyes. "Don't you worry about me," he said after a while. "They'll pay through the nose. I'm ready for those amateurs."

⁝∘⁜ *Tuesday*

*T*HE difference between Foley sober and Foley drunk was about a fifth of Irish whiskey. Early Tuesday, Art Epstein was awakened by a pounding at the door of his penthouse suite on the twenty-first floor of the Taj Mahal and as he rolled out of bed he registered that he felt fully rested although it was still an early enough hour so that no daylight was filtering through the curtains. A glance at his watch on his way to open the door told him it was six-thirty in the morning.

Foley obviously hadn't been to bed yet. "I need legal advice," the pilot said without preamble, stumbling into the room with a grin on his face and his green eyes bleary with alcohol. "Where's the can first? I just took a leak but it's a long elevator ride up here."

"Maybe I'm missing something," Epstein said to the pilot's back. "Don't you work for me? Isn't that supposed to entitle me to some privacy?"

Foley closed the bathroom door behind him and shouted through it. "Let's get some breakfast. My treat, Art. Steak and eggs, hash browns, rye toast, orange juice — how's that sound? Coffee wouldn't be a bad idea, either. Tell you the truth, I'm a little drunkie." He came out of the bathroom buttoning his fly. "I don't see how I could have just taken a leak. It must have been in some other hotel. You get room service here?"

"It takes forever," Epstein said. "They want you downstairs gambling, not upstairs eating. I'll put some clothes on."

Foley sat on the bed, leaning back on his elbows and losing his balance in the process. "I need a lawyer," he said. "I'm gonna sue the MGM for sexual harassment. They have a girl working there who won't screw me. I think that's grounds."

Epstein went into the bathroom, splashed cold water on his face and brushed his teeth.

"I'll give her another chance tonight," Foley continued, raising his voice so Epstein could hear him, "if I can get back in there. You know they got plainclothes security? Man, they moved me out of that casino so slick I couldn't believe it. I don't know what they were so uptight about. I offered to marry her."

He kept talking as Epstein re-entered the bedroom to get dressed. "Y'know, I didn't plan on getting drunk. It was a dwarf's fault.

You can help me sue Harrah's, too, come to think of it. They're dwarfists," he said, having trouble with the word. "We'll file a class-action suit. Man, talk about representing your little people. . . . You ready? Ask me, you're inconsiderate as hell. First you wake me up at some ungodly hour and then you take forever to get dressed."

Epstein didn't mind Foley's intrusion. He welcomed the diversion, in fact. Epstein knew he was unhealthily obsessed by the poker tournament, which would be starting in a matter of hours, and until it began he was glad for a distraction. Downstairs in the Taj Mahal's coffee shop the two men were given a corner booth, where Foley continued his flow of conversation while working his way through a substantial breakfast and a carafe of black coffee. "After we got the plane squared away," he said, "I took a taxi downtown and checked into my room. I'm on good behavior, okay? I mean I clean up, watch a little TV and go downstairs to shoot some craps. No problems. The casino's a tomb, though, except for poker, so I switch to blackjack for a while. But I keep getting old people from tour buses sitting next to me who hit soft nineteens. And the dealers are all on the rag. This is a cold town, Art. People here are into misery.

"Actually, I did have a couple of belts. Because I went to an empty table to get away from the ladies with the blue hair, except it wasn't a blackjack table like I thought. Which is why it was empty. The dealer's one of those Victor Charlies they got all over town now and when I put fifty bucks down, instead of dealing me cards he shoves me over some dice and a stack of dominoes. What the fuck? Turns out the game's called pai gow or something. Hell, I don't know. Mah jongg. Mooshi pork. I push the dominoes back and throw the dice and I still don't know what happened except he rearranges the dominoes and gives me a big grin and pays me off. I must be the only white guy ever played that game, because the fact is there's a bunch of Orientals standing around giggling and they give me a round of applause when I get up. I take a bow and as far as I know, right now you're lookin' at the world's only champion Caucasian pai gow player. Hell of a game. I wish I knew the rules.

"Anyway, I was walkin' through Harrah's when I notice there's action at one of the crap tables. You gotta get the picture, Art. Because the shooter's a dwarf, and I mean from *The Wizard of Oz*. I'm talking serious Munchkin here. He's got the little body, the tiny arms and legs, the big head, the quacky voice — hell, the sumbitch can't be more than three feet tall and there's no way he can even reach the table, never mind see over it. So they got him a box to stand on. He's perched up high enough to throw the dice but he still can't reach anything, so he's callin' his bets and the stickmen are placing 'em for him. Damndest thing I ever saw. He's drunk as hell but the thing is, he's hot as a two-peckered billy goat. All he's throwin' are numbers and he's got the table covered, so I get on him.

"Okay, we got us a hot, noisy table. There's magic, a rush, you know the feeling? The dwarf's crazy as a bedbug but one thing he doesn't know how to do is crap out — there just aren't any sevens on his dice. He's up there like Donald Duck going 'wack-wack-wack' and he's so excited he can't wait — he keeps tryin' to reach the dice before the dealer can hand them to him . . . What're you laughing at? This isn't a happy story, for Chrissake. I got a thousand bucks out there. I'm on every number, I'm takin' double odds, and that little fucker — get this now, he's so goddamn excited and jumpin' up and down that he throws the dice, falls off his box, and goes right with 'em. Does a friggin' swan dive right into the table.

"Jesus. You had to be there. I mean, how often do you see a dwarf in a crap table? It's like watchin' the Olympics. He does a somersault, comes up cheering, raises his arms, and everybody claps. I wanted to hold up one of those cards, you know? Order of difficulty, three-point-two. Except the croupiers don't think it's funny because maybe everybody else is watching the dwarf, but they're watching the dice and the dice are still on the table and they come up a seven. Not to mention there's chips scattered all over the place. The pit boss rules it's a clean roll — the seven stands.

"Well, now it's mutiny time. Except go argue with a pit boss, right? Rotsa ruck. But I told him if he's gonna count the dice, then he's gotta count the shooter. 'Fair's fair,' I said. 'Put that little guy on the come line and give me the back-up odds. If this is gonna cost me a thousand bucks, at least I want a chance to win a midget.' Hell, Art, any wonder I got drunk? I'm the only guy in the history of craps to drop a grand rollin' a dwarf the hard way. You want the rest of that bagel?

"Anyway, I ended up at a lounge show at the MGM. Lady sitting there with cleavage down to her kneecaps. I bought her a drink and she says, 'I want you to know I'm happily married.' I said, 'What a coincidence. I'm happily single. Where's your husband?' She says, 'Bakersfield,' and I figure I've got something going. Except after a while I saw the cigarette girl.

"I'm in love," Foley said lugubriously. After finishing all the food on the table in the course of his monologue, he was slowing up now. "I know you're in show business, boss. You're the expert on glamour. But I'm not talking glamour here. I'm talking soul, maybe religion. This cigarette girl is so fresh and pretty and sweet-looking it'll break your heart. But I mean beautiful, too. She's tall and blonde, with cheeks and a nose you want to draw pictures of and one of those pink complexions that probably glows in the dark. It's a classy hotel out there, with the chandeliers and the carpets and the uniforms and the restaurants and everything, but she's so exquisite she makes the place look like a bus depot. I didn't know if I wanted to screw her or marry her or adopt her. God damn. Sometimes when you're flyin', Art, you get a day like that, when everything's clear and just so . . . *sweet* — when you see the world differently. New possibilities.

"Here, I'll get the check. Start your day on a lucky foot. *Bonne chance* and all that." Foley lifted his cup in a salute and drained the last of his coffee. "I came on to her kind of strong, I guess, else they wouldn't have given me the bum's rush. I hear booze'll do that to a fellow sometimes. She ruined me, though. I didn't even go out to the Mustang Ranch after. For what that dwarf cost me,

70 //

I could have got three hookers, a Saint Bernard and a high colonic, but she ruined me for whorehouses. Here I am thirty-six years old and I'd rather be at the senior prom. No more drinkin' for me on this trip, boss. I'll go back there tonight if I have to wear a disguise to get in. Isn't love great? Makes you feel about as good as a crash landing. Sack time — I probably sound like a bad movie about now. Good luck out there today. I'll catch your act later."

Foley winked, pushed himself to his feet and walked unsteadily from the coffee shop. His departure left Art Epstein with a couple of hours still to get through before the poker tournament would begin.

There is a profound, almost ecclesiastical time in the daily rhythm of a Reno gambling casino, and it descends at four or five in the morning when the music from the lounge shows is stilled, the slots are quiet and only a scattering of serious gamblers remain, as grim, silent and determined as the finishing runners of a marathon race in communion with some unimaginably relentless but encouraging god of their own desperate devising. And then they, too, drift away. The planet tips, the morning light slowly arrives and the casino's pulse quickens anew, at first imperceptibly. Early rising travelers in duckbill caps, their station wagons parked at nearby motels already loaded for the day's journey, push through the glass doors from the outside, pausing momentarily in the dim light to get their bearings before aiming themselves through rows of slot machines towards the dollar-ninety-nine breakfast specials. Day-shift dealers filter in wearing black trousers and white shirts, name-tags pinned to their chests, carrying their short work aprons. At the snack bars, uniformed girls from Boise or Klamath Falls or Santa Rosa swipe at Formica counters with damp cloths, pouring coffee into styrofoam cups and serving up microwaved bear claws and cinnamon rolls. The wheel of fortune spins once, clackety-clack, for a dollar bettor. A tour bus pulls in from over the mountains and discharges a load of day-junketeers who file inside and quickly spread through the casino, to the restrooms first and then to the slots or tables.

Security cops, guarding fore and aft, trundle a money cart down an aisle. Change girls click their coin dispensers. A limping sixty-year-old in a pastel smock moves slowly along the carpet with his whisk broom and silent butler. Blackjack dealers on graveyard deal out their shift or stand idly behind their empty tables, cards fanned on the baize cloth in front of them, their gaze fixed on some distant unhappening event. Cocktail waitresses bring black coffee and bloody marys. Last night's winners sleep contentedly upstairs, but downstairs the losers and the newcomers and the compulsively possessed are beginning their long day of hope. The gambling rhythm cranks up, but it accelerates slowly. Eight or nine in the morning is a dull, uninspired time in a casino.

At that hour at the Taj Mahal, Shayna Levinson was pungling up her ten-thousand-dollar entry fee for Stretch Jackson's poker tournament. She was reluctant to part with the money but she would have been a lot more reluctant if the cash were all coming out of her own pocket. Only twelve hundred and fifty bucks of it was hers, though — the rest she'd won in the private tournament — and Shayna had to admit she liked her odds a lot better after she'd reduced them by a factor of eight. Hell, she thought, everybody in the tournament would be a long shot at the beginning anyway. That was the nature of tournaments: the more people who enter, especially amateurs, the more luck plays a part in the early rounds. During the first day even the best players would be up shit creek if they didn't catch good tickets. The longer they could last, the more their skill would begin to count for something, but first they'd have to survive the early action.

So Shayna told herself that the entry fee wasn't a donation. It was leverage. Putting up twelve-fifty to win maybe a quarter of a million? That was the kind of proposition Shayna Levinson could get interested in, and she felt an edge of aggression building within her as she counted out her money to little Archie Breen, the tournament director.

He gave Shayna a receipt and got her signature on a disclaimer for television coverage. Archie Breen was a short, barrel-chested gambler with a sailor's gait, and he was a genetic aberration — middle-aged, but with thick, dark hair, a low forehead and an unlined face, he was one of those men who would look thirty years old for most of his life. A born glad-hander, Archie Breen was gregarious and cheerful by nature.

"When's it begin?" Shayna asked him.

"Draw for seats at ten sharp," he grinned. "Sheepshearing begins immediately after."

"Then it's me for breakfast."

"Have a good one," Breen told her.

Shayna started to walk away but paused when she saw a blond man approaching the sign-up desk. He was tall and thick, like some kind of a Viking shot-putter, and he moved with a confident ease that suggested he owned the place. Archie Breen greeted the stranger with a squeeze of his arm and said, "Morning, Mr. Epstein. You're out and about early."

"Breakfast with a friend in need," Art Epstein said. He glanced at the roped-off spread of empty poker tables, a scattering of ashtrays on the green tabletops making the arena look all the more deserted. "How many signed up so far?"

"With this little lady, forty-eight," Breen said. "We're gettin' there."

Shayna couldn't resist needling the stranger. "You in the tournament?" she asked. "What're you — using a phony name? You look more like an Anderson than an Epstein."

"They'll never say that about you," he answered. "Hello again. You dealt to me once. In Vegas."

"Yeah?" Shayna said. "I don't remember. Did you win?"

"Beats me. Did I toke you?"

There was no answer for that one. "Save me a hot seat," Shayna told Archie Breen, and left, thinking *there's a cool son of a bitch*.

"That one's a tough player," Breen said to Epstein.

"Archie, you're a gentleman. You say that about everybody."

"Do I?" The shorter man laughed at himself. "What the hell, it's not my year. They're all tough if you ain't catchin'."

"When do you need me here — ten?"

"On the dot," Breen said.

"See you then." On his way back to the elevators, Art Epstein stopped to put a quarter in a video poker game, testing the waters. The screen blinked GOOD LUCK! and dealt him the jack, queen, king of spades, eight of hearts and deuce of clubs. Epstein held three cards to the straight flush and drew a jack and five of diamonds. The machine plunked a quarter into the tray for the pair of jacks, returning his bet. It's appropriate, he thought: a push. No waves, just like his gambling mood.

Now that it was finally about to start, Art Epstein felt calm about the poker tournament, but his emotions otherwise weren't under such control. When he'd checked into the Taj Mahal the previous afternoon, a phone message from Jackie had been waiting for him: *Read the script I'm sending and save a warm pillow for Tuesday night.* To take his nervous edge off, Epstein had gone out for a walk through the downtown casinos. They'd seemed like prairie-dog villages to him, full of chatter and frantic activity, and he knew he'd have to achieve the calmness of a solitary hawk soaring above. It took him a while, but he was able to distance himself from the noise and discord, to slow his adrenaline flow.

And so in a relaxed mood he'd returned to his suite at the Taj Mahal and looked through the movie script the bellhop soon delivered. Epstein didn't consider himself an expert on scripts, but this particular one, it seemed to him, had promise if they'd film it as a drama and not a comedy. Americans on the beach in Baja, a love triangle, *ménage à trois*, an R-rating — it would be cheap to shoot, too, the way things were in Mexico. The only problem was that Jackie was wrong for the part — no way could Epstein see her playing a twenty-two-year-old in a bikini. He wished she'd come to her senses about that. But hell, he thought that morning back in his room, shaving and showering and getting ready for the tournament, he wished lots of things about Jackie. And the one thing he wished above all was that she was in Reno with him. He hadn't seen Jackie for three weeks, and now at a moment when anyone else would have been psyching himself up to play cards, Art Epstein was as excited as a newlywed by the thought that he was totally, irrationally in love with his wife and couldn't wait for the day to pass and night to arrive so that he could be with her.

Stretch Jackson had been sleeping late to get through the slow part of the day and then hanging around the Taj Mahal casino at night to let himself be seen. The hotel called it public relations and the tall gambler went along with it agreeably, signing autographs and making small talk with whoever stopped to chat, meanwhile murdering Archie Breen at penny-a-point gin rummy. As the tournament host, Stretch hadn't been playing any poker in Reno because it would have been unseemly; if he'd won it would have been unfair and if he'd lost, unthinkable. So he'd lounged around drinking coffee amid the life-sized placards of himself and several times an hour the house paged him over the public-address system, hyping the act. Stretch ignored the pages. He would have ignored them anyway; it wasn't his style to do business on the telephone. Anyone who wanted to talk to him knew where to find him.

But on Tuesday his schedule shifted. He left an early wake-up call and by shortly after nine in the morning he was downstairs in the casino with Archie Breen, counting poker chips under the discreet scrutiny of a cashier and a security guard. They were putting tens, twenty-fives and hundreds into racks of ten thousand dollars each. Stretch was wearing kangaroo-hide boots, a pair of Levis so bleached and broken-in that they looked as if they would dissolve entirely in one more washing, a pale yellow snap-button shirt and an off-white cowboy hat with a band made from the skin of a rattlesnake. A cocktail waitress cruised the vicinity in case he might want a coffee refill.

"How long we gonna keep the tens in play?" Breen asked him. "They're kind of a waste of time, wouldn't you say?"

"We don't want to bomb anyone out right off," Stretch answered. "We'll give 'em their money's worth a while."

Singly or in small groups, gamblers had been drifting into the tournament area, some of them milling around and some patiently taking seats at the empty tables. Their mood was detached, through long habituation to passing idle time waiting for a poker game to coalesce, but those sitting closest couldn't help but notice when a young man with an excited air hurried down the aisle. Recognizing Stretch Jackson from the publicity posters, he asked breathlessly, "Do I sign up for the poker tournament here? Is there still time?"

And anyone watching would have noticed that although Stretch's expression remained neutral, his gray-blue eyes were sizing up the kid's foolhardy youth and inexperience. Talk about lambs to the slaughter. But Archie Breen, beaming paternally, said, "This is the place, my young friend. Feelin' lucky?"

"You can say that again," Doug McGowan gushed. "I can't lose for winning! I'm on a hot streak. I hit a keno ticket for nine thousand dollars last night — eight numbers out of ten. And I was already up over a thousand!"

As he spoke, Doug McGowan was plunging both hands into the pockets of his sports jacket, pulling out wads of hundred-dollar bills. His exuberance virtually demanded a response and Stretch drawled at him, "By God, pardner, you got enough cash there to burn up a wet mule."

"Except," Archie Breen interrupted, "no offense, but the law says you gotta be twenty-one?"

Doug McGowan laughed. The byplay was attracting attention. "Am I glad you brought that up!" he said. "Funny you should mention that. Look!" He pulled a wallet out of his hip pocket and showed a California driver's license, pointing at the date. "Twenty-one today, see? I mean it, somebody up there's smiling at me. It's like ESP. I'm gonna win money in this poker game. I know it!"

"And why not?" Breen answered. "That's what made this country great." He handed Doug an entry form and as Doug moved off to the side to fill it out, Breen shot Stretch a look and said, "Easy come, easy go. He makes forty-nine."

By then the tournament area was crowded, not just with contestants assembling but with dealers showing up to get their assignments and with tourists, too. The tourists didn't know exactly what was going on but they could tell something out of the ordinary was happening so they shuffled around, exchanging comments and hoping for some entertainment. A uniformed security guard moved through the crowd, easing the players into the roped-off area and the railbirds to the outside. The gamblers took seats at the various oval tables as if unwillingly on display, something about the scene calling a zoo to mind, creatures within the ropes contained in an area too small for their unnatural prowess. As the players waited, outwardly calm, they gave the impression that they were nervously pacing, on the prowl.

From his height, it was Stretch Jackson who first noticed over the bobbing heads a frail man moving from the periphery of the crowd towards the sign-up desk. His color was bad and his gait unsteady, but his jaw was set and his brown eyes were hard and alert. Stretch nudged Archie Breen and said, "Count out another rack." He moved to help clear the aisle for the old man but it was unnecessary; a murmuring rose up around the newcomer and people stepped aside for his progress. He acted as if they weren't there. Like an ocean liner through a swarm of tugboats, he cruised unimpeded towards his destination, leaving in his wake a babble of suddenly excited speculation.

Alone of the tournament gamblers, the big champion, Vic Houston, rose to his feet and pushed through the crowd. He stepped over the velvet rope and escorted the old man across his final steps to the sign-up desk. "By God, Stretch," Houston said, "you got yourself a tournament now."

Grinning, Archie Breen produced an entry form and said, "You're number fifty, Lee Sherman."

Stretch Jackson seemed amused by the old man's arrival. "Stakes ain't too high?" he asked.

Lee Sherman Tobias grunted, "You here to bullshit or put on a tournament?" So far he hadn't acknowledged Vic Houston's presence and now, still without looking at the big man, he shook his elbow free of Houston's grip. "Show me where to sign," he told Breen. "You can write in the rest."

When Breen led Tobias aside, Vic Houston said to Stretch, "I thought he was in the hospital. They said it was his heart finally."

"What I heard, too," Stretch answered. "Look at him — he belongs in one."

"He looks okay," Houston said.

"I seen run-over possums look better."

"He's okay," Houston said. "Don't be so hard."

Stretch touched his chest. "Me hard? I can't hardly wait to see you go easy on him. I'll buy me a Polaroid."

"That's different," Houston said. "That's poker."

"Different from what? I didn't know there was anything else."

"Aw, hell," Houston said, "I love that old boy, that's all. Tell you what — I got a grand says he makes it to the final round."

Stretch considered the bet only momentarily before shaking his head. He said, "No, thanks. Lee Sherman's got a lot of miles on him. But he ain't never been in a wreck."

Archie Breen called: "Stretch, it's ten o'clock straight up. We gonna get this show on the road?"

Young Doug McGowan didn't know he was in over his head. All he knew about gambling was that streaks come hot and cold and if you're on a hot streak, you're crazy not to ride it out. And he was on one. When he drew to a pair he tripped up or filled and when he drew to a flush he made it and when he didn't have anything to draw to he folded his hand and that was fine, too, because then it didn't cost him anything. He was up a thousand bucks in almost no time and laughing about it, trying to share his good mood with the other six players at his poker table.

Looking back, Doug understood that his keno win of the evening before had been inevitable. At dinner he'd been incredulous when he'd checked his hits against the instruction pamphlet and saw that he'd won nine G's on a ten-dollar ticket. But after a while the wads of cash in his pockets struck him as commonplace. He'd been winning at everything else, hadn't he, so why shouldn't he win at keno? It was preordained. He'd treated his three friends to dinner and drinks and the Loretta Lynn show at Harrah's, and in the dark booth in the showroom, suffused with warmth and alcohol, he and Gail joked and held hands and kissed, nuzzling each other . . . and in the motel room later, with Terry and Lisa pairing off next door, Doug and Gail had made love as he'd known they would, his twenty-first birthday drenched in an abundance of money and sex and good fortune. When you're hot, you're hot, he thought. Just like the song says.

Awakening early that morning, he'd told Gail she could find him later at the Taj Mahal, to come over and watch him win some more money, and then he'd gone next door where his luggage was and, with Terry and Lisa sharing a bed in the darkened room, he tiptoed into the bathroom to shave and brush his teeth. But Terry followed him in, curiosity showing through his sleepy countenance, and he whispered, "How'd it go?"

"Great," Doug whispered back. "Really great. You?"

"Me, too," Terry grinned. He held out his hand. "Happy birthday, McGowan. You dumb lucky bastard."

"I'm going over to play in that poker tournament," Doug said. "You bring the girls later, okay?"

"We're gonna stay another day then?"

"Hell, yes. I'm not through winning yet. You need money for breakfast and stuff?" Doug fished a hundred-dollar bill out of his pocket and pressed it on Terry, both of them giggling at the incongruity of it all.

Outside it was cold, still below freezing although the sun, or what could be seen of it through the low overcast, was well above the horizon. Snow was ankle-deep downtown, slick paths trod in the sidewalks and the center lanes of the streets churned up, slush piling in the gutters. Doug took a quick run and planted his feet, sliding across a shallow ice puddle. He scooped up some snow, tossing it back and forth between his hands, and then whirled and threw the snowball at the head of a parking meter. It exploded into powder and Doug raised his fist jubilantly. He couldn't miss at anything.

Inside the Taj Mahal, on his way to breakfast, he put fifty dollars down at a twenty-one table. The dealer, impersonal as a robot, shuffled the cards and offered him a cut. She buried a card, dealt him a blackjack and paid him off with seventy-five dollars. It was no less than Doug expected, and he walked off without playing a second hand; he wouldn't put unreasonable demands on his luck — he just wanted to make sure it was still with him. And it was. When the poker tournament got underway, his luck was there when he reached for it. He could almost visualize it, like a presence, a friendly entity hovering above the center of the table. Doug didn't ask for anything unfair. He didn't try to make good hands out of garbage or go for inside straights. But he kept getting pairs dealt to him and then he would bet or call and the hands always helped, turning into trips or full houses, and Doug took the good luck as his due and swept in the money, grinning around the table.

The player Doug hurt most in the first hour of the tournament was Art Epstein. Doug didn't know it — he was oblivious to any subtleties in the game — but Art Epstein knew what was happening and was chagrined at the irony. Except it wasn't irony, he recognized — it was farce. Everyone at the table knew the kid didn't even belong in the tournament because he was such a rank novice, and yet there he was, murdering Epstein. Whenever Doug got a hand, it just happened to be Epstein who got one, too. A run of second-best hands is the worst thing that can happen to a poker player, and Epstein was being plagued with a string of them.

The first couple of losses weren't his fault. Early in the tournament, Epstein had been dealt a pair of kings and caught a low pair to go with them. He bet but Doug kept calling so Epstein, suspecting him for trips, checked on the last two cards. Doug checked, too, but sure enough, he had three of a kind and won the pot. The next time, Epstein had trips and bet strong but Doug called every bet and last-carded a flush. Against that kind of playing, Epstein didn't have a chance; when the kid checked with the nuts and called with nothing but dreams in his hand, there was no way to figure him. Then Epstein got nailed by Doug a third time, losing to a higher straight, but at least he got off cheap since the kid didn't have the sense to stick it to him.

But by then Epstein's confidence was shaken and he proceeded to make a tactical mistake. Not against Doug, though — he caught a hand and found himself up against one of the taciturn cowboy-types, a professional gambler named Brett Overstreet. The hand cost Epstein because Overstreet played him like a guitar. And Epstein let him do it. On the fourth card he should either have folded or raised big and settled things right there, but instead he just called, indecisive, and Overstreet shoved in a big bet on fifth street. Epstein called the bet but had to fold after the next one because by then he didn't know where the hell he was. He didn't know if Overstreet was bluffing or what. Then his nemesis, Doug, beat him on another lucky hand. Stretch Jackson, who was wandering around watching the action, put his hand on Doug's shoulder and said, "Somebody better arrest this fella for speedin'."

It was a joke by then — not only was Epstein getting carved up by an amateur, and not only did the other players at the table think he was incompetent, but he actually faced the prospect of being the first player eliminated from the tournament. With the initial hour of play concluding, Art Epstein felt like a sprinter who'd fallen flat on his face at the starter's gun. But at least the stakes were still low; a run of bad luck like that later could be immediately fatal. Epstein flexed his muscles, filled his lungs and leaned back in his chair. He had to collect himself while he still had time.

The tournament had begun at ten o'clock with Stretch Jackson placing fifty numbers in a hat and the gamblers drawing for position at one of the seven tables. The last few well-wishers had moved beyond the rope, where the crowd was standing three and four deep in a semicircle by then, and the dealers had settled into their seats. Getting ready for action, the players somehow managed to give off a gloomy mood reminiscent of cattle in a feedlot, vaguely pessimistic about their future, and spectators expecting instant drama had drifted away, victims of yet another casino disappointment. Stretch Jackson and Archie Breen had circulated among the oval poker tables unracking ten thousand dollars in chips in front of each player, the gamblers rearranging the chips to suit themselves so that the stacks soon ended up in every conceivable conformation from precise neatness to ragged piles as jumbled as abstract sculpture. And the competition had begun.

The rules were simple. During the morning round, the ante was ten dollars and the minimum bet twenty. After the ante, the players were dealt two cards face down and one face up, and the player with the lowest up card was forced to bring in the betting. As further cards were dealt, the high hand showing would have to bet first. The stakes would be escalated after a one o'clock lunch break, and play would continue for as long as it took to eliminate eighteen players, leaving thirty-two contestants to begin Wednesday's session.

Warming to the action, Jerry Corbett soon felt optimistic about surviving Tuesday. Like the others, he'd begun in an apprehensive mood but he'd quickly settled down. His costume helped — Jerry was so accustomed to sitting at a poker table in women's clothing and makeup and a wig that he was able to put everything out of his mind but the immediacy of the game. In the early going he caught routine cards, either good enough to raise with or bad enough to fold, with nothing in between to complicate things, and that allowed him the luxury of tuning into the other players at his table.

Two of them were hard to read. The overweight black man, Sandwiches, and the aged champion, Tobias, were as unyielding as rock. Jerry wouldn't have wanted to be on the stage with either one; they didn't give anything away — no vibes, no clues, nothing. Just stolid obstinacy. Or was that their reputations preceding them? With time, Jerry thought, he'd figure them out. At the next table over, directly in his line of sight, was Shayna, wearing a powder-blue tee shirt with a scoop neck. Below her throat, Jerry could see the outline of her sternum and rib connections when she moved.

Earlier that morning, Shayna had noticed Jerry in his drag costume and thrown a barb at him in passing. "I know it'll be tough for you, honey," she'd said, "but try not to give the sisterhood a bad name." Sitting next to Shayna at the other table, Jerry saw, was the tournament favorite, Vic Houston, who'd already added considerably to his stack of chips. Jerry knew the starting odds had the big Texan at six-to-one where most of the field, including himself, were underdogs ranging all the way up to eighty-to-one. Houston was wearing a gray sharkskin suit with a string tie and a pearl-colored Stetson. Despite the annoyance of having Shayna at his side, Houston looked at ease, maybe even bored by the mundane matters taking place on the green table in front of him. In fact, it seemed to Jerry, Houston was more interested in watching Lee Sherman Tobias than following his own game.

Well, Tobias was tough, that was for sure. Sandwiches, too. The black man sat in corpulent repose like a Buddha, eyelids drooping and hands folded over his abdomen. But above his mustache a light beading of perspiration showed on his upper lip and it gave Jerry a feeling. Sandwiches wasn't as self-confident as he looked. Othello, Jerry thought. Macho warrior with a tragic flaw. Could it be some racial thing? Anger? Look at him sitting there, Jerry thought, stone silent, placid as an ox — and sweating. The room wasn't that hot. Jerry thought about what a black man must go through in a lifetime of playing poker with rednecks. Discrimination, insults, fights — the man's got pride, Jerry thought; he's constipated with it. The insight gave him a niche to work with, like a fingerhold for a rock-climber. So he's world-class, Jerry thought. Big deal — inside, he's another insecure human being. I'll get a handle on him. And he smiled to himself, thinking, *Were I the Moor, I would not be Iago.*

Lee Sherman Tobias was a tougher nut, though. The old man was so obviously sick that Jerry would have ignored him if it weren't that Tobias was winning every pot he got into. The best poker players aren't the ones who play the most winning hands, but the fewest losing ones, and so far Tobias hadn't wasted a chip that Jerry could tell. It didn't make sense; Tobias was weak as hell —

you could even hear his breathing — and yet he was dominating the table and Jerry was mystified at how he did it. All Jerry knew was that before anyone at the table made a bet, he looked first to see what cards Tobias was showing. But there was no pattern to Tobias's behavior that Jerry could figure out. Sometimes he looked ready to call but folded when the bet came to him, sometimes he looked uninterested but jumped in with a raise, and sometimes he did what everyone expected him to do. There was no way to read him.

Twice Jerry had playable cards but passed when Tobias came in with a raise. Both times Jerry knew the old man had him beat and both times he had second thoughts afterwards. Since few hands went all the way to the seventh card, the players usually knew only by circumstantial evidence whether they were truly beaten, but Jerry noticed that Tobias seemed to create ambiguous situations, as if he weren't merely capitalizing on uncertainty, but causing it. Jerry noticed, too, that Sandwiches and Tobias didn't mix it up much with each other, an observation he was able to use for his own benefit. If Sandwiches folded because he thought Tobias was strong, or vice versa, Jerry accepted the opinion and played his own cards accordingly. The tactic was saving him money and had injected him into the serious tier of competition, for as the second hour of the tournament spun itself out the players at Jerry's table had shaken themselves down into three levels: at the top were Tobias and Sandwiches, impregnable so far, below them was Jerry Corbett, playing well, and below him were the others, scrambling to stay alive.

Shortly before the lunch break, two players at Jerry's table initiated some serious betting. One of them was a heavyset man of about sixty wearing dark blue overalls so new that the bib was still puckered with its creases from the dry-goods shelf. He had on a long-sleeved khaki work shirt, a plum-colored tie knotted at his throat and, pulled squarely on top of his head, a duckbilled cap that said Ortho. If he was trying to look like a farmer, he was doing a good job of it. With an ace on the second round of cards making him high hand, he pushed four chips at the pot. A hundred dollars.

"Raise," said a player to his left. The raiser, showing a king, was a younger man in a shabby black sports coat. Prematurely balding, he had a waxy complexion, a pitted face, sunken cheeks, and an overbite so massive that his head resembled a skull. Animated by nervous twitches, he looked around the table with the genetic mistrust of someone who'd never seen a blood relative survive to the age of forty. He lifted eight chips from his stack and flung them at the pot. "Up a hundred."

"We've got a major wager," the dealer said, collecting cards as the other players folded behind the raise. Only the farmer called, and on the next card neither player improved. The farmer bet another hundred, and again the spectral man raised a hundred.

"And back," the farmer said.

The younger man poked his head forward like a bird. He looked at his own stack of chips and lifted off some hundreds. He weighed them in his hand, as if he were going to re-raise big, and then threw in a chip, just calling.

The dealer burned a card and dealt the fourth up cards. The farmer rose in his seat and leaned forward to squint at his opponent's hand. With neither man showing a pair, he was still high with his ace. He threw three chips in the pot.

"And three," the younger man said immediately.

"Three back," the farmer said, re-raising.

The other man hesitated, as if considering another raise, and then said, "Call."

The seventh card came, face down, and the farmer bet five hundred.

The younger man turned up the corner of his final card. "I don't believe this shit," he muttered. He reached for his cards to fold them, then changed his mind and impetuously threw five hundred dollars in the pot. "You got me," he told the farmer.

The farmer, from the look on his face, didn't seem to think so. He shook his head, made a shooing motion at the pot and said, "Ace high. I was trying to run one."

"No pair?" The younger man came back to life. He turned over one of his hole cards and said, "Ace *king*."

Now the farmer brightened. He turned over a king and a queen.

The other man showed the rest of his hole cards. "Ace, king, queen," he pointed, "ten."

The farmer exposed his entire hand. Rearranging the cards, he said, "Ace, king, queen, ten, eight."

"Son of a bitch!" the younger man cried, picking up an eight from his own hand and slamming it on the table.

The dealer intervened, spreading both hands so the players could get a clear look. But by then it was obvious — both men had been bluffing. The hand was a tie. "Needed a jack," the dealer murmured, dividing the pot and pushing half to each player. The two winners were sharing almost four thousand dollars but their actual gain was negligible — half of the antes and the first small round of betting. The rest of the pot was their own money coming back to them. By then, they were glad to get it.

Stretch Jackson, attracted to the table by the action, drawled, "First liar don't have a chance, does he?"

Lee Sherman Tobias made a face. "Cut the bullshit," he said, "Deal cards."

The tournament broke for lunch.

Brian Bates had awakened with a hangover after his night of drinking with the psychologist, Carroll Shepherd. But aspirin had helped, and a clubhouse sandwich and a dish of vanilla ice cream were restoring him as he ate lunch with his new partner upstairs in the Taj Mahal's coffee shop.

"Are you as sure of yourself down there as you look?" Shepherd asked.

"I've been so sick I don't know what I am." Bates answered. "What did I do last night? I'm not that kind of drinker."

"You're money up, aren't you?"

"Some. Could you see okay from where you're watching?"

Shepherd nodded. "You made a couple of inspired calls."

"Against the four-flush? That guy was whistlin' in the dark."

"How did you know to raise him?" Shepherd asked.

"He was playin' hearts. That's my suit. I had the deuce in the hole. My suit and my card? I played a hunch."

Shepherd winced.

"Hey, it worked, didn't it?" Bates said. "That game's not so tough. Almost everyone in it's an Okie — or a Texan, same thing. If there's one thing I'm good at, it's figurin' Okies out. I think we got a shot at the marbles, partner. What do you think?"

Shepherd smiled. "I think we were pretty drunk last night when we signed you up for this thing."

"That guy they call Hoo-Hoo?"

"Owl Avery," Shepherd said.

"Yeah. He's tough. But I can handle the others."

"A piece of cake, huh?" Shepherd said.

Bates laughed, but stopped suddenly and looked at the older man. "What am I doin' in this tournament, doc?" he asked. "What am I doing in this *town?*"

Outside, the clouds had blown away except for some high overcast and the temperature had climbed above freezing, turning downtown Reno into puddles and slush. Pep-talking himself, Art Epstein walked for ten minutes in his shirt-sleeves, across the Truckee River and around the park. Chilled through by then, he hurried back to his suite at the Taj Mahal and took a hot shower. He ate an apple and an orange and some grapes from the fruit bowl that came with the suite, and then he lay down and closed his eyes. When he went back downstairs at two o'clock, he was wearing fresh clothing and looked ready to take on the world. Maybe the break helped him, or maybe it was just that Doug McGowan started winning from other players, but during the afternoon session Art Epstein began to inch his way back.

Jerry Corbett used the lunch break to freshen his disguise. Up in his room, he shaved again to be on the safe side while Chris, aloof, watched from a distance. She hadn't left the hotel room all morning.

"Come down and watch me play," Jerry said.

"No."

"Please."

"I couldn't stand it," Chris said.

With a towel draped around his neck to protect his blouse, Jerry shaved meticulously, careful not to nick himself. When he was done, he rinsed his face with cold water, used the towel to dry off, and sat down with his cosmetic kit. "Make me up?" he asked.

"What if I won't?"

"Come on. A girl has to look her best."

Chris swiveled his head to catch the light better. She went to work on his face with her brushes and colors.

"My mind's going a mile a minute," Jerry said. "Listen to me. I'm on top of everything. Do you understand?"

"Sure."

"No, you don't," Jerry said. "Things have changed. Downstairs it's different than you think. I never asked you to watch before because it was never important before. There was always tomorrow and tomorrow and tomorrow, but this is the end of the line. I'm at peak performance and I want you to share it with me. Do you hear me? It's important."

Chris kept working. The thing about Jerry, she knew, was that he was so glib he could make anyone believe anything. Yet he had the emotions of an artist and was always sucker enough to fall for his own performance. It was a high to share his excitement, but Chris had to be on guard against the letdown afterwards.

"They've got me at eighty-to-one," Jerry told her. "I can't win this tournament. Right now I'm playing against two of the best poker players in the world. Surprise — they're better than me. *But I'm better than the others*. It's all worth it, Chris, I swear. The crap I put up with at Gardena, the months at Vegas, us being separated. This is the payoff and it's worth it. I've never been so sharp. Come down and watch. You have to."

"Why? To bring you luck?"

"The hell with luck. I don't need luck. I told you I'm not going to win. Listen. Christ, I'm thinking so fast I can't keep up with myself. We've had our priorities wrong, hon. Sometimes you dig yourself so deep into a tunnel you forget to look up into daylight. What's ten grand? We've been acting like it's the treasure of the Incas. Hell, ten grand isn't money — down there, it's a tip. The hell with the ten grand! It's just dues, that's all. When this is over, I'll earn us another ten grand. I'll go to work in a car wash or something. It doesn't matter. You were right about the money. It's lost. So forget it."

Chris said, "You're not making me feel any better. What do we do next?"

"The theater! That's the point! Poker's been a sidetrack. I'm no poker player. Ha. I came a long way to find that out. So maybe I play a tough game. Big deal. Those guys downstairs are king of the mountain. They're not human. They're going to kill me. You hear what I'm saying? After tomorrow, or Thursday, whenever, we're through with poker forever. We're going back to L.A. and we're going to auditions," he grinned, "and we're going to be big fucking movie stars! Both of us. No, don't kiss me — you'll smudge my makeup."

Chris said, "You mean it? No more gambling after this?"

"Cross my breast. Now will you come down and catch my act? Jesus, I'm putting on the performance of my life."

"Can I let on that I know you?"

"No. Don't blow my cover."

"And you'll promise we'll go to L.A. Friday?"

"Absolutely."

Chris put her lips to his forehead.

"One more thing," Jerry said.

"What?"

"Forget everything I just said."

She drew away.

"Listen, I meant it all. But eighty-to-one doesn't mean I *have* to lose. Lightning can strike. There's a fortune down there. Remember why we're here? If I win, we'll have enough to live on for ten years. So forget the odds and forget everything I just said — I didn't come here for a walk-on. We're in Reno to get rich. Hell yes, bring me all the luck you can. Because I need it, hon. Okay?"

"You've got it," Chris said. "Break a leg."

"Okay!" Jerry said.

Russell Henry was in Reno to write a magazine article about Stretch Jackson's poker tournament. He was short and fortyish, with a beard and a paunch, but he was spiffy in a white three-piece suit, white shoes and a white plantation hat. Russell Henry had a reputation in literary circles but gamblers aren't readers and the only reputation he was making for himself in Reno was that everybody who saw him figured him for a little fruit. That didn't bother him, because Henry knew that people didn't have to like him to talk to him. He was seeking truth, not data, and truth had a way of emerging when people were confronted with the unexpected.

Russell Henry was not a magazine writer by profession. He was an author. He'd published three books — two on war, one on adventure — and had the scars to show for it: shrapnel in Vietnam, frostbite in the Himalayas. Now he was working closer to home — something about money, risk and fame in America — and the magazine assignment was only a pretext to credentialize him with the Taj Mahal. He'd cover the tournament for the magazine one way or another, but in Russell Henry's larger scheme of things he was researching a book chapter, not a magazine article. He didn't tell that to anyone.

He didn't say much of anything, in fact. Henry subscribed to the theory that says when two people communicate, the rhythms of their central nervous systems synchronize; he believed that in an ideal interview, there is no giver of information and receiver of information, but rather that the information is all contained in the process. He was also capable of laughing at such pretensions and conceding that maybe he was just putting on an act to get what he needed. But after two days with the poker players, he'd discovered they were doing the same thing. Henry was feeling good about the gamblers. Catching Stretch Jackson during the lunch break, he'd decided that picking Reno instead of Atlantic City or Las Vegas had been a good idea. Reno was a cow town by comparison, but that helped because he didn't have to cope with the distractions of a larger city. He could focus his attention easier, and somewhere in the back of his mind Henry was comfortable with the idea that Reno's roots were in a more coherent past, that in Reno it was but a short reach back to the Old West.

"You're a foot taller than I am," he commented to Stretch Jackson.

"My momma was a bitty thing," Stretch said. "She used to tell me the only big that counts is inside. Course, she was churchy. My daddy said I was livin' proof you could pile bullshit higher'n most people thought."

"Did he gamble?"

"Sure did. On the crops and his liver. They both failed him. You gettin' what you need from these old boys?"

Henry shrugged. "How do you get insight?"

"Push everything you got into the pot," Stretch said. "It'll tend to concentrate your attention."

After a while Henry said, "So far there's more action in the side games than in the tournament."

"Ain't it sweet?" Stretch answered. "I do love the sound of guys tappin' out. Keep the faith, pardner. Before the tournament's over, you gonna see some alligators in the hot tub."

And so they bantered, never quite getting on the subject nor straying very far away from it. When the waitress dropped their lunch check on the counter, Russell Henry said, "Flip you for it." But Stretch said, "Your money's no good here." He left a ten-dollar bill for a tip and the two men stood up and went downstairs and back to work. The one tall and slender, the other short and paunchy, they had nothing in common except for being soldiers of fortune; in a cautious society, they took the risk of living by their wits. And he signed the check by drawing a ten-gallon hat, Henry thought. Stretch Jackson, his mark. Could it be he's not even literate?

When the gamblers returned for the afternoon session of the poker tournament, the ten-dollar chips were taken out of play and exchanged for chips of larger denomination. The stakes were raised, to an ante of twenty-five dollars and a minimum bet of fifty. That meant that a gambler who didn't get playable cards could watch his stack shrink by something like a thousand dollars an hour just while he sat there. Since nobody could afford that kind of attrition, the higher stakes had the effect of compelling more action. As a result, it was shortly after three o'clock when the first player was eliminated from the tournament. At Doug McGowan's table, an overweight man with a florid complexion and a bushy, straw-colored mustache had been playing in bad luck all day. But now he caught an ace-high club flush on the first five cards and threw five hundred dollars in the pot. "Anyone wants to draw out on me this time," he said, "it's gonna cost 'em." Nobody called the bet but Doug, who was showing a pair of deuces.

On the sixth card, Doug didn't help and the florid man caught another club. He picked it up and waved it at Doug. "In case you had any doubts," he said. Doug checked his deuces and the florid man pushed his entire remaining stack of chips at the center of the table. It was a gesture — he didn't expect Doug to call. Nobody at the table expected Doug to call.

The dealer counted the bet and said, "Eighteen hundred."

Doug looked at his hole cards and said, "What the hell." He called.

The florid man exposed his hole cards, showing the flush. The dealer dealt the final card face up, since the betting was over. He tapped his finger at Doug and said, "Let's see 'em."

Doug turned over his hole cards. They were both deuces.

"Four ducks," the dealer said. In a fluid motion, he gathered the pot together and swept it over to Doug.

"And he checked 'em," the loser said. "I can beat anything but stupidity and dumb luck." His face got even redder, but he compressed his lips and pushed himself to his feet with controlled dignity. He looked around the table and said, "Thanks for the lesson, guys." As he maneuvered his way through the tournament area, a ripple of applause spread through the crowd, the railbirds acknowledging the exit of a good sport. The florid man passed grimly through the rope and disappeared into the casino.

On the sidelines, Doug McGowan's friends Terry, Lisa and Gail were cheering enthusiastically. Doug gave them a grin and a thumbs-up sign and pointed at his stack of chips. So far, he was the big winner at his table.

Art Epstein, one of the six remaining players in the group, sympathized with the victim. There but for the grace of God, he thought. Epstein had a way to go just to get even, but he'd been picking his shots carefully since the break and had inched his way up to fifth place at the table. And that was without having any decent cards yet. It was rough going for him.

Legend had it that Vic Houston once jumped out of an airplane for fifty thousand dollars, broke his back when he landed, and lost the fifty grand while he was still lying there by betting on how long it would take for an ambulance to show up. It was a good story, but like most gambling stories it shaded the truth. The writer Russell Henry had gotten Vic Houston's account of the incident over a drink the previous evening.

"Some guy put that yarn in a book once," Houston had said. "It doesn't hurt my reputation any. People believe what they want to believe and sometimes it's downright impolite to confuse 'em with facts. Truth is, I was airborne in the war. Hundred and First Screamin' Eagles over Normandy. We jumped at a place called Pouppeville. You can't hardly forget a name like Pouppeville. What are you drinkin'?"

"Gin and tonic," Russell Henry told the waitress.

"Wild Turkey for me, honey," Houston told her. "Water back."

Henry said, "Change mine. I'll have the same."

"Anyways, I was tapped out," Houston continued. "This was maybe twenty years ago, down in Vegas. There were some sky-divers around braggin' about how it takes balls to jump out of an airplane, and I worked 'em around to a proposition. Except it wasn't for fifty grand. It was for five, and it took me an hour to get 'em up that high. I should have got me an Oscar that day."

"A sure thing, huh?"

"What I thought," Houston said, "until they opened the hatch. I hadn't jumped since I was a kid. I'll tell you, it ain't like ridin' a bike, son — you forget. And we used a static line, but this was free-fall. The gospel truth is if I had five grand, that was a bet I'd have been glad to lose. Course, if I had five grand, I wouldn't have been up there in the first place. I jumped, but if I counted to more'n three before I pulled the ripcord, that's stretchin' it. And that's all there is to the story. The rest is made up. There might have been fifty grand in side action on whether I'd hit the target, but I wasn't in on it. Good thing, too. I missed by a mile."

The drinks arrived and they sipped their bourbon. "So no broken back," Henry said.

"I broke my toe," Houston told him. "That's probably how the story started, because I limped around for a while. Nope, as soon as they got the parachute off me, I did the only one thing I had in mind to do. I got right down on my knees."

"To pray?"

"To shoot craps," Houston laughed. "How do you think I lost the five grand? It just wasn't my week."

Henry knew that Houston had stayed up all night playing poker, only cashing out that morning in time to change clothes, grab some breakfast and show up for the start of the tournament. But as Tuesday afternoon's session dragged on, the writer couldn't discern the slightest clue that Houston was playing on a sleep deficit. Houston looked amiable and at ease, the big fingers of his right hand dexterously riffling two stacks of chips, shuffling them together over and over, while he contemplated the young blonde woman sitting on his left.

"I only got two weeks for my vacation," Shayna was complaining. "You here to play cards or what?" Moments earlier she had pushed a big bet into the pot and now the table was waiting to see what Houston would do.

Houston wasn't doing anything. He just kept looking at Shayna and riffling chips.

"What is this?" Shayna asked. "The world championship stare? I'm supposed to crack under the strain?" A flicker of a grin passed over her face. "Look at this guy," she said. "The big six-to-one favorite can't decide whether to call my bet."

"Honey, that's decided," Houston said. "What I'm debatin' is how much to raise."

"I should be so lucky," she answered. "Get your money in, cowboy."

"You tryin' to talk me in or out?"

Shayna said, "In. I got you beat."

On the sidelines, Russell Henry had no idea which of the two had a hand, but if he was confused by Shayna's act, Houston didn't seem to have trouble figuring it out. Having gleaned whatever information he needed from the situation, the Texan tapped his index finger on the table in front of him. Fold. He turned his cards over without further interest, and once the hand was over Henry realized that Houston had never had any intention of calling Shayna's bet. He'd strung the moment out for reasons of his own. Some kind of test, probably. In putting Shayna through a performance, he'd learned something about her. But it works both ways, Henry thought. Shayna hadn't needed to volunteer any conversation. Well, she had her own agenda. Like himself, Henry thought, Shayna was probably trying to figure out what made Houston tick.

But the writer would have been surprised to learn that Vic Houston himself couldn't have answered that particular question on that particular afternoon. Houston had come to Reno for the camaraderie and the side games, although it was unthinkable, of course, that he wouldn't enter the tournament while he was in town. But like everybody else, he understood how strong a part luck would play in the contest in the early going. Putting him at six-to-one or sixty-to-one, it wouldn't make a hell of a lot of difference the first couple of days, but he hadn't counted on getting such a smooth run of cards in the first round. If he finished the first day with the biggest stake, he'd have leverage he could use like a weapon and, therefore, as time droned on during Tuesday afternoon's session — and now hardluck and inept players were being eliminated at the various seven tables — Houston was beginning to assess his winning chances as realistic in Stretch Jackson's tournament.

First place would be sixty percent of half a million, but he didn't especially care about the money. He was in the game for his ego, and that was a piece of irony because Houston had grown up a charity case in north Texas without ever hearing the word ego. Until he was grown, he didn't even know such a word existed. Yet for half a century it was ego that had driven him. Houston had spent most of his life prisoner of a compulsion to prove he was number one and then out of the blue one day he'd asked himself why. If he was being honest, he knew there was no way on God's green earth he could claim to be a better poker player than Lee Sherman Tobias or any of a dozen others he could name. They were the elite of the worldwide poker fraternity and on any given day, any one of them might be the best. What was the big deal about being number one anyway? Houston had been on the Johnny Carson show after the Vegas World Series and there he'd sat, the world champion, actually broadcasting to forty million Americans that he wasn't the best poker player in the country. The words had surprised him even as he spoke them. It could have been his kid talking.

There was another piece of irony. His kid. Vic Houston, who'd spent most of his life among cronies who instinctively covered their faces when a camera appeared, had a son who'd graduated from law school. Houston, with a gambler's inbred belief that formal law was somehow illegitimate, had a son he'd allowed to incorporate him. Well, people change. Maybe he was beginning to learn something from the younger generation. Or maybe he just wasn't as hungry as he used to be.

But how could he be? Houston remembered when the Salvation Army had come calling with the food baskets and pitiful little Christmas trees. He remembered the hopelessness of Wichita Falls. He remembered the empty countryside barren except for stunted mesquite trees, the cold northers, the sandstorms — they used to say Oklahoma would blow in one day and Texas would blow it back the next. His daddy had been blinded by white lightning and the Johnson family was on welfare. That was his name then, J. D. Johnson, Jr. Except there wasn't any welfare. His momma cleaned house and took in washing for people. She'd heat up a big kettle and a couple of sadirons on the wood stove and on summer days it must have got up to a hundred and fifty degrees inside. And Houston remembered it wasn't just money they did without, but electricity and gas, too. They didn't have a radio or refrigerator or books or even new clothes. He remembered when his momma sold her engagement ring for food money. It was only after his daddy died and Roosevelt got in that things began to look up a little. His momma got a federal relief job on a sewing machine and later they left Wichita Falls on a bus and moved to Houston and the first chance he got after Pearl Harbor, J.D. lied about his age and signed up for the army.

That was adios, Texas. In basic training he picked up a nickname from V for Victory and later, in the poker games on the troopship, it turned out there were two Vics. There was Vic from Memphis and Vic from Houston, which they shortened to Vic Houston, and the name must have been a natural because it stuck. He got out of the war at the age of twenty-one with a whole skin, a gambling stake and a voracious worm eating him inside.

That bankroll had carried him a long way. Hundreds of thousands of miles and almost forty years now. But lately he'd begun to think there must be more to life than beating on people. He'd turned into almost an easy touch. The pros were all rascals and they were all gentlemen, too, but Vic Houston had developed a notorious streak of generosity that set him apart from the rest. What made him tick? Vic Houston himself couldn't have answered that question because, his nobler sentiments to the contrary, inside he was still a hungry kid from Wichita Falls. He still had to prove he was best. Playing poker was what he did and what he'd be remembered for and on that Tuesday afternoon at the Taj Mahal in Reno, the worm was eating him again. Houston could have shrugged off a run of bad luck — there was no shame in losing with bad cards — but he'd been getting hands and he'd positioned himself in first place and he was feeling the old familiar challenge. It didn't matter how much money he'd won over the years or how solid his reputation was, because once again everything came down to the here and now, just like always. The wheel went around and around but it always came back to where it started. Here was the place and now was the time and in a poker game Vic Houston didn't take prisoners.

Only four of the seven players who'd started at his table were still in the game by late afternoon. Houston had personally knocked out the three who were gone. Shayna had taken her pound of flesh but it was Houston who'd tapped them out. It was his foot on their throat when they went all in and his winning hand that was the last sight in their eyes before the gate slammed on their dreams of glory. But such was his style, it was Houston, too, who eased their departure with a gentle word and led the applause for their exit. And then he went back to work. Now, of the other players still at his table, only Shayna had a good-sized stack. The rest were hanging by their fingernails and without a miracle it would only be a matter of a few hands until they went broke.

But they got a reprieve, as it turned out. Shortly after six o'clock, Stretch Jackson made the rounds announcing that thirty-three gamblers were left in the tournament; as soon as one more was eliminated, play would recess overnight. The announcement gave a struggling Art Epstein only momentary pause. He was in trouble again and merely surviving a few more minutes to make it through the first day wasn't a goal that appealed to him. After creeping back up all afternoon, Epstein had walked into a couple of disasters and his stack was down again, to three thousand and change. That wouldn't last him an hour on Wednesday.

There were four players left at Epstein's table. Doug McGowan, still on his rush, was like a magician — whenever he needed a card, he just held out his hand and it appeared. Epstein expected the dealer to start throwing him pigeons out of the deck next, rabbits, silk scarves. But Doug didn't know how to make the most of his streak, and a new pattern had developed during the afternoon. The professional gambler, Brett Overstreet — a rawboned, bearded man of about thirty-five wearing a scruffy Levi outfit, with eyes as expressionless as chips of glass — had the hex on Doug. Overstreet couldn't stop the kid, but he'd slowed him up on more than one occasion. Doug had won a mountain of chips from Epstein and the others, but Overstreet had been funneling the money from Doug to his own stack.

Of the survivors at Epstein's table, then, there were two big winners — Doug McGowan and Brett Overstreet — and two big losers. For as small as Epstein's stack was, the fourth gambler's was just as pathetic. A scholarly-looking man with tortoise-shell glasses, he'd been stoically enduring a tough day. But now he was in a hand; with two cards yet to come, he'd been dealt four cards to a spade flush.

Art Epstein had three sixes.

The situation wasn't one Epstein would have chosen for a critical play because skill wouldn't be a factor. The hand was going to come down to a matter of luck. Equivocal as Epstein's position was, he couldn't count on getting a better one and although his heart didn't warm to what logic told him to do, he had no choice.

"I'm going all in," he announced.

The dealer counted the chips Epstein pushed at him and said, "Thirty-one hundred."

The scholarly-looking man nodded, acknowledging the inevitability of Epstein's bet. He counted his own chips. A stack of hundreds. Another stack of hundreds. A partial stack. Some quarters. "I've got twenty-eight hundred," he said. He turned over his hole cards one at a time, then pushed his stack in. "Let's see a spade," he said.

The dealer slid three hundred–dollar chips back across the green tabletop to Epstein. His change. He dealt the sixth cards. They didn't improve either player. He dealt a seventh card to the scholarly-looking man. It was red. No flush. It knocked him out of the tournament.

Art Epstein collected the pot, ending the first day of play with fifty-nine hundred dollars in front of him. When the standings were posted later, that put him in twenty-eighth place out of Tuesday's thirty-two survivors.

THE FIRST ANNUAL STRETCH JACKSON SEVEN-CARD STUD POKER CLASSIC

Standings as of Tuesday evening

1.	Vic Houston, Texas	$36,125
2.	Doug McGowan, California	34,800
3.	William "Hoo-Hoo" Avery, Arizona	32,750
4.	Amateur player (Walsh), New York	31,600
5.	Lee Sherman Tobias, Missouri	30,350
6.	Professional player ("Easy"), Nevada	30,325
7.	Brett Overstreet, Texas	29,300
8.	Shayna Levinson, Washington	26,250
9.	John "Sandwiches" Treece, Louisiana	25,050
10.	Jerry Corbett, California	19,750
11.	Brian Bates, Oklahoma	17,300
12.	Professional player (DeHaven), Texas	16,400

And 20 remaining contestants ranging from $15,750 to $1,900

Starting time Wednesday: 12 Noon

At Brian Bates's poker table, five starters made it through Tuesday's round. Bates almost doubled his buy-in but he still finished a distant second at the table to the older, round-faced man they called Owl, who was obviously a better player. Owl got more action from his cards and usually ended up sitting in the right position to control the betting. A lifetime of poker would probably teach a man how to do that, Bates thought. All he'd learned himself during the day was that he'd have to play more aggressively.

Not that it mattered to him. Bates was pokered out. Gambling was boring him and it annoyed him that the tournament was costing him eight thousand bucks. He was tired of Reno. He wanted to be somewhere else. His muscles cried out for the loosening warmth of the tropics. Bates's nerves were jumping.

But his partner, Carroll Shepherd, was elated. The psychologist pushed through the crowd when Tuesday's session adjourned and grabbed Bates by the shoulders. "You're doing great," he said. "Watch — you'll be on the leader board."

"Where did you disappear to this afternoon?" Bates asked.

"You noticed? I ducked out to play some blackjack." Shepherd added quickly, "Don't ask how I did. You ready for drinks and dinner?"

Bates looked at his watch. "I'll meet you at the bar in a few minutes. I'm gonna find a phone."

He was gone more like a quarter of an hour and when he returned, he seemed distant. Straddling a barstool, he ordered a Michelob. "In a bottle," he told the bartender.

Shepherd was drinking a margarita. "Everything okay?" he asked.

Bates didn't answer. When the beer came, he tipped his head back and took a long swallow. To the psychologist, he looked like a sullen kid. For the first time since Shepherd had met him, Bates looked like the tough Okie he claimed to be.

"Anything you want to get off your chest?" Shepherd asked.

After a while Bates said, "I talked to my lawyer in Honolulu. I got a problem."

"Can I help?"

Bates shook his head.

Shepherd ordered another margarita. Halfway through it he said, "We're partners."

Bates glowered at him. "I wouldn't push that too far."

"Maybe you'd rather be alone."

"I don't know what I'd rather. I got trouble."

"People pay me to listen," Shepherd said. He finished his drink and signaled for another one.

Bates looked at him. "You get drunk every night?"

"Maybe I've got a problem, too."

"I believe it," Bates said. "You said you're a shrink. What the hell — you drink, you gamble. You some kind of renegade?"

"I'm on vacation, son. What's your excuse?"

"Screw it," Bates said. "I'm starving. You want to do the restaurant or the coffee shop or what?"

They went upstairs to the steak house, where over dinner Bates described to the older man how he'd made his money in Hawaii. He told him about the real-estate deals. He explained the down payments and the mortgage manipulations. He had to go through it twice before Shepherd understood, but on the second time around Shepherd got the picture: Bates was a little crook and he was in conflict about it.

"My lawyer says they're gonna indict me," Bates blurted out. "Turns out that Jap dentist has clout. Consumer protection division, the bastards. I ate dirt all my life and who protected me? I didn't do anything illegal, so what's with a felony indictment? You know what is?"

"What?"

"The bottom line is if they can get a conviction, that's what. Then it doesn't matter if I broke any laws. I'm in the deep shit, doc."

Shepherd asked him, "Conviction for what?"

"Fraud. Overencumbering properties. Quote, a deliberate pattern. My lawyer says give the money back."

"What do you say?"

"I don't know. If I go to court it'll cost me a fortune just to defend."

Shepherd said, "I'm not tracking. You have a choice?"

Bates took a breath. "They'll deal," he said. "I make restitution, they drop the charges."

"Can you afford that?"

"Can I afford not to?"

"How do I know?" Shepherd had switched to wine with dinner and was showing the effects. "What'll it cost you?"

"Everything I've got. Maybe more. Depends on how the D.A. plays his cards. It's a damn poker game."

"Well, that's up your alley."

"Lots of luck. This mess could cost me a quarter of a million bucks."

"What a coincidence," Shepherd said.

"What?"

"The tournament. First place prize money."

Bates blinked. "Holy shit. You're right."

Shepherd lifted his wine glass. "Welcome to the desperadoes' club."

Bates was staggered by the idea. He could go to jail, go bank-rupt — or beat the best poker players in the world at their own game?

"One way or another," Shepherd said, "we're all on the brink." He was definitely under the influence.

"Jesus, can I pull it off?" Bates wondered. People had under-estimated him all his life, but where patience and determination counted for anything, the dumb Okie was in the fight.

"The brink," Shepherd was saying, "is where it's at. The guy with the sandwich board? He could be me. That's what Reno's about. Risk. You've seen him — three-day growth, no teeth, looks like he's on chemotherapy? He walks up and down Virginia Street wearing a sign that says we cash out-of-state checks. Probably bites the head off a chicken on Friday night if he gets a chance, too. I'll

let you in on something — the difference between me and him?"
Shepherd put the ball of his thumb a fraction of an inch from his
index finger. "That much loss of control," he said. "There's your
downside. Sure I drink and gamble. I've got a good practice but
I've also got a line of credit here and a checkbook and I could blow
everything in one night and end up in a sandwich board outside
Harold's Club.

"That's the real gamble here," Shepherd said. "It's not winning
or losing money. What's money? The gamble is finding out if you
have any limits. Coming to Reno's easy — getting out alive is
what's hard. Unless you're just fuckin' around with your life. If
you're just fuckin' around with your life, then nothing matters
anyway and you might as well go out a window. But if you're
serious, you either leave here alive or you turn into a geek with a
sandwich board. Are you serious, partner? Because the guys you're
playing against sure as hell are. They live on the brink. They wrote
the book on it."

"I've been there a few times," Bates said.

"Just trying to help," Shepherd said amiably. "Give you a little
perspective. You're in the big leagues. Those poker pros have been
up and they've been down and you know what they think? They
think *what's so bad about wearing a sandwich board?* The geek's one
of them, kid — he took a risk. And that's more than most people
ever do. End of lecture. That's Reno, that's life and that's the
bottom line of the poker tournament. I say go for it."

"You're shitface," Bates told him.

"Doesn't mean I'm not worth listening to."

"Get some coffee, doc. I'm gonna call it a night."

Bates left Shepherd and went up to his room to think. He supposed it was all right to confide in Shepherd about the real-estate
deals. No harm done. But he hadn't divulged the other half of the
bombshell his lawyer had dropped on him.

His wife was somewhere in Reno.

It was just like a woman. Marlene didn't know Bates was in
town, the lawyer said. She just thought if you're getting a divorce,

you're supposed to go to Reno. She didn't bother asking anybody if it made sense. She just got on a plane.

As if he didn't have enough on his mind.

Vic Houston thought a few hours' sleep wouldn't be a bad idea. He was good for three or four days without getting down if he had to, but marathons had a way of affecting a man's judgment sometimes and there was no point in looking for trouble. So when Tuesday's tournament session broke up, he left the casino and got on an elevator to go to his room for a nap.

Another man rode with him up to the penthouse level. Houston had seen him around and recognized him because he was blond and big, even bigger than Houston. But Houston would have remembered him anyway; there was something about his attitude and the way he carried himself.

"What's it gettin' to be like outside?" Houston asked.

"Clearing up," the other man, Art Epstein, answered. "Looks like a nice night."

"Too cold up here for my bones."

"At least it's dry. You know what Mark Twain said. Coldest winter he ever spent was a summer in San Francisco."

"That ain't all they say about San Francisco."

Epstein smiled. The elevator stopped at the top floor and they got out and headed in the same direction down the hallway.

"Cards treatin' you okay?" Houston asked.

"I'm still alive. You going to give the rest of us a chance?"

Houston stopped at his door and pulled a key out of his pocket. "Son," he said, "if you gotta ask, you already in trouble."

Inside his suite, Houston took off his hat and stripped down to his socks and underwear. He put his wristwatch on the nightstand next to his bed and reached for the telephone. He dialed the desk and said, "Vic Houston, honey. You want to gimme a wake-up call in a couple of hours?"

He got back into bed and switched off the table lamp. The room went black. Up that high it was deadly quiet. Another hotel room, another night on the road. Vic Houston could sleep anywhere. He dropped off immediately.

By ten o'clock, shaved, showered and fed, he was back downstairs in the casino ready for a night's work. He took a seat in the hold-em game at the center table and signed for a stack of chips. Owl Avery and Sandwiches were in the game, and a couple gamblers from Vegas and a couple more he didn't know where they were from. One was a foreigner, an Arab from his looks, and the other was a suntanned fellow with a good-looking girl sitting next to him, practically in his lap, one hand holding a cocktail and the other resting on the inside of his thigh. He seemed to have everything in the world anybody could think of wanting. He looked bored.

"Lee Sherman around?" Houston asked.

"Haven't seen him since the tournament," the Owl said.

Sandwiches said, "I seen enough of him then."

"He's stayin' here, ain't he?" Houston asked.

Nobody knew.

The dealer was lively, a skinny, freckle-faced girl with a happy personality, and Houston liked the pace she kept. He got into the flow of the game. Most of the players knew each other well enough so that talk was superfluous. A glance, a half-smile, a gesture — those sufficed for communication. It was a comfortable pattern and Houston was enjoying himself. So a couple of hours passed before the nagging thought that had been bothering him all day surfaced again in his mind. It was between deals when he looked up suddenly and said, "Goddamn it, where's Lee Sherman?"

Lee Sherman Tobias was upstairs in a room at the Taj Mahal, furious. He'd been tired all day during the tournament, but up in his room that night when he lay down and couldn't breathe, he knew he was in trouble. He'd spent more than one night of his life lately propped up with pillows but now he felt a bad attack coming on. He was aware of his fast pulse, the noisy breathing that left him panting for oxygen. He was starting to cough up mucous and worse yet, he was swelling. When he touched the puffiness in his ankles, his finger left a dent. That was a bad sign. With the kind of heart trouble he had, they'd told him he could drown in his own fluids.

Tobias had called the hospital and told them he was coming in. They knew him there. After he'd driven down from Portland in October, he'd spent three weeks recuperating in the Reno hospital. They'd given him oxygen and morphine, adjusted his digitalis, drained him with diuretics and kept him on a diet — he'd felt okay when he checked out and flew home for the holidays. But now, after taking it easy all that time and then playing one lousy day of poker, it was starting in again. Tobias felt cheated. After his first attack, when the hospital in Vegas treated him, he'd been okay for almost a year. This time he'd only lasted two months.

He paged Archie Breen on the house phone and when the gregarious little gambler arrived in Tobias's room, he sized up the situation in a glance. "Hoo-boy," Breen said. "We'll look after you, Lee Sherman. You want me to get you a house doc or a nurse or what? A bottle? A hooker? What can I do you for? Lay down and take a load off."

"Cain't lay down," Tobias said. "I'm goin' to the hospital for overnight. Get me outta here quiet, Archie."

"Service elevator?" Breen asked. "I'll call security. We can go out the kitchen maybe. That be okay?"

Tobias nodded.

Breen reached for the phone. "You sure?" he asked. "Maybe you oughta stay in bed and we get somebody up here."

"Told you. I cain't stay in bed. Use the damn phone."

A plainclothes security guard and a hotel assistant arrived and wanted to get a wheelchair but Tobias said no. He held their arms walking down the hallway. Archie Breen rode down in the elevator with them. "Anything I can do, Lee Sherman."

"Just keep it quiet," Tobias said.

"What'll I tell Stretch?"

"Nothin'."

"I mean —" Breen didn't know how to say it respectfully. "I mean tomorrow. I gotta tell him something."

Tobias glared at him. "Forget it," he said. "I be there tomorrow."

The clouds had moved off to the east and outside it was clear and cold, the sky blue-black and the temperature down in the teens. Russell Henry stood on a street corner wearing a knee-length fur coat over his white suit and looked up at the neon hotel names on the city's skyline. Harrah's. Sundowner. Hilton. Circus-Circus. Taj Mahal. The writer imagined how beautiful the night would be in the nearby Sierra Nevada with the snow deep in the quiet pine forests, and he tried to put himself in a vacationer's frame of mind.

They treated you right in Reno, he thought. It didn't matter who you were or where you worked or even if you worked. It didn't matter how you dressed or what language you spoke or what color your skin was. As long as you had the money, they took care of you. They were friendly. They were efficient. They were indulgent. Gambling, drinking, entertainment, license — as long as you could pay for it, Reno was prodigal. The city was kaleidoscopic, Henry thought, like a big machine, an illusionist's trick, mirrors and glitter and dancing girls, a perfect device for the collection of money. Like a giant turning slot machine, it paid you off but it took from you, too, and what it took was carefully calibrated always to be more than it gave.

But oh what a smoothly integrated machine it was, Henry thought. How skillfully it engaged its many elements. There were dealers: blackjack dealers, craps dealers, roulette dealers, poker dealers, baccarat dealers. There were pit bosses. There were slot mechanics and change girls. And cashiers and security guards. And accountants and credit managers and computer operators. There were bartenders and cocktail waitresses and keno runners. Janitors and gift-store clerks and restroom attendants. Headwaiters and hostesses and wine stewards and waitresses and busboys. There were chefs and cooks and frycooks and salad chefs and silent, smiling little Orientals in aprons and chef's hats who did nothing but slice ham and prime rib at the end of buffet lines. And there were performers: singers, dancers, strippers, comics, musicians. Costumers, choreographers, sound and lighting technicians, prop men, stage managers. And room clerks and bellboys and maids and laundry workers and valets and tailors and chauffeurs and plumbers and electricians and delivcrymen and repairmen. All of them were cogs in the money-collecting machine.

Not to mention cab drivers, Henry thought, flagging a taxi and telling the driver to take him out to the MGM. Wheeling away from the curb, the driver asked over his shoulder, "What's your game, sport? Blackjack? Craps?

"Poker," Henry lied.

"Slow death. There's plenty ways to die in this town. Poker's the Chinese water torture. Craps at least you go down in flames. Blackjack's just fuckin' stupid." The driver gave his number into his radio microphone and said, "Loaded to the Muggum."

Henry loved it. *Loaded to the Muggum.* It could be the title of an article. The driver, jowly and unshaven, was chewing the wet stub of a cigar. The cab stank of cigars. The ashtray was overflowing and the front seat was a jumble of litter.

"I'm a handicapper," the driver said. "You play the horses?"

Henry said he didn't.

"I'm the best in the west," the driver said. "I know, you think that's bullshit. Bullshit it's bullshit. Fourteen factors I figure in. Took me three years to develop my system and I'm still refinin' it. I'm workin' on somethin' now, could give me an extra eight percent edge."

The cab cleared the casino district, crossed the river and headed east. Henry was thinking of how the novelist Mario Puzo had explained the lure of gambling. Puzo had written that people gambled out of a desire to be happy, that they gambled in search of the innocent happiness they had enjoyed as children. It could well be true, Henry thought — the cab driver was like a ten-year-old in his boasting.

"Couple days ago I pick a guy up at the airport," the driver was saying. "I take him to the Taj, I help him with his bags and he gives me, ya know, a good tip. Nice guy. I tell him if he needs help, he can find me at the Cal-Neva. Any afternoon, that's where I am. The guy's a crapshooter. Certain death. He shows up the next day lookin' for me. I ask him how he's doin'. 'You stuck?' I ask him. 'I'm stuck,' he says. He's stuck two grand and he's gotta catch a plane. So I put him on a horse, Chasamor, goin' off at seven-to-two. He goes a grand on Chasamor and wins thirty-eight hunnerd. I take him to the airport, he tips me three bills and flies home. You hear what I'm sayin', sport? I ain't just the best in the west — I'm the best in the east and the north and the south."

"So how come you're driving a cab?" Henry asked.

"I got insomnia."

The cab went under the freeway, made a turn into the parking acreage of the MGM, maneuvered the speed bumps and swung around to the elaborate porte cochere. Henry got out, pushed through an opaque, black-glass door, like Alice going through the mirror, he thought, and paused in red-carpeted brightness under one of the big chandeliers in the foyer. Before him swept the rich geometry of a casino the size of two football fields. The far walls disappeared in perspective and he felt himself drawn inside by the ambience as seductively as a bee attracted by a clover field. Welcome to Wonderland, he thought. Here indeed was the promise of escape to the happiness of carefree childhood. Here was total artifice, a make-believe world so removed from ordinary life, so lushly suspended in time and place that only an utter failure of the imagination could prevent someone from believing that wonderful, magical things were about to happen.

At that moment in Reno, Russell Henry was not alone in the belief.

At that moment, downtown at the El Dorado, a salesman from Oakland sat down at a blackjack table and placed a twenty-five-dollar bet. He lost, doubled his bet to fifty and lost, doubled his bet to a hundred and lost, pulled the last two remaining hundred-dollar bills from his wallet, lost again and went to the cashier's desk to write a check. He'd been off his tour bus for exactly five minutes.

At that moment at Harold's Club, a hardware dealer from Tulare had just made five straight passes on a crap table and finally, after two days of nonstop losing, had a chance to get even. He had big bets riding and back-up odds on all the numbers and he had ten for a point and he had the sudden, awful precognition that he'd pushed his luck one roll too many. He was sick with the certain knowledge that he was going to throw a seven. He shook the dice and shook them but there was no exorcising the seven that he knew was coming out to break him. He was dead. A man doesn't have a chance when destiny says lose. He gave up hope and shot the dice down the table. They came up two fives, a winner. He rejoiced and it was as if his cold fear of a moment earlier had never existed. Instead of dragging his money, he pressed his bets.

At that moment outside of town, a fisherman from Dutch Harbor, Alaska, had just bought two hookers and a dirty movie at the Mustang Ranch. One girl was blonde, one was black, both were gorgeous, and he'd paid for the night with keno winnings. His ship was docked for repairs in Seattle and he told himself, taking his pants off, that flying down to Reno had probably been the smartest and luckiest thing he'd ever done in his life.

At that moment downtown, a young man in a tuxedo stepped through curtains into a spotlight on a stage at the Taj Mahal and said, *"Good evening, ladies and gemmun. Money talks in Reno, doesn't it? Mine says good-bye. But seriously, talk about losers — I saw a guy in a casino who'd gone broke, so he just walked around making mental bets. He lost his mind."*

At that moment at Harrah's, a woman from Denver put three dollars in a slot machine, hit a row of bars and thought she'd won eighty-four thousand dollars. When the slot attendant told her that the bars were in the second payoff line, not the third, and she'd only won two thousand, she complained bitterly and threw her drink on the carpet.

At that moment at the Hilton, a man from Vancouver bought chips with a Canadian twenty-dollar bill and got kidded for what seemed the thousandth time for trying to pass money from a Monopoly game.

"*I won't say they want your money here,*" the comedian said, "*but I sent a bellboy out for a deck of cards and he made fifty-two trips. But really, isn't this a great hotel? The towels are so thick I can hardly close my suitcase.*"

At that moment at the Reno airport, eighty people from Portland on an overnight junket fretted impatiently in a plane on the runway because the buses taking them thirty minutes down the highway to Carson City were late. The delay was costing them gambling time.

At that moment in the showroom at Harrah's, a couple from Spokane sat in the audience disappointed to find out that Loretta Lynn wasn't an ice-skating star.

At that moment in the downstairs steak house at Harrah's, Shayna Levinson was having dinner with three of her backers in the poker tournament. At least they thought of themselves as her backers, although as far as Shayna was concerned she'd won the entry fee fair and square and was in the tournament on her own. But the group was drinking wine and Shayna was the center of attention and she couldn't help but join in the good spirits. Recounting poker hands from that afternoon, she said, "I'll tell you, playing Vic Houston's like trying to nail jelly to a wall. Sometimes I think poker only caters to lunatics."

The man on her right said, "It doesn't cater to 'em. It breeds 'em."

Shayna laughed with him and he said, "You've got a nice smile. You ought to use it more often."

"It better be nice," Shayna told him. "It cost my folks four grand for orthodontics."

"Money well spent," he said.

He was making a pass at her and Shayna thought that was just fine. The wine was loosening her up and she was with friends for a change and she told herself she ought to do things like this more often.

At that moment, the comedian on stage was saying, "*A woman comes up to her husband and tells him, 'I just lost twenty dollars in a slot machine.' The husband says, 'That's terrible,' and she says, 'But you lost a thousand dollars.' He says, 'That's different — I know how to gamble.' But hey, gambling's not so tough. I've got a dog that can play poker. Of course he never wins — every time he gets a good hand, he wags his tail.*"

At that moment in a restaurant at the Taj Mahal, Jerry Corbett and Chris had finished dinner and were lingering over their coffee refills. Jerry was dressed as himself and Chris was radiant in his company. She believed they'd passed through a crisis since coming to Reno and she was eager to get back to Los Angeles and the acting business, where they belonged. Chris knew now she was partly to blame for the gambling problem because she'd pushed Jerry into going after the easy money in Gardena when they were broke, so she couldn't hold the poker tournament against him. It was her fault as much as his that they'd ended up in Reno with their entire savings at stake, and once she'd admitted that to herself, her anger with Jerry had melted away. She felt better about their relationship than she had in months.

Her contentment showed. Jerry reached across the table for her hand and said, "You're practically purring. What's got you so happy?"

"Oh, nothing," Chris said. "Everything. Us."

They sat holding hands until Chris shifted her gaze and stared across the restaurant in surprise at a couple who were being led to a table. "I can't believe it," she said to Jerry. "Don't stare, honey, but Jackie Gaines just walked in here."

At that moment, the comedian on stage was saying, "*I've got a new agent but I don't think I trust him. Before he gave me his business cards, he shuffled 'em. And did you know Oral Roberts is in town? Yeah. I saw him walk through a casino and by the time he left, all the slot machines had two arms. And how about this? A guy comes up to me today and says, 'Can you let me have a hundred dollars? I'm desperate. I've got a wife and kids. They kicked us out of our hotel room. We're starving.'*"

I said, 'How do I know you won't use the money for gambling?' He says, 'Oh, no — gambling money I've got.' "

Chris said to Jerry, "I can't imagine what Jackie Gaines is doing in Reno. Should I go over and say hello?"

Jerry asked, "Will she know you?"

"Sure. I made her up for six weeks. Remember I told you she's really nice? It would be rude not to go over."

"Better not," Jerry said. "The big guy with her's in the tournament. I don't want him to recognize me."

"He won't," Chris said.

"He might. What we ought to do is slip out of here before she notices you. Come on, honey."

At that moment, meanwhile, Jackie Gaines was signing an autograph for a woman from Salinas who had intruded at her table. "I've seen all your movies," the woman was saying. "You're even lovelier in person than on the screen."

"Why, thank you," Jackie answered. "You're sweet to say it. That's a beautiful ring you're wearing. I just love turquoise."

After the woman left, Art Epstein said, "She hasn't seen all your films."

"Home movies don't count," Jackie leered. "Keep your filthy thoughts to yourself."

Epstein grinned. "I'll buy you a turquoise ring."

"You do and I'll divorce you," she told him. "That's funny."

"What?"

"Sitting over there. There was that pretty makeup girl. Chris what's-her-face. What a coincidence. I was going to say hello. Now she's gone."

"Maybe it wasn't her."

"It was her," Jackie said. "That's strange. I'd swear she saw me."

At that moment the comedian was saying, "I saw a guy with a rabbit's foot lose ten thousand bucks at a crap table. I said, 'The rabbit's foot didn't bring you any luck.' He said, 'Are you kiddin'? Think how much I would have lost if I didn't have it.' What is it with you people? You don't like gambling jokes? For Christmas, my wife and I asked our *kid what he wanted. He said, 'I want a watch.' So we let him. Oh, now you laugh. Why didn't you tell me earlier you came here for filth? We could have saved a lot of time. Friend of mine married a girl who was half-French and half-Chinese. On their wedding night she ate his laundry."*

"So," Jackie asked Epstein as the waiter brought martinis, "are you going to win the tournament?"

"I'm in twenty-eighth place."

"Is that good?"

"It's terrific. There's four people behind me."

"Poor baby. Maybe if you had a cowboy outfit." They clinked their glasses and Jackie said, "I'll bring you luck tomorrow."

"You'll go shopping and play the slots all day. I know your style."

She laughed. "Nope. I'll buy you a cowboy hat and I'm going to stand behind you and tell everyone, 'This is my husband and he's gonna whup you shit-kickers.' Or what if I let my boobies hang out and distract their attention?"

Epstein was feeling better by the minute. "It might work," he said. "Sometimes a small pair gets their attention."

Jackie had arrived an hour earlier. Up in the suite she'd showered and changed and made up, but she and Epstein hadn't made love yet and the sexual tension between them was powerful.

"Let's go somewhere," Epstein said. "Fiji or some goddamn place. I can button things up at the office in two days."

"I haven't even been home yet," Jackie said. "I need some time in the city. We could go to Mexico next month."

"For what? Oh," he said. "Baja. I read the script."

"Save it," Jackie said. "Let's drink first. Tell me about the tournament. Are you really not doing well?"

"I'm doing great. The cards aren't doing well."

"Do you have a chance?"

"Probably not. The hell with it. Tell me more about Malibu."

"I said already. It was a big snore. Classes and exercise and I got a suntan. Now I'm ready for work. What about you? Any deals brewing?"

"Nothing special," he said. "I need a new outlet."

"I told you, you can manage my career."

"Be a big-shot Hollywood lawyer?"

"You've been diddling with it, Art. Why don't you jump in? Oh, Jesus," she laughed.

"What now?"

"Look behind you."

Epstein turned and saw Foley making his way across the restaurant towards their table. The pilot was wearing tight black trousers and an open-neck velour shirt, and he had a handkerchief tied around his neck and a black beret sitting rakishly on his head. "*Bon soir, mes amis!*" he called.

"I thought Peter Sellers died," Epstein told him. "*Tres* continental, Foley. You look like an idiot."

"*Toujours gai,*" the pilot grinned drunkenly, waving the comment aside. Jackie was already rising but Foley pulled her the rest of the way to her feet and crushed her in a hug. "When are you going to leave this asshole and run away with me?" he said. "We'll hump our brains out."

Jackie kissed him on the lips. "You silver-tongued devil," she laughed. "Still breaking hearts, Foley?"

"Hell yes," he said. "Right and left. Dexter and sinister. Where'd Julius go? You've gotta meet Julius."

Only then did Epstein and his wife notice the little man who had been tagging behind Foley. His head, oversize for his squat body, barely reached Foley's waist. "Julius cost me a thousand bucks last night," Foley said, "but tonight he's gonna make up for it. Julius knows everybody in Reno. He's gonna use his influence for me. Julius, I want you to meet the one and only Art Epstein and his insatiable mistress, Jackie Gaines. This is Julius. He's in show business. He works at a topless joint."

"I goose the strippers," the dwarf said in a raspy voice, jabbing his thumb in the air. "I'm the best gooser on the West Coast. Herb Caen said that in his column."

"Julius is drunk," Foley said. "Julius has been drunk ever since I met him."

"It's like bowling," Julius said. "It's all in the wrists. Bend over and I'll drive you home."

"Julius is gonna get me back in the MGM," Foley announced. "We're gonna bribe people."

"No sweat," the dwarf said. "A little *schmeer*, a little tap dance, you know what I mean?" He bounced up and down, slapped a rhythm on his thighs and then showed his hands, palms out. They were empty. If it was supposed to be a trick, it was lost on his audience. "I'm still workin' on that one," he said. "Up at the lake I goosed Liza Minelli. She introduced me in her act. She said I give good goose. It's all in the glimmers, goosin' women." He rolled his eyes salaciously. "Goosin' men it's more physical. You give it the whole shot, up and under." He doubled over suddenly, like a football center, and when he straightened up he held a pink coupon aloft in each hand. He gave one to Epstein and one to Jackie. "Good for a free drink at the midnight show," he said. "Tell 'em Julie sent ya."

"Julius, let's move out," Foley said.

The little man bowed to the Epsteins. "It's been my large pleasure meeting you."

"*Au revoir,*" Foley grinned. "Kismet beckons."

The two left and Epstein told Jackie, "He's been molesting a cigarette girl at the MGM. They eighty-sixed him last night."

"I hope he flies better than he drinks," Jackie said. "Speaking of which —"

After four martinis they ordered dinner. Jackie and Epstein were feeling tender with each other by then, touching hands and murmuring in conversation. Their talk turned to the movie script and for a moment Epstein was lost. Jackie frowned when Epstein said he couldn't recommend her playing a twenty-two-year-old in the Baja script. "The girlfriend?" she said. "Whatever gave you that idea? I want to play the wife."

"The forty-year-old?"

"I don't know how old she is. The horny housewife. Did you read the script?"

"You mean the mature woman."

"Yes."

Epstein blinked. "I'm not usually this slow," he said. "Have I missed a rite of passage somewhere?"

"Honestly, Art. I wish you'd travel with me like I ask you to. What do you think those classes were about — how to wiggle my tush better? I'm talking about a new direction in my career."

"Drama?"

"Whatever it takes to get control," she said. "I want to produce."

"Since when?"

"Since I wised up. I can do tits and ass for another three years and then go on the shelf. Or I can start taking the business seriously. Damn it, I'm an actor but nobody knows it."

Epstein said, "You're getting me excited. If you pull off a couple of dramatic roles, you could be talking breakthrough."

"I know! That's why I want you with me. I need management. I can see it finally. For the first time, I can understand turning down work. The people in L.A. keep getting me parts but they're the wrong kind for the long run. Your judgment's so good. You can hold our feet to the fire. Besides, you can get to money people."

"I *am* money people," Epstein said. "Don't stop now. Tell me about the Baja script. Who owns it?"

"Me, if I want," Jackie said. "Us!"

And so time passed in its various ways that night in Reno. Over at Harrah's, three elevators arrived at once, the buttons lighting up in a row — *ding! ding! ding!* — and Doug McGowan cried, "Jackpot!" He was having a great time. The way Doug looked at it, he had something like thirty-five thousand dollars in tournament money socked away in safekeeping, so he could spend as much as he wanted treating his friends to a night on the town. They'd had an expensive dinner, and liqueurs afterwards, and they'd caught a comedian doing his lounge act and now they were on their way to the MGM for the late show. Not only that, but Gail had fallen in love with him — Doug could tell from the way she hung on his arm and kept ogling him — and Terry and Lisa had a good thing going, too. Doug knew he was looking and acting more than ever like James Dean. He could even feel himself walking differently, with a swagger.

Except he was running out of spending money. He'd started the evening with almost a thousand dollars in his pocket but he was down to less than half that. The trouble was that instead of winning his bets, he was losing them now. He was getting stiff hands at blackjack, fruit salad in the slot machines and crap rolls at dice. In a men's room with Terry at the MGM, he counted his cash and said, "There's plenty left. What can the show cost us, tops?"

"Thirty bucks each?" Terry said.

"So that's a hundred and twenty. What are you nervous about?"

"And another hundred and twenty for the rooms."

"Forget that. I got the rooms."

"Bullshit, man. They're in my name."

Doug put his hands on Terry's shoulders. "I've got thirty-five fucking thousand dollars. Will you stop worrying?"

"Look," Terry said, "all I know is that we're gonna check out tomorrow morning. We have to pay for the rooms and buy breakfast and I need a tank of gas. And I have exactly eight bucks on me."

"What's your lucky number? We'll put the eight bucks on a roulette wheel."

"That's not funny anymore."

"Lighten up, will you?" Doug said. "Here's three hundred. That'll take care of the rooms and you can pick up the tab at the show — let Lisa think you're treating. Okay?"

"Well, sure —"

"Okay then, no problem. What's three bills anyway? Except we're not checking out tomorrow morning," he said. "Come on, let's go put your eight bucks on roulette."

As they left the men's room, Terry said, "The girls want to be on the road first thing tomorrow, McGowan. We already stayed an extra day."

"The hell with that," Doug said. "There's money left to win in this town."

And so midnight came and went, turning Tuesday into history. At that moment, asleep in his room at the Taj Mahal, Brian Bates was lost again in the threatening shadows of the dormitory, trying to find his way through the labyrinth to a special room and the welcoming brightness of a familial Heartland. He was terrified, crying in the dark and searching frantically for the bed of the Queen of Hearts when the tangled darkness of the dormitory became the sinister jungle blackness of Nam. That was always the worst part of his dream because he thrashed and cried out and strangled in his blankets until the dark overcame him and he stopped breathing, plunging into an inky whirlpool. And then he always awoke with the shakes, his heart pounding like the thump of detonations.

Except this time he wasn't swept into the whirlpool. This time the dream continued, lifting him to a sunny island, a fragrant island with green hills and a blue lake. On the verge of waking, he felt as happy as he'd once felt in real life, so ecstatic that he laughed out loud, and then the emotion was no longer a dream but a memory. He heard his laugh and awoke at the instant he smelled a vivid fragrance — Marlene's scent — and then the perfume and the dream were gone and Bates was awake and recalling the connected dream associations, like a straight line from the orphanage to Marlene. He lay still, trying vainly to get back into his dream. He'd gone from the dark to the light, from lost to found. The dream was telling him something, he thought. The feeling of joy . . . it was from his honeymoon. It was from when he and Marlene had first been married. It was from a period in his life when he'd been accustomed to calm and happiness and the joy of sharing. It was Marlene who'd made him whole — that was what the dream was telling him, how important she was to him. And he'd run out on her.

But she was in Reno now —

And so time continued to pass during that night in Reno. Over at the MGM, Russell Henry occupied a barstool on the periphery of the immense casino, sipping another straight shot of Wild Turkey in his three-piece white suit and white shoes and white plantation hat, his fur coat draped across his lap like a shaggy carcass. There are girls and there are women and there are ladies, he was thinking, and in these days of liberation you don't know what to call them anymore or how to behave towards them anymore and the whole social situation is badly confused except in a make-believe place like a casino where everything is reduced to its essence and the women are pure and simply female. There are broad-beamed females who travel in groups, he thought, who wear harlequin glasses and stretch polyester and have thighs like trees and breasts like melons and who drink tom collinses or wine spritzers and get loud and jolly and have just a terrific time except you can't help but wonder where they ever find men brave or cowed or desperate enough to climb into bed with them when they leave the casino and go back to their hotel rooms. There are handsome, fine-boned females of impeccable grooming, he thought, who don't say a word, who sit sidesaddle at blackjack tables with their elegant legs crossed and faraway looks on their faces and who place their bets with the self-assurance of chessmasters. They smoke long slender cigarettes and remove imaginary flecks of tobacco from their tongues with long painted fingernails and if they catch you staring at them, they give you the kind of smile doormen are accustomed to receiving.

There are spontaneous, friendly females, he thought, with bedroom voices and randy smiles, who are as agreeable as house pets and will talk to anybody about anything and will listen to your life story or tell you theirs and let you buy them a drink or two or three but when they excuse themselves they don't come back and when you run into them later in a different part of the casino they're as friendly and randy as ever except they're with another guy and they don't seem to remember you from before. There are plain-looking females with weathered faces and crow's feet around their eyes, he thought, who look like they've buried three husbands who were all steelworkers except beneath their rough exterior, if you only give them a chance, they're about as tough as marshmallows. There are refreshing, unblemished females, he thought, with pink gums and white teeth and long legs and no waists and who look just like the girl next door, if you happen to have Hugh Hefner for a neighbor, and who make you believe in God because where else could such delectable creatures come from?

There are efficient bartender females, Russell Henry thought, signaling for another Wild Turkey, and this one has poured enough bourbon to drunk me up good by now, yes indeed, and I think it's time for yours truly to walk around a while. Because there are invisible mousy females and brassy obnoxious females and average housewife females and good-natured practical females who will put you in a hammerlock if you lay a finger on them. There are boobs and butts and clefts and cleavages and hips and thighs and rolls of flesh and there are perfumes and lipsticks and eye shadows and hairsprays and if because of all that you think this place reeks of sex, my intoxicated friend, you have your head up your ass. Because if this place reeks of anything, it reeks of money, and if money is power and power is an aphrodisiac, then okay, you can drag sex into the picture twice-removed, as it were. Except the place doesn't truly reek of money, either. What it reeks of is fantasy, exactly as you decided a couple of hours earlier when you were sober. Fantasy and make-believe and the magic of childhood.

So pierce the fantasy, Henry thought. Squint your eyes, my good man, and get a focus. Forget the voluptuous females for a moment and think, for example, about bellies. Yes, concentrate on tum-tums. Beer bellies and bloat bellies and bellies that should be pushed in a wheelbarrow. How do people get into such shape? Have they no pride? Bellies that fill tee shirts and bellies that sag into trousers, high bellies and low bellies and humongous protruding bellies heavy enough to sway backs. It is not all beauty here, my friend. There are also the results of dissipation and self-destruction. And what about the poor souls who can't help what they have become — the bent-over arthritics, the wheelchair-enclosed, the shaky, nearsighted octogenarians as dry and wrinkled as walnuts? They, too, have their dreams and there, my friend, is the reality amid the fantasy. There is your Reno. And don't forget the anomalies: the blind woman at the roulette wheel, the one-armed man playing a slot machine. And at this very moment, if your eyes don't deceive you, a manic dwarf pulling behind him by the shirtfront a large grinning gentleman in a beret who appears to be even drunker than you yourself.

Russell Henry had enough cash in his pocket to buy into a small poker game but he decided he wouldn't learn anything in a small game. He could afford a small game. To experience risk, he needed a high-stakes game. So he aimed himself towards the cashier's cage. He had credit cards. He would negotiate a line of credit. It was time, he thought, for some serious field research.

And so time continued to pass as morning neared in Reno. West of the MGM, between there and the casino district, Lee Sherman Tobias awakened in a hospital room at the Washoe County Medical Center, aware that he'd slipped away for a few hours of drugged sleep. He was propped up slumping forward, pillows hugged to his chest and his body supported by the overbed table. His eyes adjusted to the dim light and moving his head sideways he saw a man fully clothed lying on the bed next to him.

"I gotta pee," Tobias said.

"Lee Sherman, how you doin'?" Archie Breen asked anxiously, coming awake and swinging his legs over the side of the bed.

"I gotta pee."

"Hang on. I'll get a nurse."

"Hurry up. By God, I'm gonna piss a gallon."

Tobias discovered that he was breathing easier now than he'd been earlier. Getting rid of fluid was a good sign, too. A nurse came with a plastic urinal, Archie Breen trailing behind her, and she left the room while Tobias emptied his bladder. The nurse returned and took his pulse and blood pressure and offered him a pill.

"What's that?" Tobias asked.

"Diuretic."

"I don't want no more morphine," he said.

She gave him the pill and a tumbler of water. She adjusted his pillows and said, "Try to get back to sleep, Mr. Tobias. It's still early." She left the door ajar when she left and subdued light from the hallway filtered into the room.

"What time you got?" Tobias asked Breen.

"A little after four," Breen said. "You feelin' better?"

"I been hurt worse in crap games." Who'd said that? Suddenly Tobias remembered the dark hospital room where C. R. Cooley once lay dying, attended only by a distant relative. That miserable rainy day in Oregon seemed like a dream to Tobias, like something that had never happened. And then it seemed like only yesterday.

"Archie," he said, "listen up. Call my missus and tell her to fly here. Get the hotel to meet her at the airport."

"You mean today?"

"I mean right now. Don't give her no big story. Just tell her I said. You go on. I'm gonna sleep."

"I'll stay with you."

"No. You do what I said. I be okay. Just see the hotel sends me a car in time." Tobias closed his eyes and Breen left to carry out his instructions.

Thus dawn approached. Two hours later, in the casino district, Doug McGowan was awakened in his motel room by the telephone. Terry was calling from next door to say that he and Lisa were up, that it was time to get breakfast and hit the road.

"It's still dark out," Doug complained.

"It'll be light soon," Terry said. "Get on it. Meet you in twenty minutes."

Gail stirred on the pillow next to Doug. "Lover?" she asked. "Time to get up?"

"Not if you ask me." Doug switched on the table lamp. Gail's face, resting in a nimbus of brown hair, was glowing with contentment, and Doug peeled the bedcovers back and lay on top of her. They rocked gently from side to side and Gail hummed her pleasure until she began tickling him and he had to let her go. She got out of bed and walked naked to the bathroom.

"We don't have to go home today," Doug called.

"Yes, we do." In a moment he heard the shower running.

Well, shit, he thought, I'm staying. They can go back without me. But later, over breakfast at a coffee shop, he tried again to coax the others into staying in Reno. "What's a few more hours?" he asked.

"You said that yesterday," Terry said.

"Damn straight, and I made money for us. A couple hours here can be worth thousands of bucks." Doug distracted Gail and tried to steal a piece of bacon from her plate. She laughed and slapped his hand away and Doug went into a routine with the salt and pepper shakers, moving them around as if he were running a shell game. "Cut you for high," he said, reaching for the stack of toast and pretending it was a deck of cards.

"So what do you say?" he asked. "Here's my plan. As long as I'm winning, I'll stay in the poker game. If I start to lose, I'll cash out and we'll go home."

Terry said, "No offense, McGowan, but we haven't won a bet for about twelve hours."

"A minor setback."

"Minor? We lost every bet we made last night. We're out of walking-around money."

"Well, excuse me," Doug said, "but I'm sorry as hell my money's temporarily tied up in a poker game. I mean, all I have to show for two days in Reno is a lousy thirty-five thousand bucks. Can't you get it through your head? Listen, if it so happens, which it won't, but if I start losing and get down to twenty-five thou, I'll quit. That's a fortune!"

But the others were adamant about hitting the road. The girls didn't want to cut any more classes at school and Terry was supposed to be at work that afternoon. Outside, the day was turning brilliant. It was cold, but the upthrust of the Sierra Nevada was silhouetted against a lightening western sky entirely clear of clouds.

Back at the motel, with their luggage stowed in Terry's car and the engine idling, Doug said, "How are we fixed for cash?"

"I've got enough for gas," Terry said. "You?"

Doug grinned. "The bad news is I'm down to lunch money in my pocket. The good news is that the bad news doesn't matter. I'll call you tonight when I get home."

"There's probably a couple of planes," Terry said.

"I already thought about that." Doug did a little tap dance and told them, "I love it — I'm gonna take a cab home!"

"Kiss kiss," Gail said.

Doug held her, feeling her breath warm in the hollow of his throat. "I'm glad you came along," he said. "It was great."

"Me, too," she said.

"We'll do it again soon. Wish me luck."

"Luck." Gail kissed him. The trio drove out of the parking lot and Doug went back to his motel room. It was paid for until eleven o'clock, which was good timing. The second round of Stretch Jackson's poker tournament was scheduled to begin at noon.

►►◄ *Wednesday*

"BLACKOUT curtains," Art Epstein mumbled, waking in the dark. "You have to be a bat to maneuver in here." He felt his way to the window of the hotel suite and located a pull-cord. "Sun's coming up, gorgeous," he told his wife. "You brought some good weather."

"Let me look at you," Jackie said. "God, you're a sight in the morning. You look just like Tarzan."

"Tarzan's circumcised?"

"You know him better than I do, darling."

Epstein felt a rush of pleasure. Maybe the way they were living made sense after all, he thought. Maybe it was the separations that made their getting together so good. He was still excited by the possibilities Jackie had raised the night before about changing the direction of her career and later, relaxing over juice and coffee in the sitting room of the suite, he asked, "What turned your thinking around?"

"It's been gradual." Jackie lifted her chin. "Look at this face — it has character. I keep taking bubblehead parts and I finally realized they're a dead-end road. I'm built for the long run, honey. I look at a Jane Fonda or a Dyan Cannon or a Faye Dunaway and I realize there's life after forty —"

"A Shelley Winters, an Elizabeth Taylor —"

Jackie laughed. "Up yours. I take after my father, sweetheart, not my mother. But say we do this oddball Mexico thing where I play a woman ten years older than me, and then I follow with a dramatic role. And then go back for one more sex-bomb part, a comedy maybe, while I still have the equipment for it —"

"I like it," Epstein said. "It's what you call positioning yourself in the market."

"It's what you call getting away from typecasting, dear. I want to get three projects started this year, and for once have them all part of a master plan. But I want you to produce with me. Am I being selfish? I don't want to take you away from your own business."

They were interrupted by a knock on the door. "Open up!" Foley called from the hallway. "It's the vice squad!"

"Oh, God," Jackie said. "If that horrid midget's with him, please don't let them in."

Epstein opened the door, saying, "Isn't it kind of early —" He stopped in mid-sentence as the pilot entered, ushering a tall young blonde ahead of him.

"If you close your mouth," Foley said, "maybe a fly won't get in it. I know, you're about to say, 'Foley, we thought you'd have a hangover.' Well, I do. However, I would like you both to meet

Anita. Anita and I want to buy you breakfast. Anita, this is Art and Jackie Epstein. Art's the tall one."

The pilot looked like a different man from the night before. Gone were his scarf and beret and silly French affectations. Instead, he was dressed in a pair of creased gray slacks, a yellow sports shirt and a long-sleeved brown sweater. Combed and shaved and scented and on his best behavior, he looked as smug as a church deacon who'd just dropped twenty dollars in the collection plate.

Epstein asked, "Would you like some coffee?"

Foley nodded. The girl, Anita, said, "He'd like some aspirin if you have any, too. But he's too polite to ask."

The girl struck Epstein as someone you don't expect to encounter in real life. In a painting, maybe, or an air-brushed photograph. Her features were too perfect. It was the angle of her nose, he thought, and its relation to the curve of her cheeks. But then he realized that her mouth, the outline of her lips and the shape of her teeth, completed the geometry of her face in an essential way. And that was without taking into account her complexion, which was an amazing high pink, or her dark blue eyes or blonde hair. She glowed, and Epstein recognized that her look was natural; she wore scarcely any makeup. She was a treasure. She was wearing blue jeans and a print blouse, no jewelry, and she was high-waisted and proportioned in a way other women would kill for.

Foley put his arm around her and said, "Anita needs friendly support. She quit her job last night."

"It's no trauma," she said. "Foley's just trying to work up a load of guilt." She turned to him and said, "You didn't talk me into it. It's been coming for a long time."

Epstein busied himself with the coffee machine and Jackie said, "I'll see if I can find some aspirin. They furnish everything else here." She caught Epstein's eye and gave him a perplexed look.

Basking in Anita's attention, Foley said when the four of them got settled, "I told Art all about you yesterday. How I fell in love at first sight."

"He was so cute," Anita said. "He followed me into the employees' lounge on my break. He was talking such a blue streak that nobody could get a word in. I told him if he'd just wait five minutes I could meet him outside, but by then it was too late because somebody called security."

"I thought you did," Foley said. "That's what broke my heart."

She shook her head. "I followed you out as soon as I could but you were gone by then."

Epstein said, "Wait a minute. Pardon my interruption, but we have a mystery. Jackie and I saw this character last night and he was blasted. He was also in foul company, dressed like an *apache* dancer and obviously on his way to a debacle. Now he shows up ten hours later, stone cold sober and acting like an Amway salesman. What happened?"

"She told me to sober up," Foley said.

"Just like that?"

"I was hoping he'd come back," Anita said. "I wanted to apologize for the night before. I don't know, I felt there was something special about him. But when he did come back last night, he was drunk and had that awful little Julius with him —"

"I thought I needed him and the disguise to get back in," Foley said.

"Dear, it's only a casino," Anita said. "It's not Buckingham Palace. Believe me, the only thing anybody needs Julius for is if they get off on being goosed. But I didn't want to deal with a drunk so I told Foley to come back in an hour and be sober, or else forget the whole thing."

"True," the pilot said. "And that's one for the Guinness book. I ditched Julius, got a cab back here, took a cold shower, changed clothes, drank coffee, ran around outside in the ice — tell 'em, Anita, was I sober next time you saw me?"

"Pretty much."

"Ha," Foley said. "It was an act. *Now* I'm sober. I think. With this headache, who knows? Anyway, we talked all night and now we're driving up to the lake to plan Anita's future some more. Can we buy you breakfast first? You got time before the tournament?"

Jackie said, "I'd love it. Art?"

Anita suddenly clasped a hand to her mouth. "Oh, my goodness," she said, "this is so embarrassing. I thought you looked familiar. You're Jackie *Gaines!*"

Epstein, meanwhile, put his coffee cup down and said, "Son of a bitch. The poker tournament. I'd forgotten about it."

Brian Bates awakened with the sun and as he rolled out of bed the memory of his vivid midnight dream returned: Marlene was in Reno. For the moment he shook aside his money and legal worries. One thing at a time, he told himself; that's the only way you ever got anywhere. The first question is, do you want to see Marlene? The answer is yes. I need her. Okay, then — how do you expect to find her?

I'll have to call hotels and motels, he thought. Unless she's not staying in one. Maybe she rented a room somewhere. What a dumb-shit idea — there is absolutely no legal reason for her to be in Reno. I could call lawyers. No, hotels are better. But first I need breakfast, he thought. And I need a shower and a shave and I need to think about poker. It's a good thing I got up early. Bates fought down his tension. One thing at a time. He cleaned up and got something to eat downstairs and returned to his room, and by then it was almost eight o'clock. Going on six in Hawaii. Fuck it, he thought, he's charging me plenty; I'll wake him up at home.

Bates phoned his lawyer in Honolulu and said, "I slept on it. Tell the A.G. I'll make restitution. No, it's not a stall. They've got me by the short ones. I've got a wife and kids and I don't need a felony rap. So get the indictment killed. Just don't talk hard figures. I'll be back in town next week and we'll work out the details. And listen, call that Jap personally and tell him what's going down. I'll get back to you."

Bates replaced the receiver. With one phone call, he'd just gone from being rich to being broke. It galled him. By the time he was through with this, he'd be lucky to walk away with grocery money.

But shitty as it is, he thought, the problem's solved. Worrying about it won't help. Get on to the next one. He sat on the edge of his bed, opened the Reno phone book to the yellow pages and started dialing hotels. He began with Harrah's, the Taj, Circus-Circus, the MGM, the Hilton. They put him on hold and they piped elevator music at him and he kept drawing blanks. But he stayed at his task with the patience of a door-to-door salesman. He dialed, got through to room clerks and asked if a Marlene Bates was registered there. No, she's not. Sorry. Not here. No one by that name. He kept dialing.

Sometime later he was interrupted by a knock at his door. He opened it and saw Carroll Shepherd standing in the hallway.

"Your phone's off the hook," the psychologist said. "You want some breakfast?"

"I already ate," Bates answered. "You look like hell."

Shepherd entered the room. "I feel like hell. I tied one on last night. I also got killed at twenty-one. If you don't win the tournament, I'm going to end up in a sandwich board."

Bates looked at his watch. "Shit, nine-thirty already. Listen, doc, I need your help. Two things. First, get a deck of cards somewhere — we have to practice. And there's a tee-shirt place. I think it's on Fourth Street just off the main drag. You know where I mean? They've got a sign in the window — it says they print to order. Pay extra if you have to, but get me a tee shirt right away. I need it for the tournament. I want it to say ESP. In capital letters."

"Extrasensory perception?"

"Unless you can think of something better. Get an extra-large."

"What's the deal?" Shepherd said.

"Look, yesterday I didn't give a damn," Bates told him. "Today I need the money. Some of those guys have been playin' poker since before I was born, but if they beat me it won't be because I rolled over. I can intimidate, too. I'm gonna pump up before the tournament and play in a tee shirt. But it ought to say something to get 'em off-balance. It's a bullshit idea but it's better than nothing."

"Marginally," Shepherd said.

"Shake ass, will you? I've got other stuff to do. If I'm not here when you get back, I'll be down at the health club."

Shepherd left on his errand and Bates went back to dialing the telephone. After twenty minutes more, he had a brainstorm: travel agency. Of course. And he figured he knew which one — they'd used it before. Bates called Honolulu information and got the phone number but it was still too early back there; nobody answered when he rang the office. He changed into his sweat clothes and took the elevator down to the health club.

Shepherd found him there later, working his back muscles on a pulley row. "Mission accomplished," Shepherd said.

Bates had soaked through his sweatshirt by then. "A few more minutes," he said. "I'm just gonna do some more chins and then work my arms." His face was flushed and his hair was limp with perspiration.

"You're not going to leave your game in the locker room, are you?" Shepherd asked.

Bates didn't answer. He stepped on a stool and reached up for the chinning bar. He took an overhand grip and bent his legs backward, crossing his ankles for stability as he hung from the bar. "Hold my feet steady, doc," he said, "and fight me a little. Give me some resistance."

Bates did a set of chin-ups such as Shepherd had never seen. His grip on the bar was wide, beyond the width of his shoulders, so that his body formed a letter Y. He pulled himself up with his head forward, flattening the Y to a T when the back of his neck touched the chinning bar. He did six quick chin-ups, slowed his pace and did three more, then squeezed out a final two. Shepherd, with his hand on Bates's crossed ankles, felt in touch with a muscular strength beyond his experience. There was something atavistic in it, something of the jungle.

Bates dropped to his feet, flexed his back and shook himself, then moved over to the dumbbells to pump up his biceps and triceps. It was only when they got back to Bates's room and he pulled off his sweatshirt that Shepherd saw the effects of the workout.

"Holy Jesus," he said.

Bates threw a pose at himself in the mirror. His upper body was grossly inflated — sloping shoulders, pumped-up arms, round slabs of muscle on his shoulders and chest, a bulging V-taper, abdominals ridged like bricks. "Awesome," he said. He took a shower and emerged from the bathroom drying his hair with a towel. "Let's see the shirt," he said. "You got a *pink* one?"

"Lavender," Shepherd said. "It has religious connotations."

The tee shirt was imprinted on the front with "E.S.P." in block letters and, in smaller type below it, "Katmandu."

"What's this other word?"

"It's a holy place," Shepherd said. "If you're going to fake eastern philosophy, you might as well do it right. Except you're going to need a shoehorn."

"Just so it's long enough to tuck in." Bates pulled the tee shirt over his head and snaked it down his body. It was such a tight fit that all the definition of his overdeveloped physique showed through the fabric. "I feel like an asshole," he said. "Do I intimidate you?"

"Let's just say you don't look easy," Shepherd answered.

"Break the cards out. I have to make a call."

Bates struck gold this time when he reached the Honolulu travel agency. "The Lucky Seven Motel in Sparks?" he said to Shepherd, replacing the receiver. "Where the hell's Sparks?"

"A couple of miles down the road."

"It figures. They gave her a package deal. How cheap can you get?" Bates found the number in the phone book and dialed the Lucky Seven. But Marlene's room didn't answer. "Take a message," Bates told the clerk. "Tell her Brian called. I'm in Reno at the Taj Mahal and I want to see her."

"Who's Marlene?" Shepherd asked.

"Never mind. Shuffle the cards while I get dressed."

"You shuffle 'em. I have to be sick." Shepherd hurried into the bathroom and closed the door behind him. He was pale when he came out. "I should have done that last night," he said.

"You okay?"

"I will be. I just got rid of a fifth of Jose Cuervo. You know, if we're partners, you might try confiding in me."

"I don't have time." Bates dealt a round of poker hands on top of the bureau, two cards down and one up. "Deuce of hearts brings it in," he said. He pointed to the next card. "What's the jack do?"

Shepherd looked at the hole cards. "Jack calls."

"The seven?"

"Seven folds," Shepherd said. "What do you do with your ace?"

"Fold my ace."

"What do you mean, fold your ace? You've got the high hand showing."

"I don't bet against the deuce of hearts," Bates said. "That's the Brian card. That's *me*. Look!" He flipped over the hole cards under the deuce of hearts. They were both kings.

Shepherd said, "ESP?"

"Fuckin' A! Test my memory — turn over some cards and then hide 'em real fast."

Shepherd momentarily exposed five cards; Bates recited them by suit and number. He did the same with eight cards, and then twelve. "I'm up for this, doc," he said. "You want to see something?" Bates fanned the cards out in a serpentine, face down. "Hearts are my suit. They're my family." He let his hand hover over the deck and then plucked a card out. "Heart," he said, turning it over. It was the seven of hearts. He ran his fingers over the deck and he plucked another card. "Heart," he said. It was the three of hearts. "One more time." Slowly he slid a card out of the deck, lifted it high and slammed it down on the bureau without looking. "*Heart!*" he said as it fell. It was the queen. "*Momma!*" Let's play poker, doc! You think I'm not ready for those bastards?"

The psychologist, taken aback by the aggressive performance, looked at the pumped-up chest with E.S.P. printed across it and then down at the three red cards exposed on the bureau. "Now I'm intimidated," he said.

134 //

*

Russell Henry was chagrined. Getting drunk was no novelty to him. Staying up all night was no novelty. Suffering a hangover was no novelty. But selling his fur coat to a cab driver at four in the morning, that was embarrassing. So was dropping a thousand dollars in poker games where he'd been over his head from the beginning. I came here to write about winners, he told himself, and all I learned last night was how it feels to be a loser. It feels lousy, and I didn't need help to figure that one out. If there's one thing I know, it's that there are a hell of a lot more losers in Reno than there are winners, and they all volunteer for the job. Losing is symbolic suicide. Just listen to the metaphors, Henry thought; I got killed, I'm dying, they murdered me. You might argue that chronic losers carry a load of guilt and a great need to punish themselves, he told himself, if that weren't such a trite widespread belief already, thanks in part to Sigmund Freud. The good doctor also said that compulsive gambling is like masturbating: you keep swearing you'll quit but every time you break your resolution you get paid off with an exquisite thrill of guilt.

And that's all very erudite, Henry thought, but your time here will be more productive if you forget the compulsive losers and start concentrating on the compulsive winners. He'd seen a few of them last night, too, studying cards with all the mystic concentration of people who read entrails, arranging chips as if they foretold destiny like the count of the *I Ching*. What would a man from Mars think? The cards are as cryptic as any rune or glyph, the face cards inscribed as elaborately as the picture-writing of the ancient Mayans. Yet how many millions of people who couldn't possibly distinguish *Imix* from *Uayeb*, even with a lifetime's study, can discriminate with the most fleeting glance the king of diamonds from the jack of spades?

And the language, Henry thought — it's as inaccessible as a foreign tongue. Ace, deuce, trey. Salmon, eight, nine. Bullets. Ducks. Three ducks, Huey, Dewey, and Louie. Maverick, jacks and queens. Dead man's hand, aces and eights. Trips. A full house. A filly, a full boat, a boat. A lock. The nuts. The hammer. In the blind. All purple. A pair. Paregoric. I pass, Pasadena, Paso Robles. El Paso. And three tens, thirty miles of railroad track, hence thirty miles, hence San Jose to Gilroy. First one over wins. Read 'em and weep, friend — San Jose to Gilroy.

Outside in Reno it was clear and crisp, a winter's day to breathe deep in your lungs, punch holes in the air and yelp out loud for the pure hell of it. The sky was the blue of promises and the foreshortened mass of the Sierra Nevada rose under fallen snow that blinked a flat, dazzling white unbroken by shadows. But none of the outdoor light penetrated to the center of the Taj Mahal's casino. There, it could have been any hour on the clock except for some subtle combination of details peculiar to midday in a casino. The thinness of the crowd, the shuffling aimlessness, the lack of intensity, the too-loud noise of the slots, all combined to produce an atmosphere of waiting. Likewise the poker players, assembling for the second day of the tournament, suggested to Russell Henry a mood of momentum scarcely begun.

There was Vic Houston, rumored to have cleaned up in a hold-em game that lasted until dawn, trying to engage Lee Sherman Tobias in conversation. But the older man, looking feeble, ignored him. There was Shayna Levinson, in slacks and a sweater and makeup, who sat with her knees crossed, jiggling an ankle. She looked out to the rail when she heard her name called and gave someone a wink and a thumbs-up sign. There was the overweight Sandwiches, sitting in a chair with his thighs spread, eyes closed, only his twirling thumbs belying his attitude of repose. There was Art Epstein standing behind the rail and whispering something to his wife. There was young Doug McGowan with a grin on his face, bouncing up and down to an inner rhythm of optimism.

And there came stubby Archie Breen through the crowd, followed by the looming thinness of Stretch Jackson. A television crew had set up equipment and as the players began drawing for seats at the four remaining tournament poker tables, the TV lights came on harshly, scattering some of the railbirds. Brian Bates squinted at the glare and sent Carroll Shepherd out for a pair of dark glasses. People stared at Bates, who looked as wide as two people. They stared at Jackie Gaines as word circulated that a movie actress was among the railbirds. They stared at Vic Houston and Lee Sherman Tobias, the professionals' professionals. And they stared at Stretch Jackson, the celebrity, who for a split second seemed to disappear in darkness when the television lights clicked off.

But nobody paid any attention to Russell Henry as he wandered away from the area. He was musing on the proposition that everybody in a poker game was an equal. Young or old, black or white, rich or poor, intelligent or illiterate, as long as they could put up the ante they were the peer of the next guy. He was thinking that a poker game was a perfect extension of democracy. And he thought, making his way to his room, that the dollar sign was probably civilization's most successful symbol since the introduction of the crucifix.

Jerry Corbett, however, would have argued that money had nothing to do with the game of poker. The chips were just a way of keeping score. To amateurs the chips could buy stereos, cars, condos, but the pros knew better. Jerry Corbett had almost twenty thousand dollars in chips in front of him but he was fully aware that within the confines of the green table his stack didn't have the retail value of a bag of peanuts. Still in his woman's disguise, Jerry was optimistic; he'd drawn an easier table than the day before. Not counting himself, there were only two big winners from Tuesday in his group. One was a computer whiz from New York named Walsh, and the other was Shayna. The rest of the players at his table were losers. And Jerry figured he had a couple of other factors in his favor. First, Chris was among the railbirds now, pulling for him. And second, the TV lights and cameras made the scene more like theater, which was his element.

The stakes had been raised again, to a fifty-dollar ante and an opening forced bet of a hundred dollars. Jerry and the others eased into the first minutes of the tournament with what could have passed for nonchalance, adjusting seat cushions, restacking chips and acknowledging friends out in the crowd. At Jerry's table, the first pot was won by a player new to him, a middle-aged redhead with a high forehead. Jerry was low and bet the mandatory hundred dollars. Nobody called except the redhead, who had an ace showing. On the next card he bet two hundred. Jerry folded and the redhead raked in the pot.

"Good start, sister," Shayna said.

Jerry ignored her. He knew Shayna would be on his back all day, since there were only two other women left in the tournament and they were playing at different tables. But he could handle her. Jerry knew how to play Shayna from previous experience: ignore her mouth and concentrate on her cards. Besides, Shayna considered Jerry a lightweight so she'd devote most of her energy to harassing the computer guy. Already she'd picked up on Walsh's accent. "Hey, Noo Yawk," she said, "didja ever play with cowboys before?"

Jerry was concentrating on Walsh, too. He was about Jerry's age, with unkempt brown hair, horn-rimmed glasses and a leather jacket. Jerry tried tuning out Walsh's voice and watching him the way he'd watch a mime. He wanted to get a feel for Walsh's body language, to understand the connection between his eyes and his gestures. Walsh was quick, and as Jerry studied him he began to feel a respect for him. Then he realized Walsh was staring back and he repressed a laugh. He probably thinks I'm coming on to him, Jerry thought.

Play proceeded cautiously. Jerry wasn't especially interested in the other players at the table; by Thursday he planned to share the stage with the known champions. He intended to be in the final round with Houston and Tobias and Sandwiches and Owl Avery, and he wasn't going to let this indifferent crew knock him out of the tournament. Testing the waters, he ran a small bluff and got away with it. He settled into the routine.

Meanwhile, Shayna was counting her blessings at drawing an easy table, too. She figured she was entitled to a break after battling

Vic Houston all day Tuesday, but this was almost too good to be true, especially in a round when she needed to run up her winnings. She jumped out early, forcing her own tempo on the game. The only player in the group who worried her was the computer guy, but so far Walsh wasn't showing much. Shayna figured the other woman, Corbett, the one with the brown eyes and the teeth, was in over her head. She'd fade. It was inevitable.

Shayna had gotten laid the night before, for the first time since she'd been in Reno, and she had to admit it gave her a better attitude. Maybe she was going to find a circle of friends. That would be some change from Vegas. In Vegas all she'd had were a hundred poker enemies and that bastard Frank Bartelli, but last night with Eugene she'd found a tender companion. She could see why he was a lousy poker player; he didn't have a killer instinct. Eugene had played in the private mini-tournament that staked Shayna and afterwards had become her most enthusiastic supporter. He was a Reno local, but a roofing contractor and not of the regular gambling population, and Shayna found him easy to be around. Since he was a nice guy, there was no point to her trying to outsmart him or humble him with wisecracks, so instead she'd quieted down and accepted his gentleness.

But none of that had anything to do with the poker tournament. "Hey!" Shayna said, jumping up from her seat and pointing across the table at Walsh. "I got a pair showing, in case you didn't notice. You wouldn't see a white rat if it ran across the table." She pushed a raise into the pot.

The television reporter was a sleek brunette with high cheekbones and a hundred-dollar hairdo. "Stretch Jackson," she said, getting ready to stick a microphone in his face, "you've made a movie, you've written a book, you're reputed to be a millionaire — why do you still play poker?"

"The companionship of true gentlemen, honey," Stretch said. "The most honest men in the world are settin' right here behind us. You take a businessman, a lot of people think he's honest when he's just inexperienced. But a gambler's word's his bond. If one of these boys tells you it's gonna snow in July, you'd best put chains on your car, 'cause it's damn sure gonna get slick outside."

"Is poker fun to a professional?" the reporter asked.

"Sure is. To a gambler, the greatest pleasure in the world is winnin' at poker."

Smirking suggestively, she asked, "And the second-greatest pleasure?"

"Losin' at poker," Stretch drawled.

At Art Epstein's table, one player started the session with a miniscule stack of chips. He had a pink face so puffy that his eyes were squeezed into the barest slits, and he had a perpetual smile on his face, as if this particular poker game were the pleasantest occasion he'd ever experienced in his entire life. Within thirty minutes Wednesday, he was knocked out of the tournament.

It was a tough table. Brett Overstreet, the laconic Texan in faded Levis, was a big winner, and so were a blue-whiskered professional they called Easy and another Texan named DeHaven. All three were on the leader board and Epstein found himself relishing the prospects of the next few hours.

It had been a long time since anybody had taken Art Epstein for granted. He was reminded of years ago at law school where, with his size and California blondness, he'd been dismissed as a West Coast hick — until the class standings were posted. Similarly now, the professional gamblers were disregarding him as they maneuvered for advantage among themselves, and Epstein felt a thrill at being so casually underrated. Despite his small stack, he was inching his way up, and he was confident. He knew the others would run over him like bulldozers if he showed any fear, but he wasn't putting up a front. For the first time since the tournament began, he felt like a winner. He felt it tingling inside him. The cardboard placards of Stretch Jackson beckoned from the periphery of his vision. The streamer overhead blazoned the tournament. Lights shone on the green tables. Chips rattled, cards fluttered, the crowd pressed close, and Epstein felt a challenge. In his mind he could hear the words of the aerialist Karl Wallenda: *to be on the wire is life; the rest is waiting.*

Epstein folded his cards and pushed himself away from the table for a break. His wife was standing at the edge of the crowd, a blonde girl next to her.

"You should see yourself when you play," Jackie told him. "You're so intense. You look like you own the table."

"Give me time," he said. "You okay? Nobody bothering you?"

"Actually, I'm fabulously engrossed. I don't think you've met Chris," she said, introducing the girl at her side.

Chris offered her hand and Epstein took it, struck by the freshness and symmetry of her face. She also had a figure, which was emphasized by her blue jeans and Reno tee shirt.

"You must be a poker fan," he said.

Chris had been improvising frantically ever since Jackie Gaines had attached herself to her. "My girlfriend's in the tournament," she said.

"In tenth place," Jackie added.

Epstein looked at the leader board. "Jerry Corbett? She must know what she's doing."

"I think she has a chance to win," Chris said. "She's played in Gardena a lot."

Jackie said, "I told Chris she and her friend ought to have dinner with us tonight."

"Oh, we wouldn't want to impose," Chris said.

"Don't be silly," Epstein said. "We'd love it."

"I'll have to ask Jerry," Chris said. "Thanks very much. It's just that she might have the tournament on her mind or something."

"Ask her," Epstein said. "Excuse me — I have to get back or they'll deal me a dead hand."

Jackie walked a few steps with him. "Having fun?"

"More than yesterday."

"I love watching you play," Jackie said. "And I take back what I said about you looking like Tarzan. You know what you remind me of? A lion."

"You're bringing me luck," he said. "That's a pretty girl, that Chris."

"I know. Isn't she lovely?"

Lee Sherman Tobias sagged as the afternoon wore on. He'd felt rested after his overnight stay in the hospital but soon exhaustion crept up on him. Energy was draining from him like a slow leak and after a while the only thing holding him up were his elbows, supporting his weight on the arms of his chair. His damn luck, too, drawing a table with Hoo-Hoo and Sandwiches. Easy pickings all over the place, Houston a table away cleaning up on a bunch of nobodies, and Lee Sherman was stuck at a tough table.

Well, he'd been there before. When it came to hanging on, the pit bull hadn't been whelped that could match Lee Sherman Tobias. With fatigue invading him like a toxin, he drifted back in time. The thousand-mile drives, the lifetime of all-night games. Tobias at the wheel, hanging on. He was in the old familiar game, hearing again the old familiar music. At poker, Tobias was like an orchestra conductor who caught every nuance, who recognized instantly when someone came in a fraction of a beat late or the slightest bit off-key. Exhausted, drawing on a reservoir of stamina existing only in his memory, the old man played. By one-thirty he'd personally knocked two players out of the contest, one a woman, the other somebody with a cigar. When they exited, Tobias didn't have the strength to lift his head or join in the brief applause. He just tapped his finger weakly on the table. Deal cards.

Meanwhile, six feet away at an adjoining table, Brian Bates had fallen in love. In his wraparound dark glasses, with his hair slicked back and his massive upper arms bulging the sleeves of his tee shirt, Bates was more of a menacing figure at the poker table than he knew. He looked dangerous to the other players, if not downright vicious, and no one would have guessed that he was overwhelmed by the presence of Vic Houston sitting next to him.

Unexpectedly, in Reno, Nevada, of all places, Brian Bates had discovered his real-life John Wayne. He felt like a child enveloped by the radiance of a beloved parent. In Vic Houston, Bates saw every trait he'd ever fantasized in his unknown father, every ideal of masculine perfection. Houston was tall and husky, he had a rugged, leathery look, he was tough and ruthless but with a twinkle of forgiveness in his eyes, he was Olympian in his self-confidence, supreme in his chosen field, feared and respected by everyone in his orbit. He could back you up six paces just with a look and Bates knew that nobody in the world could wrong, insult or lay a hand on the big Texan, not without suffering a cool and dispassionate revenge.

Bates wanted to be alone with Houston. He wanted to ask him questions. He had an urge to sit in Houston's lap. With awe, with love and adoration and hero worship all mixed together, he watched Houston play poker. The Texan's movements were efficient, his expression pleasant, his comments courteous and his blue eyes fearless. His confidence was obvious and his stack of chips kept growing.

So did Bates's. Bates was playing remarkable poker. For the first time in his life, he had the chance to show his father what he was capable of, to prove he wasn't just a dumb Okie. Demonstrating his competence to the one man who counted above all others, Bates was winning money, not as he expected out of his desperate necessity, but because he was in the presence of the King of Hearts. He'd found an ally. Playing a hand, Bates caught an ace on the fourth card and nodded as if in satisfaction, although the card gave him exactly nothing, an ace up and a king down. Doug McGowan, showing a pair of deuces, bet two hundred dollars into him and Bates said, "Raise you three."

Doug hesitated. He took another peek at his hole cards and said with an uncertain grin, "What the heck — when you're hot, you're hot, right?" He called Bates's raise.

Doug was anything but hot, though. His good luck of the day before had vanished as capriciously as it had appeared, like a mirage, and suddenly all he was holding was dust. He'd been losing steadily since noon. He was drawing unmatched cards, low pairs, straights that refused to fill. Now, with three spades on the first three cards, he'd paired a deuce on the fourth card instead of catching another spade. He was tempted to throw the hand in, but he was still pushing his luck. It could just be a temporary setback, he thought; I can get two more spades or another deuce. Hell, four deuces isn't out of the question. Doug knew he had to play his hunches, because he sure couldn't get a reading on Bates. Bates terrified him. He looked like some kind of an animal.

The fifth card didn't help either player. Doug, still with the high card showing, bet two hundred again. Bates said, "Make it twelve. I raise a thousand."

Bates knew Doug was going to fold. Doug's pair of deuces had him beat but Bates wasn't worried about deuces. The deuce of hearts had already fallen — Bates wouldn't forget the magic card — and little Bobby Dee, the deuce of spades, was tucked in his own hand. Bates's only decision was how much to raise, since the kid would call a small raise for sure, and a big raise could look too obviously like he was trying to buy the pot. He wanted to drive Doug out, not keep him in, so a thousand was the strategic amount. Bates wasn't aware of thinking through to that conclusion; it simply appeared in his mind when Doug made his bet, and his raise followed immediately.

Watching the action, Vic Houston doubted that even Doug would be dumb enough to call the bet. Houston figured Bates for a pair of aces, maybe aces over, and thought Bates was too greedy; he was trying to reel the kid in before the hook was set.

Doug agonized over the raise. He scratched his head. He drank some Coors. But finally, afraid of Bates, he folded. Bates, collecting the pot, turned his hole cards over so everybody could see he'd been bluffing.

Vic Houston was surprised at reading Bates wrong and wondered where he'd made his mistake. Probably with the costume. The horseshit with the dark glasses and the muscles and the tee shirt had thrown him off — Bates maybe wasn't the fool he looked to be. Houston registered the information and filed it away.

But Houston didn't care much about the byplay between a couple of minor players. He was more concerned with how Lee Sherman Tobias was holding up at the other table. His affection for the older man went way back. When Houston had started his gambling career after the war, Tobias was already a legendary figure. Houston had heard about the taciturn loner who they said would drive a thousand miles or more nonstop in his Cadillac to any club or back room in the country where the action was big enough, but it wasn't until the early fifties, at Hot Springs, that he'd first laid eyes on him. Expecting some remarkable character, Houston had been struck by Tobias's ordinariness. Tobias was thick through the torso, and gruff to the point of rudeness, but the only memorable thing about him, except for his playing, was his eyes, as brown and ancient and unfathomable as an ape's.

And look at him now, Houston thought, still beatin' the pants off people after all these years. Seeing Lee Sherman Tobias at a poker table was like finding Bobby Jones or Gene Sarazen still on the golf tour winning tournaments from athletes young enough to be their grandchildren. He's the last of a breed, Houston thought, a living memory of the glory days of the road, and when he goes, the book'll close on a piece of history. Except he's not goin' anywhere yet, Houston told himself — Lee Sherman's a scrapper. Houston remembered a kid in the army, a lanky, tow-headed Tennessean hemstitched by a German machine gun in Normandy. Nobody could get to him and he lay crumpled for hours where he fell. When it turned dark, he walked in on his own and said, "Get me a medic. I think they shot me twice." He had seven bullet holes spaced like buttons across his body. And Houston had another memory, this one from downtown Vegas maybe fifteen years earlier. They were playing five-card stud and Tobias got into a hand with Stretch Jackson. The Stretcherman, with a pair of kings wired, was looking at an ace in Tobias's hand. He raised Tobias's bet and said, "Get out, Lee Sherman. I got kings."

"I got aces," Tobias answered, raising back.

"Bullshit," Stretch said. He raised again on third street and Tobias re-raised again.

"I told you I got aces." Tobias said.

"You got a handful of hope," Stretch drawled. In those days he was already cultivating his image as a public personality and with his ego, he was a special target for anyone good enough to nail him.

On fourth street, Tobias bet two thousand, Stretch raised him five and Tobias said, "Godammit, but I hate to be took for a moron. I told you I got aces. How much money you got there?"

Stretch counted his chips. "Seventy-eight hundred."

"Get it in, if you're so proud of them kings," Tobias said.

When the fifth and last card was dealt, Tobias took his hat off and put it on the table.

"What's that about?" Stretch asked.

"I'm bettin' my hat against yours," Tobias said. "You're goin' home in a barrel, you dumb son of a bitch." He slipped the watch off his wrist and put it in the pot. "That's a Rolex. I ain't got all the rings you do," he said, "but get out of your britches." Tobias unbuttoned his shirt and put it on the table, then stood up and took his belt off, threw it on the table and followed it with his trousers. "Your boots, too," he said.

Tobias sat down again, a scowling sixty-year-old in the middle of a casino wearing nothing but longhandles and an undershirt. "I got aces," he said.

Stretch slumped in his chair and stared at Tobias while a long moment passed. With his thumb, he pushed the Stetson a half an inch farther back on his head. Then he looked around the table at the other players, grinned, reached out and slowly turned his cards over.

"Like he said, gents, he's got aces."

Tobias took the pot without comment and started to get dressed. His cards were still on the table. That was when Houston interjected, "He doesn't have aces."

Stretch looked at Houston, then down at the table in front of him, empty of chips.

"Your marker's good," Houston said.

"How much?"

"Ten thousand says you had him beat."

Stretch didn't answer directly. "Lee Sherman," he said, "did you run one on me? You actually willin' to get nekkid, a man your age, just to buy a pot?"

Stuffing his shirttails into his trousers, Tobias said, "Take his money. I got aces."

Stretch chuckled. He was in a bind, but no one had ever accused him of being anything less than good-natured. "I just tapped out 'cause that sumbitch has aces," he said to Houston. "How the hell can I turn down a proposition sayin' he *don't* have aces? You're on."

Without a change of expression, Tobias turned over his hole card. "Didn't have 'em," he grunted.

Stretch sat still for a long time. Then he stood up and said, "Deal me out. When I lose on an instant replay, it's time for some shuteye. But Lee Sherman," he said, pointing a long finger at the older man, "next time you get undressed in front of me, you better make sure your back ain't turned or you're by damn gonna get what I just did."

Well, Stretch had style, you could always say that about him. But now, looking over at the next poker table, Houston saw a sad remnant of the man Tobias once was. Leaning forward, elbows on the table, head drooping, he looked like one of those sagging carcasses you trip over in a nursing home. Still, while Houston watched, Tobias pushed a big stack of chips at the pot and Johnny Sandwiches, his brown forehead shiny with perspiration, flicked his hand in surrender and said tiredly, "Take it."

The dealer swept the pot over to Tobias as Archie Breen walked into the tournament area with his hand raised. "Break time," he called. "Twenty minutes!"

THE FIRST ANNUAL STRETCH JACKSON
SEVEN-CARD STUD POKER CLASSIC

Standings as of 2 P.M. Wednesday

1.	Vic Houston, Texas	$52,775
2.	William "Hoo-Hoo" Avery, Arizona	42,050
3.	Lee Sherman Tobias, Missouri	37,200
4.	Brett Overstreet, Texas	35,250
5.	Amateur player (Walsh), New York	34,750
6.	Professional player ("Easy"), Nevada	33,500
7.	John "Sandwiches" Treece, Louisiana	32,175
8.	Shayna Levinson, Washington	31,850
9.	Brian Bates, Oklahoma	31,750
10.	Jerry Corbett, California	26,225
11.	Doug McGowan, California	25,200
12.	Professional player (DeHaven), Texas	19,650

And 10 remaining contestants ranging from $17,200 to $5,150

Play to resume at: 2:20 P.M.

Of the thirty-two gamblers who'd survived Tuesday's competition, ten were eliminated by Wednesday's first break. The remaining players would be recombined at three tables — two games of seven players and one of eight — and the stakes increased again, the ante to a hundred dollars and the opening forced bet to two hundred. The gamblers drew for new seats and exchanged their twenty-five-dollar chips for hundreds, high-carding each other to round off the odd amount. That accomplished, most of them wandered off, leaving the tournament area temporarily abandoned.

The television reporter grabbed Shayna Levinson and Jerry

Corbett, signaling her crew to start the camera. "The two surviving women in the tournament," she announced. "How does it feel?"

"Ask me when it's over," Shayna said.

"At the halfway point, two women and twenty men," the reporter continued. "Are you rooting for each other?"

Shayna gave her a look. "You're kidding. I'm rooting I knock this one out."

The reporter turned to Jerry. "Jerry Corbett. An amateur at poker, a female, playing against the best gamblers in the world — how do you rate your chances?"

Show biz, Jerry thought. This airhead makes fifty thousand a year and all she has going for her are cheekbones and a hairdresser. He smiled demurely, looking at Shayna, and said, "I'd like to believe there's still a place for amateurs in the world."

Jerry drifted out of camera range and the lights clicked off. Shayna moved over and said, "Was that a crack?"

Jerry widened his eyes. "Whatever do you mean, dear?"

Doug McGowan, meanwhile, had approached Archie Breen and asked, "Can you cash my chips for me, or do I do it at the cashier's window?"

"Beg pardon?" Breen said.

"Where can I trade my chips?"

"For what?"

"For money," Doug said.

"Casino chips? They take 'em anywhere, kid. The cashier, the change window, anywhere."

"I mean my poker chips," Doug said. "They aren't the regular casino chips."

Breen said, "Just leave 'em on the table. They're safe. We got our eye on 'em."

"That's not what I mean," Doug said. "I want to cash out. Can you do it, or Mr. Jackson, or who?"

"You want to cash out," Breen said. He was starting to get it. "Out of the tournament?"

// 149

"Yeah," Doug said. "My luck turned sour. Enough's enough, y'know? I'm gonna be smart and quit winners."

"You want to cash out of the tournament? You don't want to play anymore?"

"Right," Doug said. "I dropped ten thousand today. That's my limit."

Breen let out a soft whistle. He touched Doug's arm and said, "Hang on a sec." He walked over to where Stretch Jackson was seated at a table, arranging names for the leader board. "A little situation, Stretch," he said. "The kid over there wants to cash in."

Stretch said, "What's his problem?"

"Nothin', except for bein' about half a bubble off plumb."

Doug was watching them from ten feet away. Stretch crooked his finger and Doug hurried over.

"Take a load off, pardner," Stretch said. "Archie tells me you want to cash out."

Doug sat down. "Yeah. Time to hit the road."

"First prize is sixty percent of the buy-in," Stretch told him. "That's three hundred grand."

"I'll settle for what I've already got," Doug said. "I was hot earlier, but now I'm salty."

"I know the feelin'," Stretch said. "But the thing is, neighbor, if everybody quit winners, then we wouldn't have any prize money to give out. You savvy?"

"How do you mean?"

"It's what you call elimination. Only way to get out is if you lose your stack."

"Aw, no," Doug said. "That's not fair."

Breen said, "It's tournament rules, kid. Same for everybody."

Doug looked at the two men. "That's suicide. I mean, I'm not some famous gambler. I can quit even, can't I? I can get my ten thousand back."

Stretch shook his head. "Face it, son. You're in up to the withers."

"But it's my money."

"Nobody's sayin' otherwise," Stretch told him. "It's all of it yours, for as long as you can hang onto it."

Doug stood up with a sick look and walked away.

"You can put a fork in him," Stretch told Breen. "He's done."

Meanwhile the television reporter, who'd eavesdropped on the conversation, brought Doug over to her camera and said, "Doug McGowan. Youngest contestant. You started today's round in second place. And now —?"

Doug was stunned. "I don't know. This is crazy." He blinked at the lights. "Are we on television?"

"Correct me if I'm wrong. You didn't understand this is a freeze-out tournament?"

Doug said, "Hey, yesterday I turned twenty-one, you know? I'm here with friends, I'm having fun, I'm on a hot streak, so I get in the poker game. Now they tell me I have to win it all or lose it all. This is gonna cost me a fortune."

"But you can still win," the reporter said.

"Yeah? You want to back me?"

Until then, Doug hadn't pictured his winnings as a specific amount. He'd just enjoyed a euphoric feeling that his next couple of years were taken care of. A new car, a nice apartment, some clothes, some tapes, maybe a trip somewhere. He hadn't sorted it all out. He just knew he was rich. He actually had twenty-five thousand dollars. And now he might as well flush it down the toilet. He was dazed at the magnitude of his disaster.

Upstairs in their room at the Taj Mahal, Jerry Corbett said to Chris, "So you had a little excitement. How'd you do?"

"I ad-libbed like crazy," she said. "You and I are neighbors. You're married but your husband isn't into poker, so you brought me along for moral support. We're sharing a room here. You play mostly in Gardena."

"Good for you. And she bought it?"

Chris stuck her tongue out at him. "You're not the only actor in town."

"What's my husband do for a living?"

"It didn't come up. You decide."

Jerry laughed. "I love it. He's a mortician."

"Oh, no," Chris said. "Be fair."

"Okay, a computer programmer. Naw, that's too obvious. How's this? He's a high-school gym coach. A closet queen. Ha! His name's Duke. Duke Corbett."

"You're really enjoying this, aren't you?"

"Hell yes," Jerry said. "You, too. Didn't you get a kick out of improvising down there?"

"Actually," Chris said, "I did get a tingle. It's been a long time since I've acted."

Jerry hugged her. "Damn right. Tonight we'll put on a real performance."

"Where?"

"At dinner."

Chris pushed him away. "You're not going to accept that invitation!"

"I wouldn't miss it, hon."

"You don't have any limits!" she said.

Jerry was grinning. "Don't pick on me. I'm just a normal guy who jumps off rooftops for a living."

The recklessness of the idea suddenly appealed to Chris. "It could be a kick," she said. "But what if we don't pull it off?"

Jerry threw his hands in the air. "So we get caught. Big deal. Come on, make me up or I'll be late getting back. You know, if I come in sixth, we get our ten thousand back. Fifth, and we make a profit."

"Sit still," Chris said. "Do we actually have a chance?"

"Not on paper. But we've come this far."

Brian Bates used the break to go up to his room and phone the Lucky Seven Motel in Sparks. But Marlene didn't answer the ring.

"Check her box," Bates told the clerk. "See if she picked up her messages."

"Empty," the clerk said.

Bates hung up and only then noticed that the red message light on his own phone was blinking. "Let's go back down," he told Carroll Shepherd.

"You're sure speeding today," the psychologist said. Shepherd had recovered from his hangover with a few carefully spaced beers and wanted to talk about poker. Following Bates down the hallway to the elevator station, he asked, "Are you getting good cards? How come you're doing so well? Tell me about it."

"Jesus Christ, doc, I'm working to stay out of the poorhouse. What's the surprise? You must have thought I could do it — you bankrolled me."

The two men were silent in the crowded elevator, but at the ground floor as they exited into the din of the casino, Shepherd asked, "Have you been bluffing? Did you run any good ones?"

"A few. That big guy Houston is too much. What do you think of him?"

"I've got two grand invested. I wish he'd drop dead."

"That's a shitty thing to say," Bates answered. He picked up his message at the desk. It was on Taj Mahal stationery in handwriting he recognized, Marlene's carefully curlicued longhand: *Brian — No answer at your room. I'm in the hotel. Will check back. What are you doing in Reno?* Bates told the clerk that if a woman asked for him, to send her to the poker tournament.

"I don't have time to go searching," Bates told Shepherd. "The break's over."

"What's she look like?"

"Five-two, brown hair, a cute nose, good figure. You can't find her with that description."

An hour's nap and a cold shower had brought Russell Henry back to life. He entered the casino looking like a new man, in Levis, a plaid snap-button shirt, a rough-out vest, tooled-leather boots and a cowboy hat. "Who do you like in the tournament now?" he asked Stretch Jackson.

Stretch winked. "You curious or lookin' for action?"

"Just asking."

"Houston wins."

"What if I was looking for action?"

"I'd need odds," Stretch said. "He ain't in the barn yet."

They were playing at three re-grouped tables. As a joke during the break, someone had scattered a handful of sunflower seeds in front of Hoo-Hoo Avery's position. Taking his seat as the tournament resumed, Avery used a cocktail coaster to sweep the seeds carefully into an ashtray. "Owls don't eat seeds," he announced. "Owls are carnivores." With a dignified air, he nodded at Art Epstein and said, "Good afternoon. I played you in Vegas, didn't I?"

"You killed me in Vegas."

Avery gave a little smile and looked pointedly at Epstein's modest stack of chips. "They say history has a way of repeating itself."

"They also say generals are always ready to fight the previous war."

Avery raised his eyebrows. "A learned adversary?"

The dealer interrupted, sweeping seven hundred dollars in antes into the center of the table and dealing a round of cards to start the game. "Four of clubs brings it in," he said.

"Who?" Avery asked.

"Four of clubs."

"Who?" Avery asked.

"Hoo. I get it." The dealer tapped his finger impatiently at Doug McGowan, who pushed two hundred dollars into the pot on his low card showing.

The Owl can afford his little jokes, Epstein thought; just look at his stack. No wonder he's unruffled. Epstein watched Avery calmly follow the betting, with his round head and flat ears, his spectacles and tiny hooked nose. The Owl raised the opening bet five hundred and Doug folded in a hurry. The dealer pushed the pot to Avery.

Art Epstein had eleven thousand and change in front of him, a pittance, but he was on the rise after the terrible start he'd gotten Tuesday. He felt like a runner who'd pulled up lame in the opening stretch of a mile race but had stayed on the track and somehow begun to close the gap. He was still a straggler, but he was keeping contact. He leaned back in his chair, surveying the table. This was the competition he'd come to Reno for: smug Avery, a World Series champion, sitting two seats to his right, and the sick but still formidable Lee Sherman Tobias, a three-time champion, sitting two seats to his left. Three other men at the table were unknown to him, but Epstein had to consider them serious competition if they'd gotten this far. Of the group, only Doug McGowan looked forlorn and out of place, like a broken marionette that had been tossed carelessly into a chair.

Doug was hoping for inspiration. He felt defeated, despite his sizable mound of chips, and the only strategy he could think of seemed pathetically primitive: he'd call the opening bet only if his first cards were three of a kind, three to a flush or three to a straight. Lacking any of those, he'd fold. At that rate he could hang on for a while, although it would still be a one-way trip downhill, but he didn't know what else to do; he couldn't play his luck when it wasn't there. As hands were dealt and Doug kept donating hundred-dollar antes, he was so preoccupied with feeling sorry for himself that he didn't notice he had fans behind the rail. Thanks to the TV reporter, word had spread that Doug hadn't understood the tournament rules and he had supporters in the crowd. Like spectators anywhere, they were rooting for the underdog. Their sympathy went out to the tousle-haired kid with the good looks and the sagging hopes. But as the afternoon progressed, Doug didn't give his fans anything to cheer about. He folded, hand after hand.

At that stage of the tournament, Doug McGowan wasn't alone in adopting a new game plan. Conditions were changing and subtly, at all three tables, the gamblers were shifting strategies. No longer was it so necessary for them to make the most of every pot; minimizing losses was becoming just as important as maximizing gains. The winners began to wait for their best shots — they had the bankrolls to cripple when the circumstances were right, and in the meantime they could lay back and let the losers scavenge for survival.

Yet there was no standing still in a poker game; if you weren't winning, you had to be losing. Vic Houston continued to move ahead, stealing antes by raising on the first round when he had position. The other players knew he was bluffing a lot but nobody knew exactly when, so he was getting away with it. Meanwhile he was baiting a trap for Brett Overstreet, in his opinion the only serious competition at his table. Since Overstreet couldn't let Houston dominate the game, he'd have to come after him eventually, and that's when some big money would change hands.

The rest of the players at his table were incidental to Houston. Four were short on chips and the fifth was the blue-whiskered Vegas professional who went by the inappropriate name of Easy. Houston had Easy's number. A nervous gambler, strictly a percentage player, Easy was taking a safe line: he'd concede the first couple of places to the champions and try to outlast everyone else for a piece of the lesser prize money. So at Houston's table that just left Bates, the muscleman in the dark glasses, for him to figure out. The kid had balls, Houston gave him that, but he mixed it up in too many hands. He was taking money from the losers but it was risky business because sooner or later he was going to get committed to a serious pot and walk into trouble.

Brian Bates, for his part, knew the risk he was running. But he didn't have any choice about it because he also knew he couldn't win by being passive. Winning players didn't wait for things to happen, they caused things to happen. He realized that his aggressive game might cost him, but he knew that with any other strategy he wouldn't have a chance at all. They'd eat him alive if he sat around waiting for perfect hands, and if he had to tap out it didn't matter to him when it happened, today or in tomorrow's finals. Bates was playing for the money, not the glory, and he was pushing hard.

Yet as time passed, he felt as if he were swinging at shadows. He must have been active in half the pots but he couldn't seem to make contact with the big winners. Somehow they avoided him. He came out throwing leather like a club fighter but couldn't connect with anything solid. Anyone else might have let the frustration affect his judgment, but Brian Bates was a man who knew how to hang on to an idea. Yesterday the tournament had been a diversion for him, a drunken whim of his and Shepherd's, but today he was playing for his life. He might lose to better players or luckier players, but if there was one thing he knew you could carve in stone, it was that nobody in the tournament had a chance in hell of beating Bates by wearing him down.

Especially not with Vic Houston, the King of Hearts himself, sitting next to him. Bates drew power from Houston's presence. He was winning hands he had no business winning and sidestepping danger with some newfound sixth sense of warning. His stack had grown as big as Easy's or Overstreet's and he had to restrain himself from nudging Houston and showing him, "Look how I'm doing, dad!"

But the real dogfighting was going on at the third poker table. There, four players with comparable winnings were slugging it out. Shayna Levinson felt besieged. Johnny Sandwiches had to be watched every second and Walsh played like a damn snake. Those two were a handful by themselves, but Shayna found herself fighting off a constant threat on another flank from the Corbett woman, who was still playing over her head. The rest of the players at the table weren't exactly pushovers, either.

But Shayna's frustration was nothing compared to Sandwiches's. As usual he seemed placid, almost stuporous, behind his half-closed eyelids; Sandwiches gave away no secrets with his looks. But inside he was disgusted. Last night he'd dropped a bundle in a side game and today bad cards were on him like stink on a skunk. It can happen — sometimes your luck turns cold and that's all there is to it. Sandwiches hadn't had a break yet in the tournament. All day Tuesday he'd had Lee Sherman Tobias to cope with, and then this morning he'd drawn Lee Sherman again and the Owl, too. Now he was finally at an easy table for once and he couldn't draw flies. With the rotten cards he was catching, there were two women at his table he couldn't even beat. Meanwhile, he noticed, Houston was playing with people he'd send a taxi after.

Of the group, Jerry Corbett was the only player enjoying himself. He sensed Sandwiches's melancholy and he felt anger coming from Walsh, who was letting Shayna get to him. Jerry got a kick out of Shayna; she was on top of her form, a real nuisance. She was forcing a jerky, staccato rhythm on the game, trying to keep everyone off balance, and it was working for her.

Except with Jerry. He distanced himself, denying her a reaction. It was pure method acting — he went back to the beach at Ensenada with Chris, mellowed out on a languid evening, calmed by the soothing sounds of a tranquil surf, and Shayna couldn't reach him. He simply wasn't there for her. Yet the less of a response she got from him, the more she tried for one; and the harder she pushed, the more Jerry retreated. It was work for her but it was kid stuff for him, a theater game: without touching him, Shayna had to move him. But Jerry wouldn't move. Serenely, he was upstaging her.

She had her chair turned around now and was perching on her knees, gaining height. "Whatcha got?" she asked, pointing at Sandwiches, who'd opened for two hundred on his low card. "What's he bettin' on?"

"A three," the dealer said.

"Clubs or spades? All I can see is black. Huh," Shayna said, "I got another winner." She threw two hundred in on a seven showing.

"Keep talkin' — maybe you'll convince yourself," Walsh told her. He threw four chips at the pot. "Raise it two."

That put it to Jerry, who had a pair of aces in the hole. He figured Walsh, with a king showing, for either two kings or a hidden high pair. Shayna might have anything. She put two chips down in front of her and counted five on top of them. Jerry was supposed to notice that she planned to re-raise when it came back to her. She wants me out, he thought. Or else she wants a cheap card.

"Hey, Scary Jerry — it's on you," Shayna said. "Wake up and smell the coffee."

Jerry sat up and looked around the table, as if his mind had been wandering. "Call," he said quietly. He put four chips in front of him, purposely so close that the dealer, in reaching for them, had to turn his back on Shayna.

Sandwiches folded. On the next card, Shayna paired her seven. "Five hundred," she said.

Walsh hesitated. For a moment he looked like the brain in a math class working out answers in his head while everybody else punched their calculators. "Raise five," he decided. "Play for a thousand."

"Goodness," Jerry said, thinking: he's got the kings and he wants me out. He leaned forward to peer at Walsh's cards, and then Shayna's, and then he looked at his own hole cards.

"Hey, sister, either fish or cut bait, okay?" Shayna said.

Ignoring her, Jerry called the raise and said timidly to Walsh, "I think I'm donating to you."

Walsh wasn't impressed. "That'll be the day, lady."

With the next card, Jerry felt a rush of satisfaction; he'd played it perfectly for the way the cards fell. Shayna caught another seven, which gave her three sevens showing, and Walsh paired his king. Jerry caught a lonely-looking ace — except he had two more in the hole.

Now Shayna had a problem. She couldn't check with trip sevens showing, yet she had to figure Walsh, sitting behind her, for trip kings. She bet a thousand, hoping it would go around.

Walsh raised a thousand.

Jerry didn't do anything immediately. He knew Shayna didn't want the sevens. She'd probably gone in on three to a straight and then stuck around because she was high on board and the bets were cheap. Her sevens looked good but she didn't have anything to back them up. Walsh, he knew, had the three kings.

Jerry pretended to think things over. Then he re-raised two thousand dollars.

"*Shit!*" Shayna said. Corbett was so goddamned stupid she was trying to buy a pot just because she had position. The raise killed Shayna. She knew she had Corbett beat and could drive her out with another raise, but she had Walsh sitting behind her and she couldn't beat *him*. There was nothing Shayna could do. She was in a bind. Caught between a winning hand and an idiot raiser, she had to fold. She turned her cards over in irritation and then yelped with disbelief when Walsh did the same. "What? You *fold?*"

"Against trip aces? Yeah," Walsh said.

"You got a leak in your sunroof, you moron!" Shayna screamed. "She doesn't have aces. With aces, she raises on third street. What do they teach you in New York — to throw in winners? You cost me a pot!"

Walsh said, "Listen, mouth, you got enough trouble playin' your own cards. Suppose you don't try to play mine."

Raking in the chips the dealer pushed over, Jerry murmured, "That's a nice pot." They'd paid six thousand bucks without even getting to see his cards. Jerry loved it. He knew he could have milked the hand for more money but at the moment it was more important for him to keep undermining Shayna's confidence. Later, he'd collect.

Doug McGowan knew he wasn't playing in enough hands and he also knew everybody at the table was wise to him: all they had to do was raise the bet and he'd fold. He was at a polite table. The Owl, who was in love with the sound of his own voice, had some kind of verbal competition going with the big blond guy, Art, but they kept it quiet and mostly between deals. The old guy, Tobias, kept quiet, too, except for his breathing. So the table was civilized.

But that only meant Doug McGowan was getting sliced up in a nice courteous way. It was still the death of a thousand cuts.

But for a moment he came to life. Dealt the low card showing, Doug bet the mandatory two hundred dollars and nobody called him. Nobody. He won the antes. It was only a six-hundred-dollar win, but it was the first time in an hour he'd won anything at all. "One in a row," the dealer winked at him. And to his surprise, Doug heard a cry from the crowd of "Yay, underdog!" He turned around and saw railbirds smiling at him and friendly fists upraised in encouragement. While he looked, somebody called, "Go get 'em, Doug!" and a good-looking girl caught his eye and gave him a thumbs-up sign. Doug grinned back and waved. That's more like it, he thought — nobody else in the tournament had a cheering section. Suddenly he felt special again. And sure enough, on the next hand he was dealt a queen-jack in the hole and a queen up. It wasn't the three of a kind he'd promised to wait for but it was a good start and he knew, like yesterday, that help was on its way.

He caught a jack on the next card, giving him two pair and making him high on board. He felt a full house coming. He bet a thousand dollars and everybody folded but the Owl, who raised him a thousand. Sure, Doug thought, he knows all he has to do is raise and I'll get out. But I've got a surprise for him this time. Doug raised back a thousand and the Owl, with a comic grimace, quickly folded his hand.

"Two in a row," Doug told the dealer, raking in chips. From behind him he heard another cheer. This time he turned and pumped his fist in the air.

On the next hand Doug was dealt a four-five in the hole and a six up. Straight! he thought. He felt it in his bones, just like yesterday. He stayed in the pot, along with the big blond guy and one of the losing players, a heavyset man with a dark mustache.

Doug caught a seven on the next card, giving him a four-five-six-seven. That's more like it, he thought; this is the way the game's supposed to go. His next card would be an eight to make it three wins in a row for him.

"I'm going all in," the man with the mustache announced. "Thirteen hundred." He had a pair of tens showing.

Art Epstein thought: that's a break. Epstein didn't have a hand yet, but he had the king-ten of diamonds up and the jack-queen in the hole and it was the cheapest draw to a straight flush he'd get for the rest of the tournament, he knew that. The mustache probably had two pair, and with a decent stack of chips he could have made Epstein pay through the nose to see any more cards.

Epstein called the bet. So did Doug. On the next card Doug caught the eight he was expecting, which made his straight. Art Epstein caught a black nine for a higher straight, hidden. The man with the mustache was all in for the pot, so he wasn't a factor in the betting anymore. Epstein checked to Doug. Doug bet two thousand dollars and Epstein started to throw his hand in. Then he pretended to reconsider and took another squint at his hole cards. He wouldn't have tried such a cheap stunt against anyone but this green kid. "One time," he sighed, and called Doug's bet. The dealer separated the four thousand dollars in a side pot.

On the next card, Epstein and Doug both caught threes. It gave Doug a three-four-five-six-seven-eight, which didn't improve his hand, but a six-card straight looked better to him than a five-card straight and he took it as a further good omen.

Epstein checked again, and Doug bet another two thousand. Epstein managed to sound resigned. "Hell, I'm in this far," he said. That made eight thousand in the side pot. If I did to small children what I'm doing to this kid, Epstein thought, they'd put me in jail. But he couldn't work up even a twinge of guilt; it was Doug who'd killed him with blind luck yesterday, hand after hand, and gloated about it. Epstein appreciated the fine hand of justice. He'd win more from Doug in this one hand than Doug had won from him in a dozen yesterday.

The seventh card was dealt face down. Epstein checked without looking. Doug caught a deuce, for a seven-card straight. Three in a row, he thought — I'm back in the tournament.

"I bet two thousand again," Doug announced.

Epstein still hadn't looked at his last card. He said, "Raise you two."

Suddenly Doug didn't understand. The blond guy had garbage showing, a three-nine-ten-king. Was he bluffing? He hadn't even looked at his last card. What was going on? Doug was aware that the other players were watching him. He knew he had to call, but should he raise back? He was disoriented. All of a sudden he couldn't figure anything out. But people were expecting him to do something.

"I'll see you." Doug threw his chips at the side pot and turned over his hand. "Straight," he said, "deuce to the eight."

Epstein shook his head. "Not good enough. I went in with a king high." He exposed his first two hole cards, showing the straight: nine-ten-jack-queen-king.

As the dealer pushed the big side pot over to Epstein, the man with the mustache, who was still in for the smaller original pot, turned over his hole cards. "I'll be damned," he laughed, with the obvious relief of somebody who'd just gotten a reprieve, "I filled up. Last-carded a boat."

"Full house over here," the dealer said, arranging the cards for Epstein's benefit. Before pushing the chips over to the man with the mustache, he reached out and perfunctorily turned over Epstein's seventh card. For a moment the table went silent. It was the ace of diamonds.

The smile died under the man's mustache. "A straight flush?"

"Royal," the dealer said. "You win it all," he told Epstein, and pushed the rest of the chips over to him.

Again Doug McGowan heard clapping from behind the rope. But this time the applause wasn't for him. The railbirds were acknowledging the man with the mustache, who stood up and threaded his way through the crowd, another plucky gambler who'd tapped out.

Doug knew he was dead — now he was one of the lost players sitting with a small stack of chips in front of him and time running out. Glumly, he saw the end. Betting an eight-high straight into a royal flush? If he needed final proof that he was out of his league, that was it. But no hard feelings. "Good hand," he told Epstein.

"Tough luck," Epstein answered. He didn't like the way he'd won the hand — it was as subtle as a rape — but he was in contention now, for the first time in two days. He put out his hundred-dollar ante for the next hand but folded when the bet came to him. Looking out at the spectators, he saw Foley in the front row, waving at him with a foolish grin on his face, and Anita, the ex-cigarette girl from the MGM, standing next to him. Epstein thought they looked like they'd been in the rack all day. Then he noticed that Foley wasn't just waving, but beckoning to him. Epstein shook his head. He held up his wrist and pointed to his watch. But the pilot wouldn't accept an excuse. He held up his own hand, fingers spread, and swiveled it in the air. Then he lifted Anita's hand and swiveled it, too. They were both grinning like idiots.

Epstein got up from the poker table and walked over. "Your timing's as good as ever," he said. "I'm hot." To the girl, he said, "Hello again." Then he noticed — they were both wearing rings. "What is this? You got engaged?"

"That's your problem, boss," Foley said. "You're old-fashioned."

"You won some Crackerjack prizes? I just had a royal flush. What's going on?"

The radiant look on Anita's face gave him the answer. "I'll be damned," Epstein said when it sank in. "You got married. You did, didn't you?"

"Up at the lake," Foley laughed.

Epstein's first impulse was that they were kidding him. But they weren't. Foley had his arm around the girl and she was gazing up at the pilot in adoration. Epstein shook Foley's hand and kissed the bride. "I know people gamble in Nevada," he told her, "but aren't you carrying it to an extreme?"

"I've never been so sure of anything in my life," she answered.

From the light in Anita's eyes, Epstein believed her. Who was he to sit in judgment? His own marriage wasn't the most conventional one in the world. "Can we celebrate tonight?" he asked. "I have to get back to the game. What are your plans?"

"Tonight. Hell, yes," Foley said. "We'll be here. Go knock 'em dead."

"We're rooting for you," Anita said.

Epstein started for the poker table but detoured when he spotted Jackie back in the crowd. He made his way over and asked, "Have you seen the newlyweds?"

"Isn't it crazy?" she said. "But crazy wonderful." Jackie was dabbing her eyes with a Kleenex. At Epstein's look, she said, "Well, somebody has to cry at a wedding." She tugged at his lapel and pulled him down for a kiss. "They're in love. Anita said it was inevitable, so why waste time?"

"Don't cry, sweetheart."

"I'm happy. Everything's so lovely."

"That's what I think, too," Epstein said, "but nobody gives a damn about my royal flush."

Sitting back down at the poker table, he saw that another chair was empty and they were down to five players. The kid, Doug, was gone, and so were his chips. "Who did it?" Epstein asked. He looked at the Owl. "You did. You turned carnivore on that poor kid while I was gone."

"Who?" Avery said. "Who, me? The Owl is innocent." He pointed at Lee Sherman Tobias. "It was that turkey buzzard."

"Tap city," the dealer said. "Trips against two pair."

As the dealer shuffled and they put their antes out, Tobias grunted at Epstein, "Wasn't much left to him when you got through."

Epstein was dealt a pair of sixes and gave a loose call. He felt good about Jackie and he felt good about himself and he felt good about life and he wondered how the hell he'd allowed this tournament to distort his priorities about what was important in his world. It was just another lousy game of cards. And when you got down to it, who cared about a poker game?

Brian Bates did. The game demanded all of his concentration and he couldn't even let Marlene into his mind to mess it up. He'd get her squared away later. She was among the railbirds now and God only knew what she was thinking anymore, because Bates sure didn't. Carroll Shepherd had found her after all, as she was trying to see through the crowd and locate Bates in the poker tournament, and Shepherd had gotten Bates's attention and called him away from the game.

Marlene had only had two things to say. One, that Bates looked ridiculous showing off in a tee shirt, to which he responded, "There's a reason." And two, that she had no intention of letting him call off the divorce, to which he said, "Everything's changed. We have to talk. The doc can tell you why I've gotta keep playing cards right now." He moved to kiss her, but she averted her head.

Figure it out later, he told himself. One thing at a time. For now he had to pay attention to the game. Everybody at the table used a different architecture to stack their chips, so amounts were hard to tally, but Bates estimated that he was the biggest winner at his table except for Houston. It warmed him to know the big Texan was aware of it. It strengthened their kinship. Money was moving around faster now and the dumb Okie was gaining on everybody. Okay. He played cards.

At four o'clock, Archie Breen interrupted the tournament and called another break.

THE FIRST ANNUAL STRETCH JACKSON SEVEN-CARD STUD POKER CLASSIC

Standings as of 4 P.M. Wednesday (Semifinalists)

1.	Vic Houston, Texas	$57,600
2.	William "Hoo-Hoo" Avery, Arizona	54,000
3.	Lee Sherman Tobias, Missouri	46,900
4.	Amateur player (Walsh), New York	41,800
5.	Shayna Levinson, Washington	40,600

6.	Brian Bates, Oklahoma	39,900
7.	Brett Overstreet, Texas	37,900
8.	Jerry Corbett, California	37,500
9.	Professional player ("Easy"), Nevada	31,800
10.	John "Sandwiches" Treece, Louisiana	28,400
11.	Art Epstein, California	25,500
12.	Professional player (DeHaven), Texas	17,800

And four remaining contestants ranging from $14,200 to $3,500

Play to resume at: 4:30 P.M.

They were down to sixteen players. During the break, the television reporter asked Stretch Jackson for an analysis. "There's three World Series champeens left," he told her. "That's Houston, Hoo-Hoo and ol' Lee Sherman, and they in the one-two-three spots. Fact is, between 'em they already got most of the money."

"Are you saying that if a player's good enough, poker isn't the gamble everybody thinks it is?"

Stretch looked at her as if she were retarded. "If poker wasn't a gamble, missy, we'd all be at the crap table. What I'm sayin' is players come and go but talent has a way of stayin'."

"And with your talent," she asked, "what would your strategy be at this stage?"

"I only got one strategy," Stretch said. "In Korea, there was a marine general got himself surrounded. He told his men, 'Boys, we got enemy in front of us and enemy behind us and to the left of us and to the right of us. They won't escape this time.' "

Walsh, the New Yorker, used the intermission to locate his wife at a blackjack table. Looking at a dealer's face card, she'd been dealt a fifteen. "Should I hit it?" she asked.

"What's the count?"

"I don't know."

"If you're not countin'," Walsh said, "why don't you just hand 'em your money? Hit it."

She scratched her cards on the table and the dealer gave her a nine to break her hand. "Thanks a lot," she said. "How are you doing?"

"It's a tough game," Walsh said. "Believe me, it ain't like chess. In chess, you've gotta be able to back up your bullshit."

In fact, Walsh was worried. He knew the only reason he was in fourth place was that he'd been getting cards. But how long could it last? Poker wasn't like bridge or backgammon or other games he knew. In poker, you needed intuition. The elite players mystified Walsh. He didn't hear voices like they did. All he knew was logic and numbers.

Upstairs in the room, Chris asked, "What's the status now?"

Jerry said, "They're putting us at two tables of eight. We'll play down to twelve people and call it a night."

"I saw a couple of players with teeny stacks."

"They won't last. I wish I knew what to do."

Chris said, "More of the same, I'd think."

Jerry handed her his wig to comb out. He lay back on the bed. "I don't know, hon," he said. "Sooner or later I'll have to back off and play for position. I wish I knew when. Look what we're up against. There's Houston and Tobias and Avery. That's three. Then there's Easy and the black guy and Overstreet. So that's six professionals we know about. Shayna's the next thing to a pro. The computer guy's supposed to be a genius. And who knows about the others? I can't beat 'em all. I have to finagle to come in sixth."

Chris sat next to him and massaged his temples. "Poor baby. It's hard work, isn't it?"

He grinned. "I love every minute of it."

"Why don't you try to come in first?"

"Too risky."

"But you said you've written off the money."

"I don't want us to leave here broke."

"If it's for me," Chris said, "I don't care about that. It's my fault you got started in this. If you want, I think you should play it all the way out. This is a long way from Gardena, hon. Don't compromise for me, not after you've come this far."

Jerry reached for her hand. He lay silently for a while and then started chuckling.

"What is it?" Chris asked.

"Deborah Kerr in *Tea and Sympathy.*" Affecting a seductive voice, Jerry said, "Years from now, when you talk about this — and you will — be kind."

Lee Sherman Tobias had a problem. The diuretic was working on him and he couldn't make it to the can on his own. Next thing I'll be carryin' a bag on my leg, he thought. He would have asked Archie Breen for help, but Archie was busy counting chips with Stretch, so he asked Vic Houston to walk him. It was either that or pee his pants.

Houston felt awful. Lee Sherman was dead weight hanging from his arm. Their pace was a crawl. "Haven't seen you around for a while," he said.

Tobias concentrated on putting one foot in front of another. "I been to home for the holidays."

Houston knew that was shading the truth. Tobias hadn't been in Vegas since summer at least, not long after he'd won the World Series. That was when the rumor started that he'd had a heart attack. Houston didn't want to believe it, but a bad ticker was about the only explanation for the shape Tobias was in. Houston didn't know what to say. He wanted to put his arm around the old man's shoulders and give him a hug. Close friendships weren't one of the rewards of a gambling life. There were guys you'd known for years, guys you'd stake to thousands of dollars on a handshake, guys you understood better than you understood your own family — and you didn't even know their last names. But Tobias was a thoroughbred. Vic Houston wanted to blank from his memory this long painful crawl to the can and back.

Owl Avery was expounding to Russell Henry. "There are three kinds of people in the world," he told the writer as they strolled to the bar. "There are people who make things happen, there are people who watch things happen, and there are people who walk around saying, 'What happened?' Poker, young man, is a game of action, not reaction. To succeed, you are obliged to attack. Poker is the most aggressive activity you can engage in without getting out of a chair. You can quote me on that." At the bar, he ordered a club soda.

"Same for me," Russell told the bartender. To Avery he said, "In your opinion, then, a player's personality can overcome the law of averages?"

"Tut," the Owl said. "Averages are not a consideration. The average person in the world has one boob and one ball. Average is as close to the bottom as it is to the top. The average person believes, because he's never questioned what he's been told all of his life, that he shouldn't jump from a deck unless there's a lifeboat waiting. I'll tell you something, son — sometimes you have to jump anyway."

"How do you know when?"

Avery pulled a cigar from his shirt pocket and smiled as he unwrapped the cellophane. "If you have to ask," he said, "you can't afford to find out. As George Washington put it, 'I have heard the bullets whistle and there is something charming in the sound.' "

"Who?"

"George Washington."

"Who?"

The Owl frowned at Henry and lit his cigar.

At first, Marlene Bates had drawn the natural conclusion that her husband had followed her to Reno. But now she knew otherwise, and Brian was trying to persuade her that the coincidence was significant. Upstairs in the hotel room, Bates had taken off his

tee shirt and was pointing to the lettering on it. "E,S,P," he said.
"Where's your faith? Karma, kismet, whatever they call it — there's
a reason we both ended up in this town, and it's caused by a bigger
power than either one of us."

"Baloney," Marlene said. "I can't believe you wore that shirt in
public."

"Yeah? Since noon it won me ten thousand dollars."

"You won it, Briny, not the shirt."

"Maybe. Hell, I don't know." Bates crumpled the tee shirt and
threw it on the carpet. "I feel like an asshole wearing it, I know
that." He pulled a loose-fitting aloha shirt out of the closet and put
it on.

"I phoned my mother," Marlene said. "I talked to the kids and
told them you said hello."

"They're another reason."

"Last month you didn't think so."

"I was wrong," Bates said. "How often have you heard me admit
I made a mistake? Well, I made one. I'll say it for the rest of my
life if you want. I owe you one."

"I'm not keeping score," she said.

"You don't give a damn, do you?"

"I give a damn. You're the one who walked away. Having that
law office serve divorce papers on me? But I'll get over it. Just
don't tell me how I feel."

"Okay," he said. "You care and I care, too. That's a start, isn't
it? We can work this out. I'm reimbursing all those people. You've
been on my case about that."

"It's not exactly your own idea."

"Hell it isn't. I could fight 'em in court. But it's you and the
kids who'd suffer. What would I get if I lost — a few months' time?
I could do that standing on my head."

"Always the tough guy."

"I'm just me," he said.

"That's the whole point," Marlene said. "You're only you. You don't think you need anyone. Well, I can't live with somebody with that attitude. Why should I? I tried. It doesn't work. You were right."

"I'm talking to a wall," Bates said. "I wasn't right. I did a bad thing and I'm sorry. I apologize. I kept asking you to change and that was wrong of me. I told you about the dream I had. I need you, Marlene. You don't have to change. You're fine the way you are."

"Well, thank you very much, and that says it all. I happen to know I'm fine. The problem with our marriage isn't about me changing. The problem is about *you* changing —"

"The waterworks again," he said. "Just once, I'd like it if you'd turn off the faucets when we talk."

"Women cry," she said. "So do men."

"None I know." Bates had never seen his wife so resolute. "I'm canceling the divorce," he said, "and inside you know I'm right. Think about this. You've heard me talk about Reno. You knew I wanted to come back here and settle the score. You didn't come to Reno by accident. Unconsciously, you knew I'd be here."

Marlene didn't know what she thought. A talkative, over-wrought Bates was nobody she was familiar with. "What about your own unconscious?" she asked. "You came here in a state of mind and right away made friends with a psychologist. I wonder what that says."

"That's just a coincidence. And it wasn't right away. Anyway, he's a drunk."

"In other words, my coincidences mean something and yours don't."

"I don't want to argue," Bates said. "I have to get back to the tournament."

On that, at least, they agreed: Bates needed to win the prize money. But Marlene was shaken at seeing her husband in such an agitated mood, so unsure of himself. For him to beg her, and tell her about his dreams, was unprecedented. It wasn't in his personality to get that tense, she thought, and certainly not over a poker game, no matter how high the stakes.

West of Reno, the sky over 1-80 at Boomtown was clear but the sun was low in the mountains and the wind blowing down from Donner Pass carried a numbing cold. At an on-ramp to the freeway, Doug McGowan stamped his feet and blew on his hands. He could have borrowed money for bus fare — somebody in his rooting section probably would have made him a loan — but it would have ruined the ending to the story he was already constructing in his mind.

"Nevada?" he was going to be able to tell people years from now. "Boy, does that bring back memories. I used to hang out in Reno when I was underage. I remember one time up there just before my twenty-first birthday. I took a college coed with me. Goddamn, but she was built. I always wondered what happened to ol' Gail. She was a real sweetheart. Man, Reno was cold and snowy — this was in January — and we were inside in a warm motel in a king-sized bed and we fucked and sucked till hell wouldn't have it. You know what it's like when you're young.

"Anyway, I got on a hot streak you wouldn't believe. I'd left San Jose with maybe a hundred bucks, figurin' to give the tables a try for a night or two. I mean, I was workin' at a pizza joint for the minimum wage. But I started winnin' at poker and blackjack and then I hit a keno ticket for ten thousand bucks."

He'd throw in a little chuckle then, when he was telling the story later. "I had hundred-dollar bills comin' out of my ears," he would say. "There was another couple with us and man, we're drinkin' the best booze and eatin' the best food and seein' all the best shows. I mean I'm feelin' no pain, right? So I get in one of those high-stakes poker games. Remember Stretch Jackson? The gambler they made the movie about — big tall skinny guy in a cowboy hat? Well, he's puttin' on like a tournament, so I get in it and I'm hot as a two-dollar pistol, you know what I mean?"

It would work into a good story. Doug would embellish it by describing Houston and Easy and Sandwiches and the Owl, world-class players. "Oh, yeah, I played with those guys," he'd say, and he'd tell how he was the youngest player in the game and got up twenty-five grand and had his own cheering section and was interviewed on television. And it would all be *true,* that's what he liked. Then he'd do a transition and tell about losing to a royal flush and he'd describe Tobias, that old wreck of a guy who must have been seventy years old, and how Tobias had tapped him out with trips against his two pair.

"Aces and eights," Doug would say with a forgiving laugh. "I sure learned why they call it the dead man's hand. That was some trip to Reno, all right. No shit, I was down to pocket change and I ended up hitchhikin' to get home. But like they say, one day chicken, the next day feathers." He'd shake his head in memory about then and let the story drift to its conclusion. "Standin' there on Interstate Eighty with my thumb out, the temperature below freezin' . . ."

Soon it would be dark on the highway. Already shadows had disappeared and the luminance was fading from the day when a cream-colored Mercedes sedan braked to a stop. Doug grabbed his suitcase and ran for the car. Inside, the warmth from the heater was luxuriant. The windshield on Doug's side fogged up momentarily from his breath and then cleared as the Mercedes pulled back on the interstate and began accelerating. He held his hands over the defroster vent and looked at the driver. She was a woman, or a girl, actually, and good-looking.

"How far you going?" she asked.

"All the way," Doug said. "Over the hill. San Jose."

She looked Mexican, or Filipino maybe, with straight, shiny black hair and dark brown eyes. "Been to Reno?" she asked.

Doug said, "Yeah. A trucker took me this far. Kind of a short hop."

The girl couldn't have been more than twenty. She smelled good, and she had clean white teeth when she smiled. "How'd you do?" she asked.

Doug relaxed in the leather seat. Smiling back at her, he said with a nonchalant toss of his hand, "You know what they say — one day chicken, the next day feathers."

174 //

The highway peeled off behind them. Willie Nelson was on the tape deck. When he sang "On the Road Again," the girl laughed. "They're playing my song." After a few miles, up in the darkening mountains, she glanced sideways at Doug and said, "I can't help staring. Did anyone ever tell you you look just like James Dean?"

Sandwiches Treece, viewing the world through half-closed eyelids, sat at the abandoned poker table with his hands resting on his abdomen and thought about a visit to New Orleans. He still had a stake. He could move in with his brother, do some fishin' while he waited out the cold spell. They could keep this damn winter weather. But the trouble, he knew, was you couldn't wait out a cold streak. You had to play it out. It was like God kept an account book. You had so many bad hands comin' and it didn't matter how long a vacation you took tryin' to hide from 'em, they'd still be waitin' when you came back. You had to work your way through, keep knockin' at the door until it opened again. Sandwiches sighed. He knew he could play it out a lot cheaper in New Orleans than Vegas and eat better while he was at it, but he'd miss the action in Glitter Gulch. He didn't need a vacation. What he needed was some good cards.

Easy dropped into a seat next to him and asked, "How's it goin', bro?"

Sandwiches said, "Look at the blackboard."

"I know what y'mean." Easy had a silver dollar in his hand and was running it back and forth across his knuckles. "Fuckin' cards," he said.

"Amen to that."

"Fuckin' Houston."

"He gettin' to you?"

"Fuckin' Reno."

Sandwiches turned his head to look at the other man. Easy was scowling. He did something with the silver dollar and it left his fingers, landed on the edge of the table and rolled back to him as if it were on a string. "Wanna go partners?" he asked. "Fifty-fifty? One of us might catch fire."

Sandwiches showed the courtesy of pretending to think about the offer. Then he shook his head and closed his eyes. If even Easy was readin' him for a loser, he thought, he was definitely in the deep shit. His car was at the Vegas airport. He could fly out tomorrow, pick it up and head east. He wouldn't even have to go into town.

By then, the other players were wandering back to the tournament area and taking their seats. Easy was still worrying the silver dollar. "Fuckin' tournament," he said.

Except for two breaks, the poker players had been gambling since noon; they returned to the two reorganized tournament tables as if to a familiar routine. Casual passersby, attracted by the crowd and the banner overhead and the occasional bright glare of the television lights, stopped to watch out of curiosity but didn't entirely understand what they were supposed to be looking at. There didn't seem to be enough noise from the poker games for anything momentous to be happening, and the area didn't seem focused or organized. Off-shift dealers stood around. Cocktail waitresses circulated. Players wandered from their seats. Some of the eliminated contestants lingered in the area to watch the action, and others were gambling in the half-dozen side games going on at nearby tables. But still, from time to time an electric moment would announce its own importance. In the tobacco haze that hung over the tables, action would seem to freeze at a particular game. The only movement might be the stroking of a mustache, the puffing of a cigarette or the riffling of a stack of chips. Finally the tension would break when a player folded, patting the tabletop, or else counted out a bet and pushed it into the pot.

But a bystander might wonder what the chips represented in real money. Here, for example, at the two tables where the television lights were set up, there were remarkable stacks in front of some of the players. To an unknowing tourist, it stood to reason that the chips were ones and fives, or maybe fives and quarters. But why so many? And why the TV lights? Why the crowd pressing close behind the velvet rope? If huge amounts of money were at stake, wouldn't there be some noise, some excitement, some animation? Look at the calm, self-assured big man in the gray suit and bolo tie and pearl-gray Stetson — he had an avalanche of chips in front of him, enough to fill a small shoebox. Surely a casual bystander could be forgiven for not concluding that Vic Houston's stack was composed entirely of brown hundred-dollar chips. Except for the few dozen purple ones, which were five-hundreds.

For the losing players, the tournament was becoming a war of attrition as the winners jockeyed for position, cautious about committing themselves. Unlike a Friday-night social game, which everybody involved understood would end at midnight or one or two in the morning, Stretch Jackson's tournament would continue indefinitely for all purposes, and there was no benefit to anyone's pushing hard to make the most of the hour, to loosen up or get reckless as the clock moved towards quitting time. There was no quitting time. The tournament wasn't a fight against the clock; it was a battle of bankroll against bankroll, the only object being to stay alive and survive to the end, whenever it came.

So as Wednesday's play dragged on, the winners, biding their time, came to resemble moray eels or similar predators that lunged with devastating effect from hiding — from rocks or caves or tunnels or camouflage — and then retreated as swiftly. Big bets won the antes. Bluffs went unchallenged or else were quickly abandoned. Play became a matter of probe and test, slash and run, as the antes and forced bets inexorably ate into the losers' diminishing stacks. And as afternoon turned into evening, the larger casino itself seemed to undergo a sea change. The noise level pulsed like a surf. Tides of visitors washed through the aisles and around the gaming tables, day-gamblers carried by an ebbing current swirling with night-gamblers collected by the next gathering wave of the endless cycle.

Brian Bates felt the change. He stopped scrapping for every pot. He was playing at a reassembled table against two players new to him, the old guy Tobias and the big guy Epstein. Like Vic Houston, who was in the same group, they were invested with an authority as unchallengable and final as a judge's. Sin, and they would punish. Err, and they would convict. But Bates was learning to play it their way and he readjusted his game. He had a stack to protect, too.

Tobias got hot for a while. He looked as if he belonged on a gurney, so who could figure him? But what goes around, comes around: the heat moved from Tobias to Bates, who jumped in aggressively. He felt respect from the others for his own authority, sensed them withdraw. Houston's turn came next; he took a big pot from Easy, then nailed one of the losers. Minutes later Tobias administered the *coup de grace*. The spectators applauded a good sport and suddenly there was one less gambler in the poker tournament.

Just feet away, at the second tournament table, Owl Avery was feeling pestered. Sandwiches he'd known for years. Brett Overstreet he was familiar with. But those two weren't turning out to be his competition at the new table. Instead of the professionals giving him a bad time, three young amateurs — two of them women — were buzzing around him. They seemed to have brought an animosity from their previous table, triggered by the noisy blonde. Shayna nagged and harangued, she stalled and she speeded up, and the Owl could see she was anathema to Walsh, the young man in the leather jacket. Shayna's technique was no mystery to the Owl: get somebody angry enough and he'll call your bet when he shouldn't, just because he hates you, and that's when you shove it home. But the third newcomer, the Corbett woman, was inscrutable to Avery. She seemed withdrawn, unaffected by Shayna's needling, yet somehow she completed the trio.

Well, the Owl thought, I'm sorry to inform you of this, my young friends, but the torch hasn't been passed to a new generation yet, not in poker it hasn't. Avery wasn't worried. But he was annoyed. He felt like a bomber pilot swarmed by pesky little fighter planes, and there was always the chance one of them might get in a lucky hit.

It was Sandwiches who was getting cut up by the strafing, though. It wasn't his week, and that's all there was to it. He knew that on any given day he was a better player than anyone at the table, the Owl included. This just didn't happen to be the day. Stretch Jackson, watching the action, gave him a look of sympathy before wandering over to the other table. Sandwiches followed the tall man with his eyes and muttered to no one in particular, "Man, he look like there been a famine."

"No shit?" Shayna said. "You look like you caused it."

They put up their antes. Overstreet, who hadn't been able to get anything going, called for a new deck. The dealer sent cards around the table. Play continued. Time passed. At a quarter to six, the tournament was winnowed down to its final twelve players. They adjourned until Thursday.

THE FIRST ANNUAL STRETCH JACKSON SEVEN-CARD STUD POKER CLASSIC

Standings as of 5:45 P.M. Wednesday

1.	Vic Houston, Texas	68,900
2.	William "Hoo-Hoo" Avery, Arizona	63,400
3.	Lee Sherman Tobias, Missouri	52,600
4.	Brian Bates, Oklahoma	50,800
5.	Shayna Levinson, Washington	50,300
6.	Jerry Corbett, California	50,000
7.	Amateur player (Walsh), New York	47,100
8.	Art Epstein, California	37,800
9.	Brett Overstreet, Texas	28,500
10.	Professional player ("Easy"), Nevada	22,700
11.	John "Sandwiches" Treece, Louisiana	18,400
12.	Professional player (DeHaven), Texas	9,500

Starting time Thursday: 2 P.M.

The contestants disbanded. Pushing a microphone at Brian Bates, the television reporter was saying, "Fourth place in the competition going into tomorrow's final round. Top amateur, trailing only three world champions. How does it feel?"

Bates averted his head and kept walking but the reporter sidestepped, staying with him. "You're obviously a bodybuilder," she said. "Earlier today you wore a tee shirt. Now it's a Hawaiian shirt. Why the costumes? Are they part of your game plan?"

Bates still didn't answer. He maneuvered around her and made his way to the casino's main aisle where he was accosted again, this time by a small man of his own height wearing a cowboy outfit.

"Russell Henry," the stranger said. "I'm with the press. A few words?"

Carroll Shepherd had zeroed in on Bates, too, and was hovering close with a bottle of beer in his hand and a loose grin on his face. Bates took Henry's arm, spun him around to the psychologist and said, "Talk to my manager."

Still moving away from the crowd behind him, Bates reached out for Marlene's elbow and propelled her up the aisle to the elevators. Their argument resumed upstairs in his room.

"I'm not spending the night here," Marlene told him. "I've got my own room."

"What's the idea — some kind of punishment?" Bates asked. "How many times do you want me to say I'm sorry?"

Marlene said, "I think we should make plane reservations out for Friday."

"I'm not thinkin' past tomorrow," Bates answered. "Jesus Christ, one thing at a time!"

"Are you okay?"

"Yes, I'm okay!"

"Then calm down," she said. "I don't want you to apologize. I don't want you to be angry. I'm not angry. It's just that things are complicated and I think we should keep our heads."

"Things aren't complicated," Bates said. "You're making them complicated. The only thing that's complicated is the goddamned poker tournament, and I can handle that if you don't mess up my head."

"What do you want me to do, Brian?"

"I want you to stay here. I want you to act like my wife. I want you to sleep with me."

"I can't. I told you how I feel."

"Are you getting a kick out of this? Is that it?"

"Briny, I've never seen you this way," Marlene said. "I'll help if I can. If you need moral support —"

"I don't *need!*" He whipped off his dark glasses and slung them across the room. "Can't I get through to you? I got along fine all my life without a mother — I don't need you to mother me!"

"This isn't helping," Marlene said. "I'll talk to you tomorrow."

After she left, Bates sat on the edge of his bed. He couldn't figure out why she was acting that way. What was he doing wrong? He looked at his hands, which were trembling. He clenched them into fists, but still they shook, more and more violently. He couldn't control them.

Downstairs in the casino, Carroll Shepherd was telling Russell Henry, "I've given it a lot of thought, believe me. What it gets down to is an attitude towards risk. You said you're a freelance writer. Okay, a lot of people would consider your occupation reckless because you don't have a steady salary —"

"I'm all right on risk," Henry interrupted. "I'm trying to come at it politically. The poker player as politician. Look, in politics, you can argue that the facts don't matter. The only thing that matters to a politician is what people *believe* to be the facts. Vietnam, for example. Or hell, Central America. In poker, the actual hands — the facts — don't matter, either. What counts is what you can make somebody else believe you have in your hand —"

"I want to go back to risk," Shepherd insisted. "You can't understand this town unless you understand the guys in the sandwich boards. Topless dancing, oil wrestling, we cash Canadian checks. Look, will you take ten minutes and come outside with me? I want to show you someone. When you see the geek, you'll know what I'm talking about. Come on. Hey, you want a drink first?"

*

Outside, the temperature had dropped to twenty degrees but the sky was still clear. Shayna Levinson took a cab home. Inside her apartment, she turned the radio to some slow music and drew water for a bath. She was coming off an adrenaline high. In two days of the tournament she'd played against Houston, Sandwiches, Overstreet, the Owl — all the top pros except Tobias — and she'd held her own. So far, nobody was running away with the tournament. Tomorrow they'd crank up the stakes again, and Shayna figured she had a shot at the big money.

After her bath, she shampooed her hair and dried it, turned the radio dial to a rock station. She was coming back up, and the thought of a game with a bunch of tourists had a magnetic appeal. Casino poker was like sex that way, she thought; no matter how often you've done it, or how recently, the anticipation would always build inside you until you knew irresistibly that the next time it was going to be something new again, and better than ever.

She phoned Eugene, her companion of the night before. "Want to get together a little later?" she asked.

"Sounds great," he said. "Have you had dinner yet?"

"Thanks. I mean later. One or two, something like that."

"Oh, hell," Eugene said. "Give me a break, kid. I get up in the morning."

"Well, I'm going downtown to play poker," Shayna said, "so I'll be busy for a while."

"Forget the cards tonight. I'll come by."

"Are you kiddin'? No way. Not with all the easy money in town."

"Some other time then," he said.

"Don't get mad about it."

"I'm not mad."

"It's how I make my living, you know."

"No problem," Eugene said. "We're just out of synch tonight."

"Well, pardon me all to hell for calling."

"I'm flattered," he said. "Good luck, kid."

Well, fuck you, she thought.

*

There were six of them for dinner at the Taj Mahal's steak house: Art Epstein and Jackie, Jerry Corbett and Chris, and the newlyweds, Foley and Anita. Jerry was still in his female disguise, and Chris, a nervous wreck about the deception, was drinking screwdrivers to get through the evening. To her horror, Jerry was ordering the same. Anita was sipping a white wine but Foley, on his best behavior, was sticking to club soda. Epstein and Jackie were drinking martinis.

They had already toasted the newlyweds and now a grinning Foley raised his glass in return and said, "To our poker players, who thanks to the cocktail waitress are rapidly becoming a high pair."

They drank to that, and Jerry giggled. "Duke would die." The others looked at him and he said, "My husband. I want to break the bank at Monte Carlo and Duke wants to break two hundred at the Freeway Lanes. It's what you call a failure of communication. But I have a toast, too," Jerry said. "To our lovely and talented actresses. To Chris, my dear friend and neighbor, and to the incomparable Miss Jackie Gaines."

"Hear, hear," Epstein said. "Soon to be actress and producer Jackie Gaines."

Jackie accepted the toast with aplomb but Chris was mortified. "Honestly, Jerry," she said, "you can't compare me with —"

"Do you really act?" Anita asked her across the table.

Chris said, "Well, yes, I do. I mean I have, but —"

"She's too modest," Jerry interrupted. "You shouldn't hide your light under a bushel, dear. Didn't you tell me you're a member of the Screen Actors' Guild?" To Jackie, he said, "She's done commercials, she's done wonderful bit parts —"

"Jerry, please!" Chris said. "You're embarrassing me."

Jerry put a hand to his lips. "Goodness — have I made a *faux pas?*" There was something so comically ingenuous in his surprised expression that the others laughed.

Over dinner, Art Epstein was amused to see that Anita was bringing out the Jewish mother in his wife. Jackie huddled with the girl in animated conversation while Foley beamed, apparently in love with the whole world. Earlier in the day the elopement had struck Epstein as ridiculous, but he was getting used to it and now it made as much sense to him as anything else. Why not take a grab at happiness when it floats your way? Hell, he thought, they'll probably stay married forever. Who was he to sit in judgment? Epstein had known he wanted to marry Jackie twenty-four hours after he'd met her.

Epstein felt a glow as dinner progressed. His wife still excited him and his infatuation with Jackie was enhanced, if anything, by her maturity in comparison with the two younger girls. There were no lines in Jackie's face, no droop to her posture, nothing specific Epstein could isolate to define Jackie as a woman and Chris and Anita as girls. But she had a look, maybe of wisdom. Or experience, or patience. Something, anyway. Maybe humor. They were some special trio of females in any case, Epstein thought. In her own way, Chris, the makeup stylist or actress or whatever she was, was as much of a knockout as Anita. Anita's appeal was more subtle — it came from her bone structure and coloring — but Chris's looks leaped out from the flesh: she had bigger eyes, a toothier smile. The camera would treat her better, Epstein thought. And the fourth woman at the table, Jerry Corbett, seemed perfectly at ease despite finding herself among three beauties. Although Epstein had expected Jerry to talk about the poker tournament, she seemed more interested in drawing Jackie out about the profession.

"In *California Comedy*," Jerry was saying, "you played a girl who kept writing suicide notes to her fiancé. Remember?"

"Don't ask," Jackie said. "I remember that turkey. How do you remember it?"

"I saw it."

Jackie laughed. "*You're* the one."

"You wrote the notes right-handed, didn't you?"

"Yes."

"But you're left-handed."

"That's just business," Jackie said. "You want the audience to follow the action, not the handedness. You're very observant."

"I'm fascinated by acting."

"Do you do any?" Epstein asked.

"Me? Heavens, no," Jerry said. "Just on Saturday nights with Duke."

"Jerry!" Chris said.

Again Jerry clasped a hand to his mouth and rolled his eyes. The effect was comic. "He really would kill me for that. Ooh, no more vodka for me tonight."

Epstein didn't think Jerry was as drunk as she was pretending. "You bluff in poker," he said. "That's acting."

"It's different," Jerry said. "I could never be a theater actress, never." He shook his head vehemently at the idea, although nobody was disagreeing with him.

"You know what?" Foley said. "Anita could be in your Mexico movie."

"Like hell," Anita said.

"Sweetheart, be quiet," Foley told her. "I'm your agent now. If I'm going to fly ferry to Mazatlan, we'll get you on the payroll, too. They're rich. They can afford it."

"He talks like an agent," Jackie said.

"I can see it now," the pilot went on. "Anita Foley in a Jackie Gaines production of an Art Epstein blockbuster of a —"

"I hate to disillusion you, sugar," Anita interrupted, "but I tried modeling once. It didn't work."

"Why not?"

"My features wash out. I photograph without eyebrows or a nose."

"I don't believe it," Foley said. "Does that mean you're not going to be able to support me?"

Chris said, "I could make you up, Anita. You're so pretty. I'll bet it would work."

"See?" Foley said. "We're over the hurdle. When do we screen test?"

"Chris could do it," Jerry announced.

Jackie agreed. "She did wonders with me."

"I mean," Jerry said, "she could act in your film." Chris began to protest but Jerry overrode her. "You said you'll want new faces," he said to Jackie. "This girl is a real talent. Maybe it's improper to bring this up at your party, and I apologize. No — I don't, either. Isn't that how it's done in the business — you use your contacts? I'm sorry if this is embarrassing, but Chris is too modest to push herself. Chris dear, you've got an agency. Couldn't they contact Miss Gaines? I do apologize," he said. "It's the vodka talking. But I know how good Chris is and if she got a chance, you'd see it, too. You'd thank me."

"Test 'em both," Foley said grandly. "Break out the cigars — I feel like an executive!"

Jackie and Epstein were looking at Chris as if they hadn't quite noticed her before. She colored, but she raised her chin and said, "I've had training. I am an actor."

Jackie said, "You understand the deal isn't together yet." She looked at Epstein, who gave her a noncommittal shrug. "But we're certainly open to suggestions."

Upstairs later, Chris asked, "How did you get the nerve for that?"

"From screwdrivers," Jerry said, sitting on the bed to take off his shoes.

"Three cheers for Smirnoff, then. You did great! I just hope she puts the deal together."

"If the husband's in it, she can do anything she wants. I hear he owns half of San Francisco."

"I want to start classes again next week," Chris said. "Can we afford it?"

Jerry held a shoe in front of his face like a microphone. "We'll have that story tomorrow. Now this," he said, and took off his pants.

*

Downstairs in the casino, the side games continued into the night. "I oughta take a vacation," Vic Houston said. "I don't know why I keep doin' this."

"You've got a reputation to uphold," the Owl told him. "Mr. World Champion of the Johnny Carson show."

"I got a couple grandkids now." Houston smiled sourly. "Silver-spoon little bastards. You know how much money I got?"

"How much?"

"Beats me. Between Uncle Sam and my kid, I can't keep track. All I know is I can't go broke, the way things're set up. Takes away all the fun."

"Get some of it in the pot," the Owl said.

Houston turned his cards over. "Thanks. I seen a full house before."

Between deals, the two men carried on their intermittent conversation. Houston said later, "Gettin' too old to play golf. My kid says go fishin'. Can't bet on a fish. My wife says get a Winnebago and we'll drive around the country. Ain't a white line on the road I don't already have memorized."

"We get jaded," the Owl said. "Once upon a time I thought a dollar cigar was the height of luxury. Then it was a Lincoln Continental. You know what it is for me now?"

"A hard-on?"

They put their antes in the pot. "Times change," Houston said. "They'll be two hundred people in the World Series this year. They oughta raise the buy-in. It's gettin' like the Boston marathon."

"Tell me about it," the Owl answered. "The first time I came to Reno, you could park your car at the curb on Virginia Street. Remember? Harold's Club was the biggest place in town."

"Ol' Pappy Smith," Houston said.

"No high rises. No traffic. No crowds."

"There ain't enough room here now to whip a dog," Houston said. "You bettin'?"

"Not into your trips."

"What trips? You don't see no trips."

"I've never seen my cat's fleas, either. But I know she's got 'em."

They played on, as familiar as next-door neighbors. If out in the aisle spectators paused to gawk at them as celebrities, they seemed unaware of it. "What's the craziest thing you ever saw happen in a poker game?" Houston asked.

"There've been too many to single out. It seems women were usually involved."

"I saw a guy take a shit on the table once."

"A private game, I presume."

"In Hollywood. He was some kinda movie big shot. They said he did it whenever he lost big."

"A fifty-thousand-dollar laxative," the Owl said. "Now there's a luxury I hadn't considered."

In the summer, Russell Henry imagined, Virginia Street between Circus-Circus and the Cal-Neva would teem with people. The sidewalks would fill with a promenade of tourists just like any other resort in the West, whether it was Aspen or Carmel or Jackson Hole or Disneyland or you name it. Even now in the dead of winter, people were out on Virginia Street. In the clear night, in the neon brightness, they jaywalked from casino to casino or beckoned for taxis or hurried afoot, hands in their pockets, on their way back to their rooms to call it a night. Standing on the sidewalk beneath an overhang, as unmoving as a statue, a squat, bandannaed woman stood bundled up against the cold. She gazed at nothing, as if she'd lost all interest in her surroundings, and she held in one hand the small mittened fist of a young girl who kept vigil as patiently by her side. The woman's other hand rested on the handle grip of a baby stroller in which an infant slumbered, swaddled in blankets, while inside at a crap table the husband and father gambled away his paycheck. Not far down the street, had Russell Henry but noticed, a policeman approached a blue-jeaned Indian leaning against a building and said, "Remember what I told you, Joe."

The Indian made no response. As far as he seemed to be aware, the policeman didn't exist.

"What's in the sack, Joe?"

Still the Indian didn't acknowledge the other's presence.

"I'm taking you in," the policeman said.

Still without looking at the policeman, and in a hoarse voice that didn't carry beyond the length of his arm, the Indian said, "I'm not goin' in."

Suddenly, so fast that Russell Henry wouldn't have noticed even if he had been looking, the Indian was no longer upright but was face down on the sidewalk, a smear of blood staining his upper lip. The policeman had a knee on the Indian's shoulders and was cuffing his wrists behind his back. A patrol car appeared at the curb and within a minute the scene was cleared.

Russell Henry walked into the Taj Mahal. Again, had he been looking, he would have seen a shrunken, white-haired woman in a cotton washdress standing splay-footed at a row of slot machines. She was grinding her dentures, her lower jaw jutting forward, and wearing a single white glove she worked two machines alternately, taking nickels out of a waxed paper cup to feed the slots and pulling the handle of one machine with her gloved hand while the drum of the other clattered to a stop. Had Russell Henry been attending closely, he would have seen a strange look come over the woman's face, a startled grimace, a sort of momentary annoyance. Then he would have seen her sag and go down, bouncing off the machine behind her as she collapsed, her gloved hand reaching up in vain for a final pull of the handle even as another woman slipped over to claim the machines, which might have been ready to jackpot.

Russell Henry was on a sleep deficit. He was suffering from a sensory overload. He was thinking: there are no winners in this town. There are thousands of losers — and he called them losers, not gamblers, because the only gamble they took was on how long it would take for the house odds to grind them down — and if there were even a handful of winners, they were among the poker players. His people. And Henry knew that he didn't understand the poker players and would never understand the poker players. Stretch Jackson's tournament was no more to them than a diversion. The tournament was hardly a blip in their cash flow. The side games were where they played for real money, and the secrets of their casual transactions in the side games were not accessible to an outsider. Sign your name for a line of credit, hand over a stack of chips and tear up a marker, borrow a stake from a friend — or is he repaying a loan? — it was mystery money, subterranean money moving without a trail. Henry wondered if at any given moment even the players themselves knew who among them was money ahead or money behind.

The casinos were voracious maws, Henry thought, great swirling suction machines. He was temporarily obsessed by Orientals, who seemed to be gambling everywhere. Chinese, Vietnamese, Japanese, Malaysians — wherever he turned he saw Orientals, tiny alien Orientals and loose-limbed native-born Orientals, sober and industrious and determined Orientals who managed in their grim resolve to make the recreation of gambling look like a kind of ethnic penitence. Then he found himself noticing legs everywhere, spike-heeled, mesh- or nylon-covered legs of cocktail waitresses and keno runners, intriguing curves of thigh and calf, scissors glimpses of flesh that were so ubiquitous, free looks in every direction, that they failed even to stimulate desire. Thighs, perfumes, hairdos, eye makeup, lipstick, breasts, amazing cleavages, all of it came gratis with the casino decor, mere background for the money machine.

Henry was haunted by a couple he'd seen at breakfast that morning. He'd been at a dollar-ninety-nine buffet breakfast, all you can eat, up an escalator flight at a busy joint where they moved the customers in and out fast, tables small and close together, efficient Chicano busboys collecting dirty dishes with a clatter. Eating alone, dulled by his drinking and his poker losses of the night before, Henry had noticed a young couple two tables away. They were sitting across from each other, talking earnestly with a lot of eye contact. They were black and in their mid-twenties, both of them arrestingly handsome. The girl had Caucasian features and wavy hair and was dressed immaculately, in white slacks and a green silk blouse and jade earrings. She gave off the aura of a capable young executive, like someone on the way up in television or banking or public relations, and just the sight of her would make the meanest bigot concede that there might be some merit in affirmative action. Likewise, the man with her looked as clean and fresh as if he'd just stepped out of a hot shower. He was darker, African black, in sharply-creased khaki trousers and a sky-blue polo shirt. He was a broad-shouldered, big man, six-four or -five if he stood up, Henry guessed, and muscled like a basketball player. He had a huge helping of food on his plate, scrambled eggs and hash browns and sausage links and ham and sliced tomatoes and biscuits, and a side plate of grapes and honeydew and cantaloupe and syrupy figs and plums. He ate methodically, stuffing his mouth, and he gripped his knife and fork, one in each hand, like farm implements. He scooped his food and ducked his head to get at it, like a man who'd never before in his life had the remotest acquaintance with silverware.

He was an athlete, Henry knew that. He had an athlete's size and build and discipline. He was also dumb as a post, and it showed. He'd gone through college on a ride, Henry was sure of it, and all he had to show for four years of higher education were a scrapbook of clippings and no more useful knowledge of coping in the world than how to sink that fadeaway jumper. He was sweet, simple, a tender, well-meaning young man, and he was trying as hard as he could except it wasn't good enough. He was going to lose the girl, if he hadn't already lost her, and he didn't know it. But the girl knew it and that showed, too. She had a future but his was behind him, not for lack of heart or lack of ambition or lack of trying, but for lack of luck. He'd been born with the right looks and the right body and the right reflexes, with everything right about him except his color and the ghetto he grew up in.

Watching them, Henry ached with melancholy. Such a pleasant, sincere, deserving young couple. And so doomed. At the breakfast table, Russell Henry had forgotten for a while that he was in Reno.

He'd drifted out beyond the make-believe world of the gambling casinos and could have been anywhere in America. He was sad, and the memory came back and depressed him that night inside the Taj Mahal, where he paused for a moment at the poker area to observe the side games. A cardboard cutout of Stretch Jackson in sequins and a fringed jacket beckoned to him. What a smile. Hiya, pardner. Easy money, pardner. Jump right in. Ante up and make your fortune, pardner. Henry turned and trudged up the aisle towards the elevators.

Behind him as he walked off, a bony, horse-faced gambler pulled a chair over and sat down at a table behind Vic Houston and Owl Avery. He wore the doleful expression of a farmer who'd just had his tractor repossessed. He seemed known to the two men, and in a lull between deals he said, "I'm busted, Vic. Loan me a couple hundred to get to Vegas?"

"I can't hear ya," Houston answered.

"Be a pal," the man said. "Hoo-Hoo?"

The Owl shook his head. "It's against my firmest principles."

"Well, shit," the man grumbled, but not as if he were surprised by the refusals. After a while he said, "Lost on a flush. Lost on a full house. It's not like I ain't catchin'."

The Owl said, "I know the feeling well."

Houston nodded at that. "Happens to Hoo-Hoo here every ten or twenty years hisself."

After watching a few more hands, the man said, "Hell with it, then. I might as well stick around and play hold-em. Borrow me a stake?"

"What'll do ya?" Houston asked.

"Five grand?"

Houston reached into his trousers pocket and pulled out a packet of bills rolled with a rubber band. He handed it to the man, who thanked him, but not as if it were a big thing, and walked off. Neither gambler bothered to make a note of the loan. Houston and the Owl anted up without comment as cards were dealt around. The game continued.

*

Brian Bates was in serious trouble this time. There were dormitories and there were dormitories but this was the worst one ever. It was a hootch not a dormitory and how Charlie got into the orphanage in Oklahoma was something Bates couldn't understand except he knew it wasn't fair. He was too innocent to die. He was just a kid, struggling on chubby legs in the dark and the labyrinth when Charlie knew the maze by heart, ran it as fast as rats, came after him in every corridor. He heard ricochets, felt the rush of shrapnel. For Bates there was no sanctuary in Heartland this time, there was no Heartland in Nam, Heartland was from years ago when they used to hit him but they never tried to kill him, not all of them, not like this, not with his heart pounding, going thump thump like incoming, like the shock wave of the waterfall in the gorge ahead, the whirlpool. Bates was drenched in sweat, sopping wet with hot perspiration as he ran and dodged and suddenly he was swimming, trying to swim but getting sucked downstream again, down and under, suffocating again in the thump thump of the whirlpool, on his back whirling faster and faster and above him was the clear blue and the bright green foliage, palm trees, a fragrance, the thump thump of rotor blades flipping him over, going headfirst now, free-falling into the inky whirlpool, the bottomless foxhole. He had no breath left, he could die in one of these nightmares, and he landed on something soft, someone cushiony who pulled him away and rolled over and over with him down the sand to safety as Bates hung on, first to a leg and then struggling upward, humping his way upward to embrace a body as they stopped rolling and the fragrance returned, the enveloping fragrance of Marlene and his own terrified shouting that awoke him. He flung his pillow, kicked out of his blankets and lay panting, shivering as the sweat chilled on his naked body, as frightened awake as in the dream where he was hugging Vic Houston, desperately embracing him like a child a father, pleading for help . . .

A mile away, in a hospital bed in a room at the Washoe County Medical Center, Lee Sherman Tobias lay trussed like a chicken. He was propped up with pillows and he had rubber tourniquets tied around his left bicep and both thighs. A pair of tubes directed oxygen into his nostrils from a cannula that snaked across his upper lip. His breathing came in gasps and his eyes were open and staring.

In the hallway outside the room, Archie Breen hovered nervously while a doctor conferred with Tobias's wife. "The tourniquets may look frightening," the doctor was saying. "They're merely to retard venous return. We're trying to clear his congestion."

Edith Tobias had steel-gray hair, a lined face and flinty, gray Missouri eyes that looked as if they'd stared down a lifetime of catastrophes. "He's put on weight," she said. "He must be eatin' okay."

"Well, that's the edema," the doctor said.

Standing close to Edith Tobias was a younger man wearing tortoise-shell eyeglasses and a blue suit. His name was Harmon and he was a lawyer. He asked, "Is it all right to go back in?"

"Just don't excite him," the doctor said. "If he tires, let him sleep."

"Is he sedated?" Harmon asked.

"Not at the moment. The morphine's worn off."

Archie Breen said, "Doc, he wants to get back in the poker tournament later."

"That's out of the question."

"It's not for twelve hours still."

"Believe me, he won't feel like leaving his bed."

"I believe you," Breen said miserably. "Who's gonna tell *him*?"

Edith said, "He's a mule. When he gets his back up —"

"We don't have to bother the doctor with that now," Harmon interrupted. "If it becomes a problem, I'm sure the hospital can —"

"It won't become one," the doctor said.

Leaving Archie Breen to fret in the hallway, Edith and Harmon entered Tobias's room. The invalid stared at them. "Am I dyin'?" he asked.

"You been through worse," his wife answered.

"Bull. I don't want no more dope. It puts me out."

Edith started to say something but again the lawyer interrupted. "We'll tell them," he said. "For now, you can help yourself most by relaxing."

"They got me tied up like a Boy Scout," Tobias grumbled. "Harmon, you look like your daddy."

"I'll take that as a compliment, Mr. Tobias."

"He doin' okay?"

"He sure is, as long as the fish are biting."

When Tobias spoke again, he told the lawyer, "I want Edie provided for."

"Mr. Tobias, that's the last thing in the world you have to worry about."

"I know the house is paid," Tobias said. "But they ought to be some money."

A nurse came into the room. "It's time to rotate again, Mr. Tobias," she said. "Just lie still now. You don't have to move." She tied off his right arm with a rubber strap and then slowly loosened the tourniquet on his left arm. "Comfortable?"

"Is it supposed to be?"

She felt his pulse. "I'm afraid not entirely."

"Well, it ain't."

"This is the last rotation," she said. "We'll start removing them soon. You're breathing easier now, aren't you?"

"I'm breathin'," Tobias said. When the nurse left, he looked at the other two. "It's my heart. Nothin' I cain't do about it."

"You need rest," Harmon said. "Take the strain off."

"I am restin'."

"He's had it before," Edith said. "It keeps comin' back."

Harmon said, "I'll be in the lounge. You all must want to visit."

"Damn it, wait up," Tobias said. "I asked about the money."

"What can I tell you?"

"How much is there?"

"Well, we'd have to prepare an accounting."

"They oughta be a hundred thousand anyways. And you gotta take care of the sonabitchin' taxes."

Harmon said, "Mr. Tobias, you know your holdings are worth a great deal more than a hundred thousand dollars."

Tobias looked at his wife. "You know what he's talkin' about?"

She said, "They watch over it. You never asked before, Lee Sherman."

The lawyer pulled a chair next to the bed and sat down. Carefully he said, "Mr. Tobias, back when my father was still a young lawyer, you were already entrusting the firm with large amounts of money. That was more than forty years ago."

"I know. I sent it to Edie to bank. I'm askin' how much is left."

"It's not exactly a matter of what's left," the lawyer told him. "Your investments have, ah . . . appreciated substantially. You have equity positions. Your real property holdings are extensive." Harmon glanced at Edith but got no help from her stolid expression. "Very extensive. I'd estimate your net worth, conservatively speaking, at ten or twelve million."

"You shittin' me."

Harmon said, "I assumed you had some idea."

Tobias said, "Edie? Did you know?"

"I don't spend much," she said.

"How much in cash?" Tobias asked the lawyer.

"I couldn't say offhand. In liquid accounts, certainly six figures."

Tobias was quiet for a while. Then he said, "Can Edie get hold of the cash?"

"Yes. Of course."

"Okay, then. I'll be go ta hell. I don't mind tellin' you, Harmon, I'm obliged."

"I'll wait in the lounge," the lawyer said.

After he left, Edith told her husband, "You oughta do somethin' nice for him. He got the tickets and flew with me and all."

"Don't tell no one you're a millionaire. Hear, Edie?"

"The airplane wasn't any worse than ridin' a bus," she said. "You gained weight, Lee Sherman. You ain't dyin'."

"I was coughin' up bad. It's my heart."

"Reno's two hours earlier," Edith said. "I put my watch back."

"Get Archie in here."

Edith asked Archie Breen into the room and Tobias told him, "That lawyer fella needs a room. Don't let him pay for nothin'. What time's the game?"

"Two o'clock."

"Get me a car here in time. You go on now. Edie'll stay."

Breen left and Edith sat down. "They got a thing like a merry-go-round for the luggage," she said.

"Hush. I gotta sleep." Tobias closed his eyes but the nurse returned in a few minutes and he watched her unstrap the tourniquet from his left thigh. He flexed his leg weakly and coughed, bringing up a pink froth.

The nurse wiped his mouth with a tissue. "Try to rest," she said. "I'll be back in fifteen minutes to undo your other leg."

Tobias watched her as she left the room. Ten million was too abstract an amount to mean anything. He understood the forty grand in cash the Taj Mahal was holding for him. And he understood the couple of hundred grand in the poker tournament. That was real money. He could put it in his pocket. Ten million was just a number. But it sounded awful good. If it had been in his nature, the old man might have smiled.

Shayna Levinson rang a bungalow door chime in a subdivision southeast of downtown Reno. In a minute the porch light came on and Eugene opened the front door, wearing a pair of striped pajamas.

"I'm sorry I snapped at you," Shayna said.

Eugene was half asleep. "That's okay. What's going on?"

"It's freezing out here," she said. "You gonna invite me in?"

"Huh? Sure." He jiggled something on the screen door and pushed it open. "What time is it?"

"A little after three."

"Some hours you keep, kid. I'm not in shape to be much of a host."

"I don't care. I just don't want to be alone tonight."

"Did you go downtown?"

"Yeah, it was worth it," she said. "I'm up about four grand. Hey, look, I won't bother you. I just need some company."

"You've got it. If you don't mind my snoring." Eugene walked back to his bedroom and got under the covers. "Turn off the light when you're ready."

Shayna got undressed except for her panties and tee shirt. She got into bed and snuggled close to Eugene. He moved his arm so she could rest her head inside it. "I'm nervous about tomorrow," she said.

"Not you."

"Yeah, me," she said. "But I don't want to talk about it. I just want to zonk out."

"Be my guest."

After a while Shayna said, "You're a sweet guy, Gene." But by then she was talking to a man asleep. She moved over to the other side of the bed and when she awoke in the morning, she was alone. Eugene had left her a glass of orange juice and a pot of coffee, along with a good-luck note.

☙ Thursday

I T had been a blindingly clear sunny morning up at the south shore of Lake Tahoe. Snow blanketed the Sierra Nevada at that altitude and the sky above was the pale, pure blue of winter, with the flat rippleless surface of the lake itself a deeper blue, its distant edges scalloped by a mirrored reflection of the surrounding mountains. But now the weather was deteriorating. The higher limbs of the pine trees at lakeside 'were beginning to toss, and gray cloud tops were bubbling over Tahoe's western slopes as a storm in the Sacramento Valley pushed its way inland.

Art Epstein and his wife had an enviable view of the panorama. They were lingering over brunch at a window booth in a restaurant atop a high-rise casino-hotel. "Foley and Anita are so cute together," Jackie was remarking.

"And they say romance is dead," Epstein answered. "I feel like a chaperone at the sock hop."

"Is Foley an alcoholic?"

"Naw. He likes to fly too much."

"I'd hate to see him mess this thing up."

"He's only half the clown he pretends to be, love. Did you know he has a doctorate?"

"In what?"

"Atmospheric physics, meteorology, something like that."

"Then he could teach," Jackie said.

Epstein patted her hand. "Yes, dear. I love the way your mind works. You're in the world's most dissolute business and you want all your friends to be respectable."

"I just want him to be able to take care of that girl."

"She looks like she can take care of herself. You don't plan to test her, do you?"

Jackie shook her head. "She's stunning but it's not the look I want. Anyway, she's not interested. Art, it's beautiful up here." Jackie waved her hand at the view. "Two days ago I was smearing myself with sunscreen in Malibu. Now this. You sure know how to surprise a girl."

"It works both ways, sweetheart. Two days ago the most important thing in my life was a poker tournament. Now I could give a rat's ass."

"Why not?"

"Because you've got me all excited about producing a movie. And turning your career around? Playing an older woman, that's a challenge. Next thing you'll tell me you want a baby."

"Play fair," Jackie said. "You can't bring me to a winter wonderland with a couple of newlyweds and then try to knock me up. That's taking advantage. Of course I want one. Just not yet."

"Is there a schedule I should know about?" Epstein asked.

"Get that look out of your eye," she said. "It's bad enough I'm in an emotional state — one of us has to keep his head. The schedule, darling, is first we produce three pictures for me. Then we reassess."

"Or you could do three, and three more, and three —"

"I don't mean that at all," Jackie said. "Listen. It makes sense. First I play a forty-year-old in the Baja movie. With us producing, if you're with me —"

"If? I'm ready to rent an Arab's house in Bel Air right now."

"Then I do a drama. Then my T & A swan song, and after that I don't need my figure any more."

"On the Baja movie?" Epstein said.

"Yes?"

"That girl Chris has a certain appeal. Considering she spends most of the film in a bikini."

"I thought of that. The question is whether she can act. And with who."

"I'm turned on by all this," Epstein said. "You're making me feel like a kid."

"I keep telling you we should see more of each other."

"I thought that was my line."

"No, sweetheart. Your line is, 'I'm callin' yer bet, pilgrim, an' raisin' ya fer all ya got.'"

"That's the worst John Wayne I've ever heard."

"You were expecting maybe Rich Little? Win the tournament, Art. That's what you came here for."

"I'm giving it my best shot. But those professionals are damned psychics."

"Then do this for me," Jackie said. "Look like a champion. You know that king of the mountain expression you can get?"

"No."

"Yes, you do. The Tarzan look. You can make those other players look like pygmies. Do it for me. Damn, you're a hunk."

She slid over in the booth and kissed him but they were interrupted by Foley and Anita, who had been making their way across the restaurant. "I thought we were the horny newlyweds," Foley said. "Gang, we'd better hustle if we're going to beat the weather."

The clouds had moved overhead by then and the wind outside had picked up. Snow flurries were blowing across the highway when the four of them piled into the rental car. Driving down the highway to Reno they stayed ahead of the worst of the storm, but by the time they descended to the Carson Valley they had their headlights on and were plowing through slush.

The final day of Stretch Jackson's poker tournament began with the same two tables of six players who had adjourned the night before. The tables were set up adjacent to each other on their long axes, so a spectator walking up the aisle of the Taj Mahal casino would pass a good twenty feet of championship poker as close as the players' comfort and the slight barricade of the waist-high velvet rope would allow. Most of the brown hundred-dollar chips had been taken out of play and replaced with purple five-hundreds, but the exchange still left sizable stacks at some of the empty seats as starting time drew near.

The television reporter had already taped more than enough interviews and color to put a show together, but now she was hoping for some stirring drama as the day progressed. "Honey, I don't know what you call drama," Stretch told her. "These folks ain't exactly playin' for rent money."

"How long do you think the tournament will last?" she asked.

"Depends," Stretch said. "We'll keep crankin' up the stakes."
He grinned. "I'd have it over in an hour if I was in there, but some
people do like to drag things out."

Walsh, in his leather jacket, was the first contestant to enter the
tournament area and sit down, counting his chips and rearranging
them into stacks that suited him better. As if his appearance were
a signal, other players began drifting in from around the casino.
Vic Houston and Owl Avery arrived together, separating to take
their seats at different tables. Shayna Levinson, dressed and made
up for the cameras, sat down. She turned her back on Walsh but
made some comment to Sandwiches and the Owl, who ignored
her.

Next to the blackboard, a revised list of odds had been posted.
Bettors could get three-to-two on the favorites, Houston and Avery.
Lee Sherman Tobias was at four-to-one; Sandwiches, Easy, Brett
Overstreet and Shayna Levinson were eight-to-one underdogs, and
the remainder of the players were long shots at twenty-to-one.

Brian Bates moved pugnaciously through the gathering crowd,
like a little tank. He sat down, reached into a pocket of his sports
jacket for a pair of dark glasses and, like the others, began counting
and restacking his chips. While he was at it, Tobias shuffled slowly
towards the table, supported at the elbow by the Missouri lawyer,
Harmon. Tobias dropped into his chair as if he'd misjudged the
distance. He was wearing a snap-button shirt with a fleur-de-lis
pattern and a western hat with a scarlet feather in the band, but the
rakish effect was ruined by soft bedroom slippers beneath the swol-
len bulge of his ankles.

Stretch Jackson leaned over the dealer's shoulder at one of the
tables and told the players, "The ante's two hundred now, and low
hand'll bring it in for four hundred." He held fingers up to make
his point. "We gonna play 'til there's nine left, then we'll take a
break and put y'all at one table. Any questions?" There were none.
Stretch patted the dealer on the shoulder and moved over to the
other table and made the same announcement. The dealers broke
out new decks, discarded the jokers, fanned the cards front and

back for inspection, mixed them while they were face down on the table, then gathered and shuffled the cards and started to deal.

Away from the poker tables, the mood of the casino was carefree for that early in the afternoon. The storm outside had closed the Sierra passes and for all practical purposes Reno was snowbound until the weather abated. There was nothing for the tourists to do but drink up and make the most of the situation, which was what they were doing, but the frivolous mood of the casino stopped at the perimeter of the poker tournament. There, inside the roped-off area, in the tobacco haze and under the lights, serious business was going on.

DeHaven, the Texas professional, was the first contestant to be eliminated Thursday. A pale, slight man with a chin beard that gave him the appearance of a sagacious goat, DeHaven had held a monopoly on twelfth place virtually from the start of the tournament. But being twelfth out of fifty players was a lot different from being last out of a dozen. He'd been suffering a steady decline since the previous afternoon and his bad luck continued when Thursday's play began. After two rounds, the antes and forced bets had eroded his stack by almost half. Then, drawing a pair of kings and sevens, he went all in for his last pot. He lost to Art Epstein's trip tens and was knocked out of the tournament.

Tens were sticking to Epstein. Whenever he was dealt one, he seemed to catch a second or a third, and once already that afternoon he'd drawn the ten he needed to fill a straight. His good luck amused him — Epstein was feeling too cheerful about everything else to care a hell of a lot whether he won the poker tournament. On the opening day, when he'd been lusting for victory and losing pot after pot to Doug McGowan, every bad hand had been a knife in his ribs. But that memory didn't seem as if it came from the poker tournament. Now that he was coasting instead of straining, Epstein's luck was fine and he was enjoying himself.

He couldn't say the same for the other players at his table. For Vic Houston, maybe. In his tailored gray suit, with a pearl-gray

Stetson resting lightly on his head, Houston was playing with his usual calm omniscience. Nothing seemed to rattle Houston, although what was actually going on inside his unreachable mind was anybody's guess. But if Houston and Epstein were at ease, it was obvious that nobody else at the table was having the slightest bit of fun. Brian Bates was wound up so tight that he was muttering to himself. Tobias, who looked too sick to be in the game, had placed a big bed pillow against the edge of the table as a cushion and was leaning into it for support. More and more, between hands, his eyes were closed. Easy, the blue-whiskered Vegas professional, had self-pity written all over him; his stack was shrinking and if he didn't get some help soon, he was going to find himself in the same bind that had finished DeHaven.

At the other tournament table, meanwhile, the gambling was more artful and deceptive. Jerry Corbett was even managing to deceive himself. After debating various strategies all morning, he'd finally sat down to play Thursday with every intention of laying back for the duration of the tournament. He'd protect his stack and let the others eliminate themselves while he hung on for sixth place. But since he couldn't let the strategy become obvious or the other players would rip him apart, he'd have to give the impression he was mixing it up. And the way to accomplish that, he decided, was to stick around for the cheap betting and even try to steal some pots early, before the raises got too big. It was a sensible strategy except for an unexpected problem: it was working too well. It turned out that he was catching cards and thus, despite his intentions, Jerry found himself engaged in one hell of a poker game. He kept telling himself that soon, after another round or two, he'd go back to his original plan, but in the meantime he was winning pots. And he loved being so cool about it. The hotter the action got, the more placid and self-controlled did he require the reserved Ms. Jerry Corbett to act. What a role. What a performance.

His aloofness was driving Shayna Levinson to new heights of frustration. There was no way, Shayna thought, that frigid Gardena bitch could have lasted this long in the tournament. Shayna threw out her women's lib comments, her Gardena insults, her sexual innuendoes, and none of it worked. She couldn't get to Corbett. But she was having better luck against Walsh, who'd lost his self-possession. Walsh had one speed now: fast. He'd convinced himself that he couldn't get inside the minds of the other players, that trying to figure them out, in fact, only messed him up. So he was doing what he knew best, which was playing the odds. He was betting on the reality of what he could see on the table, not on the illogic of what might or might not be happening in somebody's imagination, and he stayed in or out, bet or raised, checked or folded, all instantaneously. Walsh hadn't lost his nerve; his bets were big. But his game was devoid of subtlety.

With the turmoil of emotions churning at the table, it was Owl Avery's kind of game. He felt energy coming from the action, lifting him. He imagined himself airborne. He felt like a soaring owl with a sharp, panoramic overview, and when he swooped, he struck without effort, nailing his prey with absolute precision. At the height of his skill, sustained by the energy of the table, Avery knew he was unbeatable.

Sandwiches knew it, too; he'd been there a few times himself. Some days you manage to pull everything together and there isn't a player in the world who can lay a glove on you. But you still need the tickets, Sandwiches thought. You can lose with good cards and once in a while you can even win with bad cards, but not in the long run. In the long run, a string of bad cards is bound to break your back. Sandwiches was playing at the height of his game, too, and his skill was the only thing keeping him in the tournament. Three times in the past half-hour he'd gone all in, and three times he'd heard a hush fall over the crowd behind him, felt the tension of the moment as the spectators waited to see if this would be the hand that broke him. And three times he'd stayed alive. But Sandwiches knew that was no way to win a poker tournament, not without tickets. No matter how shrewd you were, you couldn't expect to keep coming back from the dead.

But the axe fell on Brett Overstreet first. For too long on Thursday, the denim-clad Texan simply hadn't been a factor in the game. He'd gotten clipped early on a couple of second-best hands, once by Shayna and once by the Owl, and he'd retreated behind his diminished stack. Overstreet wasn't a talker, and in his unbroken silence at the table he'd become all but invisible to the other players. When he was down to five thousand dollars, he pushed his stack in against Jerry Corbett. Like the others, he continued to ignore the evidence and rated Jerry the weakest player at the table.

Overstreet went all in on a pair of kings showing. Jerry raised five thousand with an ace-queen up. It was a perfect bet; the players behind him folded, not interested in drawing against his likely pair of aces, and that left just Jerry and Overstreet in the pot, with Overstreet all in. In fact, Jerry didn't have a hand yet but was gambling on the momentum of Overstreet's own bad luck. It paid off. Overstreet paired fours to go with his kings but Jerry caught a second ace and a pair of nines to win the pot.

Overstreet saw it coming. "Good hand," he told Jerry, standing up.

"Bullshit," Shayna said. "She had position, is all."

Jerry didn't say anything. He just demurely accepted the chips the dealer pushed in his direction while the spectators gave Overstreet a round of applause. Overstreet hadn't been anybody's sentimental favorite but he'd come in eleventh in the tournament and the railbirds were generous in acknowledging a tough player. He tipped his hat and threaded his way over to the bar for a shot of whiskey. Behind him, the game continued.

Nothing in his thirty-five years of existence had prepared Harmon, the Missouri lawyer, for the sight of Lee Sherman Tobias playing poker. Except maybe, he thought, when they'd put a man on the moon. It was Harmon's nature to be awed by the incredible capacity of the human genius, by the improbable and glorious achievement that was mankind. Surely, he thought, no species in God's kingdom was as visionary as *homo sapiens*, dreamed such fantastic dreams, exemplified such noble and unquenchable emotions. Harmon held in reverence the potential of the human race and the holy, insatiable spirit of the individual soul, striving for the stars.

Alone of all the people in the Taj Mahal casino, the lawyer knew how sick Lee Sherman Tobias was. Earlier that morning at the hospital, the doctor had been outraged when Harmon negotiated Tobias's release. "He'll die," the doctor said. "I can't put it any simpler. He's suffering congestive heart failure."

"He knows," Harmon answered. "He'll sign a release."

"It's out of the question," the doctor said. "He'd be signing a death warrant."

"He's an unusual man."

"And he's seventy-five years old. Where's the wife?"

"In the room. I represent her." Harmon put his hand on the doctor's arm. "If you can talk him into staying, that's great. But otherwise we'll check him out."

"Don't be idiotic," the doctor said. "We've gotten him through the worst of it. He has a strong will. He's recovering."

"How long would you give him?"

"He could live a year."

"Or a week?"

"A week, a month, a year, two years. The disease isn't intractable yet. Pardon me."

The doctor went into Tobias's room. Harmon waited in the hallway, thinking that Edith Tobias was no help. Maybe she didn't understand. Or more likely, in her primitive wisdom, she understood plenty. But in any case, she remained as stolid as a farm animal. Edith had nothing to say except that whatever her husband wanted, that's what had to be.

The doctor was steaming when he came out of Tobias's room. "This is a goddamned mockery," he told Harmon. "Have you ever seen acute pulmonary edema?"

"No."

"Consider yourself lucky. You will, if you don't get in there and talk sense to him!"

"I've been trying for two hours, doctor. You see what I'm up against."

"I'm holding you responsible," the doctor said. "This is criminal! I wash my hands of it."

Harmon accepted the responsibility, confident that he was doing exactly what his father would have done in the same circumstances. Among Harmon's earliest memories were his father's stories about Lee Sherman Tobias, who took on all comers without asking for quarter, a lonely gladiator girded for battle with naught but his wits and a stout heart. "I don't endorse gambling," Harmon's father had told him years ago, "even though it's said there's no gamble involved when Lee Sherman Tobias sits down to play poker. But I respect the man and I want you to remember why, son. He's as honest as the day is long. But that's only part of it. Uneducated, all but illiterate, he has made himself into a wealthy man. But that's only part of it — anybody in this country who's willing to work hard can acquire wealth. I respect the man, though he's a gambler by profession, because he has never complained nor begged favors nor flinched from adversity. From humble origins he set out to become, *on his own*, the best practitioner in the world at what he does. He's tried with all the heart and soul the good Lord saw fit to give him, and that's the mark of a man in this world, son, committing to something and never giving up. He'll probably die at a poker table some day and if that's the destiny he wishes, he's earned the privilege."

Until now, Harmon had been acquainted with Tobias only as a mythic figure, but he knew the gambler was responsible to no small extent for his own reverence at the glory embodied in the unconquerable individual. Look at that old soldier, Harmon thought. It may be his fate to die at a poker table, but it's not going to be this poker table. Harmon had taken what precautions he could: he'd hired an ambulance, which was parked outside on standby, and he'd hired a registered nurse, who was sitting with Edith Tobias off to the side of the tournament area. Harmon himself was standing behind the velvet rope, as avid a spectator as the devoutest railbird.

He knew he was looking at but a spectre of what Tobias must have been in his prime, but even so his heart leaped. He was watching a living legend. Just look at him, Harmon thought, hanging on, doing what he knows how to do better than any man alive. He'll make it. One man alone, sublime, unquenchable.

As Harmon watched, he saw that something decisive was happening at the table, that some moment of crisis had arrived. "Easy's goin' all in," he heard somebody say. The nearby crowd murmured, then hushed. Tobias, resting against his pillow, had pushed a mound of chips at the pot. The stacks collapsed and Tobias waved his fingers feebly at the dealer, who restacked and counted them. The dealer returned some to Tobias and then reached out and put his index finger on the table in front of the man they called Easy.

The TV lights clicked on and for a full minute Easy sat motionless in their bright glare. Then he said, "I call." He put the rest of his chips in the pot and exposed his hole cards. He swiveled in his chair, finding a familiar face in the crowd, and pantomimed an elaborate shrug as the dealer dealt out the hand. When the final card fell, Easy was already rising from his seat, a dead duck. The crowd applauded. Easy was gone.

"Twenty-minute break," Stretch Jackson announced.

THE FIRST ANNUAL STRETCH JACKSON SEVEN-CARD STUD POKER CLASSIC

Standings as of 3:40 P.M. Thursday (Finalists)

1.	Vic Houston, Texas	85,000
2.	William "Hoo-Hoo" Avery, Arizona	80,500
3.	Jerry Corbett, California	69,500
4.	Shayna Levinson, Washington	65,100
5.	Lee Sherman Tobias, Missouri	53,800
6.	Art Epstein, California	52,300
7.	Brian Bates, Oklahoma	51,200
8.	Amateur player (Walsh), New York	34,600
9.	John "Sandwiches" Treece, Louisiana	8,000

Play to resume at: 4 P.M.

For the first time in the tournament, all the surviving players were going to find themselves facing each other around the same poker table. The stakes were going up again, too, the ante to three hundred dollars and the opening forced bet to six hundred. That meant there would be more than three thousand dollars in the pot before anybody even called the first bet. The legendary gambler Nick the Greek once said that the only difference between winners and losers is one of character. In the hours ahead, the nine finalists in the First Annual Stretch Jackson Seven-Card Stud Poker Classic would have a chance to demonstrate whether that was to be the case.

First they drew for position. Archie Breen removed the ace through the nine of hearts from a deck of cards, mixed them up and spread them face down on the table. Walsh shot his hand out and plucked a card. It was the five. That gave him the fifth seat, counting clockwise from the dealer. Quickly, before anyone else could act, Brian Bates reached for a card. Hearts were his suit — it was an omen. But a good one or a bad one? His draw would tell. "Deuce!" he cried. Bates needed a good sign; after playing a winning game for two days, he'd run into a brick wall. Suddenly he couldn't get ahead of anybody and it was time to get the magic working again, the old ESP. So he grabbed for his card before anybody else could beat him to it. "Deuce!" he cried, and turned it over.

It was the nine.

His cousin Earl! Of all the lousy cards to draw! In Heartland's whole imaginary good-spirited bunch, there were only two rotten relatives. The nine and the seven. Earl and his kid brother Mickey. They were ugly troublemakers, odd-numbered instead of sym- metrical even-numbered cards, and they were mean. If anyone could spoil a Heartland reunion, it was Earl, the hard-knuckled adolescent bragging about his nine-inch dick, his sneering face dis- figured by pockmarks like the pips on the card. And Mickey grew up to be just as bad. They'd run away from home, riding the rails out west, and little Brian was glad when he'd heard they got crushed by a freight train. Good riddance. But now he'd picked the damn card.

And Vic Houston picked the seven! Bates winced. Him and Vic picking Earl and Mickey? The signs were terrible. When the old guy who looked like death warmed over picked the Brian card, the deuce, Bates felt sick. With a foreknowledge of doom as ominous as in his nightmares, Bates slid into his seat at the dealer's right. Sure enough, the nigger sat down next to him. That put the cork right in the bottle.

Sandwiches lasted exactly one pot. On the first hand, Brian Bates was low and opened for the forced six hundred dollars. The players folded around to Houston, who raised a thousand with an ace showing. That put it to Sandwiches, who was unimpressed. He figured Bates to fold behind him, which would leave just himself and Houston in the pot. Two people — he couldn't get better odds than that, especially when Houston didn't have anything to back up his ace. Sandwiches called the thousand and Bates folded.

The next card gave Sandwiches four cards to a high straight. Houston bet another thousand and Sandwiches went all in with his remaining forty-one hundred dollars. Houston called. When the seven cards were dealt, Sandwiches ended up with a pair of jacks. "San Francisco marriage," the dealer said. Houston won with two aces, which he'd had all the way.

For Walsh, it happened too fast. He wasn't ready for it. Consolidating the tables into a single game meant that he was playing against strangers again, and he needed time to adjust. But Sandwiches disappeared before people were even settled into their seats. With his departure, Bates and Houston eased their chairs around the curve of the table to get some elbow room. Epstein spread out by sliding to his left and Walsh shuffled a foot or two in that direction himself, moving away from Shayna. Tobias coughed, sounding wheezy.

Walsh was nervous. Casually in the first damn hand, Houston had won almost eleven grand and knocked a player out of the

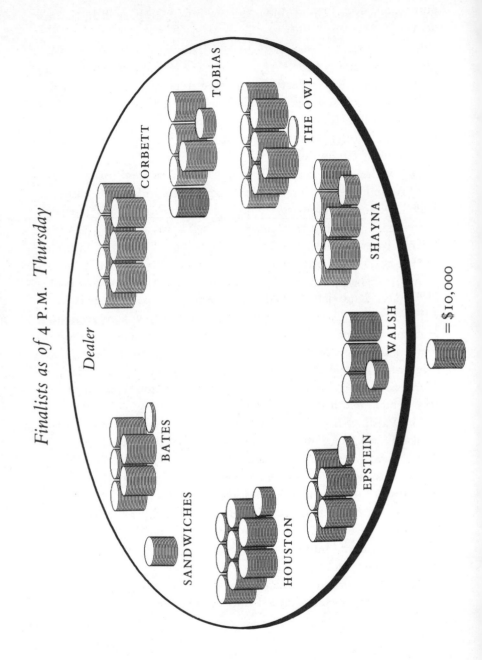

Finalists as of 4 P.M. *Thursday*

CORBETT

TOBIAS

THE OWL

Dealer

SHAYNA

BATES

WALSH

SANDWICHES

EPSTEIN

HOUSTON

= $10,000

tournament. Zap. Just like that. Walsh hadn't played against Houston yet but he knew him by reputation and was worried about him. And about Tobias, too. Walsh folded his cards in the second hand. He had the smallest stack of chips on the table now. The big blond guy on his left, Epstein, was new to him, and so was the squat thug in the dark glasses. Hell, Walsh thought, the only people at the whole table he'd actually played against so far were Hoo-Hoo and the two women, and they'd all been beating him.

As Walsh watched the second hand develop, the Owl folded on fourth street, leaving just Shayna and Bates in the pot. Bates had bet a thousand dollars and Shayna was stalling, pretending to make up her mind. She drummed her fingers on the table while Bates stared at her. Shayna looked back at him and asked, "Are those your shoulders or are you smuggling watermelons?" To Houston she said, "His cards don't scare me — I'm afraid he'll hit me."

Houston ignored her. Except for Walsh and possibly Bates, there wasn't a player left in the tournament Shayna was going to be able to throw off balance with her chatter, but she had to give it a try. She called Bates's thousand and on the next card she bet two thousand into him. "In case you can't see through those shades," she said, "I got a pair showing."

Bates glowered at her. He wasn't used to being needled, especially not by a woman. He hadn't expected to find himself playing against two women in the final round of the tournament anyway. The quiet one wasn't in his line of sight but he had his hands full with the noisy one for now, and she had him beat with trips as sure as he had a hole in his butt. Bates wasn't about to start chasing cards, not at those stakes. He folded.

"Smart move." Shayna threw her cards in and said in an aside to Jerry Corbett, "One for the sisterhood."

My luck, Walsh thought; I had to draw a seat next to her. "Why don't you zip it up?" he said.

"Another country heard from," Shayna laughed, raking in her chips. "The kingdom of wimp."

Owl Avery won the next hand. And the next. Both times, he raised the opening bet a thousand dollars and nobody called. He tried it again in the next hand and Houston re-raised him a thousand. The Owl reacted with a startled gesture, imitating W. C. Fields, and quickly threw in his cards. Houston smiled. The two men were so accustomed to each other that their bets were routine ninety percent of the time. Decisions that might have seemed inscrutable to outsiders were automatic for them.

The byplay wasn't lost on Walsh. He's clownin' around at these stakes and I'm dyin', Walsh thought. These guys don't play cards, they read minds. From now on I stick to backgammon. I can lose ten grand an hour here on the antes alone.

Jerry Corbett was doing some calculating, too. There were eight players left, which meant he had to outlast two of them to win a piece of the prize money. Jerry wasn't dreaming about winning the tournament anymore — in his mind, he'd already conceded first place to either Houston or the Owl. It was a minor miracle that he'd come this far, but he couldn't congratulate himself yet because his original and still pressing idea was to win some money and to do that, he still had to outlast two more players. Or one, actually, because Walsh was dying on the vine.

But who would it be? Not Houston or the Owl. He couldn't count Shayna out, so she made three. Epstein? Jerry hadn't played against Epstein yet but he'd had a chance to watch him at dinner the night before and the guy was Mister Cool. With his bucks, it figured. He made four.

Tobias? I'm going around the bend, Jerry thought; that's crazy. But look at him. When Jerry had played against him Tuesday, Tobias had merely looked old and frail. Now he looked like a corpse. Just listen to his breathing, Jerry thought. And it's not an act. But for Christ's sake, I'd have to be an idiot to count Lee Sherman Tobias out. He makes five.

So that leaves the bodybuilder, Jerry thought. After Walsh, I have to outlast Bates. Jerry couldn't get a good reading on Bates because of the seating arrangement, but he could feel the vibes coming off and they told him Bates was twitchy. What he needs here is finesse but instead he's trying to muscle his way through, Jerry thought. He's wound up like a dime-store alarm clock and Shayna's already started to tighten his springs. Bless her for once.

The cards came out. The Owl was low and brought in the betting. Epstein called. Bates called. Jerry Corbett called with three spades. On the next card he caught a fourth spade. Bates bet a thousand on what looked like a pair of kings. Jerry just called, getting a cheap draw to a flush. The Owl dropped without further interest and Epstein hesitated.

Art Epstein toyed with his chips. He had a look on his face that stopped just short of being a smile. Jerry Corbett amused him. She was trying so hard to look like a pushover, but you could see through the act if you watched her eyes. They were too shiny and alert. He'd noticed the same thing at dinner the night before: Jerry didn't miss a nuance. Epstein was enjoying the idea that Houston, Tobias and the Owl weren't the only assassins at the poker table. They were all killers, and the challenge stimulated him. The pot looked too easy; Epstein folded.

That left only Brian Bates and Jerry Corbett in the hand. On the next round, Jerry caught a third spade showing. Bates bet a thousand. Jerry counted out some chips and raised five. This time Bates hesitated.

Bates had the king of hearts in the hole. Houston's card. He didn't want to fold it. Folding it would show lack of belief. It would be traitorous. Not only that, but he had the king of diamonds to go with it, and a pair of cowboys sure as hell beat anything he saw in Corbett's hand. What is this shit, he wondered. First I get chased out by that smartass cunt and now the quiet one comes after me. Women don't belong in a poker game. I go in two hands and they're both against women. Marlene was out there with the spectators and somehow that depressed Bates. He reviewed what he'd seen of the hand so far. The old guy'd been dealt Lenny and the New York guy'd had Marv. That made two spades on the outside, three showing, and eight left in the dormitory. She must have the

/ / 2 1 5

flush. Reluctantly, with a gloomy feeling that the king of hearts had let him down, Bates folded. The dealer pushed the pot over to Jerry.

The finalists were settling into the game. Except for Tobias and Walsh, they'd all gone into a pot now, feeling each other out. They'd been throwing feints and jabs, not serious punches, but they were beginning to warm up. They'd start pounding. And they all knew that while they were working each other over, they'd be looking for the chance to land a blockbuster. They'd be softening each other up because that was part of the game, but they knew sparring wasn't the way to win a tournament. The only reason you wore somebody down was to set him up for the haymaker. The sucker punch.

The list of tournament prizes was displayed next to the leader board, beside one of the big cutout placards of Stretch Jackson. Hand-lettered on a sheet of poster board, it said:

$500,000 IN CASH PRIZES!

First Place	(60%) —	$300,000
Second Place	(20%) —	$100,000
Third Place	(10%) —	$ 50,000
Fourth Place	(5%) —	$ 25,000
Fifth Place	(3%) —	$ 15,000
Sixth Place	(2%) —	$ 10,000

Chris could visualize the dawning of a miracle, a bright golden sunrise expanding in her mind's eye. Jerry had been telling her all along to take things a day at a time, and now he was in third place. He'd been realistic about the Reno scheme from the start; it was Chris who'd been the anchor, dragging him down about money. But he could actually win the tournament, she thought, and even if he came in second or third, they'd still collect a fortune. To think that last month she'd felt on top of the world because they had a little nest egg stashed away. That was her problem, Chris realized — she hadn't been thinking big enough.

But she'd gained a different sense of herself. She was emboldened, especially after dinner the night before when she'd climbed right up on the high wire with Jerry. Now Jackie Gaines had attached herself to Chris in the spectators' gallery and if Jerry was putting on a performance at the poker table, Chris was doing the same on the sidelines. Jerry was a woman? Okay then, Chris was the loyal friend and neighbor. Jackie Gaines, the movie star Jackie Gaines, was at her elbow making small talk like an old friend? Big deal. Chris could handle that. Hadn't Jackie told her about the script of her next movie? Weren't they considering Chris for a co-star? What was there to be timid about? Jerry had nerve? So did Chris. They were partners. She was an actor, too.

"They all adopt *personas,* don't they?" Jackie was saying. "Look at that table. You've got the governor of Texas, an economics professor, a cabana boy, a computer nerd, a guerrilla fighter —"

"Which one's that?" Chris asked.

"That awful blonde. Can't you see her in an Israeli uniform carrying a machine gun? And look at Art. The chairman of the board."

"Announcing a stock dividend," Chris said.

"Or a merger. Wait." Jackie grabbed Chris's arm as Epstein picked up a stack of chips and put them in the pot, turning to look at Walsh in the seat to his right. "Art's the only one playing with a grin," Jackie said. "I think it's cute."

As they watched, Walsh fidgeted in his seat. He looked at Epstein, looked at the pot, peeked at his hole cards. Then he leaned back and didn't do anything for a moment. Finally he gestured with his hand. Take it. Epstein gathered the chips.

"How would you cast my friend Jerry?" Chris asked.

Jackie looked at the far side of the poker table, where Jerry Corbett sat next to the dealer in apparent meditation.

"With a great deal of caution, dear," Jackie said. "No offense, but she looks like a housewife killing time while the turkey roasts. Am I right that there's more to her than meets the eye?"

"That would be telling," Chris said.

They were joined by Foley and Anita, who pushed up behind them in the crowd. "Hey, Art's still hanging in there," Foley said. "Good for him. And your girlfriend, too, Chris. All right! Jackie, it's really coming down. We're not flying home tonight."

"Were you outside?"

"We went to the MGM. They've got the snowplows out. Anita wanted to gloat over what I'm rescuing her from."

"I had some good-byes to make," Anita said. "I'm so glad to get out of that job. I won't miss this town for a minute. I'm going to take pilot training."

"Like hell," Foley said. "I'm enrolling you in computer school. Six months of class and you can support me. What's the old guy doing — taking a nap? That's what I call confidence."

"I think he's sick," Chris said. "He hasn't been doing any betting or anything."

Foley said, "He must be one of those unconscious gamblers you hear about."

Dusk came quickly with the winter storm. Big wet snowflakes floated through the neon illumination of downtown Reno, mottling the artificial brightness and giving Virginia Street a pointillist appearance. Sandwiches planted his feet carefully as he made his way through the slush to the Hilton. Nothing was flying out of the airport, which put him in the classic gambler's predicament: stranded in town and down on his luck. All he could hope to do was wait things out cheap. He unbuttoned his coat and shook off the snowflakes when he entered the Hilton's casino. At the poker lounge, they put him in an empty seat right away. He bought in for fifty dollars, surrendering to the ignominy of a small-stakes game. Sitting at the table were three tourists, a couple of gimlet-eyed locals who watched his arrival with paranoid suspicion, and the blue-whiskered Easy, riffling a stack of dollar chips. Sandwiches laughed. Easy gave him an embarrassed look and said, "What the hell — it's action, ain't it?"

*

Carroll Shepherd was drinking again, and so was Russell Henry. They were sitting on barstools at the Taj Mahal. "My guy's gonna come in seventh," Shepherd said.

"What makes you think so?" Henry asked.

"Good question, asshole. Because there's six players left better'n him."

"Good answer," Henry said.

"Which means," Shepherd said, "this is gonna be a fifteen-thousand-dollar week for me. That's a personal record, if you're taking notes. Don't use my name — my patients wouldn't understand."

"How come I came here to write about winners," Henry said, "but the only people willing to give me interviews are losers?"

"Because that's Reno's second-favorite indoor sport," Shepherd told him. "Feeling sorry for yourself. I dropped four grand at the Circus, two at Harold's Club, three here, fifteen hundred at the MGM and maybe a grand at Harrah's. Plus expenses, plus two grand backing a loony in the poker tournament. Is that fifteen thousand? Close enough. It'd be a great life if I could afford it."

"I should have gone to Vegas," Henry said. "If I had to spend a week on a story I don't know how to write anyway, at least I could have done it in good weather."

"The kid's gunnybags," Shepherd said. "Very unprofessional choice of words. Don't quote me. I took a chance he's a great poker player and he turns out to be a space cadet. You know what I do now?"

"What?"

"I go back to San Mateo. I call my broker and tell him to dump the high-tech stock. I'll take a bath but at least I can write it off, so this trip costs me maybe only eighty cents on the dollar. You want to talk about losers? How's that for rationalizing? Then I'll put on my tweed jacket and stay sober for six months."

"I could write a first-person piece and do a tap-dance through it," Henry said. "Me and Hunter Thompson."

"The water wagon's okay," Shepherd said. "It beats the hell out of vomiting blood at two in the morning. But around June I'll tell myself I'm fifty-nine years old and I don't know I've got that much time left. I'll ask what's the harm in a few days at Reno with my friend Jose Cuervo, and here I'll be. Put that in your story."

"You were right about risk," Henry said. "That's what the story's got to be about. I want to put on a sandwich board."

"It's too cold out."

"So I'll wear it indoors. Come on. It's time for gonzo journalism."

"It's finally come to that, has it?" Shepherd said. "Well, I just happen to know the alley where those guys hang out in bad weather. Drink up."

Brian Bates was dealt two hearts in the hole: the deuce and the king, his own card and the Vic Houston card — and his first card up was mama, the queen of hearts. The signs couldn't be better. Across the table from him, Walsh opened for six hundred dollars. Betting clockwise, Epstein called, Bates called and Tobias called.

Walsh paired fours on the next card and bet a thousand. Epstein folded but Bates, who'd caught a black card, stayed in. So did Tobias, showing two mismatched cards. The dealer burned a card and dealt another round. Walsh and Tobias didn't get any apparent help, but Bates caught a fourth heart. He'd felt it coming — he was going to make his flush.

Harmon, the lawyer, pressed closer to the rope. Tobias hadn't gone in a pot for a long time; he'd seemed to be napping through most of the hands, resting on his pillow. Harmon told himself it was an act. He hasn't been getting cards so he's been milking the situation, that's all, setting the stage for a big move. His art is subtle, Harmon thought, as ephemeral as a skywriter's, disappearing in a moment and leaving nothing behind but a memory.

Walsh bet two thousand. Bates called and so did Tobias, spilling his chips. Harmon, on the sidelines, knew there were signals in the betting that he couldn't decipher. But he knew Tobias was in control. As the dealer sent out the fourth up cards, Harmon rose on his tiptoes for a better look.

Walsh watched carefully, too. This was his pot and he could build it into a big one if he got the breaks. Walsh was already sitting on a full house: he had a pair of fours and a seven showing, but he had a four and a seven in the hole and that gave him a winning hand if he ever saw one. It didn't matter what he drew for his last two cards, but he wanted the other players to improve so they'd stay in.

Bates caught a third heart showing and Walsh thought: beautiful — he made his flush. Now help the old man. Tobias was showing an eight-nine-jack of different suits, going for a straight. Give him a ten, Walsh prayed. But Tobias caught another nine, giving him a pair of nines showing and making him high on board. He checked immediately.

Okay, he's out, Walsh thought. But I'm going to take that flaky weightlifter apart like a goddamned Tinkertoy. Walsh bet two thousand dollars, the same as he'd bet the previous round. He knew that Bates, with a flush, had him figured for trip fours and would come back with a raise. And that, Walsh thought, is when I separate him from his jockstrap.

Up to a point, Walsh had everything figured out perfectly. He couldn't have known that Bates was holding cards invested with secret magical significance, but as it turned out that played right into his strategy. Because when Bates made his heart flush, he knew he'd caught the winning hand. The early promise of his mama, daddy and Brian cards had been fulfilled. A sensible part of his mind told him to drive Walsh out of the pot with a big raise so he couldn't make a full house on the last card, but Bates didn't listen to it. He'd stopped being sensible hours ago. The poker game was as unreal to him as one of his dreams by now, and he was putting his faith in signs. He knew the special cards wouldn't let him down. The king of hearts was protecting him; it would keep Walsh from filling up. So he wanted the New Yorker in the pot. His problem was to keep the old man in, too, with his straight. He had to bet just enough to convince Tobias and Walsh that he didn't have his flush yet.

Bates raised five thousand dollars.

Walsh thought: got him — the son of a bitch is hooked in the gonads! I'll call him this time and rape him on seventh street. It was Walsh's kind of hand; he had hard data. But he didn't reach for his chips right away. He didn't want to seem eager. First he waited for Tobias to fold. The dealer put his finger on the table, pointing at Tobias, and said, "Up to you, Lee Sherman. Costs you seven thousand."

And that was when Walsh's airtight logic failed him for the final time in the tournament. Tobias coughed.

All Harmon saw from the sidelines was that Tobias fumbled for his chips, coughing, and as he bounced on his pillow he wheezed something to the dealer that Harmon couldn't hear. But Tobias managed to push some chips out and Harmon watched as the dealer stacked them. He counted fourteen purple chips. Seven thousand dollars. Then he counted a stack of ten. And another stack of ten next to it. And another, and another. "He raises twenty thousand," the dealer said.

The TV lights clicked on. Under his chin, Tobias's pillow was stained pink. That old fox, Harmon thought — he checked and raised! As the lawyer watched, Walsh rose from his chair and stared unbelievingly across the curve of the table at Tobias's cards. Tobias, coughing, hugged his pillow.

"I don't have twenty," Walsh said. "I'm going all in." Quickly, he counted the chips in front of him. "Eleven thousand eight," he said to the dealer, moving his stack towards the pot, but the dealer extended a hand, stopping him from pushing his chips too far. If Bates called, they'd have a side pot.

Tobias continued to cough. In the flat white glare of the television lights, Harmon saw the pink stain spreading on Tobias's pillow. He turned to locate the registered nurse in the crowd.

Meanwhile, Walsh had the uneasy feeling that he'd missed something. But what? He had a full house, for chrissake. The pot was going to make him well. So why did he suddenly feel worried? What was the old man raising on?

Vic Houston could have told him. Owl Avery, too. It was obvious. But the Owl, in the seat next to Tobias, wasn't paying any attention to the pot. He was looking at Lee Sherman instead. Tobias was trying to say something. Across the table, Vic Houston was looking at Tobias, too, unaware that in the seat immediately to his left, Brian Bates was staring at him with deranged horror.

Bates's mind was bubbling. The synapses in his brain were crackling with poker equations. The first combination, the obvious one, was that the old man had a straight and since Walsh called his raise, then Walsh must have him beat with a full house. And if Walsh had a full house, that meant he had Bates's flush beat, too. But if he, Bates, could figure out that Walsh had a full house, then the old man sure as hell could figure it out. And the old man *raised*. So he must have a *higher* full house. Then why did Walsh call his raise?

The questions bounced through Bates's mind instantaneously and were followed just as immediately by the answer: because they're both fuckin' crazy, that's why! *I've* got the winning hand. Walsh has trip fours and the old man's bluffing, that's what's going on here. The old man checked originally, and Walsh didn't bet like he has a full house. So my raise was perfect — it fooled 'em both, just like I wanted. Bates ran the hand through in his mind, the discards printed like photographs in his memory, and he didn't see any tens. The old man's got a ten in the hole sure as shit, he thought, either a ten-seven or a ten-queen, which means he's got the straight. And that means I've got him beat. I've got both of 'em beat. They're tryin' to run one on the dumb Okie, and are they gonna be sorry.

It wasn't like Bates to move so fast. He barely had enough money to call Tobias's raise, and after he put his chips in the pot, he was left with practically nothing in front of him, maybe a couple of thousand. And instantly, he was terrified by the thought that he'd made a mistake. Vic Houston wasn't helping him. Bates looked at Houston to get a confident nod for his play, a conspiratorial wink, something, some sign of approval, but Houston ignored him. It was as if Houston didn't know or even care that his son was sitting right next to him. Instead, he was looking across the table at the coughing old man.

Bates felt trouble. Houston was rejecting him. The king of hearts refused to help him. He knew he'd somehow fucked up horribly, but he was losing touch. Vaguely, Bates was aware that the dealer had separated a side pot from the main pot and sent the final round of cards around. But it didn't matter. The big pink stain on the old man's pillow was in the shape of a heart. The old man, coughing, said something or did something, but it didn't matter because Bates saw a sight in the casino that destroyed what was left of him. The dealer told him the old man had checked and Bates said, "He checks? I check," and stared in horror beyond the table at the front row of the crowd of spectators. What he saw in his agitated state was the surreal sight of Carroll Shepherd and Russell Henry laughing and prancing, actually *prancing,* the sadistic bastards, each encumbered by a big sandwich board strapped over his shoulders that said I LOVE RENO. Except instead of the word "love," the sandwich boards had its symbol, a huge red heart. That made two hearts Bates was staring at, the deuce, a pathetic abandoned fool.

Lee Sherman Tobias had built a monster pot. More than eighty thousand dollars in chips sat in the center of the table and under the television lights all hell was breaking loose. Stretch Jackson and Archie Breen were trying to calm things down as the dealer figured out the hand. Harmon and the nurse had barged through the rope and were hovering over Tobias as Vic Houston, on his feet, yelled at the television people, ordering them to turn off their lights and get their camera off Tobias.

Tobias was oblivious to the confusion. He hadn't meant to check the last bet but he was losing his vision. His eyes hurt and he was seeing everything yellow, although that wasn't the worst of his problems. He was coughing up pink froth, great gouts of it like whipped aerated blood, but that wasn't the worst of his problems either. His worst problem was that he couldn't breathe. He was suffocating. He couldn't talk. He could only cough, and flop, and cough.

He'd won the pot. They'd decided that. But meanwhile the ambulance attendants had wheeled a stretcher in and Tobias felt himself being lifted. His mind registered something cold and wet beneath him. Melting snowflakes. A face loomed over him. He knew from the shape and the hat that it was Houston. Tobias couldn't draw air. His mouth was wide open, gasping for a breath, and he managed to cough out, or tried to, "I'm out. Cain't make it."

He had the winning cards of course, a full house. He'd had three jacks wired all the way. The hand knocked Walsh out of the tournament and reduced Bates to a pittance. The dealer pushed the pot over to Tobias's empty seat as Stretch Jackson waved his arms over the confusion and announced a break in the tournament until they could get reorganized.

THE FIRST ANNUAL STRETCH JACKSON
SEVEN-CARD STUD POKER CLASSIC

Standings as of 5:50 P.M. Thursday

1.	Vic Houston, Texas	$105,100
2.	William "Hoo-Hoo" Avery, Arizona	97,500
3.	Lee Sherman Tobias, Missouri	94,200
4.	Jerry Corbett, California	71,000
5.	Shayna Levinson, Washington	69,100
6.	Art Epstein, California	61,200
7.	Brian Bates, Oklahoma	1,900

Play to resume: as soon as possible

Tobias's stretcher disappeared into the casino, security guards breaking a path through vacationers who grudgingly stepped aside for it, while behind it at the poker table, the television lights continued to pour their flat white glare over the disorder. Before calm could restore itself, Vic Houston started to cry — he sat down in his seat with tears blinking over his eyelids. Houston hadn't understood the words Tobias had wheezed at him as he was wheeled off, but he'd caught the drift of the message and he knew he couldn't kid himself anymore that Lee Sherman was hanging on. Tobias was being carried off the battlefield for the serious kind of attention you only find in a hospital. Houston had too much country in him to hide his natural feelings for a friend — without embarrassment, he pulled a big white handkerchief out of his back pocket and mopped his face.

Brian Bates couldn't stand it. His sudden isolation was too painful. In his most private and secret fantasies, Bates had anointed Houston the king of hearts, the very daddy card itself, and now Houston sat next to him crying in public. Men don't cry! Houston had deceived him. The king of hearts hadn't helped him as a hole card, had withheld his magic, had openly ignored him, rejected him, betrayed him in front of the whole world. He was a fraud. Bates had no daddy. No momma. He was alone, alone again, always and completely alone. At the sight of Houston crying, he groaned.

At first Bates didn't hear the sounds he was making. He was broke. He'd lost the hand. The magnitude of his desolation overwhelmed him and he pounded his fist on the green tabletop. He was under indictment. He'd lost his money. He'd lost his wife. His home. His children. The shrink was laughing at him. Everybody was laughing at him. He was desperate and pitiable, with no resources remaining, no inner strength left to draw on.

Bates sobbed out loud. He didn't know he was doing it. His chest was tight, his face hot, his eyes burning, and he moaned and pounded on the table. The TV lights were splashing him, the players and the nearby railbirds staring at him, but he was in too much pain to notice. He was still alone after all the years, in the jungle blackness again, in Nam, trapped in the labyrinth, drowning in the whirlpool, defenseless in his nightmare. He needed help, somebody to protect him.

Marlene had hold of his arm and was pulling him to his feet. He grabbed her by the shoulders and begged for help. She said, "Briny, come," and slowly, as his surroundings came back into focus, Bates

226 //

realized he was the center of attention at the table. In an agony of shame and misery, he clung to his wife and allowed her to hurry him off from the poker tournament, into the crowd, away from the bright lights that illuminated the shine of his tear-stained face.

In the silence left by his departure, Shayna Levinson looked around the table and said, "What is this all of a sudden — a soap opera?"

Stretch Jackson had an arbitration problem. While the players waited, he and Archie Breen conferred for a few minutes and then returned to the group. With Breen at his side, Stretch sat down, leaning forward and speaking no louder than necessary for his drawl to carry across the table. The gathering would have struck a casual passerby as incidental except for the overlarge stacks of chips sitting on the table. And the TV lights, still glaring. The television reporter, out of the camera's frame, had her arm extended with a microphone pointing at Stretch Jackson.

"Here's the story," Stretch told the players. "First, y'all been at it for two hours. So we gonna raise the stakes. The ante's goin' to five hundred and low hand'll bring it in for a thousand. Ya got it?" Again, he held up his fingers to make his point. "Okay. Now, about Lee Sherman. The rules say you can leave your seat for ten minutes but after that, you play a dead hand."

"So to speak," Shayna said.

"But that don't apply here," Stretch went on. "They takin' Lee Sherman to the hospital, so it ain't like he's on a ten-minute break. What we gonna do is withdraw him from the tournament." He waited a moment for the information to sink in. Then he said, "About his money. I don't like this any more'n y'all, but we gotta divide it."

"Hell we do," Houston said.

"There ain't no way around it." Stretch handed Archie Breen a printed sheet of tournament rules, which they'd all received with their entry forms.

"Rule Six," Breen read. "If a player withdraws from the tournament, his remaining money will be divided equally among the remaining players."

"You're jumpin' the gun," Houston argued. "Let's break for an hour. Give Lee Sherman time to get fixed up and get back."

"I'd go for that," Art Epstein said.

"Second the motion," the Owl chimed in.

Softly Stretch said, "Amen. I appreciate it. But the fact is, Lee Sherman ain't comin' back in an hour."

"We don't know that," Houston said.

"Yeah, we do," Stretch said. "Archie?"

Breen said unhappily, "He's been in the hospital the last two nights. He shouldn't even of been here today. He signed out against orders."

"You know that for a fact?" Houston asked.

Breen nodded. "I was over there. The doctor said they almost lost him once. He ain't gonna be back today. They wouldn't of let him out, except he had a lawyer. He didn't want me to say anything," Breen added lamely.

"Damn," Houston said. He lifted his hat and brushed his hair back with his hand. "Then give him his money. He won it."

"Cain't," Stretch said. "Wish I could."

The words sat there awkwardly until the Owl piped up. "Friends, let's give Stretch a little support," he said. "Fair's fair. We have a problem but Stretch didn't cause it. He's trying to solve it."

"Man, this is such crap," Shayna complained. "What about Mister Macho there?" She pointed at Bates's empty seat.

Stretch said, "He's got ten minutes."

"That's not what I mean. He's down to a couple of antes. We do it your way, he gets a free buy-in. That's bullshit."

Jerry Corbett offered quietly, "I think we should hear Shayna's plan."

Shayna shot him a venomous look. She didn't have a plan. She just didn't want Bates getting a free ride back into the tournament.

Stretch stood up and said, "Okay, that's it. We'll divvy up Lee Sherman's chips and get back at it." He added, almost as an afterthought, "Good luck." The implication wasn't lost on the players: the poker tournament had finally been narrowed down to its six prize-winners.

Epstein couldn't resist saying to Shayna, with a grin of transparent insincerity, "*Mazel tov.*"

"Up yours," she answered.

With the distribution of Tobias's chips, each player received a bonus of almost sixteen thousand dollars. They high-carded each other to round off the odd hundred dollars; Bates, who hadn't returned, was automatically declared a low draw. Meanwhile Archie Breen and a security guard were bringing in racks of pink chips and exchanging them for the brown hundreds and most of the purple five-hundreds. The pink chips were worth a thousand dollars each. When the swap was completed, a new dealer, a woman this time, shuffled and cut the cards. The tournament resumed.

THE FIRST ANNUAL STRETCH JACKSON SEVEN-CARD STUD POKER CLASSIC

Standings as of 6:05 P.M. Thursday (Prize-winners)

1.	Vic Houston, Texas	$121,500
2.	William "Hoo-Hoo" Avery, Arizona	113,000
3.	Jerry Corbett, California	87,000
4.	Shayna Levinson, Washington	84,500
5.	Art Epstein, California	76,500
6.	Brian Bates, Oklahoma	17,500

Upstairs in his room, Brian Bates ducked his head into a basin of cold water. Marlene handed him a towel and as he dried off he looked at her with an unaccustomed meekness, aware that within a short span of minutes their relationship had undergone a basic change. He'd cried in front of her. He'd sat on the bed while she'd held him, and he'd cried in her arms. Things between them couldn't be the same after that. On the collar of her blouse there remained a smudge of wetness from his tears. She looked at him steadily as he finished with the towel and said, "You needed to get that out of your system."

Bates didn't answer. Had she sounded smug, he would have hated it. But she didn't. She was still her. He was still him. The earth hadn't opened up and swallowed him. Yet something deep inside had changed with his crying jag. He felt emptied. And despite his problems, he felt a floaty sense of relief. He could handle his problems. Somehow he'd manage. He looked sheepishly at Marlene.

She said, "I know it bothers you, Briny. Breaking down in front of those people."

He wanted to deny that he'd broken down but his intuition warned him against it. He wasn't the only one whose mood had changed; there was something different about Marlene, too. She was softer. For the first time since she'd showed up in Reno, she seemed receptive to him. Sensing the importance of his behavior during the next few minutes, Bates told her exactly what he was feeling. He said, "I need you. I don't have a life without you."

"I need you," Marlene said. "What are we going to do?"

Now her eyes were wet. "Hey, don't cry," Bates said. "We'll be okay."

"We can't start over," she said. "We are where we are."

"I know."

"Where are we?"

"I don't know." Bates found some Kleenex and sat on the bed next to her, drying her tears. "We're in trouble," he said.

"I know." Marlene put her head on his shoulder. "You have to go back to the game," she said.

"I can't."

"We need the money."

"What else is new?"

"Are you laughing?" she asked.

"Do I sound like I'm laughing?"

"Yes." Marlene pushed herself away to get a look at his face. "You *are* laughing," she said.

Bates raised his hands. "I don't know what else to do. We hit bottom. We're still here."

"You're laughing and you're crying," she said.

"I'm not crying. I don't cry. I tried it once and didn't like it."

"Whatever you say." Gently, Marlene took the Kleenex from him and dabbed at his cheeks.

"You're laughing now," Bates said.

"Because we're in such a mess."

"I've been having nightmares. Did I tell you?"

"You always have nightmares."

"These are bad. But they have good parts, when you're in them. Do you think I need a shrink?"

"Do you think so?"

"I don't know. I'm partners with one here. *He* needs a shrink."

"Let's go back downstairs," she said.

"I can't. I made a fool of myself."

"It doesn't matter — they're strangers. Do it for the money. Briny?"

"What?"

"This is going to sound terrible. You know how I always said you didn't have to be John Wayne for me? How it was okay to show your emotions?"

"Yes."

"Well, it's true. But it's okay to be John Wayne sometimes. I'll be with you."

"Marlene?"

"What?"

"I think we're all fucked up."

"So what else is new?" They left the room and walked holding hands down the hallway to the elevator bank. "Do you still have a chance to win?" she asked.

"I don't see how."

"Then why are you laughing?"

He kissed the tip of her nose. "Same reason you are."

The elevator arrived. They stepped inside and pushed the down button.

After Tobias's chips were distributed, the five players left at the table anted up and resumed the final round of the poker tournament. Clockwise from the dealer, they were Jerry Corbett, Owl Avery, Shayna Levinson, Art Epstein and Vic Houston. To Houston's left was Brian Bates's empty seat with seventeen thousand, five hundred dollars sitting in front of it. Houston, dealt a deuce up, opened for the mandatory thousand dollars. The dealer took a pink chip from Bates's stack and put it in the pot. Bates's hand was showing an ace but that was immaterial because Bates wasn't there.

Jerry Corbett was showing an ace, too, but he had nothing in the hole to back it up. He knew somebody was going to make a run at Bates's stack of chips but with three players sitting behind him, Jerry had bad position. Reluctantly, he folded. That put it to the Owl, whose analysis was identical to Jerry's. The Owl didn't have a hand either, but his situation was marginally better because he only had two players sitting behind him. The Owl figured it was worth a shot. He called the thousand.

Shayna Levinson, on the Owl's left, didn't know what to do. She'd already decided that if the Owl raised, she'd fold, and if he folded, she'd raise. So instead, she thought, the son of a bitch just calls. Go figure. Shayna had a pair of deuces in the hole, which were all but worthless, and she still had Epstein behind her to worry about. She knew she ought to fold but she also knew that, one way or another, Bates's stack would be in the pot before the hand was over. She called the thousand, flipping a pink chip in with her thumbnail, and instantly knew it was a mistake because sitting where he was, Epstein had to raise. She should have made the raise herself; at least then she might have learned something.

Epstein, showing a queen, raised five thousand dollars.

"Surprise, surprise," Shayna said. There was no mystery to anybody at the table about what was going on. Epstein had position, first of all, and second, he had a hand. How good, they couldn't say. A pair of ladies maybe. Houston, who had garbage, folded without a second thought. As soon as he did, the dealer counted five pink chips from Bates's stack and deposited them in the pot.

That moved the bet back to the Owl, whose chances of improving weren't worth five thousand dollars to him. He folded.

Shayna said, "Thanks a lot, Hoo-Hoo." His pass left it to her to keep Epstein honest. She kicked herself for not raising earlier. If she had, she'd be in the driver's seat instead of Epstein. The question was how strong Epstein was and how good her own two deuces were. Not very, she knew, since Houston had already folded a deuce.

She said, "I want to make sure I understand." Shayna ignored the woman dealer and asked Stretch Jackson, "I can tap Macho out but he can't win the pot, right?" She knew the answer. She was just stalling to see what kind of a reaction she'd get from Epstein. He could be bluffing. Maybe she'd pick up a clue if she could make him nervous.

"I still say it's a lousy rule," Shayna complained. "This isn't poker. It's fish in a barrel." She separated five pink chips from her stack and put ten more beside them, threatening to re-raise. Epstein didn't care. He just smiled, and it was obvious to Shayna that he was no more worried about her raising than he was about a chandelier falling on his head. "Aw, the hell with it," she said, folding her cards. "I didn't come here to rip off some guy who can't defend himself."

Jerry Corbett said, "Dear, even for you that's a cheap shot." The tone of the remark brought a chuckle from Houston and the Owl.

Shayna colored and said, "You should know about cheap, dear."

The pot had eighteen thousand dollars in it, with another eleven thousand still sitting at Bates's empty seat. One more bet and the money would be Epstein's. Even before the dealer sent the next card around, Epstein shoved eleven pink chips in the pot, pointed at Bates's stack and said, "He's all in."

Then two things happened. One, the dealer gave Epstein a second up-card and plunked another ace on the table at Bates's hand. Two, as the dealer moved the last of Bates's chips into the pot, Bates materialized from out of nowhere. He popped into view from behind Epstein's back, slipped past Houston in a hurry and dropped into his seat at the table. "What's happening?" he asked.

"He's eligible!" Shayna said, extending her hands over the pot. "He got back in time!" She shot Epstein a malicious look.

The dealer, keeping her eye on the pot, crooked an index finger for help. Stretch was there, leaning over the table. He said, "Play it out."

Bates, puzzled, asked, "What is it?" The change in his appearance since he'd fled the table in tears was remarkable. He looked fresh again, and composed. Stretch explained the situation to him and Bates said, "You mean to tell me I left here with two thousand bucks and now I'm in for that pot? You mean part of it."

"The whole thing, pardner," Stretch told him.

"There's gotta be forty grand in there," Bates said.

Shayna was enjoying the sudden turnaround of Epstein's fortune. She'd love to see him taken down a peg. "Two of the best," she said. "Master Bates and Epp the schlepp. It's show-and-tell time, fellas."

Art Epstein looked amused. For some reason, he was starting to laugh. When Bates turned over his hole cards, exposing the case ace, Epstein roared. On the sidelines, Jackie started laughing, too. "What is it?" Chris asked her. "Beats me," Jackie said, "but Art's sure having fun." Jackie's laughing started Chris laughing, and the laughter spread from the two of them to the nearby railbirds and then rippled through the entire spectators' gallery. The poker players, in the bright wash of the television lights, were suddenly surrounded by an epidemic of hilarity. Stretch grinned, playing to the crowd, and the Owl started jiggling with amusement, which triggered a bark from Vic Houston. Even the dealer began to laugh, holding up the play of the hand.

"What's so funny?" Shayna demanded.

Jerry Corbett restrained himself, but he knew what the hilarity was about. It was a delayed reaction to Tobias's collapse. The old man had been carted off unceremoniously, and in the heat of the moment and the confusion that followed, the players hadn't ventilated their feelings. Now, with the flimsy excuse of Epstein breaking up, they were using laughter as a catharsis. Jerry felt a rush of camaraderie for the other five. For the first time, they were a group.

Epstein, meanwhile, was trying to explain himself. "I don't have a hand," he said. He flipped over his hole cards, disclosing that his queen wasn't even paired. "I've got position, I run one, and I lose to a guy who's not even here? I think that's funny. I'm such a hotshot I can't even beat an empty chair!"

But there were still three cards to be dealt before the hand was over and as the table calmed down, the dealer resumed her work. The next two cards didn't help Bates but they gave Epstein four to an inside straight, king high. He needed a ten to fill it, although if Bates paired anything to go with his three aces, a straight wouldn't be good enough. Still, Epstein thought, tens had been sticking to him.

His luck held: Epstein's seventh card was a ten. That meant Bates had gone from losing the hand to winning it and back to losing it, all without having the slightest say in the matter, and he still had a chance to win it if he caught a full house. His last card came out — a split-second of suspense as it dropped — and it didn't match anything in his hand. He lost to the straight. Bates was out. Epstein had leap-frogged into third place in the tournament.

Stretch kept the award ceremony brief. He held up a thick, banded packet of hundred-dollar bills for the crowd's attention. "Ten thousand dollars," he announced, waving the cash. "Neighbors, give a hand to the sixth-place winner. Brian Bates, a mighty tough player."

Bates accepted the money and Stretch's handshake. "Can I say something?" he asked. The lights were in his eyes and a microphone was in front of his face and since nobody stopped him, he said, "First I want to thank Stretch Jackson for being fair to me. I want to thank the Taj Mahal. And I want everybody to meet my wife. Come up here, honey."

Marlene stepped over the rope and into the lights. Bates put his arm around her. "I want you to see who I was playing for," he said. Bates had lost his audience by then but he didn't care. A grin split his face and he said, holding up the money and squinting into the casino, "Two grand of this is yours, doc. But you better hurry to collect it, because we're takin' the first plane back to God's country."

Even before he finished, the television lights blinked off. But Bates didn't feel deserted, not with Marlene's arm wrapped tightly around his waist. The last time the crowd had seen him, he was crying. Now he was laughing. They probably thought he was crazy, but at the moment Brian Bates didn't care what anybody else in the world thought. Right there on the casino floor, he kissed his wife and closed his eyes and saw all the bright lights he needed in his life.

The five remaining players settled down. The laughing jag was over, the melodrama behind them, and the contestants dug in for a siege of serious gambling. There wasn't enough of a gap between Houston in first place, with one hundred and twenty thousand dollars, and Shayna in fifth place, with eighty-three thousand, to give any player a distinct advantage. It would take a lot of five-hundred-dollar antes to make a dent in anybody's stack, and anyone who wanted an edge was going to have to find a way to create it. The bigger the stakes got, and the fewer the players, the less the tournament's outcome would depend on luck and the more it would depend on skill and guile.

Alone of the remaining players, Vic Houston knew he was going to win. They were well past the hazardous opening rounds of free-for-all and once the game got this close to the wire, he was in his element. Houston couldn't conceive of not winning; he only had to play his game. Owl Avery was just as confident about his own chances, except for the minor question of whether he could whip his old friend Houston at the end. But he knew it would come down to that. Hoo-Hoo could guarantee it; inevitably it would be him and Houston left at the table, at which point you could take

236 / /

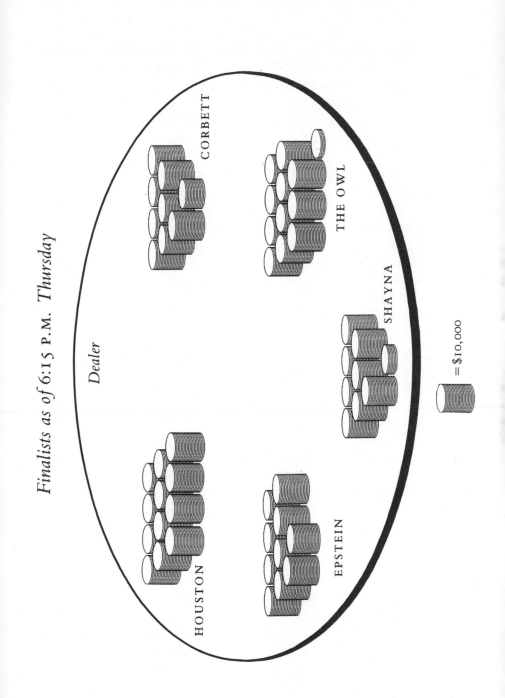

Finalists as of 6:15 P.M. Thursday

CORBETT

THE OWL

SHAYNA

Dealer

HOUSTON

EPSTEIN

▌ = $10,000

your pick, even money. There remained only the pesky matter of eliminating the amateurs, and the Owl figured that problem would take care of itself in short order.

In Art Epstein's opinion, however, the game wasn't as cut-and-dried as the professionals thought. Epstein was the only player left who'd had to scrap to get to the final table, and he felt stronger because of it. Unlike the others, he'd played the first half of the tournament in rotten luck, catching a string of second-best hands against the unconscious kid. But he'd maneuvered the mine field; the kid was long gone and Epstein was in third place. Besides, he had a secret weapon, which was that he didn't give a damn. He was having too much fun. After two days with Jackie, his grim attitude about the poker tournament had melted almost into nonchalance and he was playing better because of it. Epstein had found his groove.

Neither Jerry Corbett nor Shayna Levinson were thinking about winning. They were thinking about cash. Shayna, who was only in the tournament for twelve hundred and fifty dollars of her own money, was already assured of at least fifteen thousand on her investment. But that was if she only came in fifth, and she didn't see any good reason why she couldn't beat Corbett and Epstein. Shayna figured she had third place all but sewed up, for fifty grand. And who could say she wouldn't take it all? One thing she knew was that she wanted the win more than Houston or the Owl. They already had their reputations but this was Shayna's big chance to make hers. She just had to be careful not to step into quicksand. And she had an extra incentive, too, because she was goddamned if she'd let Corbett come in ahead of her. It suited Shayna fine that they had a woman dealing; it reminded her of how far she'd come since her own early days and it goaded her to keep fighting.

Jerry Corbett was getting tired; three days of nonstop acting had sapped his stamina. But he was feeling mellow — he'd be the happiest man in the world to come out of the tournament in fifth place. He thought back to September, when he'd decided to risk his nest egg in the tournament, and he thought of how as recently as the night before he'd been reconciled to losing the money and chalking it up to experience. But now, guaranteed no worse than fifth place, he was on top of the world. Hell, he could still win the whole ball of wax. He hadn't been in trouble yet, had he? The others still thought he was a woman, for pete's sake. He had their number and they didn't know anything at all about him. Take it a scene at a time, he told himself; you could still be in for a long night of poker.

All five of them played on the cautious side during the next hour or so, waiting for good cards, and the game developed a pattern. After the antes and the forced opening bet, there would be thirty-five hundred dollars in the pot. The typical raise would be two thousand dollars, sometimes three and once in a while five thousand. Usually the raise came from the high hand showing, but whoever made it, the raise was taken as a clear signal by the other players and what it said was: *I've got winning cards right now.* Anybody who wanted to draw out against the best hand would have to pay to do it, and they all understood that the next raise wouldn't be trivial. Once a player got committed to the pot, the price of poker could suddenly get steep.

Casual spectators soon became bored; the game didn't manifest any of the high drama they expected from no-limit poker. The hands were usually settled in the first couple of rounds of betting, and the winning cards were never exposed because the player holding them never got called. After a while, even the more sophisticated railbirds were growing restless. "I'd rather watch paint dry," somebody muttered. But they knew the tedium would continue until the cards warmed up or somebody at the table decided to change his strategy. The players weren't in a hurry, though; they had all the time in the world. As far as they were concerned, the name of the game was patience, not poker.

Shayna felt as if she were in a game with four department-store dummies. She was the only animated player at the table, the only one giving it any chatter. She stood up, she turned her chair around to straddle it, she hassled the dealer, harangued the other players —

not that any of it accomplished anything for her. The three men stayed slumped in their seats, playing the game with their wrists and fingertips, speaking in monosyllables if they said anything at all, only their eyes showing any life. And Corbett kept that stupid smile on her face, Shayna thought, sitting there like she had a Hershey bar in her mouth and an icicle up her ass.

Art Epstein broke the pattern for a moment. He raised five thousand on an ace and won the antes. On the next hand he did it again, and on the hand after that he raised five thousand on a seven showing. The others let him have that pot, too, and by the time they realized he'd run a few on them, it was too late to do anything about it. He dropped out of the next hands, playing tight again. But he'd netted nine thousand on his little spurt and wedged the game open a hair. After that, nobody bothered with two-thousand-dollar raises anymore. They escalated to a three-thousand-dollar minimum as if by unspoken agreement.

The TV reporter said to Stretch Jackson, "I thought we'd get some excitement by now."

"It's there, honey," Stretch told her. "You just cain't see it. When the targets are shootin' back, it tends to change the nature of your huntin' style."

Shayna called, "How about a new deck?" The dealer obliged. She collected the red deck she'd been using, squared it up and held it over her shoulder. Archie Breen took it and handed her a blue deck. She discarded the jokers, fanned the deck on the table to check it front and back, then mixed and shuffled the new cards. A cocktail waitress circled the table, emptying ashtrays. Shayna and the Owl told her to bring more coffee. Houston ordered a shot of Wild Turkey. "Water back, honey," he said. Epstein ordered the same and said, "Beer chaser."

Jerry Corbett didn't order anything. On the next hand, he won four thousand dollars by calling the Owl's raise on the first round, then raising five thousand himself when he paired up on fourth street. The Owl folded. But Hoo-Hoo won the money back on the next hand, from Epstein. Then Epstein won five thousand from

Shayna. Shayna won three from Houston. With the new deck, money was moving around the table faster. The pots were still small, but a feeling came off the game like that of an ice jam about to break.

Jerry Corbett called the Owl again, for nine thousand. The Owl turned right around and won it back. He would have won a lot more if Jerry had called his raise, but Jerry had second thoughts just in time. Whoops, he thought, I almost stepped off the cliff on that one. It's amazing, he thought; the man gives off nothing. No vibes. No body language. No emotions. Nothing. Hoo-Hoo, and Houston, and more and more Epstein, too — they're ice. The only player Jerry could read was Shayna, and he'd figured her out a long time ago. As usual, she was riding him, but Jerry was picking up an undertone of desperation in her voice and he thought he knew why. Houston and the Owl weren't mixing it up with each other. If one went in the pot, the other tended to stay out. That was because they respected each other, but Jerry knew there was another factor involved; they were waiting. Why look for trouble when it was inevitable that the two women would try to knock each other out of the game? Jerry knew Shayna had figured that out, too, and then it struck him: she was buying into it. She was willing. She can't reach the others but she thinks she can get to me, Jerry thought. That was the edge he was hearing in her voice, and it suddenly suited him fine because it gave him an idea. It was chancy and he'd need a break, but what the hell, he thought — he was money ahead anyway and it was time somebody broke the game open.

He set the trap. The next time Shayna raised, Jerry stayed with her. Another card came out and Shayna checked. After hesitating, so did Jerry. On fifth street Shayna bet five thousand and stared across the table at Jerry. He allowed a perturbed look to cross his face, then folded his cards and said in a small voice, "I didn't think you were that strong, dear." It was the first time he'd spoken to Shayna in an hour.

"You have to pay to find out, dear," Shayna said.

Jerry sat out the next few hands and then went into another pot with Shayna. Except this time he got caught between her and Houston. Jerry and the Texan had both called Shayna's raise and on the next round of betting, she put ten pink chips in the pot and said, "I've got you beat, cowboy."

Houston didn't argue. "I believe you do," he said, and folded.

That put it to Jerry. He didn't do anything right away. He just frowned, as if he had a headache. I should get an Oscar for this, he thought. He wished Chris could share the experience with him. Jerry knew Shayna had a hand and wanted him in the pot. Almost like an electric current, he could feel every cell in her body pleading for him to call the raise. He reached for his chips. But then he pulled his hand back and looked at his hole cards. He pursed his lips. It was uncharacteristic behavior for him. He seemed to have lost his focus. He reached for his chips again but changed his mind a second time. "I think you're buying, Shayna," he said, sounding doubtful.

"There's one way to find out, sister," Shayna answered.

Jerry shook his head and muttered to himself, "She's buying." He folded his cards slowly, as if it caused him pain. Shayna raked in the pot and Jerry said to Owl Avery on his left, "She bought that one. Wouldn't you say?"

The Owl tapped an ash from his cigar and said, "Victor didn't think so."

Jerry contorted his face, then closed his eyes and took a deep breath, visibly forcing himself to relax. He seemed to have gone through a crisis. Almost immediately, he sat forward and rearranged his chips, putting them in stacks of ten for counting. His two indecisive calls against Shayna had cost him about ten thousand dollars and if anybody suddenly looked worried and unsure of himself, maybe even on the verge of doing something desperate, that was Jerry Corbett. He sat out the next few hands. Surreptitiously he rearranged his chips into uneven stacks, as if he didn't want to be caught counting them. None of his behavior was lost on the other players and Jerry only hoped he wasn't overdoing it. He knew they all had him pegged as a loser; he was finally just giving them some evidence for their belief, baiting his trap. But he still needed a hand.

He caught the beginning of one. Jerry was dealt two jacks in the hole and a four up. He opened for the thousand dollars. The Owl called with an ace. Shayna, showing an eight, raised three thousand and Epstein and Houston both folded behind her. Jerry waited.

"C'mon, sister," Shayna said. "Fish or cut bait."

Jerry said, "I really wish you'd stop calling me sister."

"Tough," Shayna said. "You in or out?"

"I'm in!" Jerry said impetuously. He thought: *she's got a pair of eights, maybe an ace kicker.*

Quietly, the Owl put three thousand dollars in the pot, too. *A low pair, playing the percentages,* Jerry thought.

The dealer burned a card, then dealt around. She dropped a jack on top of Jerry's four. The Owl caught a three. Shayna paired her eight. "Pair bets," the dealer said.

Shayna said, "Well, well, well. What do you say we make it six thousand? Three on each."

She's got trip eights, sure as hell, Jerry thought. Both of his up cards were clubs. He stalled again, trying to look like somebody agonizing over whether to chase a club flush. Shayna wanted him in; he could feel it. He glanced to his left at the Owl's up cards, as if he were worried about the Owl re-raising.

"Wake up, Jerry, they're throwing dirt on you," Shayna said. She added, "Sister."

Jerry flinched. Putting a tremor in his voice, he said, "I don't think you have anything." He put six pink chips in the pot with a quick motion that suggested it wasn't his idea, that his hand was acting on its own against his mind's better judgment. The Owl folded behind him; no surprise in that. Just Jerry and Shayna were left in the pot.

Another card came out, the third up card. Jerry was aware beneath his concentration that the audience's restlessness had quieted. His heart was thumping and he could feel his adrenaline flowing, but he had to use the pump to make his excitement look like fear, not confidence. He'd hooked Shayna, but was he good enough to land her? Jerry caught a four as the cards dropped, giving him a hidden full house, with only a pair of fours showing on top. Shayna's hand didn't improve.

"Pair of fours are new," the dealer said. "Eights are still high."

"Eights bet ten thousand," Shayna said.

Got her! Jerry thought. He knew Shayna had him figured for four to a flush, maybe two pairs or, at best, trip fours. Any way she could see it, she had him beat with her three eights and she didn't want to lose him. That's what her ten-thousand-dollar bet was about. Any less would look too obvious, any more could scare him out. Ten thousand was just right to suck him in. Then on sixth street she'd jam it home.

Jerry could barely contain himself. Chrissy, Chrissy, he thought, why can't I share this with you? The pattern was so perfect. He'd set it up beautifully. He'd begun the bluff twenty minutes earlier, setting the stage for exactly this possibility. Twice before he'd gone eyeball to eyeball with Shayna and blinked. Now she'd think he had to brazen it out. Pride alone wouldn't let him back down a third time. But more than that, he'd been giving every indication that he'd finally cracked up after three days in the pressure cooker. Whatever he did now would look like desperation, a frantic last grab at luck because his self-control had shattered.

His hand shaking, Jerry called Shayna's ten-thousand-dollar bet. Again the cards came out, the fourth up cards. Neither player helped. "Eights still talk," the dealer said.

Shayna knew exactly what she was going to do but she took a moment, pretending to calculate. Her act was pathetically transparent to Jerry: she wanted him to think she was unsure of herself. I knew it six months ago in Gardena, Jerry thought. I spelled it out for Chris that night in September. Poker's my game. Against Jerry, Shayna might as well have been playing with all of her cards exposed. He could see right into her. And strangely, he felt a tender affection. Maybe that's how the lion feels towards the antelope, he thought, the coyote for the lamb. One might have to die so the other can live, but the killing isn't done in enmity or hate. It's done in love. In a peculiar way, now that she was his, Jerry loved Shayna. But he had to fight the feeling. His big scene was coming up and he couldn't let love interfere with it. Or could he? Maybe he could at that. He was an actor — he'd give them acting. If he couldn't do it on method, he'd do it on technique.

The pot had more than forty thousand dollars in it, two years' pay for some people. The money meant nothing. It was only chips. Jerry was at one with Shayna. He knew she heard the silence, too, felt the crowd's tension every bit as much as he did. They were at the center together.

"The eights say twenty thousand," Shayna finally said, breaking the stillness as something like a sigh rippled through the crowd. They knew she had him; Jerry was in too deep — he had to call. Inch by inch Shayna had lured him in and now the noose was dropping over his neck. Jerry watched Shayna act out her role too late, with too little. Trying to look like someone whistling in a graveyard, like someone making a show of false courage — oh, how she was scheming to get him into the pot — Shayna said as Jerry hesitated, "Don't let anything stop you but fear or better judgment." And added the final insult. "*Sister.*"

Jerry ignored the bet. He looked at Shayna and said, without inflection at first, "Sister, huh? Do you know how long you've been handing me that crap? Months. You started it in Vegas. You've been jabbing me with it here ever since we started. You know something? You're acting like a horse's ass. Sisterhood doesn't mean shit to me."

Shayna looked at him as if he'd lost his mind. "Sisterhood doesn't cut any ice," Jerry said. "Maybe you've got a sex problem. Maybe you've got a personality problem. Maybe you've got a mental problem. But one thing you can take to the bank, you've sure as hell got a poker problem." The hell with method — he could do it on technique alone. To feel love and show outrage? Jerry was pulling it off. With his voice hardening and dropping, he said, "I'm not your sister, you pinhead. I'm not anybody's sister!"

From the sidelines, Chris was the first to see it coming. She recognized the move. An instant later everybody saw it, although it didn't register immediately. Jerry's hand went to his head and ripped off his wig. Only then did the TV lights blink on, and for a further moment the spectators stood immobile, as if caught in a freeze frame.

At the table Jerry was saying, "Now — do you want to play poker or do you want to play women's lib? Because I've had it with your bullshit." Still his hands were moving, unbuttoning his blouse, digging out the falsies and tossing them away. Now Jerry felt the shock wave from the crowd, sensed the rumble, heard the hoots beginning. He saw Shayna's eyes widen, her mouth gape. "I don't think you've got a hand," he said. "I think my three fours beat you. I think you're full of it. I think you've been full of it all day. I'm calling your twenty" — he'd eyeballed Shayna's stack down to the last chip —" and I raise you forty-one thousand bucks. Now, make up your mind whether you want to bullshit or play cards. And take all the time you want, *sister,* because I'm going up to my room to change clothes."

Jerry Corbett pushed his entire stack into the pot, all but two chips, a pink one and a purple one, and he stood up and told Stretch Jackson, "I'm in all the way. I'm in for the last card and I'm tapping that bitch out if she calls. And I'm taking a ten-minute break starting now, okay?"

Stretch shrugged, conceding the point, and Jerry left the poker table in a hurry, sidestepping the television reporter, pushing himself like a fullback into the pandemonium he'd caused and elbowing through the crowd into the main aisle of the casino. Halfway to the elevator bank he felt Chris run up from behind him and grab his hand. Jerry pulled her forward, moving fast, and not until he was sure he was out of earshot did he stop and give her a hug, lifting her off her feet and saying jubilantly, "I nailed her, honey! We're in first place!"

*

Up in their room, Jerry went to work on his face with cold cream and a towel. "Lay out some clothes for me, will you, hon?" he asked. "I don't want to get hit by a time call like that Bates guy."

Chris sorted through the closet. She was caught in a confusion of emotions. On the one hand, she was relieved that the charade was over, even though she'd been enjoying her own acting role. But on the other hand, Jerry had changed things too abruptly. He'd been doing so well; Chris worried that this quick switch would ruin his luck. But most of all, she didn't understand what he was up to.

Jerry was beside himself with elation, though. "God damn, but I set that up exquisitely," he said. "Chris honey, that was the best poker sequence I've ever put together. Ever!"

"Are you going to tell me what your hand is?"

"Full house. I've got jacks full and she's going to call!"

"How do you know?"

"Because there's a hundred and twenty thousand bucks in the pot, sweetheart. And she thinks I've got three fours! I've got the hex on her more ways than you can count. Chrissy, I'm running a number on her I started a half an hour ago."

He was working with soap and water now. "How can you be so sure?" Chris asked. "I don't understand why you left the table."

"It's part of the bluff. Besides, if I stuck around down there, I'd scare her out of the pot. Look at this puss — I can't keep a straight face. But we have to get back." Jerry looked at his wrist. "Oh, terrific," he said, taking off his woman's watch and replacing it with a man's Timex. "Anything else?" he asked.

"Just your earrings."

"That's cute. Look, I know I'm flying high," Jerry said, "but don't worry — I'm on top of things." He climbed into a pair of trousers and put on a shirt and sweater. Combing his hair in the mirror, he winked at Chris. "I wish I had a cowboy outfit. Let's go, love." He took her hand and as they left the room he said, "Just so you know. There's a way she can beat me. But she'd have to catch the case eight to do it. That's about a fifty-to-one shot."

// 247

"I'm not worried if you aren't," Chris said.

"Do I look worried? Hey, I'd be the first to congratulate her. Maybe this sounds crazy, but I like the girl. She's making us rich."

Jerry Corbett had analyzed Shayna's situation perfectly. She was in a jam. In the first place, she was surrounded by bedlam. The crowd was whooping and cheering in the background and even Houston, Epstein and the Owl had broken out of their cocoons to laugh at Jerry's unmasking. Shayna's first impulse was to protest Jerry's legitimacy in the tournament, but before she could do anything she saw her friend Gene standing chest to chest with Stretch Jackson arguing the case for her. Shayna had forgotten that Gene was in the casino. She was disoriented; in her concentration on the game, she'd lost track of time. Stretch, looking as amused as everybody else about Jerry's stunt, ruled that Jerry was within his rights. In no time at all, what had been a serious poker tournament had disintegrated into a sideshow.

Shayna was struggling. Everyone around her was having fun and games, which was terrific for them — but she was the one on the spot. In the middle of chaos, she had to decide whether to call the damn bet. She couldn't think of a good reason not to, except that somewhere inside her brain something was screaming at her that she'd been set up. Worse yet, she had the sick feeling that everybody in the Taj Mahal except her knew exactly what Jerry had in her hand. Or his hand — Shayna still saw a woman sitting there. Shayna knew she had an obvious play, but for the life of her she didn't know what it was. And there she sat, in the spotlight, with everybody waiting on her. And laughing.

She had to think it through. If she called and won, she was in fat city. But if she called and lost, she was dead. If she folded, she was still alive. She'd be in trouble, way down in last place, but she'd still be alive. But how could she fold? The son of a bitch has three fours, she told herself. Or four to a flush. But that's crazy — he's not going all in on four clubs.

Shayna tried to conjure up an image of Jerry's face as he sat there pulling falsies out of his blouse. Nothing. He looked fruity, is all, in short hair and lipstick. His expression was no help. But in the earlier hands, she thought. She could see him in the earlier hands and he was sure as hell starting to lose it. There you go, she thought — it's a desperation move. That's why he ran away from the table, because if he stuck around, she'd be able to see right through him. He'd give away how hopeless his case was. Going all in on a four-to-one shot at making a flush? That's it. That's the key. He went in on a wing and a prayer and didn't have the balls to stay there and tough it out. There's your answer.

Shayna was embarrassed that it had taken her so long to decide; she had a reputation to maintain. But everyone was still waiting on her and hell, the situation was so obvious to her now that it was laughable. No wonder everyone was loose. They were on her side; it was Jerry they were laughing at. She even heard one of the railbirds joking about it. "One guy leaves on a stretcher," he was saying, "one guy throws a fit, another one turns faggot — they ought to charge admission." Shayna relaxed, trying to make it look as if she'd been stalling on purpose so everybody could milk the last drop of fun out of the escapade. She winked at the woman dealer — there is a sisterhood, she thought — and said in an easy tone, "If everybody's through giggling, do you think we can get back to the game? I happen to have forty-one thousand bucks here that says him or her, take your pick, whatever he is, doesn't catch a club."

She thought she heard Art Epstein on her left say softly, "He doesn't need one." But that was a moment after she'd pushed her stack in, thereby committing the most expensive mistake anybody had made yet in the first annual Stretch Jackson poker classic.

Afterwards, Shayna waited for the fury to hit her, for the anger and fantasies of revenge. But the feeling didn't come. More than anything, she was still groping for an explanation when Stretch Jackson awarded her the fifth-place prize money. A full house? *Jacks* full? Shayna had been flabbergasted when the dealer turned over

Jerry's hand. Not in her remotest calculations had she considered the possibility that he had a pair of jacks in the hole. She didn't know who the hell Jerry was, what kind of magician or actor or card hustler or God knew what, but she understood that he'd set her up like the greenest mark in the world, had led her into new terrain beyond her depth. She was supposed to be the tough poker pro but he'd blindsided her, knocked her right off her props. And not only that, but he'd made her like it. Instead of fury, Shayna felt a kind of dazzled pride that she'd been a principal player in a poker hand people would be talking about for years. Stretch was giving her fifteen grand in cash and she was blinking into bright lights and hearing people clap for her.

The applause was honey. Shayna hadn't planned to make a speech but she found herself waving the prize money aloft and saying, "First of all — ladies, this is for all of us!" She heard more cheering and felt a stupid grin on her face. "Where's my group?" she asked. "I know you're out there." She squinted through the lights and located some upraised arms. "For you, too!" she said. "Folks, there's seven people out there who backed me in the tournament. Dinner's on me tonight. Gene?" She laughed and blew him a kiss. "And how about the champions? There's a lot more poker left to play!"

She might have gone on grinning and babbling, but Jerry Corbett materialized next to her and took her free hand, raising it high with his own. His appearance made Shayna even more giddy. Without his makeup and wig and women's clothes, Jerry looked like a stranger to her, but a familiar stranger. His face was the same but not the same, and his personality was entirely different. His brown eyes were bright and alive and his smile could knock you down.

"Shayna's the champ!" Jerry said. Still the crowd was applauding. "She didn't know it, but she's been the only woman in the game for the past two days. Come on, let's hear it. This isn't a great woman player — this is a great *poker* player! Next year she'll win. And we love her!" Jerry pulled Shayna to him for a hug in the limelight. As he kissed her on the cheek he whispered, "That's an exit line, kid. Always leave 'em cheering."

Stretch Jackson announced a twenty-minute break in the tournament and Archie Breen began removing the last of the five-hundred-dollar chips from the game, exchanging them for thousands. The stakes were going up again when play resumed.

THE FIRST ANNUAL STRETCH JACKSON
SEVEN-CARD STUD POKER CLASSIC

Standings as of 7:40 P.M. Thursday

1.	Jerry Corbett, California	$170,000
2.	Vic Houston, Texas	124,000
3.	Art Epstein, California	104,000
4.	William "Hoo-Hoo" Avery, Arizona	102,000

Play to resume at: 8 P.M.

Vic Houston and Owl Avery stayed in their seats for a few minutes. "You asked about crazy things I've seen in poker games," the Owl said. "I told you, usually there's a woman involved."

"There was a time once I thought I had a lucky hat," Houston said. "I was on a rush that must of lasted three months."

"I remember," the Owl said.

"Naw. This was years ago."

"In Vegas. You sold it to a guy for five grand."

"You remember that?" Houston asked. "Damn, those stories stick around. We gettin' old, Hoo-Hoo."

"And you bought it back from him."

"Not the way you think," Houston said. "That's the point. As soon as he put on the hat, he started winnin'. He was killin' me. What was his name? You remember?"

The Owl said he didn't. "I just seem to recall that he looked undernourished."

"Well, it don't matter," Houston said. "He got me way down and then said he'd sell me the hat back for ten grand."

"That's the story I heard," the Owl said.

"Except it didn't happen. He did me a favor, that guy. Because I stopped thinkin' about the hat and started thinkin' about what I should've been thinkin' about all along, which was the game. That's when I got back to winnin'. *He* was thinkin' about the hat and I broke him. I bought it back, okay, for a hundred bucks. I took that off him, too."

"And of course you haven't been superstitious since," the Owl smirked.

"I don't know. Anyways, I've played with morphodites before." Houston beckoned Archie Breen over and asked, "Any word about Lee Sherman?"

"He's holdin' up, I guess," Breen answered. "I called over to the hospital. They got him in intensive care."

"They lettin' in visitors?"

"I suppose."

"Then let's get the game over."

"That's kind of up to you guys," Breen said.

"Crank up the stakes and we be done in an hour," Houston told him.

"Or well done," the Owl chuckled.

"What do we have — ten minutes still?" Houston said. "I'm gonna stretch my legs." He stood up and wandered off. After a moment, so did the Owl. Temporarily the poker table was abandoned, except for a half-million dollars in chips distributed among four stacks at the remaining seats.

As a female impersonator, Jerry Corbett had been demure and aloof, but out of his disguise he was peppy and gregarious. He also looked about ten years younger. After congratulating Shayna, he grabbed Chris's hand and made a beeline for the small group surrounding Art Epstein, where he apologized for dinner the night before. "You were gracious hosts," he said, "and I was sailing under false colors. Please don't blame Chris — I twisted her arm."

"That's not true," Chris said. "I'm a grown-up. I do what I want."

Epstein and Jackie wouldn't accept an apology. As far as they were concerned, there was nothing to apologize for. They were too entertained by the development and fascinated at the blossoming of Jerry's new personality. "So you two," Epstein said, making an ambiguous motion with his wrist, "are . . . a couple?"

Jerry, with his arm around Chris, gave her a hug. "Very special friends," he said.

Jackie asked, "And Duke?"

"Duke?"

Jackie was obviously enjoying herself. "Duke Corbett," she said, "who gets his acting lessons on Saturday nights?"

Jerry laughed. "I'm sorry. It was too tempting."

Foley couldn't contain himself any longer. He'd been standing with Anita, a big grin on his face, and shaking his head in admiration. He recognized in the new Jerry Corbett an audaciousness as unrestrained as his own. "What you've gotta do, Jackie," Foley said, "and pardon me for interrupting because I know it's none of my business, but this guy's an actor, right?"

"Damn right," Jerry said.

"Can you do *men?*" Foley asked. "I mean Jackie, Art, you're looking for fresh new faces." He flapped his arms as if everything were obvious. "Here's your couple! Reno's trying to tell you something."

Jerry said, "I didn't mean to take advantage —"

"Don't apologize," Jackie said. "I'm ahead of you both. Personally, I'm impressed as hell." She looked at Epstein for a reaction.

He lifted his shoulders. "You sure fooled me."

"Hey, don't get me wrong," Jerry said. "I'm not exactly bashful. I'd love the chance. And I'll knock your socks off."

"He will, too," Chris promised.

"It's worth a test," Jackie said. "I'd want to see you together, see what the chemistry's like. You understand we're not in a position to make any decisions yet. But we can meet on it in L.A. I can promise that much."

Jerry excused himself. He still had to talk to Stretch Jackson. "My name's the same," he told him. "Same address and everything else. I didn't fudge on the entry form. It didn't ask for gender. I want to thank you for backing me up."

Stretch looked down at Jerry from his height, veiled amusement in his gray-blue eyes. "Shoot, usin' your real handle's more than most of these old boys do," he said. "I'm just wonderin' what you got in mind for a second act."

Meanwhile, with the tournament about to resume, Art Epstein had taken Jackie aside and was telling her he thought he had Owl Avery's number. "He's a tough bird," Epstein said, "but there's something about him, some intellectual arrogance. I can feel it. With half a break, I can beat him. That'll leave just me and Houston, and he's the one I want."

"What about Jerry?" Jackie asked. "He's in first place."

Epstein said, "Jerry? He's finished. Kiss me for luck?"

Jackie did. Watching her husband move back through the crowd to the poker table, where play was about to begin, she wondered how he knew so much, where he got his confidence. As well as she knew him, he could still awe her. He was her lion.

Outside, the snow had stopped coming down. High clouds still occupied the nighttime sky but they were floating east and through them the faint blue luminance of the moon was occasionally shining. Russell Henry and Carroll Shepherd had been drinking coffee and walking in the cold and they were sobering up. "Your paradigm is nice and neat," Henry was telling the psychologist, "but it's only a model for losers."

"Are you trying to insult me?" Shepherd asked.

"I can buy the sandwich board as a metaphor," the writer said. "I'll probably even use it in my story. But it doesn't have anything to do with the poker players."

"You don't think the geek was a poker player?"

"Maybe. But he damn sure wasn't one of *those* poker players. Those guys are no closer to walking the sidewalk than we are. I know, you want to believe you can sink that low. Be my guest. But it won't happen. And it could never happen to the poker players. Hell, they're not gamblers — they're bankers. They can raise fifty grand on their signature. Believe me, going broke for them doesn't mean carrying a sandwich board. It means driving a Buick. It took me three days to figure it out, but I've got a way into my story now. I'm going to show those guys as intelligent and very goddamned successful capitalists."

Back inside the Taj Mahal, the two men made their way to the poker area. "Hey, look at that," Shepherd said, pointing at the leader board, "my guy came in sixth. I'll get my two grand back."

"What'll you do with it?" Henry asked.

"Pay bills."

"I'll bet you blow it."

Shepherd shook his head. "No way, Jose. I've had it for this trip. First thing tomorrow I'm driving home, stone cold sober."

"Q.E.D.," Henry told him.

Later it would seem obvious and predestined, a natural result of the logical progression of events: Jerry Corbett didn't stand a chance in the poker tournament once he dropped his disguise. The ante had gone to a thousand dollars and the opening bet to two thousand, but the higher stakes had nothing to do with Jerry's collapse. His problem was that he suddenly didn't know what role he was supposed to be playing. As the matronly female Jerry Corbett, quiet and inscrutable, he'd been a mystery to the other players, but as the young actor Jerry Corbett, impulsive and charismatic, he was a pushover. For all the threat he posed, he might as well have been Doug McGowan reincarnated at the tournament table. Not that he was as inept as Doug had been — his stage instincts kept working and he could still read the other players from their body language. But for the first time they could read him, too. Jerry knew they were on to him but he couldn't do anything about it. He was

/ / 255

floundering. He'd never played serious poker as himself before and without a character to play, without the contours of his shrewd female *doppelgänger* to inhabit, he saw what he'd become as soon as the game resumed: just one more Reno sucker getting his clock cleaned by the pros.

Later he would concede that he probably hadn't tried very hard to protect himself, but he wasn't in a mood to try. He was feeling too happy-go-lucky. Finally, after the better part of a year, he was able to relax and enjoy playing a loose game of poker. After his long stint in the salt mines, after all his months of tight, self-controlled gambling at Gardena and Las Vegas, after an endless treadmill of monotonous, grinding-it-out poker sessions, Jerry could luxuriate in sprawling at the table and throwing chips around. Besides, the pressure was off. He was already a winner. He was going to collect twenty-five thousand dollars, but the money was only part of it. He'd pulled his act off. He'd played his role out all the way to the last scene of the last act and proved he could hold his own in the heady atmosphere of world-championship poker. Not only that, but as a bonus, he'd gotten the promise of a screen test for him and Chris. How could he help but feel like celebrating?

So Jerry talked it up. He kept a line of chatter going at the table and he ad-libbed with the spectators. He played a loose game and for the short time he remained at the table he became the driving force in the tournament. Thanks to his betting, the raises went to double and triple what they'd been earlier. He broke the game wide open, and the lead shifted from player to player as pots of forty and fifty thousand dollars became commonplace. Jerry knew he was pushing the action recklessly, but it was the only way he had a chance. He knew he was out of his league with these guys. He couldn't beat them with skill so he had to hope to do it with luck. Big pots would help him if he caught good tickets, and if he didn't, he'd be dead anyway.

It took forty-five minutes before Jerry had to go all in. Art Epstein tapped him out, moving into the lead, but it could just as easily have been Houston or the Owl who finished him off. Whoever delivered it, the *coup de grace* was inevitable. Jerry took his beating like a man, accepted the twenty-five thousand dollars in fourth-place prize money that Stretch Jackson awarded him, received the audience's cheers and applause with a deep stage bow, and to Chris, watching from the sidelines, Jerry had never in his life looked as good to her, or as happy, as he did losing one hundred and seventy thousand dollars in the final round of the first annual Stretch Jackson poker classic. "I make it just under four thousand bucks a minute," one of the railbirds said.

And so they were down to three. A fresh dealer took a seat at the table, a man this time, with slick black hair and a black mustache and the pale complexion of someone habituated to the indoors. He had soft, sure hands and sharp eyes and a personality that was all but nonexistent. Silently he dealt around from his left, to Owl Avery at one curve of the table, to Art Epstein across from him, to Vic Houston at the other curve of the table. Three big men, two of them stocky and one corpulent, who had been playing poker now for seven hours. From behind them a television camera closed in, hovering first over one's shoulder, then another's. Word had spread through the Taj Mahal and filtered to the other downtown casinos that Stretch Jackson's tournament was nearing its climax. Maybe. It depended on the three men sitting at the table. Would they come out charging, or would they lay back and wait to pick their shots? Gradually the crowd thickened behind the velvet rope, railbirds jostling each other and craning for a better view. The players seemed unaware of the assembling spectators. They watched the dealer's quick, pale hands and followed the cards that turned up in the bright cone of light falling on the green tabletop.

Elsewhere in the casino, with the Reno money machine spinning merrily in high gear, people ignored the poker tournament. Black-jack players on their high stools slid cards under their chips. Crap-shooters leaned across siderails, pressing their bets and shouting for numbers. Keno players prayed and marked their tickets, and throughout the casino slot players pulled handles and kept the drums clattering, filling the Taj Mahal with background noise like am-

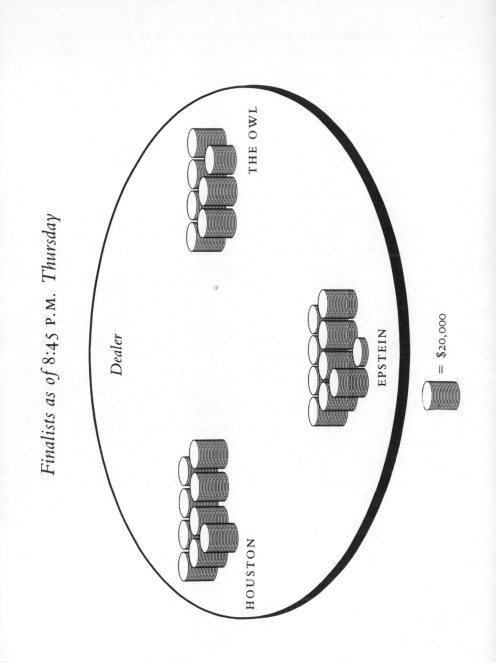

Finalists as of 8:45 P.M. *Thursday*

Dealer

THE OWL

HOUSTON

EPSTEIN

= $20,000

plified radio static. Even in the poker area, where a banner spread overhead and placard silhouettes of Stretch Jackson beamed welcome to one and all, players at a half a dozen side games were absorbed in the rise and fall of their own fortunes, selfishly unconcerned with the destiny of other gamblers even an arm's length away.

But the half-million dollars in pink chips on the tournament table had a magnetic attraction of its own, and the spectators remained. To the players, the money meant nothing. It had no more purchasing power than Monopoly scrip. The chips were just counters, weapons in a psychological battle but otherwise worthless. Art Epstein had to convince himself that what he was doing was worth doing. He didn't need the money. He didn't need the glory. He was up against two of the best poker players in the world and nobody expected him to win. He should have found it easy to succumb to his doubts, to loosen up like Jerry Corbett and throw in the towel. It was only a game, for pete's sake. What did it matter? What mattered to Epstein was that he and Jackie had re-connected. Their uncertain partnership had found a new solidness and that was of preemptive importance to him. Compared to his future with Jackie, how could he get excited about a poker game?

Houston opened for two thousand dollars. The Owl raised five. He's trying to suck me in, Epstein thought. He's loaded. Epstein passed, wondering how he knew the Owl had a hand. I don't know how I knew, he thought, I just knew. "Loosen up, son," the Owl teased. "If God wanted us to hold on to money, he'd have put handles on it."

"Like he did on our dicks?" Epstein said.

Hubris, he thought. The old Greek sin of arrogant pride. Hoo-Hoo's inflated with it. What was the Russian aphorism? "The only place where sin is inevitably punished is on the chessboard." Maybe so, Epstein thought. But there are sins of judgment, which after all are only mistakes, and sins of character, which count for something. But Epstein didn't want to pursue that line of thought. If you start judging the Owl, he told himself, if you hold him in moral balance, he's got you beat. That's what he wants you to do. He wants you to get emotional about him. Then, hubris or no hubris, he'll pick you clean before you can blink.

Epstein raised five thousand dollars on the next hand. The others folded. It's not so tough, he thought. If you get a hand, bet it, and if you don't, get out. Sure. And if you believe that, I've got some nice lake frontage in Florida I'd like to talk to you about. What's working against me, he thought, is that these two guys know each other like twins. But there's a flip side to that — they don't know me from Adam. If it's hard for me to read them, it stands to reason it's just as hard for them to read me. Hell, I can't even read myself in this game. I fly in here three days ago wound up so tight I have to walk around the block for a half an hour just to calm down. I get beaten to a pulp the first day by an adolescent. I play catch-up for most of the tournament. I don't even make the leader board until the semifinals. And then I get euphoric and say the hell with it because I've fallen in love with my wife all over again. That's a poker personality? Ha. No wonder I'm hanging in. If I can't figure out what I'm doing, how is anybody else supposed to?

Epstein played. The game was mechanical, nobody taking chances, the bets obvious. In his concentration Epstein began to feel distanced from the outside world. He was aware only of the here and now and the moment of waiting for the next card. But in the back of his mind, Epstein's ruminating turned up a kind of an answer for him. The game was worth playing for the simple reason that there was no reason not to play it. It's like climbing a mountain, he thought. You wear yourself out, you fatigue yourself until every muscle in your body tells you to quit, but you keep going, one step after another. And it's not for reasons that have to do with any great cosmic philosophy. It's not to conquer an enemy and it's not to conquer yourself, Epstein thought, and it's not for that greatest self-aggrandizing rationalization of all, to focus all of life's mortal elements into a single monumental challenge and in subduing it, to find out who you are. That's a laugh. You do it for the view. You do it because it's fun. You go to the top and see it through, like any job, because once you're committed to it, once you're most of the way there, why the hell not finish it? Epstein wasn't doing anything more important at the moment than playing poker and that was reason enough to play it well. And so much for intellectualizing, he decided. He intended to win the tournament on the grounds, simple, silly or maybe but probably not profound, that he couldn't think of a single good argument in favor of losing the tournament.

Vic Houston noticed that Epstein shifted in his chair, settling in. But Houston himself was getting impatient. If someone doesn't start gamblin', he thought, we'll be here all night. The Texan was indulging himself in a slight annoyance with Hoo-Hoo. The sumbitch is keepin' away from me, he thought. He's willin' to hammer on Epstein and he's willin' for me and Epstein to hammer on each other, but he ain't willin' to try hammerin' on me. It was an oily side of the Owl's character that Houston had seen before. Let's you and him fight, huh? What chickenshit. If he wants the championship, Houston thought, he's gonna have to come get it.

The Owl was low and opened for two thousand dollars. Houston pushed twenty thousand out. It was a crazy bet; the size of the pot didn't justify it. The Owl folded. The next hand played out the same way. And the next. "Hoo hoo hoo," the Owl said, and on the sidelines Archie Breen murmured to Stretch Jackson, "Looks like the price of poker just went up."

In a matter of minutes, Houston had won twelve thousand dollars. It wasn't enough to matter, Epstein thought, but it was a sign. You run a few and it doesn't necessarily mean you had cards, it just means you caught the other players off-guard. But it gives you momentum because you might have had cards. Were you bluffing or on a rush? By the time the other guys have to ask, it's too late; and meanwhile you're three hands to the good and as far as anybody knows, you've got the heat. Steal enough antes that way and after a while it does make a difference. Epstein knew one thing for sure: he couldn't outplay Houston and the Owl with a short stack. Not those guys.

Houston was low on the next hand and opened with two pink chips. The Owl called and Epstein raised ten thousand dollars on a king showing. He had nothing to back it up; his raise was sheer bluff. On his left, Houston didn't fold. He didn't call, either. He didn't do anything. He just stared at Epstein. Epstein stared back. Thirty seconds passed. A minute. Two minutes. Holy shit, Epstein thought, he's going all in. He's going to push a hundred and ninety thousand bucks into the pot. Epstein didn't know what secrets his face was giving away, if it was giving any away, but when Houston shifted his glance, Epstein knew he'd learned more about poker in those two minutes than he'd discovered up to then in twenty years of playing the game. Houston's eyes were fathomless. He's capable of anything, Epstein thought. The man is beyond my comprehension. For the first time in his gambling career, Epstein had looked into the abyss and it froze him to the core.

But Houston folded, and so did the Owl. Epstein, stone-faced, swept in the chips with the knowledge that in that long moment of discovery, something inside him had broken free. It was as if a stopper had come unplugged. If Houston had called the bet, it would have been curtains for Epstein — but Houston didn't call. And Epstein knew why. It was because in his own frigid eyes Houston had looked into the abyss, too. Finally Epstein understood what Jackie meant when she said he looked like a lion at the poker table.

And so the game shifted gears again. The pace slowed but the tension tightened. The spectators felt it. It wasn't a game of cards now, but a game of nerve. There were no winning hands, just winning bets. The pots were as big as forty minutes earlier, when Jerry Corbett had made his kamikaze run, but there was no sense of recklessness or desperation to the betting. There was only icy control. Art Epstein felt as cold and remote as a dead star. His hands moved with confidence, he saw himself placing chips and turning cards, but he was numb, his moves dictated by the inflexible certainty of absolute zero. Later he would have no concept of how much time elapsed. For the here and now he was conscious only of the balanced purity of three sides of a triangle: himself, Houston, the Owl.

They were joined in some manner that went beyond the physical. It was chemical, a bonding of atoms and molecules, or psychic, a synchrony of brain waves. Epstein heard nothing, saw nothing, felt nothing, but he would forever remember the two faces — Houston's square cheeks and solid jaw, the deep crow's feet around his impenetrable ice-blue eyes, the slanted hat-brim shadow across his broad forehead; and the Owl's roundness, his flat ears and small hooked nose, lenses magnifying his murky gray eyes, his double chin, the cigar plugged into his wet mouth, the moist sheen on his smooth pale skin.

Long moments passed that Epstein couldn't account for — seconds, minutes, hours? Houston riffled his chips with one-handed dexterity, calculating and waiting. The Owl removed his boots and sat cross-legged in his chair, his feet tucked under him. Epstein would remember some things. The silence. Occasional moments like Houston taking a sip of Wild Turkey, the Owl polishing his spectacles with a tissue, himself standing up at one point, leaning on the back of his chair to stretch his arms and shoulders.

The Owl went all in against Houston once, and won. Epstein remembered that. He remembered betting fifty thousand dollars into the Owl and driving him out of the pot with nothing but the strength of his gaze and the force of his concentration. He remembered the Owl's stack dropping below a hundred thousand, then dropping below eighty thousand and staying there. He remembered Houston getting on a run, building his stack to over three hundred thousand at one point. Epstein remembered his own stack diminishing, and then a hand where they all three stayed until fifth street, himself raking in a pot of close to a hundred thousand dollars. And then the Owl's stack smaller yet, this not a memory but a fact now as Epstein became aware of his surroundings again, sounds and details rushing in on him, the noise of the casino suddenly in his ears as if a volume knob had been activated.

It was like the twist of a kaleidoscope, the quick refocus of a camera. Epstein found himself back at the poker table like someone startled out of a dream. Television lights were bleaching the color from the Owl's face and all around him Epstein could feel the tense anticipation of the crowd. Epstein had gone in on a pair of nines, raising Houston's opening bet by ten thousand dollars. Houston had folded, the Owl had called, and now the dealer sent around their second up cards. The Owl, showing two face cards, checked. Epstein bet twenty thousand and the Owl sat like a statue.

Art Epstein had an urge to jump to his feet, shake his neck loose, do calisthenics. He felt like a man coming out of anesthesia. He was aware of his body again, his breathing, his clothing, all the mundane details surrounding him in the Taj Mahal casino. He was back from wherever he had been, from whatever icy remote place had been dictating his behavior. In the face of his bet, the Owl was supposed to fold — his stack was down and Epstein had been mauling him. But the Owl sat meditating, so still that he could have been in a coma.

Then he slowly unfolded himself, almost like a butterfly. Raising himself on the arms of his chair, the Owl slipped one bent leg out from under him, then the other. He leaned over, found his boots and slipped them over his stockinged feet. He took his dead cigar from the lip of his ashtray, tapped it clean and relighted it, rotating it in his mouth to get an even burn. Then he looked at Epstein.

"I've got your nines beat," he announced, and he pushed his stack in.

Quickly the dealer counted the bet, lining the chips up in ten stacks of five. "Thirty more to you," he told Epstein. "He's all in."

Epstein squinted, turning his head from the glare of the television lights. The ropes around the tournament table had been moved into a horseshoe and the crowd was pressing in on three sides. Among the railbirds Epstein saw Easy and Sandwiches standing together, and scattered among the faces he noticed that Shayna and Walsh had returned. Brett Overstreet was there in his scruffy Levis and, closer to Epstein, directly over his right shoulder, he saw Jackie with Foley and Anita, Jerry Corbett and Chris.

The Owl had a high pair, Epstein figured, maybe two pair. With his nines beaten, Epstein should have folded. Five minutes earlier he wouldn't have had to think about it; in his cold, abstracted state he would have known instinctively what to do. And if just he and the Owl were left in the game, he was sure he'd fold. But the ominous presence of Vic Houston on his left skewed his calculations. Whatever happened in this hand, he'd still have Houston to contend with afterwards. And something told Epstein it would be a mistake to fold. He couldn't beat Houston by playing the percentages. To beat the Texan, he'd have to gamble.

The spectators thought the critical hand was the one they were watching, the one between Epstein and the Owl. It wasn't. In Epstein's mind, the game was still triangular and it was for Houston's benefit that he silently turned up his hole cards, displaying his lonely pair of nines. The crowd relaxed, the hush broken. Nobody expected Epstein to call the Owl's raise; everybody assumed he was showing his losing cards to the television camera. But Epstein gave them a treat. In the full glare of the spotlight he made what everybody in viewing distance knew without a doubt was a classic blunder, thereby validating what they all secretly suspected anyway, that they belonged in the tournament as much as he did, that they could play the game as well as any so-called champions, that all you needed to play good poker was self-control and a few breaks. Epstein counted out thirty pink chips and said, "Call." With his bet, the pot had a total of one hundred and twenty-nine thousand dollars in it.

Three cards were yet to come. The dealer burned a card and dealt one faceup, first to the Owl, then Epstein. Neither player helped. He burned another and dealt again. Still no help. "Last card," he said, and dealt two more. Again neither player improved. Epstein finished the hand with a pair of nines lying exposed on the table.

The Owl's first two hole cards were still face down. All he had to do was show a pair and he'd win the pot. Deliberately and without expression he turned his hole cards over, one at a time. No pair. The Owl had seven unmatched cards.

Epstein didn't say anything. It was up to the Owl to make a gesture. But the Owl just tapped his fingertips on the table and rose from his seat as the television reporter pushed her microphone in Epstein's face. "Share your secret with us?" she asked. "How in the world did you know he was bluffing?"

"How did he know I was?" Epstein answered. He didn't like the change in the mood. They were going to break again and raise the stakes. People were milling around, but Epstein wanted to hold on to his focus. The toughest part of the tournament was still ahead of him.

Stretch Jackson awarded the Owl a wad of cash, ten packets of hundred-dollar bills bundled together, fifty bills in a packet. The Owl declined to make a speech. He looked as glum as someone who'd just lost a tournament, not somebody who'd come in third. But before he disappeared, lifted by the crowd's applause he dredged up a sour smile and said, "I shall return."

Epstein stood up, taking a look at his wristwatch, and was surprised to see it was only a few minutes after ten. He would have sworn it was two or three in the morning. Houston, still sitting at the table, looked as fresh as if he'd just had a nap and a hot shower. Epstein went to join his group as Archie Breen carried a piece of chalk to the blackboard and updated the tournament standings. He wrote:

V. Houston, $276,000
A. Epstein, $224,000

Art Epstein was in no mood for small talk. He was out among the spectators and people were trying to shake his hand and pat him on the back. He took Jackie's elbow and moved through the crowd with her to the elevator bank. Up in their penthouse suite, he took off his jacket and shirt and rinsed his face. "Hell with it," he said. "I'm going to shave, too. Sweetheart?"

"What?" Jackie was in the other room, looking outside through the curtains.

"Come talk to me, okay? Just don't say anything important."

"It stopped snowing," she said. "The moon's out." She leaned against the bathroom doorjamb. "It looks to me like your adam's apple gets in the way."

"Houston's not human," he said.

"I'm so proud of you. Does that count as something important?"

"I played in a trance for an hour. I don't know if I can get back into that psyche."

"You missed a spot."

"Where?"

"There."

"That's my cheekbone. I don't grow hair on my cheekbone."

"You put lather there."

"I didn't put it there. It splashed there."

"It's not important. Here, let me," Jackie said when he reached for his after-shave. She cupped some liquid in her palm and patted his face. "It smells like gin and tonic," she said. "Does it sting?"

"It's not important." Epstein combed his hair and changed into a fresh suit. He put on cufflinks and a tie. "How do I look?"

"Like the great Gatsby. How do you feel?"

"Punchdrunk. We never got dinner. I could ask for a break if you want."

"It's not important."

"Thanks. Let's go back. I guess I'm ready."

"What is important?" Jackie asked.

"Beating Houston."

"Anything else?"

"Not losing to him."

"Am I important?"

"Do you play poker?"

"No."

He touched her cheek. "Then you're the most important."

Out in the hallway she said, "Art?"

"What?"

"Have I told you lately?"

He pushed the elevator button. "All the time, love."

Jackie stepped closer and put her arms around him. "Just one thing," she whispered into his ear. "After you win and they ask how you did it?"

"Yes?"

"Don't say because the competition was gentile."

The elevator doors opened on their laughter.

Vic Houston was a five-to-three favorite in the last-minute odds, with the insiders backing Houston. "I'd keep that camera rollin'," Stretch Jackson was advising the television reporter, "because you gonna see some action. The game ain't gonna drag out."

"How do you know?" she asked.

Stretch said, "Honey, I got the scars. This is where Houston turns alligator."

The spectators began reassembling when Art Epstein returned. Two of the side games even broke up as gamblers vacated their seats to wander over and watch, but they left their chips on the table since they didn't expect to be gone long. Epstein stepped through the velvet rope and saw Houston not far away, talking with a pit boss. Noticing Epstein, the Texan detached himself from the conversation and came back to the tournament table. "You want a dinner break?" he asked.

"Not especially."

"Me, neither," Houston said. "How 'bout we eat after? Winner buys."

"You're on," Epstein said.

A new dealer was at the table, a small, dark-skinned man whose name-tag said Jaime. He sat silently on his seat cushion, a fresh deck of cards fanned face-up in front of him in an arc. Stretch said,

"We goin' to two and four now. Unless you fellas'd rather step it up?"

Houston said, "Five and ten?"

"That'd move it along," Stretch said, looking at Epstein.

"Sure," Epstein said.

"Okay, then." Stretch dropped his hand on Jaime's shoulder and said, "Got it, amigo? Five ante and ten to bring it in."

Jaime nodded and began checking the faces of the cards spread in front of him. During the break, Epstein's stack of chips had been moved to the far curve of the table, where Owl Avery had been sitting. Epstein started sliding them back to his own seat.

"Hold it," somebody called. It was the television cameraman. "Aren't you going to sit over there?" he asked.

"No," Epstein said. "Why?"

"I thought you'd want to face each other. You know, across the table."

"Do I tell you how to shoot film?" Epstein finished moving his chips and sat down where he'd been sitting before, across from the dealer at Houston's right.

"I have to move my lights, then," the cameraman said.

Jaime had flipped the fanned cards over and was checking the backs. That done, he mixed and shuffled the deck, but meanwhile Stretch held up the deal until the cameraman could rearrange his awkward tripodded light standards. During the delay, Archie Breen made his way to the table and tugged at Stretch's sleeve, pulling the taller man away. Whatever he had to say didn't take long. Epstein heard Stretch say, "Aw, no. No. Aw, shit, Archie."

Houston stood up and walked over to see what the problem was. Epstein followed. Stretch and Breen both looked miserable. Breen put his hand on Houston's arm and said, "It's Lee Sherman, Vic. He didn't make it."

"He's gone?"

Breen raised his shoulders helplessly. "About twenty minutes ago. I called over to the hospital."

"Sweet Jesus," Houston said.

They were standing next to an empty poker table. Houston lowered himself into a chair and, without seeming to be aware of the gesture, took his Stetson off. He pulled a handkerchief out of his pocket and blew his nose.

Stretch said, "I better make an announcement."

Epstein felt like an intruder. He left Houston sitting by himself and returned to his own seat at the tournament table where Stretch Jackson, in the glare of the TV lights, raised his hands for silence.

"Folks," he said, "there's gonna be a few minutes' delay. We just got some bad news." The crowd quieted further to hear him, but for a moment Stretch didn't seem to have any words. He looked around the crowd, fastening his gaze on familiar faces. Before he continued, he unself-consciously removed his hat. "Lee Sherman Tobias passed on tonight," he said, "over at the hospital. I don't know what else to say. He was world champeen a bunch o' times. A lot of us knew him." Again he paused. "I thought y'all oughta know." Stretch retreated from the lights and went back to where Vic Houston was sitting.

Epstein waited. He watched Jaime sit patiently with his deck of cards, and over the dealer's shoulder he saw Houston and Stretch talking. They seemed to be arguing. Epstein was aware of a uniformed security guard hovering behind him, keeping an eye on Houston's untended stack of chips. After a while, Stretch beckoned to Epstein. He stood up and eased past the guard over to the two gamblers. He stopped a pace away but Stretch reached out and pulled him closer. In a quiet voice he said, "Vic's gonna forfeit to ya."

"Bullshit," Epstein said.

Houston's eyes were red. He said, "I'm goin' over to the hospital."

Epstein was surprised at how much older the two men looked without their cowboy hats on. With thinning hair revealing the shape of their pale fragile skulls, they could have been his uncles. "We can take a break," he said.

"That won't do it," Houston answered. "We're playin' with Lee

Sherman's money. It ain't right." He looked at Stretch. "I said before we shouldn't of divvied it up."

"Damn it, Vic, .there wasn't no other way to call it," Stretch told him.

"It's blood money," Houston said. "It's one thing if a man takes sick. This ain't the same."

"Look," Epstein said, "if that's the problem, let's give it back. What was it — ninety thousand, something like that? Take it out of the prize money."

Stretch winced. "That ain't a good way to handle this."

"It's not the point anyhow," Houston said.

"Give it to his widow," Epstein offered. "Let her pick a charity if she wants."

"That ain't it," Houston said. "There's a principle. I'm not gonna play a tournament over Lee Sherman's dead body. I owe him better."

"He'd want you to play it out, wouldn't he?" Epstein asked.

"Son, you livin' on some other planet," Houston answered.

Stretch couldn't resist a smile. "Ol' Lee Sherman, he'd say fuck ya both and take the money."

Even Houston grinned at that, and once again Epstein was reminded of what an outsider he was to the professional fraternity. "Well, what about me?" he asked.

"I'm givin' you first place," Houston said.

"You're not giving me shit," Epstein told him.

"Take it," Houston said. "I don't need the money."

"You think I do?"

Houston glared at him. "You want to play it out?"

"That's why I'm here."

"Then let's finish it." Houston stood, put on his hat and went back to the tournament table. Epstein followed him.

Again the television lights clicked on. The crowd's murmur stilled as Houston and Epstein each anted five thousand dollars. At a sign from Stretch, Jaime shuffled and cut the cards and dealt out the poker hands. Houston was low with a four showing. He looked at his hole cards, then picked them up and let them flutter to the table, face up. He had an eight and a six of mismatched suits. "I'm puttin' you all in," he told Epstein. Making a trap with both hands, he shoved in his huge stack of more than a quarter of a million dollars in chips.

Epstein heard a confused babble erupt from the crowd behind him, and one voice above the others: "Jesus H. Christ!"

Epstein had the ten of diamonds showing. He looked at Houston but might as well have tried to stare down the Sphinx. He lifted the corners of his own hole cards, then turned one of them over. It was the ten of clubs. He smiled as if at a private joke. Tens. They were still sticking to him. "Look at this," he said, and turned over his other hole card. It was the ten of spades.

"Okay, now you won it," Houston said. "Satisfied?"

Epstein sighed. "I guess." He reached out languidly, picked up his three tens and flipped them at Jaime. "Fold," he said.

Houston glowered at him.

Epstein heard the noise from the railbirds behind him grow louder in disbelief. "And fold," he said. "And fold. And fold." He patted his palm on the table. "I was out of line," he told Houston. "You lost a friend. I shouldn't have pushed you into this. So be it." He extended his hand. "I don't want charity any more than you do. Call it a draw?"

Houston shook his hand. "Done."

"Flip you for the trophy."

"It's yours," Houston said. "I already got a doorstop."

"Talk about pissin' in the soup," Stretch complained. "You fellas just boogered up my tournament."

Epstein gestured to the applause that had begun and was spreading through the crowd. Getting to his feet, he asked, "You hear anybody complaining, pardner?"

The winner's trophy was almost three feet high. Art Epstein didn't want it engraved. He took it the way it was, carried it away from the table and presented it to Jerry Corbett. "I don't know if you're going to be a movie star," he said, "but you earned this souvenir if anyone did. It's the Taj Mahal Oscar for best actor. Take it and don't argue."

Jerry Corbett laughed. "You mean go now and sin no more?"

"Something like that."

Jerry held out the trophy for Chris. "What do you think, hon? Should I mend my ways?"

She kissed him on the cheek. "Fat fucking chance."

Before Vic Houston could leave the casino for the hospital, Epstein ushered Jackie over to introduce her. "For what it's worth," he said, "you'd have beaten me."

"Maybe not," Houston answered.

"You don't have to be polite. Jackie loves me anyway. You would have won."

Houston tipped his hat. "I guess we'll find out next year."

Epstein put his arm around his wife. "Somehow I doubt it," he said.

Later, when they were alone, Jackie asked, "So did you get what you came here for?"

"I won the trophy."

"You gave it away."

"It wasn't what I came here for," he said.

The banner was struck. The silhouette placards came down. The Taj Mahal's graveyard shift carted off the extra tournament poker tables and trundled slot machines back into their place. Sometime after midnight in the casino, Stretch Jackson sat down at a hold-em game. Owl Avery was at the table. DeHaven was there. Brett Overstreet. Others of his acquaintance. They acknowledged his arrival with nods or muted howdies.

Stretch rubbed his hands together. "How sweet it is," he said. "I been like a kid outside a candy store all week, but look out. I'm through refereein'. I come to play."

"You come to bullshit," Overstreet said.

Stretch called for a rack of chips. When they arrived, he initialed a marker and arranged his stack into a conformation that suited him. He put a cigarette in his mouth and slid down in his seat, using his thumb to push the brim of his Stetson back an inch. By the time he was settled, a cocktail waitress had appeared at his side with a cup of coffee thick with cream and sugar. Stretch tipped her by putting his room key in her hand. She laughed and slapped at his wrist. Stretch winked, took the key back and put a chip in her palm. He anted and soon was lost in the old familiar rhythms. Between deals the gamblers occasionally bantered back and forth. Later somebody broke the silence by saying, "Well, I wonder where old Lee Sherman is at now."

"He's in poker heaven," the Owl answered.

Stretch looked at his cards, riffling his chips out of long comfortable habit. "No way," he said. "We ain't none of us gettin' off that easy." Surrounding him he heard the background noise of the casino, felt the beat of its pulse and the shape of its dreams. "We're all goin' to hell when it's over," he said. "We already been to heaven." He beamed a radiant smile and raised the bet. Somewhere in the casino a crapshooter gave a joyful cry.